SQUALL LINE

• A NOVEL •

M ary A nne C iviok

Published by Wheatmark
2030 East Speedway Boulevard, Suite 106
Tucson, Arizona 85719 USA
www.wheatmark.com

Publisher's Note
This is a work of fiction. Any references to real people, events, establishments, organizations, or locations are intended only to provide a sense of authenticity, but are used fictitiously. All characters and incidents are drawn from the author's imagination. The publisher and author do not assume and hereby disclaim any liability to any party for any loss or damage caused by errors or omissions in *Squall Line*.

Cover painting by Mary Anne Civiok
Cover and author photos by Guillermo Escudero

Manufactured in the United States of America

ISBN: 978-1-62787-366-6 (paperback)
ISBN: 978-1-62787-367-3 (hardcover)
ISBN: 978-1-62787-368-0 (ebook)
LCCN: 2015957936

rev201601

Dedicated to my loving husband, Rich

The human heart is like a ship on a stormy sea driven about by winds blowing from all four corners of heaven.
—Martin Luther

CHAPTER 1

The heavy scent of orange blossoms wafted through the open windows as Meghan Walcott hunched over her kitchen table, trying to focus on her work. Booming car stereos punctuated the night, and palm fronds rasped against each other in the desert wind. Her gaze fell on her chipped nail polish and her mother's wedding ring on her right hand. She swallowed hard. Mother's Day was nearly over, and she was glad to put the dreaded holiday behind her.

Hoping that music would lift her spirits, she turned on the radio and heard "Unforgettable," the haunting father-daughter duet made by Natalie Cole decades after her father's original recording. It was the first song she and Bryan James had danced to when their friendship had taken a romantic turn. Tonight she was struck by Natalie's ability to reach back in time and create something so sublime with her late father.

She heard a vehicle slow down and stop in front of her house, engine idling. Since a rash of break-ins in her neighborhood during the past few months, she'd found herself tuning in to every little sound. She hurried to the front bedroom, closed the door to block out light, and squinted through the blinds. She felt the driver might be watching her home, but couldn't get a good look at him. She rushed from room to room, checking the locks and closing windows and blinds. She heard the car speed off.

Meghan liked living near the high school where she worked, but sometimes wondered if Bryan had been right that she'd have been better off staying in her grandfather's townhome after he died. She would have felt safer next door to Bryan in the gated foothills community, yet she couldn't shake the memory of Grandpa Walcott lying there in the living room on a hospital bed, his pale, thin form hooked up to an oxygen tank.

She'd moved instead to the adobe bungalow where her grandparents had first resided in Tucson. Its Mexican tile work, thick walls with nichos for her pottery, lush garden, and large citrus trees embodied the warmth and loving spirit of her grandparents. Sometimes she could almost smell her grandma's fresh-baked cinnamon bread or picture the three of them playing canasta around the kitchen table. She shoved her notes aside, switched to a classical station, and made herself cinnamon toast and a cup of tea.

When Beethoven's "Moonlight Sonata" streamed through the airways, she was drawn into the dreamy, mysterious piece that had always been her favorite. Her eyes stung with tears. Something about this particular rendition was especially moving. When it was over, she listened for the name of the pianist. She decided to download the song as soon as she finished the agenda for tomorrow's faculty meeting; then she could relax in her recliner with the latest novel for her book club.

She dabbed at her eyes and got back to work, adding her plan for orchestra students to play classical music in the cafeteria during lunch hour. She was convinced that it would do wonders for student morale and reduce behavior problems. She proofread what she'd written, ran the spell-checker, and pressed PRINT. She waited for the whir of the printer in the next room.

Instead, deafening explosions blasted through the house.

She dove under the kitchen table and crouched beneath it. Cool night air flooded the room through a broken window.

Her mind raced. Had a bomb gone off? Gunfire? Maybe a drive-by! Was someone still outside—or even *inside* her house?

She couldn't see anything move from her vantage point under the table. She held her breath and listened. Only barking dogs and the rustle of leaves could be heard over the pounding of her heart.

Hand trembling, she reached up into her knife drawer and groped around for the only weapon she could think of—a carving knife. She winced as she cut her finger on a sharp edge. Then she grabbed her purse with her cell phone and crept into the pantry. She quietly closed the door and dialed 911.

The operator asked whether she was injured and if anyone else was in the house with her.

"I'm okay," she whispered, "and I *hope* there's no one else here."

"The police are on their way. I'll stay on the line with you."

She fumbled in her purse for a bandage, taped up her finger, and wiped a smear of blood off her cell phone.

After what seemed an endless wait, the dispatcher said, "Two police officers are outside your house and are about to knock on your door."

At the sound of knocking, Meghan ventured out of the pantry, crunching across the living room through broken glass. "They're here," she told the operator. "Thank you."

She edged the front door open, trying to control her trembling. At first she didn't see anyone. Then a uniformed police officer stepped out from behind the doorway, his hand near his holster. A second policeman approached from the north side of the house.

The tall, dark-haired officer showed her his badge. "I'm Officer López from the Tucson Police Department, and this is Officer Butler." Butler had a crew cut and military-style mustache. "We have a report of gunfire at this address."

"I'm the one who called for help. I think somebody just fired gunshots into my home!"

"Is anyone else here with you?"

"No. I live alone." She fought to control the quaver in her voice as she agreed to let them check the premises. Her face burned as López's gaze fell onto the large carving knife on the entryway table. "I grabbed that for self-defense."

"Okay. Just leave it right where it is. Can you show us the damage? Then we'll check your house and yard to make sure they're secure."

She nodded, gesturing toward the shattered window and the damage in her living room. López took notes. Shards of glass covered the front room, and her favorite Hopi pot lay in pieces on the floor. Then she spotted bullet-sized holes in her recliner.

Suddenly things started to go black. She grasped the back of the couch to steady herself.

"You'd better sit down, ma'am." López guided her to a chair in the kitchen, his voice calm and reassuring. "Put your head down between your knees and breathe deep."

She did as directed, breathing deeply. Her vision returned and the ringing stopped.

"They're sending over a couple of night detectives and a crime scene tech," said Butler from the kitchen. "Maybe I should call her an EMT."

"I'm fine." She needed to get a grip, or she could wind up in the ER. She sat up slowly. "It's just that . . . at this time of night, I'm usually in that chair reading."

"Good thing you weren't there tonight," said López.

"That's for sure. I'm going to sit right here for a few minutes. I'd like to call two friends of mine to come over."

"Fine. Just so they don't interfere with the investigation."

She called her best friend, Kate O'Neil. There was no answer, so she left a message.

As she was leaving Bryan a message, he cut in, "What in hell's going on? Are you okay?"

"I'm fine, but gunshots were fired into my house! Two police officers are here with me."

"I'll be right there. Be careful, darling."

She flinched as a beam of light flashed through the window; then she realized Butler was outside checking the yard. Later she heard him return through the back door and open the pantry. The thought of a stranger surveying her clutter of birdseed, sheet music, yarn, and cans of food made her cringe. Reorganizing the pantry was one more job she'd put off until summer vacation.

Two more officers appeared at the door. Detective Irena Sandoval had long black hair, and there was a young man with rimless glasses. She thought he might be the crime scene tech. As Butler was leaving, she overheard López bring them up to speed and inform them that he'd stay on to secure the scene.

At work, she saw herself as cool under pressure and on top of things. Now her thoughts ricocheted around in her mind, and she was having a hard time keeping track of who was doing what.

The tech took photos of her recliner, then slipped on latex gloves and pushed long tweezers into one of the holes in the stuffing. He retrieved a large bullet, photographed it, and dropped it into a small plastic bag that he put into a box. When he reached for a second bullet, Meghan started to feel queasy again. She took a deep breath, headed back to the kitchen, sat down, and ordered herself to snap out of it.

Detective Sandoval sat down across the table from her. "Are you up to answering a few questions?"

"Go ahead." As many times as she'd been interviewed by the police at school about students who were being victimized or were in trouble with the law, she found herself struggling to answer basic questions. She had to pull herself together, starting now.

"Where were you when you heard the gunfire?"

"I was sitting right here at my kitchen table. I dropped to the floor, then crawled to the pantry and called 911."

"Good move. Have you noticed anything suspicious around your home lately?"

Meghan told the detective about the car that had stopped out front, and how she'd felt the driver was watching her house before he sped off. She couldn't describe him or the car. It might have been a midsize sedan, and she could only say it was a darker color. She thought it was a man but wasn't even sure of that. As a witness, she felt pretty useless.

"Can you think of anyone who's got it in for you, or who would have any reason to do this—like an angry ex-husband?"

"No. I don't have an angry ex or any enemies that come to mind." Meghan hesitated. "But I'm assistant principal at Central High. As the main disciplinarian, I'm probably not the most popular person there. But I doubt any of our students would do *this*."

"Someone did. Try to remember if anyone's threatened you."

"I will. Tomorrow I'll go over the list of students I've had to suspend or expel and see if anything jogs my memory."

"Good. Call me if it does."

Minutes later, Meghan heard Kate's VW pull up to the house. She'd recognize the sound of the Bug's rusted-out muffler anywhere.

Kate burst into the room, her wild mane of carrot-colored curls smashed down on one side and her eyes puffy. She must have been asleep when Meghan called. Kate reached out with her thin, freckled arms to embrace her friend. "Thank God you're okay. What happened?"

"Somebody fired a gun through my window."

The color drained from Kate's features as she spotted the chair. "Looks like they were aiming at your recliner."

"Maybe they got the wrong house," Meghan said. "Or it could be some random drive-by."

"In a drive-by, you usually get more scatter," said López. "These bullets are clustered."

Goosebumps rose along her arms. "So someone might have stood there, firing from right outside my window?" Had someone tried to kill her?

"It's too soon to come to any conclusions," said Detective Sandoval, glaring at Officer López. "We've just started gathering evidence from the crime scene."

López went red in the face and headed out onto the front porch.

Kate put her arm around Meghan's shoulder. "Maybe one of those drug dealers you busted at school did this to scare you. Anyway, let me help you clean up this glass."

"You'll have to hold off until we're finished with the crime scene," said Sandoval.

"Right. No problem." Kate turned to Meghan. "I could help you clean up tomorrow. Tonight you can stay over at my place."

"Thanks. I'll take you up on that. I don't want to stay here tonight."

"Neither would I," said Kate. "Now let's call someone about fixing your window."

"Good idea." Meghan checked her cell phone for the number of a glass company she'd used last month after vandalism in the chemistry lab. She was relieved to hear they had someone on call that could be there within the hour.

One of the detectives was back outside, apparently checking again for footprints or signs that the shooter might have been standing near the house. Then she saw him heading next door. She hated the thought of her neighbors being pulled into this.

When she retreated to her room to throw a few things into her overnight case, she noticed her white chenille bedspread was pulled up on one side. An officer must have looked under the bed in search of an intruder. Her mother's handmade quilt was still neatly folded at the end of her bed, yet her home no longer felt like her private sanctuary from the outside world.

Tires spun in the gravel driveway and came to an abrupt stop. Sandoval looked out the peephole. "There's a man getting out of a white Mercedes."

"He must be the other friend I called." She felt a flood of relief.

As soon as Bryan entered, he took her in his arms and held her. She longed to curl herself into his body and remain there, safe in his embrace.

He surveyed the room with intense blue eyes, his strong, angular features etched with concern. "You can't stay here!"

His steel-gray hair was tousled, and he wore faded jeans and a blue denim shirt. She was used to seeing him in a sport jacket, chinos, and a polo shirt. He was as handsome as ever, but he looked tired and upset. Old enough to be her father, he was a dynamic and youthful sixty-three, but tonight he looked more his age.

"I'm not staying here tonight. I'm going to Kate's."

"Kate's place is no safer than yours."

"I'll be fine," reassured Meghan. "Kate can follow me to work in the morning."

Meghan did feel safe with Bryan, and she was still moved by the warmth of his embrace. But she'd promised Kate, and she needed to talk. Kate had always been there for her since they'd become friends thirteen years ago, when they were new teachers at Central High. Bryan had a way of steering conversations away from stressful topics to things that were more pleasant, and tonight she needed to vent.

His face reddened. "Don't you suppose that whoever fired into your home knows where you work? Maybe you should take tomorrow off."

"I can't quit my job." She felt her stomach knotting up. She'd never seen him so upset.

Officer López stepped into the room. "Who is this guy?"

"This is my friend, Bryan James."

"And as your friend, I say you should come with me." His voice was getting louder.

"Take it easy, sir," said López. "The lady's made other plans."

Bryan's face darkened. "Let me explain. I have a state-of-the-art alarm system and live in a gated community with a guard. Her friend lives in a neighborhood with a higher crime rate than *this* one."

Kate went crimson, looking ready to explode, but for once she kept her thoughts to herself.

López eyed Bryan. She noticed the officer's subtle shift to a heightened state of readiness, his hand closer to his side. Detective Sandoval had stopped taking notes and was watching. Meghan needed to tone things down a notch.

She placed her hand gently on Bryan's arm, steadied her voice, and made an effort to sound calmer than she felt. "I'll be okay. I really appreciate your coming down here. Just having you here makes me feel so much better. I wonder if you'd do us a huge favor and follow our cars when we leave to make sure we get to Kate's house okay."

"Of course." Bryan's coloring started to return to normal.

Minutes later, the doorbell rang again. "Glass repair," a voice called out.

She opened the door. "Thanks for getting here so fast."

"I live close by, and I'm on call tonight."

The repairman measured the window. "Eight by four, like you said, but if you want this same type of window, it's going to be a special order. We haven't stocked these for years."

"I do want the same window type, but what can I do in the meantime?" She envisioned sitting up all night, guarding her house with a shotgun, like one of her students had done after a home invasion. The school social worker had discovered that the boy's sudden drop in attendance was because he was protecting his family at night and sleeping by day.

"I carry plywood with me. I'll get this boarded up for you and put your order in."

"I'd appreciate that."

As he worked on the window, Meghan and Kate tried to talk over the pounding in the front room. Bryan paced.

Finally Detective Sandoval stepped into the kitchen. "We're wrapping things up." She handed Meghan her card. "I wrote your case number on the back. Call me if you remember anything more about the car or driver, or anyone who might want to harm you."

"I will. Thanks for all your help."

Meghan drove behind Kate's old lime-green VW, with Bryan following in his Mercedes.

He waited out front until the two women were inside. Several minutes later, he called to inform them he was leaving. "If anyone bothers you, call 911; then call me—no matter what time it is. You're both welcome to stay at my place. I can come back down and get you."

"I appreciate that," said Meghan, "but we'll get along fine."

Kate sank into her couch as Bryan drove off. "I told you he was a control freak."

"He's just worried about me. I wish you weren't so down on him."

"I once served on a nonprofit board with him. He gets results but can be pretty controlling."

"He's used to running his own business. We're all upset right now, and Bryan wasn't himself tonight."

"How can you be so sure? How well do you really know him?"

"I've known him for years." Bryan had been a friend of her grandparents since they'd moved to their townhome. He'd been playing Scrabble with her grandfather when they'd first met. She'd joined in, and it had soon become a Sunday tradition. He'd even taken her grandfather to musicals when she couldn't make it.

After her grandpa's death, Bryan continued to play Scrabble with her on Sunday afternoons and escorted her to the remainder of the season's musicals. He helped take her mind off her grief and impressed her with his thoughtfulness. He was a true gentleman. Comfortable evenings together evolved into dates, and by Christmas, they were seeing each other twice a week.

"Yet in all that time he never mentioned his family or his past?" asked Kate. "Sometimes I get the feeling he's hiding something."

"Let's not go there tonight. My head's killing me. Bryan and I enjoy each other's company. What's wrong with that?"

"What's wrong is that you've had to be a caregiver for all these years. Now you've finally got a chance to get on with your *own* life—to marry and have a family, like you've always wanted."

"I'm too old for that now." Meghan had started taking care of her mother and family when she was fifteen, after her mother became ill. After her mother's death, Meghan had continued looking after her dad and younger brother. During her late twenties, she'd juggled teaching with the care of her grandmother; and then for the past four years, with the care of her ailing grandfather. Now she'd lost everyone except her brother, who was stationed overseas. Her dream of having her own family grew dimmer by the day.

"A friend of mine from yoga just had a healthy baby boy at forty-two, and you're only thirty-six. You'd make a wonderful mom, and you deserve that chance."

"You're the last one I'd expect to be pushing marriage." Kate's brief marriage to an abusive man, plus her mother's ugly divorces, had soured her on the subject.

"Marriage may not be for me, but I've had the good fortune to be a foster mom to Erin, and I wouldn't trade it for anything."

Kate could be relentless once she got started, and Meghan was starting to regret her decision to spend the night with her. Instead of getting a chance to vent, she felt she was being backed into a corner. Whether the man in her life had any interest in marriage or children was the last thing she wanted to think about tonight.

Meghan stood up abruptly. "I don't want to talk about this now. Not tonight. I'm going to get ready for bed."

After her shower, she appeared in her nightgown and robe, nail polish paraphernalia in hand. Meghan never fussed with her long, thick hair, and her idea of makeup consisted of sunscreen and a few swipes of lipstick, but she tried to be diligent about her nails.

"I'm sorry about what I said about Bryan," Kate said. "He ticks me off sometimes, but my timing was terrible. I've just been a bit on edge lately."

"What's going on?" Meghan shook her bottle of Apricot Ice polish.

"You've got enough on your mind tonight without hearing about my worries."

She set the bottle of polish down. "Now you've got to tell me."

"It's just that Erin's shut down on me. I'm afraid something's wrong."

"She *was* pretty evasive at her birthday dinner." As her godmother, Meghan had been part of Erin's birthday celebrations since Kate had become her foster parent four years earlier. Now Erin was a nineteen-year-old freshman at the University of Arizona. Meghan had first known her as a top soprano in her choir and had been there for her when she'd first reached out for help.

Kate removed a framed photograph from the mantel. The girl in the photo was a beautiful young woman with strawberry-blonde hair and sparkling green eyes. Erin could have passed for Kate's natural child and often did. The photographer had captured her radiance.

"Last month she told me she was modeling for some photographer," said Kate. "I got upset when she refused to tell me anything about the guy, including his name. I thought it had blown over, but today she gave me this photograph as a Mother's Day gift. It was done by *him*."

"It's a terrific portrait."

"I shouldn't bring this up now, after all you've been through, but when my phone rang tonight, I was afraid something had happened to her."

"Just keep in mind that this is her first year in college. Kids that age value their privacy." Meghan rubbed her temples. "Who knows? Maybe the guy's okay."

"Then why won't she talk about him? She's had to keep secrets from people all her life in order to survive, but not from *me*." Kate's eyes brimmed with tears. "I worked so hard to build a relationship between us where we could always be completely honest with each other."

Meghan laid her head back in the chair, suddenly overcome with fatigue. "Erin's a great kid, and she's always been resilient. We'll find some way to get through to her."

"I hope so," said Kate. "I just want her to have the chance to reach her potential. But she can't get there by hiding the truth."

"Not everyone's as open and honest as you are, Kate."

CHAPTER 2

The flag snapped, and dust devils drove students quickly to class, sweeping leaves and papers upward in spirals of wind. Dappled sunlight danced on the reddish earth beneath the large pepper tree, and the shadow of a hawk skimmed along the courtyard. With her bulging briefcase slung over her left shoulder, Meghan hurried toward her office at Central High, one of the oldest schools in Tucson. She squinted against the biting, fine-grained sand. Something about the hot desert winds set everyone's nerves on edge. She didn't need that today. Suddenly she yearned for the cool spring days of Maine.

After she and Kate had finally gone to bed last night, Meghan had only managed three hours of restless sleep. Unless they'd fired into the wrong house, someone wanted to terrorize or even kill her. It could be anyone—maybe one of the students watching her right now.

Meghan took in the school campus and parking lot, willing her mind into focus. Two girls carried a large piñata into the school, bracing it against the wind. She loved Tucson's many cultures and celebrations, like Cinco de Mayo, rodeo week, and Tucson Meet Yourself.

As choir director she used to eat, sleep, and breathe her job. She'd loved transforming students with untrained voices into a harmonious choir, and helping with the school's mariachi band. But a week after her grandfather's death, she'd been tapped to fill in as assistant principal. Still numb with grief, she'd accepted the position. It was a logical step toward her goal of making a real difference in education. Yet as the main disciplinarian, she often dreaded coming to work.

A crowd of students was forming near the flagpole, and it looked like a fight was brewing. Michael Roosevelt, her fifth-period aide, and Tony Montoya, a known gang member, were in the center. Meghan had been told that Tony's mother was a drug addict and that he'd grown up on the streets.

Warm, witty, and a natural leader, Michael was an athlete who'd been on the honor roll. As her student aide, the amiable African-American junior provided a bright spot in her day, but he'd gone into a tailspin after his parents split up.

She glanced over her shoulder, hoping to spot the campus monitor or the school resource officer from the police department. She called them, leaving messages to get over to the parking lot ASAP, but there wasn't time to wait for backup. She'd have to deal with it herself.

Ω

Michael's heart sank as he saw Miss Walcott storming across the parking lot, her long hair blowing in the wind like a wild mane. She looked almost fierce. He liked working with her in the front office and was learning a lot. She was caring and fair, and was helping him get through some tough times. The last thing he wanted was to get on her bad side.

Suddenly Tony shoved him to the ground.

Michael got up and brushed himself off. "Back off! What's your problem?" He didn't want to get in trouble again or cause his mom more grief.

Tony got in Michael's face. "What's wrong? Daddy ain't here to babysit you no more?"

Hands still at his sides, Michael glared at Tony.

Without warning, Tony pulled out a butterfly knife. Then someone pressed one into Michael's hand. He flipped it open and shifted into survival mode. His dad had taught him to fight. He followed Tony's eyes, stance, and hands. Every muscle was tense, ready to do battle.

Meghan approached the group just as the knives were drawn. She ordered the crowd to let her through, summoning her sternest tone of voice. "There's no fighting on this campus!"

The boys froze. She stepped into the center of the conflict. Her eyes locked on Tony's. "I need you to close those knives and turn them over to me," she commanded. Then she turned to Michael. She knew he respected her, as she did him. She was counting on it.

Michael hesitated for an instant, closed the knife, then handed it to her. She felt a flood of relief.

She glanced back at Tony, who flashed his empty palms at her. "No weapon, miss," he smirked.

She was glad to see the SRO from the police department heading their way.

Not far behind was Kate, with her blazing-red explosion of curls and the sunlight gleaming off her silver Concho belt.

"I'm sure you don't want the police to search you in front of your friends," Meghan said.

Tony glared at her with undisguised anger; then he reached down into his boot, retrieved the knife, and dropped it on the ground.

The excitement over, the crowd quickly dispersed.

Now she needed to call in the parents and suspend both boys. She'd already made several unsuccessful attempts this year to contact Tony's mom. She was determined to meet with her this time, if it meant going to the home or to the bar where she worked. Though Tony had a thick file of discipline referrals and a police record, she believed there was still time to help him turn things around.

Once the officer left with the boys, Kate turned to Meghan. "That's crazy, what you did. You really scared me."

"Michael wouldn't hurt me."

"He wasn't the only one involved." Kate frowned. "You took a huge gamble."

"I was the one in charge, and someone was about to get hurt."

"Maybe *you*."

"I'd already called for backup. A big part of my job is to make sure this school is a safe place—but sometimes I feel like a jail warden."

"You better start thinking about your own survival."

Meghan pushed her hair away from her eyes. "I know."

"Good." Kate hesitated. "Erin's roommate finally answered my call this morning and told me she's on her way to class. It's a big relief, but I still need to find a way to talk with her."

"I can go with you to her apartment after school."

"Rusty's going with me."

"Rusty Barnes?" Rusty was the tall, lanky, new biology teacher from Austin. Meghan had seen him talking with Kate in the hallway.

Kate nodded. "He's the only Rusty I know."

The five-minute warning bell rang, and the few remaining students filed into the school. Kate rushed off to her first-period class.

୬

Meghan felt warm, despite the damp breeze of the swamp cooler hitting the back of her neck. Across her desk sat Michael and Mrs. Roosevelt, with their chairs drawn as far apart as possible. They avoided each other's gazes. The anger and humiliation radiating from Michael and his mom seemed to generate a heat of its own.

A bank loan officer, Mrs. Roosevelt normally was a power-dresser, with perfectly coifed hair, and professionally manicured nails. This morning she wore scuffed loafers with slacks. Her hair looked uncombed, and two of her artificial nails were missing.

Meghan pushed aside an unruly wisp of her own hair, wishing she'd worn it up off her perspiring neck. She scanned Michael's permanent record card and turned to his mother. "I'm afraid he's been involved in another incident."

Mrs. Roosevelt looked at her son. "Another fight?"

Meghan knew there were a few troublemakers who resented Michael. They were probably jealous because he'd always been a star athlete and top student. A few of them seemed to be ganging up on him after his dad, the head football coach, took off with a student teacher. She'd have to find a way to put a stop to it, but for now, she had to suspend both boys. Though she hated to add more stress to his family, there'd been many witnesses to their weapons being drawn on the school campus. If she suspended only Tony, they'd say she was playing favorites.

"Michael has done excellent work up until last quarter, but lately he hasn't been turning in all his assignments, and he's been getting into fights. He was very cooperative when he turned the knife over to me this morning, so I was able to stop the fight before it took place. But this is the third incident, and there were weapons involved."

Michael looked her straight in the eye. "Someone put that knife in my hand."

"I believe you." She took a deep breath. "Can you tell me who gave it to you?"

He shook his head. "I don't know. They were behind me."

"But you were in the wrong place at the wrong time again," his mother said.

"So I should just stand there and get stabbed?"

"Of course not. You need to defend yourself. But you have to stop getting set up like that. You've got to steer clear of those kinds of people."

"They keep coming after me."

"I'll try to get to the bottom of that," said Meghan. "It needs to stop."

"Yes, it does. We don't need this kind of trouble," said Mrs. Roosevelt. "I'm sure you've heard by now that his father left us."

"I was very sorry to hear the news." Everyone knew about their trouble at home, as the affair involved faculty members.

She knew that Michael had been proud of his dad. He'd been a respected coach and teacher, as well as a devoted father who'd attended school functions and had taken Michael and his friends camping. As an All State quarterback, Michael had been following in his dad's footsteps until several months ago, when his father had taken up with the student teacher. He'd come home one day to announce to his wife of twenty years that it was over. Four weeks later, he'd resigned. He and his young lover were rumored to be teaching on some remote island in Alaska.

"I know this must be very tough," Meghan said. Kids could be cruel, and Michael bore the brunt of his dad skipping out on the football team midseason. Suddenly she felt tired—very tired from hearing the heartbreaking stories of her students. The freedom cry of one parent so often meant the powerful jaws of a trap slamming shut for the rest of the family. She wondered if there had ever been a time like this when individuals so avidly pursued their personal dreams, leaving behind such a wake of nightmares for their children.

"Of course it's tough," said his mother. "But it's no excuse for him to let his studies go or to get into fights. I'm working two jobs now." She turned to Michael. "You need to do your part."

"I'm trying." His voice broke.

Meghan blinked hard and looked away. He was a good kid. Michael had made such an effort to cope with everything that had been thrown at him, but her role gave her little choice. "Our social worker has a counseling group for students who are under stress or whose families are going through changes. It might help to have someone to talk with."

"Fine with me, if he wants to go. But my son is a very private person, Miss Walcott, and I respect that."

"Everyone already knows too much about my business." His eyes were fixed on the floor.

Michael had a point. "I'll find out what's available off campus. Right now, I need to write this up. I've no choice but to suspend you for three days. It's district policy." Meghan detested her job more by the minute.

"Do what you have to do." Mrs. Roosevelt gripped her handbag tightly, then dashed off her name on the forms. "Thank you for your time, Miss Walcott. I need to take him home and get to work. Let me know about the counseling. I'll do whatever it takes to help my son."

Meghan glanced up at the clock. She had six minutes to get to the cafeteria and call the faculty meeting to order. After the meeting, she'd take Tony home and race back to meet with some irate parents whose son had been kicked off the baseball team for missing too many practices. She'd already been contacted by their attorney.

She still needed to find time to go over the list of students she'd suspended to see if it brought anything to mind regarding threats against her. She checked her wallet for Detective Sandoval's card and found it stuffed in front of the one-dollar bills.

She felt a headache coming on—the kind that closed in around her temples. She hoped there would be some coffee left in the teacher's lounge and that it wouldn't be the dregs. It was going to be a long day.

CHAPTER 3

A man and woman sipped margaritas on a secluded patio overlooking the tennis courts at the Tucson foothills resort. Manicured cactus gardens, flowers, and Mexican fan palms lined the path to the main building. Beyond the tennis courts, the Catalina Mountains jutted skyward.

"Your friend, Mr. James, is creaming the number-one seed," observed the blonde with the deep tan.

"So I see," said Sarducci, a short man with an olive complexion and intense brown eyes that reminded her of her deceased husband.

Their heads turned back and forth as they followed the game. The older man positioned himself in the ad court and pounded the ball down the alley.

"He's on a winning streak," said Sarducci.

"Don't be bitter," said the blonde, aware that Bryan James had defeated Sarducci Saturday, 6–3, 6–4. "Maybe he can join us later for a drink."

"Forget about it," Sarducci said. "I love the old reprobate, but he's not your type."

"You attorneys never trust anyone."

"You're a social butterfly, and he's almost a recluse."

"Nonsense. He serves on two nonprofit boards that I know of."

"I've been thinking," said Sarducci. "Have you ever thought of moving away from here and starting a new life for yourself?"

"I don't want to move away. Besides, it wasn't me they were after." Her husband had been killed by a car bomb eight years ago. She figured if they'd wanted her dead, she would be.

"But it wouldn't hurt to get some . . . new associations."

"The same could be said for you. You could go somewhere where you weren't known as DA to the Mob."

"Lower your voice. That was a long time ago."

"There's no one around to hear us," she said.

"No reason to get careless."

"So now you're some kind of PI?"

"Just a retired tennis bum."

"Whatever you say. And Bryan James *is* my type."

She liked to watch him play tennis. He played with such fierce but controlled intensity. Too bad he always left right after his shower instead of joining friends for drinks. Devouring him with her eyes, she watched him stride to the net. Lean and muscular, he shook hands with the man he'd just defeated. Now he'd be at the top of his bracket—not to mention that he ran a successful engineering firm and owned a lot of land.

She watched him take off his sunglasses and wipe his brow. His eyes were an intense blue against his ruddy complexion and silver hair. His appeal was understated and his manner reserved, but judging from his tennis game, the reserve was superimposed over an intense, aggressive personality.

✧

On the court below, as Bryan shook hands with his opponent, he envisioned Meghan at courtside, smiling proudly. He pictured himself gently pushing aside her long, chestnut hair and kissing the back of her neck. Even during his tennis games, thoughts of Meghan invaded his concentration. He was still shaken by the attack on her home last night and upset about her refusal to spend the night with him. It was a wonder he'd been able to win the match after tossing and turning most of the night, then running around in the heat of the afternoon sun.

It was mid-May and already time to start scheduling tennis before work, while it was still cool. He wiped off his forehead, took a swig of water, and headed to the locker room.

Why in hell had they gone to dark paneling and a medieval look when they'd remodeled? All wrong for the Southwest and a complete waste of money. His feet sank into the plush maroon carpet as he removed his shorts and headed for the shower. He tried not to think of Meghan. In all these years, he'd been careful not to get too involved with anyone. He needed to get a grip.

❧

Bryan could see the entire valley from the balcony of his townhome in the foothills of the Catalina Mountains—the jagged peaks of the Tucson Mountains to the west, the rounded Rincons to the east, and the majestic Santa Ritas, halfway to the Mexican border.

His meeting with an important developer had gone well, and it was time to celebrate with a glass of Chablis. The developer had bought a large ranch northwest of town and wanted Bryan's civil engineering firm to design a planned community with small shops, pedestrian walkways, parks, swimming pools, and substantial open space left as natural desert. It was the first project in years to tap his creative interest.

He'd recently begun to enjoy a single glass of wine before dinner, and the sense of grace and control it signified to him. He may have been a binge drinker in his youth, but he'd recently concluded that he probably hadn't been an alcoholic. He was a different person now, and after years without touching the stuff, he decided he could begin to drink again, in moderation.

The wind was picking up, and a pall of dust hung over the city. He decided to finish his glass of wine in the den while he looked through his mail and watched the news. He reached for the remote and clicked on the TV. He wasn't sure why he made such a point of watching something so consistently disturbing. He was convinced that the human psyche wasn't meant to cope with all the worst disasters around the world each day, yet he tuned in to the news, like everybody else.

He learned that another border tunnel with a large cache of marijuana had been discovered; and that a body had been found in the desert. There was an investigative report on a phony home improvement business that had gone door to door, scamming local homeowners.

Suddenly the camera zoomed in on the perverted shrink Meghan had helped put behind bars. Why were they showing old footage of that predator, smiling arrogantly as he'd been escorted off to jail four years ago? He turned up the sound.

". . . escaped from prison in what appears to be a carefully orchestrated rescue involving a laundry truck. Authorities warn that the escapee, child psychiatrist Dr. Karl Devrek, could be headed for Tucson, where he ran two halfway houses for emotionally disturbed girls before he was sentenced to prison."

Bryan flipped to another channel. Same story.

He'd been uneasy about Meghan testifying against Devrek to begin with, but she was bull-headed. She'd been determined to do the right thing, no matter the consequences.

He left her messages at home and on her cell, then remembered she had choir practice on Monday nights. He grabbed his car keys and headed to the garage.

✢

Despite the gunfire last night and a hectic day at school, Meghan decided to attend choir practice rather than go home to a house full of broken glass. She figured it might help calm her nerves, but her lack of sleep and food soon caught up with her. Her voice was off, and she started feeling light-headed. She toughed it out for a while longer but excused herself an hour before practice was over and slipped out the back door of the church.

A deep bass rhythm reverberated along the avenue from passing cars, and she noticed it seemed darker than usual. Where were the parking lot's lights that always came on around sundown?

Instead of following the sidewalk, she slipped through an opening in the dense oleander hedge into the dark parking lot. The rustle of leaves in the wind didn't drown out the sound of heavy footsteps behind her. She wished she'd never left the church alone.

She walked faster, scanning the parking lot, then hesitated. All the cars looked empty except for a white SUV parked beside her car. She could make out someone sitting inside it. She debated whether to turn around and try to see who was following her or to make a run for her car. Her keys were already in her right hand, but she was uneasy about the man in the SUV next to her car. Maybe she should hurry back inside.

The footsteps were still gaining on her. She quickened her pace again, heart racing.

A powerful hand gripped her arm. She spun around. "*Bryan!* What are you doing here?"

"Keep your voice down and follow me to my car. I need to tell you something."

"Let's go back inside the church."

The SUV sped away, lights off.

"The guy who just tore out of here was kneeling beside your car when I got here. I couldn't tell what he was doing. When he saw me watching, he got back into that RAV4."

"I saw him too."

"It was dark, and I hoped he couldn't see *you*. That's why I didn't call out to warn you. "

"What are you doing here?"

"I need to tell you something. But just wait here in my car, with the doors locked. Give me your keys." He handed her his.

"My Buick for your Mercedes. Sounds like a good trade," she joked.

Bryan headed across the parking lot with a flashlight, circled her car, opened and closed each door, and looked around inside. He opened the hood, checked the engine, and slammed the hood shut. Then he got down on the pavement and eased under the car with his flashlight.

When he crawled out from underneath, he brushed himself off, crossed himself, slid into the driver's seat, and turned on the ignition. He drove her car around the lot, braked several times, and finally pulled up next to her.

"I can't believe you did that," she said. "If you thought there was a bomb, we should have called the police. They must have a bomb squad."

He got in his car and relocked the doors. "I don't think he had a chance to do anything yet. I was just being cautious."

"By turning on the engine and risking your life?"

He shrugged.

"Where did you learn to check for a bomb?" she pressed.

"I read a lot." He turned to her. "The reason I drove down here to meet you is that the psychiatrist you testified against broke out of prison two days ago. They just ran a news alert on Channel 4 that he might be heading to Tucson."

"*Devrek?*"

He nodded. "What if he had something to do with the gunfire into your house?" He spoke in a low voice. "I was afraid he'd track you to your choir practice. Looks like he might have."

She shivered. "I should notify the police."

"They can't provide you with a full-time bodyguard," he said. "That's what you need now, damn it."

"If it turns out he's behind all this, then Erin's in danger too." She dialed Kate and left her a message about Devrek's prison escape, adding, "See if you can find Erin and get her somewhere safe. Then call me."

"So what do I tell the police?" she asked Bryan. "That a guy was parked next to my car and drove off without his headlights on?"

"When I saw him kneeling beside your car, I got his license number. I'll make the call. Can you give me that card with your case number on it?" Bryan made the report, asking the police to call his cell when they arrived, as he and Meghan would be waiting inside the church.

"I need to fill in the choir director," she said. First, her neighbors had been disturbed and now her friends at church.

They followed the walkway to the side entrance. The door was open, and the organ was playing. They went down a corridor to the main chapel and sat in the back until there was a break. The choir director decided to continue with practice, but said she'd make sure everyone left together.

Meghan's mind jumped back and forth between the alarming events of the last twenty-four hours and visions of a hamburger and fries she wanted when she got out of there. She wasn't used to skipping meals.

Two patrol cars met them in the parking lot. Bryan was invited into one of them to give his statement, while Meghan waited with the other officer.

Then it was her turn. She recognized Officer Carlyle as the one who'd spoken last month to several classes about drug prevention.

"You're the new principal over at Central High, aren't you?" he asked.

"Assistant principal."

"Tell me what you saw."

"I hate to bother you with this. It's probably nothing, but there were shots fired into my home last night, and the detective in charge of my case told me to report anything else suspicious." She showed him Detective Sandoval's card with the case number.

He opened his laptop. "I'll pull up the information."

"It was dark. All I saw was someone sitting in an SUV, parked next to my car. It sped away with no headlights. My friend, Bryan James, told me he'd seen the driver kneeling beside my car. He was afraid he might be tampering with it. He was able to get the plates."

"Is there anyone who might want to hurt you?"

"Like I told the officer last night, I'm the school disciplinarian. I'm usually the one who has to call in the police when there are assaults or illegal activities on the school campus."

"Your friend reported you had some dealings with an escaped prisoner," said Carlyle.

"I testified against Dr. Devrek in court over four years ago regarding the molestation of a minor girl in one of his halfway houses. That's what got him sent to prison. Mr. James heard on the six o'clock news that Devrek escaped from prison two days ago. He came here to warn me."

"Do you think Devrek might want to hurt you?"

"I did feel threatened by him, right after his conviction."

"Tell me about the threat."

"As he was led out of the courtroom in handcuffs, he glared at me. Under his breath I heard him say, 'You made a big mistake.' He looked at me with such malice, I felt it was a threat."

"Did you report it?"

"I considered it, but I figured he'd have plenty of time to cool off in prison. And what could be done about an ambiguous comment like that? He could always claim he'd meant that I'd made a 'big mistake' about his guilt. But if he *is* after me, then his victim, Erin O'Neil, could be in even more danger than I am. She's the girl who testified that he'd raped her. Now she's nineteen and the foster daughter of a friend of mine."

"Erin O'Neil." He noted her name. "So you think the girl might be at risk too?"

"With Devrek escaped from prison? Yes." Meghan explained that Erin was a freshman at the University of Arizona and lived with roommates in an off-campus apartment. She gave him her goddaughter's address. "I'm very concerned about her. Could someone from the police department check on her?"

"I'll put in a request. I'm going to step outside to make a call."

"I'd like to make a phone call too, if that's okay."

"Go right ahead."

Meghan pulled out her cell phone and left another message for her friend. Kate rarely kept her cell phone on and sometimes didn't check her messages for days. Frustrated, she tried to call Erin but had no luck there either. With Devrek at large, they needed to find Erin fast.

She'd never forget the day when Erin broke down and told her what was going on. Erin had been a ninth-grader in Meghan's fourth-period class. Erin had always kept to herself, worked hard, and had one of the best voices in the choir. When she'd returned from winter vacation a week late, she'd been sullen, unkempt, and unwilling to sing. Meghan had asked her to stay after class.

Seated beside Meghan's desk, Erin's strawberry-blonde hair had fallen in an unwashed tangle across her pale skin, hiding her eyes and pretty features.

"You've been one of my most conscientious choir members, and our best soprano. But lately you don't seem to be singing much. Is there something wrong?"

Eyes cast down, Erin mumbled that she'd do better. When Meghan offered to give her extra practice sessions during lunch hour, Erin's eyes filled with tears.

Meghan handed her several tissues but resisted her instinct to give her a maternal hug. "I get the feeling that something's really bothering you."

Erin finally whispered, "I can't tell anyone."

"Maybe you should."

Erin talked about her classes, her difficulty in making friends, and problems with other teachers. Finally she confided, "It's just that . . . sometimes I feel really down."

"You feel depressed at times?" Meghan fought her urge to go find the social worker, fearing the moment might be lost.

"Like I shouldn't be here." Erin's mouth trembled.

Meghan's heart pumped faster. She'd attended workshops on suicide prevention and had memorized steps to take if someone confided suicidal thoughts. She'd hoped she'd never have to use what she'd learned, but if she did, she didn't want to blow it again.

She knew she had to ask the question. It was important to be direct, but the words almost stuck in her throat. "Have you thought about . . . killing yourself?"

Erin nodded.

"When was the last time you had those thoughts?"

"This morning," Erin said in a soft voice.

Meghan felt her throat tighten but did her best to sound calm. She focused on inhaling and exhaling slowly. She needed to keep Erin talking, to find out if she had a concrete plan. God willing, she could prevent *this* suicide.

Meghan tried to push from her mind the terrible image of her father wading alone into the icy waters of the Atlantic Ocean. Though no one had been there to see him, it was a vision that had tormented her for the past seventeen years, one that might haunt her until the day she died.

She took another deep breath to stave off her rising panic and asked the next question. "Have you thought of how you'd do it?"

Erin looked down at the cracked linoleum, tears falling onto her legs. "With a razor blade in the bathtub."

Red flags number three and four—*method and location!* Meghan could hardly breathe. Her mind raced ahead. She would call Erin's therapist over at the halfway house where she was in treatment, and they could get her the help she needed. She did her best to project calm. "How long have you felt this way?"

"Since he . . . since he started . . ."

"Who started?" If she couldn't reach someone in charge this afternoon, Meghan would bring Erin over to the mental health crisis center.

"Since that doctor started . . . doing it to me." Erin began to sob.

"Doing what to you?" Meghan handed her the entire box of Kleenex.

"You know." Erin paused, still crying. "He makes me have sex with him."

"Your *doctor* makes you have sex with him?"

"Dr. D, the shrink at the halfway house where I live. Over vacation, he made me stay at the house when the other kids went to the Desert Museum. He said it was a 'consequence' for 'acting-out behavior'."

"Dr. D?"

"His name is something like 'devil-wreck,'" said Erin.

The fine hairs on Meghan's arms stood on end. Dr. Devrek, the respected child psychiatrist. *Forget notifying the halfway house.* She had to call Child Protective Services and the police.

"How long has this gone on?"

"Since school let out for vacation."

"About four weeks ago?"

"I guess. But you can't tell anyone about this. He said he'd find my mom and kill her if I told. I don't even know where she is, but he said he'd track her down. Please don't tell anyone, Miss Walcott!"

But of course Meghan needed to report it. The hardest part had been convincing Erin to tell the police and social workers what had happened, then to retell it again in court.

Somehow Erin had found the courage.

When Officer Carlyle got back in the car, his expression was sober. "I ran the plates. The car Mr. James saw in the church parking lot was stolen this morning and was just found abandoned on West Speedway, near the freeway."

"Erin's apartment isn't far from there! Could they send an officer over to check on her right away?"

"We can do a welfare check and notify her about the escape of the prisoner, and we can ask if she's noticed anything suspicious. But if you think she's in danger, you might want to get her somewhere safe for a few days."

"That's easier said than done. I've been trying to reach her and her foster mom. I'll stop by her apartment after I leave here."

"If you're right that this escaped convict is after the two of you, you'd be making it very easy for him."

"I hadn't thought of it that way. But *somebody* needs to find Erin and protect her."

"Is she hard to find?" asked Carlyle.

Meghan felt her head beginning to throb again. "Sometimes it can be hard to . . . get in touch with her, now that she's in college."

"Unfortunately, there's not much we can do, even if we do find her, unless something happens. We can tell her how to file a restraining order, but that would be pretty useless against an escaped prisoner with nothing to lose."

Her stomach started to hurt. "I see your point."

"And keep in mind, it could be someone *else* who's after you."

"Of course. Whoever it is, I hope you find them soon."

Officer Carlyle opened his car door, signaling the end of the interview. "Please contact the detective assigned to your case if you notice anything else unusual. Try to change your daily routine and avoid going anywhere alone."

"Everyone knows I'm at the high school every day."

"Unofficially, if you were my wife or sister, I'd help you disappear for a few days until this guy is back behind bars. You and the girl, both."

"But I need to be at work tomorrow."

"It's your decision." The officer came around the car and opened the door for her.

Bryan was waiting in her car. As Carlyle drove off, Bryan told her that he'd been able to get a call through to Kate. "Kate and someone named Rusty were headed over to Erin's apartment to see if they could bring her back to Kate's. Bryan opened the door to the Mercedes. "We can pick up your car in the morning."

"I'm not leaving it here."

"Then you can drive *my* car, and I'll follow in yours. Don't let anyone pull in between us. I'll be right behind you until we get to the guard gate. Then I'll pull ahead."

"Fine." She was too tired and hungry to debate which car she drove.

CHAPTER 4

Campbell Drive wound high into the foothills of the Catalina Mountains, their rugged peaks looming ahead, ghostly white in the moonlight. Meghan could make out a set of headlights behind her and hoped it was still Bryan, driving her car. As she drove higher into the amphitheater of foothills homes, each tier of houses was more luxurious and commanded a better view of the city lights.

Normally, this was a favorite drive of hers, but tonight she felt like she was racing across the surface of an alien planet, tightly gripping the steering wheel with perspiring hands. The desert felt hostile, with its poisonous creatures and plants armed with spines. Every set of headlights could be Devrek or someone else trying to track her down.

Bryan pulled past her in time to be waved through the security gates, leading her along a winding, saguaro-studded lane that reached even higher into the foothills. As soon as she drove his Mercedes into the garage alongside her car, the heavy metal doors lowered behind them. She felt a wave of relief as they stepped inside.

He disarmed the security system and rearmed it for Occupied—Delay.

Gina, a golden retriever with sweet, sad eyes, bounded toward Bryan and skidded across the tile floor to await a hearty greeting. Sensing that things were different tonight, she sniffed him, then ambled off.

Meghan headed for the living room and collapsed into the white leather sofa. The high ceilings; white walls; bold, contemporary lines; and view of the city lights were grounded by the terra-cotta floor. A large, illustrated volume about southwestern gardening rested on a Noguchi freeform glass coffee table. Bryan's well-worn Herman Miller chair, bright cushions, and Navajo rugs saved the room from seeming cold and sterile.

"I'm going to heat up some lasagna from last night," he said. "Would you like some?"

"Thanks. In the meantime, have you got any crackers or a banana? I really need to eat something right now."

"Of course." Bryan reappeared moments later with a tray of cheese and crackers, grapes, and a banana. He turned on the TV, pushed aside a Two Gray Hills Navajo rug from the living room wall, and dialed the combination to a safe. He swung open the thick metal door and took out a stainless steel revolver.

"I thought you hated guns."

"I do." He shoved the bullets into the chamber and set the gun on the table.

"Do you think we were followed?" she asked between bites.

"Not that I could tell. But look at the position you put yourself in tonight, alone in a dark parking lot, after what happened last night."

"I didn't know about the prison escape yet—and I can't stop living."

"But sometimes it seems like you've no thought whatsoever for your own safety."

"That's not true." She retrieved a can of pepper spray from her purse.

"Precious little help against a gun."

"Maybe not."

"Listen, he said. "It's on the news again."

"Dr. Karl Devrek, local psychiatrist and convicted child molester, escaped from prison two days ago, and may have fled to Tucson," reported the TV newsman. "Authorities are investigating a possible link to a fatal car-jacking of a woman in northwest Tucson."

Now he's *killed* someone?" cried Meghan.

"Let's hope not. But I wouldn't put it past him."

The phone rang. Bryan's jaw tensed as he glanced at the caller ID number. "It's the guard house." He picked up the phone and listened. "Send them up, but no one else tonight. And please notify me at the first sign of anything suspicious."

Bryan disarmed the alarm, opened the garage door, and returned from the kitchen with the pasta. As he picked up his fork to eat, Kate burst into the room, flushed and perspiring.

"Have a seat," said Bryan. I'll make you up a plate of lasagna."

"No thanks. I just wanted to talk with you two in person. I got your messages, but I can't find Erin. Rusty and I couldn't get anywhere with her roommates. I told them it was urgent that I reach her, but I didn't go into any details. One of them got downright hostile and said Erin was old enough to make her own choices."

"I can't believe they were so uncooperative," Meghan said.

"Neither could I. How are *you* doing?"

"I'm fine," said Meghan. "I just want to help you find Erin. I told a police officer tonight that Devrek was in prison because of what he did to her and that we'd both testified against him. He said they'd try to do a welfare check on her tonight."

"The police were there before we arrived, but she hasn't been back to her apartment since she left for class this morning." Kate's voice quavered. "What if he already has her?"

"Don't say that." Meghan said. "Let's go search for her right now."

Bryan faced Meghan, red-faced. "You were told by the police to stay away from Erin because the two of you together could place you both in greater danger!" Then he turned to Kate. "The guard said there was a man with you."

"Rusty's out in the car."

"Please tell him to come in."

"We can't stay. He's in the car making calls on his cell. We're trying to contact all her friends. Unfortunately, most of them have lost touch with her since high school."

"I can make calls, too," Meghan offered.

"You've got your hands full right now. I've got six friends calling everyone on the list."

"Did you call Jackie Arland and Brittany Dryden?"

"Yes, but if you think of any other names, let me know. I'm glad you're staying here tonight with Bryan. Otherwise I'd be worrying about you too."

Meghan took another bite of lasagna, wondering if Kate were trying to make up for the negative things she'd said about Bryan the night before. Yet Kate always said just what she meant.

Kate paced back and forth. "Erin's roommates think she's with her photographer friend, the one she was modeling for."

"Modeling?" Bryan frowned. "Have you met this purported photographer?"

"I'm afraid not. Erin wouldn't give me his name."

"That says it all," he said. "Did you file a missing person report?"

"Not yet. Her roommates told the police that she went to class today and is probably spending the night with a friend. They reported that I check on her too much and harass them. In other words, the problem is *me*. But they don't know her boyfriend's name either."

"When I talked to the police, I stressed that she could be in serious danger," said Meghan.

"I hope that'll help," said Kate.

"They damn well need to do something," interjected Bryan. "I'll call the chief of police and tell him Erin needs to be a priority."

"Go right ahead," said Kate. "He'll probably tell you to contact the detective on the case, like they did when I called. And he might ask if twenty-four hours have gone by and remind you that she's of age to make her own decisions."

"Hasn't she always?" Bryan asked.

"Exactly what do you mean by that?" Kate demanded.

"Hasn't she always done whatever she wanted?"

Kate turned crimson. "Are you saying I just let her run wild?"

"Don't put words in my mouth."

"You're a wonderful mother," said Meghan. "Erin's so lucky to have you in her life."

"I'm out of here." Kate stormed out the door, slamming it behind her.

"I wish you could try to get along with her," Meghan said. "She's done an amazing job as a foster mom, considering everything that Erin's been through."

"I'm aware of that," said Bryan. "I just think your goddaughter could have used more discipline to make up for the apparent lack of it in her early years. She seems like a good kid with a lot of potential, especially in her art. That's my take on it."

Meghan turned to Bryan, surprised. "I didn't realize you knew about Erin's talent in art." She'd assumed he wasn't particularly interested in her goddaughter or in art. His home was decorated with American Indian rugs, pottery, and woven baskets, but not a single painting.

Bryan moved to the kitchen and started sorting through his mail. "I've seen some of her work. She came out to my office a couple months ago and wanted permission to do a pen-and-ink of my building. She showed me a portfolio of her work. It was excellent."

"I don't recall you ever mentioning it."

"If I mentioned everything that happened every day, you'd be bored to tears. I told her to go ahead and draw my office and I'd buy it from her when it was finished."

"I'm sure she'd give it to you."

"I thought it might boost her self-confidence to sell her artwork."

"I suppose it would. She may be having a tough time handling her freedom, but Kate's done everything in her power to encourage Erin with her art."

"That girl always had too much freedom, if you ask me."

"How could Kate make up for Erin's first fourteen years of being raised by a drug addict? Who but Kate would have even tried?" Why couldn't the two most important people in her life get along?

"Let's drop it. If you like, I'll run your bath. You need some time to relax."

"That sounds good." She took her plate to the kitchen, then headed to the whirlpool spa.

The terra-cotta floor and fixtures were trimmed with white and cobalt-blue Mexican tiles, as was the sunken tub. The bathroom opened to a balcony that overlooked the city. Outside the window, dwarf sago palms and potted red geraniums provided privacy without blocking the view.

Her neck and back ached. It seemed as if every cell in her body was sore, and she was exhausted from lack of sleep. She stepped gingerly down into the hot water, grateful for the chance to be alone. Bryan had supplied fresh towels and a handmade bar of lavender soap. He was always thoughtful and considerate. Sometimes it seemed as if he met needs she didn't even realize she had.

Bryan couldn't stop thinking of what would have happened to Meghan if she'd been in her favorite chair last night or if he hadn't met her tonight in the church parking lot. He admired her dedication to her students and her courage to stand up for her convictions, yet these were the very qualities that could get her killed. Sometimes, she seemed oblivious to danger.

He knew she was upset about her goddaughter, who was as dear to Meghan as if she were her own daughter. The temperamental teenager needed to learn self-discipline, as well as to believe in herself, or her artistic talent would go to waste. Once things settled down, he'd discuss it more at length with Meghan and encourage her to find a discreet way to relay the message on to Kate. He would not attempt to convey his ideas to the girl's high-strung mother again.

Bryan knocked on the bathroom door and entered with a glass of Chablis and a recent issue of *Sunset Magazine.* "Something lighter to occupy your mind." He placed it on a magazine holder that swung over the tub.

"I really appreciate all you're doing to help me."

"You deserve more. Take your time, darling. Your things are hanging behind the door. I could use another shower myself. I'll be down the hall."

Bryan had poured her warm baths before, often when she'd had a tense day at work. It wasn't easy for her to get her mind off the daily crises at the high school. At first, she'd been annoyed when he'd consistently steer conversation to more pleasant topics, though lately she'd begun to treasure their quiet dinners together and welcome the respites from pressures of work. He helped her take time to appreciate simple things, like a desert sunset or a great cup of coffee. She'd come to value his gift for creating a comfortable space, insulated from outside pressures.

According to Bryan, Meghan needed to learn to compartmentalize work from leisure. She figured he spoke from experience. Though they'd known each other for years, and had dated for several months, she sensed he held some essential aspect of himself apart.

Was Kate right that she didn't really know him? Alarming thoughts spun through her mind, and she was starting to get a pounding headache. Had Devrek been the one who'd fired into her home? If not, who had? Had someone tried to plant a bomb in her car? Was Erin in danger?

Finally, the tension in her muscles responded to the heated jets of water that exploded against her skin, and the wine was starting to take effect. The valley looked like a jewel box of glittering gems from the oversized tub high above the city. Even tonight, Bryan created a sense of refuge from the outside world.

Gina nosed her way through the door, wagging her tail. She flopped down beside the whirlpool bath. Now and then the retriever stood up to peer into the tub. Meghan reached up to rub behind her ears.

Finally, she dried herself with the thick towel and stepped out onto the cool tile floor. Hanging on the back of the door was a silk gown and matching robe for her to slip into. She ventured down the hallway, letting herself be drawn into the sheltered, serene world of Bryan's creation.

The French doors leading to his bedroom were open. A vintage Navajo Storm Pattern rug lay at the foot of his bed. Candlelight flickered on the walls.

Bryan reclined on the king-size bed. He seemed to watch her with the expectancy of a new groom. He arose, never taking his eyes from her as she came to him. He took her face in his hands and kissed her.

She nestled into his arms, finally feeling safe.

"Are you sure you don't want to sleep in the guest room tonight, darling? I know you need to get your sleep tonight."

"I'm not sure of anything at the moment." She pulled him closer.

He embraced her gently, then forcefully. Bryan was the consummate lover—considerate, passionate, and sensitive. She gratefully lost track of time and place, drifting off to sleep in his arms.

In the middle of the night, she was awakened by the howling of coyotes. She thought of Bryan turning on her car ignition in the church parking lot. He'd been ready to die for her. She reached for his hand and fell back into a troubled sleep.

He stands frozen in the bedroom doorway of the small farmhouse. Through layers of gauze, he sees the two lovers look up in panic. He tries to cry out but cannot. He hears two blasts. Then everything goes black.

Bryan awoke in the middle of the night, drenched in sweat, his head throbbing. Meghan was asleep, safe and sound, by his side. The nightmare began a thousand different ways, but the ending was always the same—except that this time the woman was Meghan.

He thought of her last night in her bath, her hair pulled off her neck with a scarf and her hazel eyes sparkling. Her smile had warmed him to the bone.

Then he rolled over, cursed his sore shoulder and knees, closed his eyes, and tried to return to the nightmare so he might finally remember. He tried to visualize the two of them. He willed the terrible scene to unfold, to no avail.

He arose, crossed himself, stumbled to the bathroom, and splashed cold water on his face. With his gray hair disheveled and wrinkles deep as crevices, he viewed himself in the mirror with great displeasure. He'd managed to maintain things on an even keel all these years. He needed to keep it that way.

CHAPTER 5

Eddie spotted Erin waiting on his back steps, her face an angry red. His desert bells clanged in the wind, as if in warning.

"Where were you all day?" she demanded. "I just about had a heat stroke waiting here."

"Why in hell did you come here anyway?" he snapped. "This isn't your day."

"I need to talk with you about something."

"I don't have time." Eddie stormed into his small rental home with Erin right behind him. He surveyed the place with disgust. The floor and bed were littered with dirty clothes, and the sink overflowed with dishes. An odor of garbage intermingled with the scent of marijuana.

Damn! He had to figure things out fast and didn't need Erin around to distract him. Dr. Devrek had broken out of prison! Worse, somehow he'd found out that Eddie was hitting on Erin. The *good doctor* had contacted him, demanding that he deliver Erin to some treatment center in Vegas, promising a generous sum if he made the delivery. Devrek would take it from there.

Eddie's gut feeling was to slip across the border to a place where he could lay low until the law caught up with the deranged shrink and locked him back up. But there was always a price to pay for crossing Devrek.

Eddie would never forget the time one of the male techs confronted Devrek with his concerns that someone at the center was molesting the girls. The tech had been blackballed and was never able to work again in the mental health field in Tucson. Not long after that, the guy's sister was raped and her house set on fire. Eddie had no doubt who was behind it. The shrink was sadistic—and vengeful.

An old friend who'd worked as legal assistant for Devrek's defense attorney had let him in on a few creepy details from the shrink's background that couldn't be used in court. As a kid, Devrek had set fires and beat up on handicapped kids. No surprise there. He'd been sent to juvy and had wound up in special education, labeled "emotionally handicapped." But Eddie had him pegged as a sadistic sociopath.

Like a rattlesnake, the doctor had managed to shed his deviant identity and criminal record. Eddie figured his special ed. records were probably destroyed five years after graduation, like his own, and that he must have been able to get his juvenile records sealed. But Devrek had been accepted at the university and made it all the way through school to become a psychiatrist. The bastard was smart, but had no business in a helping profession—or anywhere, except behind bars.

Now he was back on the loose, demanding Eddie do his bidding and bring him Erin. And here was Erin, big as life. Maybe he should go with the psycho's plan, *then* slip away.

"I wanted to surprise you." She grabbed a Diet Coke from the refrigerator.

"I hate surprises."

"Well, excuse me."

"Look, this isn't a good time."

"See ya," she snapped. "And don't expect me to come back."

"Hold on a minute." He'd probably live longer if he did exactly as he was told. He hadn't planned to follow through on Devrek's orders, but Erin had presented herself to him on a silver platter, and the thought of getting on his bad side made his blood run cold. The guy was a dangerous predator. He needed to stall a few minutes while he figured out what to do, which wasn't easy in his current state.

He touched her arm. "Sorry, babe. Why don't you go ahead and stay?"

"Make up your mind."

"Since you're here, we can have some fun. And let's do another photo shoot. We can add some pictures to your portfolio—something more cutting-edge."

"I told you I'm not into that kind of thing."

"If you want to make it as a model, you need to show a range of work. And it's not like I haven't seen you nude." He flashed Erin his sexiest smile. "There's nothing more beautiful and authentic than a photograph of a nude, when it's artistically done."

"Not if it's *me*. And it was your idea for me to do modeling, not mine."

"Let's just try a few shots. If you don't like them, we'll tear them up."

"You'd better."

Eddie changed the lenses and moved the fill light slightly to the right. "Hold it just like that." The girl on the sofa was pale, her skin translucent in the artificial lights, and her long, strawberry-blonde hair draped strategically over her shoulder. Her green eyes seemed focused at a point beyond the lights, and a thin, freckled arm lay aesthetically across her slightly protruding abdomen.

He should have his head examined, hooking up with the chick that got Devrek sent to prison, but she was so hot. Eddie had been outside the courtroom four years ago with the other photographers. The only difference was that he'd been working for Devrek, photographing the jurors and the two females who'd testified against the doctor. He'd taken some very nice shots of Erin. Trouble was, he'd blown one up into a poster and hung it in his bedroom and hadn't been able to get her out of his mind since.

Four months ago, he'd spotted her studying alone in a crowded coffee shop near the university. He'd asked if he could sit at her table and inquired about what she was studying. When he found out it was art, he threw a lot of jargon about composition and lighting into the conversation and did an impassioned spiel about the great impressionists.

When Erin expressed interest in having her portrait done as a Mother's Day gift, he'd gone to his car to retrieve his portfolio. He'd quoted a price that was way too high, then offered to do it for free if she'd give him permission to add her photograph to the portfolio. Erin bit on it, hook, line, and sinker, as had so many others.

As promised, he'd done her portrait, and it had turned out to be one of his best. He'd convinced her to study under him, and then he had seduced her. Unlike most of the others, Eddie continued to invite her to his place. He'd made sure they stayed below the radar and had never appeared with her in public. How in hell had Devrek found out— from prison?

The chick had no idea that Eddie had once worked as a psych tech at a halfway house run by her rapist. Dr. Devrek had once caught Eddie taking lewd shots of one of the girls. He'd called him into his office, closed the door, and threatened to fire him and report him to the police. Then the shrink had stroked his sparse, pathetic beard and drummed his fingers on the desk. "Maybe there's a way out of this mess. We could have a kind of arrangement." When Devrek turned around to adjust the blinds, Eddie noticed a dark, ugly mole on the back of his neck.

Devrek had gone on to suggest that Eddie would need to be more discreet and should be sure to pass along any especially interesting photos to *him*. In turn, the shrink would not turn him in to the police and would compensate him well. Eddie had allowed himself to be blackmailed and wound up supplying the pervert with a steady stream of child porn.

Working for Devrek had definitely helped Eddie's bottom line and had given him a start in the business. But the shrink gave him the creeps. Eddie knew he wasn't much better himself, taking nude shots of the patients who were minor girls and selling them online. But the doctor had set himself up as a respected authority in the community. He'd duped people into believing he was a caring and trustworthy expert in the care of young people.

Eddie had heard Devrek cleverly use a Freudian term in a staff meeting to twist a girl's hysteria about being molested into a case of *transference* involving past abuse—when she was actually being raped by her own shrink. Eddie had left the staff meeting early to puke his guts out.

Before Erin had come forward, no one had ever had the balls to stand up to the bastard, and the psycho had enjoyed free rein with all the girls. Who would believe *them*, with their thick files of severe behavior problems and well-documented track records of compulsive lying?

Eddie wished to God he'd never laid eyes on Devrek and had been relieved when the creep was locked up. Now the bastard expected Eddie to jump to his tune again—but this went way beyond taking pictures of nude girls.

He and Erin could head for the border together, but if he didn't do as he was told, he knew the good doctor would take speedy revenge on them both. Maybe he should drop her off in Vegas and make an anonymous report to the police just before he crossed the border.

"Can you turn down the cooler? I'm getting cold," she said.

"Don't move. I'm almost done. *Girl with Child*, I'll call it."

"That's not funny in the least."

"You got that right."

She was irresistible, in a fragile sort of way. She looked even younger than her nineteen years and possessed a rare, highly sought-after blend of innocence and sensuality that projected so well from his photographs. He kind of liked her. She was different. She had big dreams for herself and even for him. But the whole Erin thing had been too risky from the start. It was his own fault, and now he'd gotten her knocked up.

"Chin up, just a bit. How about a slight pout? That's right." He was walking a fine line with the little bitch, and everything was going wrong. Now he'd run out of time.

"I've been thinking," she said. "I'd like to try painting a live model. Not a nude, but someone who would hold still long enough for me to finish the drawing. That would be so great. My friends at the U only pose for a few minutes; then they get bored and leave."

"Right. With your talent, no problem." He couldn't believe the chick's big head. He thought of Miss O'Neil, the redheaded bitch who'd once tried to cram English lit down his throat. He'd like to see her face if she found out what he was doing to her daughter.

"I think I'll head up to Vegas for a while," he said. "I need to make a run up there in the morning. Ride along—we'll have some fun."

"I've got finals coming up."

"Don't worry. We'll be back in time. No problem."

Erin looked at Eddie—slender, with dark hair. He was wearing his burgundy silk shirt that showed off his tattoos. He was compelling, in a cold sort of way. His eyes seemed to bore right through her when he took off his mirrored shades. He was the kind of guy who had things under control. He drove the best car, dressed cool, and played by his own rules. And there was this sensitive, artistic side to him. He was intense about his photography, like she was about her art.

At first, it seemed like he took her seriously as an artist and taught her some of the principles of photography that applied to her field. She'd felt they were on the same wavelength. But lately Eddie was pushing her into more and more revealing poses.

And now she was pregnant. She'd come by today to talk about the baby, holding out hope that they could raise their child together, but it still didn't seem like the time to bring it up.

Erin wished she could think of a way to have the baby without Kate finding out. Her foster mom was the only one who'd ever believed in her, other than Miss Walcott. Maybe she could go away for a while, have the baby, and give it up to a family that could provide a good home.

Kate was going to be disappointed in her. She'd made a point of stressing hard work, self-respect, and responsibility, and had made it clear that she didn't want Erin to have to sacrifice her future because of something like drugs or an unwanted pregnancy.

"Tell you what, babe," Eddie said, turning off the lights and unzipping his jeans. "You want a model? You got one." He stood naked in front of her, then mounted her with a creepy smile that made her stomach churn.

Erin felt disgust. He'd made love to her before, but this time she felt used.

Afterward, Eddie got right up and took off to get beer and cigarettes, promising her a Dove Bar. Erin rifled through his dresser drawers for a match. She wanted to be well on her way to getting stoned before he got back with the chocolate bar. Maybe it would help her block out the sickening feeling that something was terribly wrong.

She looked everywhere for matches to no avail. She found a bureau in the back of the closet and jimmied open the bottom drawer. It was stuffed with twenty-dollar bills. A poster with a rubber band around it was on top.

As she started to pull it out, she felt a sharp blow across the back of her head. She fell forward, gashing her forehead on the bureau.

"What did you do that for?" she asked, her eyes wide with disbelief. "And where'd you get all that money?"

"I told you to stay out of my stuff! If I can't trust you, even for a few minutes, why don't we just forget it?"

"Forget it, Eddie? *Forget* it?" Her forehead was bleeding, and her eyes stung with tears. "What about this?" She touched her abdomen.

"What about *this*?" he shouted, raising his hand and striking her again and again, even in the stomach. "Do what I tell you to do, you little bitch, or next time I'll kill you." His eyes betrayed an unyielding cruelty she'd never seen in him before.

He silenced her hysterical screams with an undershirt tied across her mouth, then bound her arms and legs, leaving her sobbing on the closet floor.

Later that night, he untied her and gave her the chocolate bar. He promised not to hurt her again, but she must never again disobey him. He told her she needed to be taught discipline.

He wasn't the first person to tell her she needed more discipline. There were teachers all through school who'd said the same thing. Maybe he was right.

"I shouldn't have gone through your stuff. I'm sorry." She hurt all over, down to her soul, like she'd hurt as a small child when she was beaten by her mother. Maybe she deserved this kind of treatment—but Kate and Miss Walcott had spent four years trying to convince her otherwise.

He returned later to brush away her tears. "Take it easy, babe. It's going to be okay." He rocked her like a small child.

The next morning, she awoke to the disturbing sound of his voice. "Get yourself dressed, and let's get out of here. I'm sick of hanging around this rat hole."

Feeling numb, she gingerly washed herself up. Her jeans and blouse were still folded neatly over the back of a chair. Her hands trembled as she put them over her badly bruised legs and stomach. To think that last night she'd planned to bring up the subject of the baby and their future together!

That was never going to happen. But she felt she'd better go along with him, at least for now. Maybe the weed would calm him down.

"Eddie, why don't you give me a joint? I need to mellow out."

"That's more like it." He lit one, then inhaled and exhaled with relish until he couldn't hold it anymore without burning his fingers.

"What about me?" she asked.

He took out the roach clip and passed it to her, laughing.

CHAPTER 6

Sunlight shone through the open window, and Meghan heard the cooing of doves. She'd overslept and would have to rush to make it on time for breakfast with Kate. Every Tuesday morning, they met for an early breakfast at the Prickly Pear, north of the university. Today they had a lot of catching up to do.

She picked up the phone to let Kate know she might be running a few minutes late, but the line was in use. She was surprised to hear the familiar voice of Dr. González, her superintendent of schools. She covered the mouthpiece so no one would hear her eavesdropping.

"I see your point," said her boss. "I'll look into the possibility of a leave of absence."

"Thanks. I'm just concerned that someone might be targeting her," said Bryan.

"Hopefully not. See you Saturday for mixed doubles. I don't know who they've assigned us for partners, but at least mine won't be Chelsea," Dr. González said. "We decided we'd rather stay married." He and Bryan laughed, then hung up.

Meghan stormed down the hall to Bryan's office.

He looked up from his desk. "I think you should get away for a while."

"I can't believe you meddled in my career like that! I'll make my *own* plans," she said. There are still two weeks of school before summer break, and I'm on an extended contract."

Bryan's face reddened. "You listened in."

"I was about to call Kate when I heard my boss on the line."

"We were setting up a tennis match, but the most important thing to me is your safety. I'm sure the school district can manage without you for a while, and he happens to agree."

She was too angry to continue. "We'll have to talk later. I have to get ready to go."

"Why don't you invite Kate here for breakfast? It would be a lot safer. I'll whip up some eggs Benedict, and leave the two of you alone to talk."

"Thanks, but we always go to the Prickly Pear." He was becoming downright overbearing, and she needed to hold her ground.

"Suit yourself, but try to be careful, for once."

Meghan arrived first at the Prickly Pear, a popular restaurant that had once been the winter residence of a prominent mining family. With hand-carved beams, thick adobe walls, and rounded archways, it retained the gracious southwestern charm of many early Tucson homes. Great food, proximity to the university, and a comfortable ambience made it a haven for students and locals.

Meghan seated herself under a large acacia tree that shaded a handful of tables in the inner courtyard. Freshly cut hyacinths in china vases adorned the wrought iron tables, and the air was permeated with the aroma of fresh roasted coffee, cinnamon, and baking bread.

As Kate entered the courtyard, she moved with the flowing grace of a dancer and the free spirit that she was. She turned heads wherever she went. Today she wore one of her colorful full-length skirts, a jade-green blouse, and bright beaded necklace that Meghan recognized as Erin's handiwork. With Kate's panache, not to mention her natural beauty and slender figure, she could pull it off.

She loved Kate's exotic look, but Meghan was more comfortable at work in a classic dress or suit, with turquoise jewelry or a simple gold or silver necklace.

Kate ordered strawberries in a cantaloupe bowl and nine-grain toast with prickly pear jam, while Meghan chose a Denver omelet, cottage fries, homemade biscuits, and freshly squeezed orange juice. She glanced at her watch. It was already 6:45.

"Any word from Erin?"

"Nothing so far. Last night, Rusty and I checked out every college hangout we could think of. Then we went back to her apartment. Her roommates told us to butt out."

"Unbelievable. Do they know about Devrek?"

"Probably not, and it's not my place to share it. But I told them I've reason to think she could be in danger."

"The police showing up last night to check on her ought to have given them a clue."

"You'd think so," said Kate. "I need to find her today to let her know what's going on, in case she hasn't seen the news about Devrek's escape."

"I wish I could talk to them myself, but the police warned me against going to her place."

"I know. And I'm worried about you too. Have you been able to get any sleep?"

"I slept a little better last night." Still seething about Bryan's call to the superintendent, Meghan felt like spewing out her frustration to Kate but didn't want to give her any more ammunition against Bryan.

Kate bit into a large strawberry. "I've been thinking. Some gang might be trying to scare you into stopping your crackdown on drugs at school."

"You could be right."

"What about Tony, the one who's always getting in trouble? You should have seen him glare daggers through you yesterday when you broke up that fight."

"He's an angry kid."

"Just keep an open mind and be careful. No more heroics."

"I had to make a split-second decision, but I promise to be careful." She spread honey on her biscuit, then tried to wipe it off her fingers. "After work, I'll help you look for Erin."

"I appreciate it, but I'm going to wait and see," said Kate. "Her roommates are sure she'll be back after class today."

"I hope so. Then we can get her to somewhere safe."

Kate speared another strawberry with her fork and raised it to her lips. "But what about you? Why don't you get away from here for a while?"

Meghan spilled coffee on her dress and dabbed at it with her napkin. "Sounds like you've been conspiring with Bryan."

"Now that's what I'd call paranoid. But maybe he's right this time."

"Maybe so, but—" There was a loud crash in the courtyard. Meghan ducked.

"It's okay. A waiter just dropped a tray."

Still shaken by the crash, Meghan's hands trembled so much that she set her fork down and placed her hands in her lap for a moment. Then she picked at the rest of her breakfast, gulped down the last of her coffee and asked for the check at 7:16.

By 7:22, they were in their cars headed to Central High. Meghan had to stop at every light but one, and traffic near the high school was backed up for blocks. When she finally arrived, fire trucks blocked the entrance. The uproar seemed to center around the administration wing.
She forced her way through the crowd.

Meghan's secretary, Lupe Alvarado, tearfully embraced her. "Gracias a Dios you didn't come in early like you often do, Miss Walcott!"

Finally, the fire department and police allowed the administrators and a few faculty members into the building, and Meghan was escorted down the hallway by an arson detective. Though the fire was out, smoke still lingered. When she saw nothing burned, she started to feel relieved.

Then she caught sight of her office. There was graffiti on the glass showcase in front of it, and the words, "Next time school will be in session, bitch." The entire room was gutted. All that remained on her blackened desk were the ashes of paperwork she'd thought was so pressing. An old photograph of her with her parents and younger brother was burned beyond recognition.

Tears came to her eyes and bile rose in her throat. She raced to the restroom and was sick. As she wiped off her perspiring face, someone banged on the door.

"It's Kate. Are you alright?"

"Lost my breakfast, but I'm okay."

Kate and Lupe were waiting outside the door when she came out.

"Let's head on over to the nurse's office," said Lupe, guiding her by the arm.

"I'm fine. But that was my only copy of that photograph."

"Why don't you lie down here on the cot and rest for a bit," directed the school nurse.

"Just for a couple of minutes." She lay down, closing her eyes. She felt a cool cloth placed over her forehead.

Minutes later, she heard the voice of Mr. Weiss, her principal. She opened her eyes and saw him seated beside her cot. She sat up.

"In five minutes, I'm going to set off the alarm again, for the students to come back inside," he said. "There's no damage anywhere but your office. I think you should go home for the rest of the day. Get some rest."

"I have to finish the summer school schedules. What I've done so far . . . is gone. I need to start over."

"Ángel Orozco did them for years. I'm sure he wouldn't mind doing it."

Ángel was one of the best counselors she'd ever met. He cared about his students and knew every angle on how to get them into the classes and colleges they wanted.

"Sounds like it's all been decided," she said.

Bryan stood in the doorway. "Kate told me what happened. I can take you home."

"I'll drive myself home, but could you walk me to my car?"

Students watched and whispered as they waited in long lines to reenter the school, and three local TV camera crews filmed their exit. Her face felt warm as the cameras zoomed in, reminding her of the day four years ago when Devrek's verdict was announced. She wondered if the arsonist might be there in the crowd, enjoying the show.

Her stomach churned as she drove. When she pulled up to her house and saw her boarded-up window, she remembered she hadn't had a chance to clean up the broken glass yet. She led Bryan around to the back door, and they entered through the kitchen.

Once inside, Bryan crushed her against him as if he were afraid to let her go. He led her to a rocking chair in the kitchen, plumped a pillow behind her head, and pulled up a chair beside her. He took her chin gently in his hand and looked into her eyes.

"Listen to me, darling. I want you to listen very carefully."

"I'm listening."

"I don't want anything to happen to you. You need to go away for a while, where no one can find you. You're in real danger, whether you want to believe it or not. I've done some checking, and what I've learned concerns me even more for your safety."

"I shouldn't have to leave. I'm not the criminal. What happened today looks like it was done by some angry kid in a gang. There was a lot of graffiti around my office."

"Or you may be facing a psychopathic killer," he said quietly. "Either way, you could be in serious danger. You can leave this evening and be thousands of miles away from here before anyone knows you're gone. When Kate called me about the fire, I got in touch with a contact of mine across the country. I don't want to say much about it now, but it's all arranged."

"You can't be serious."

"School is out in a couple weeks anyway, and the school district will support you on this."

"I can't believe you intervened in my career again like this, without my permission. I need to talk with the superintendent myself."

She pulled out her cell phone and scrolled to his number. "I need to speak with Dr. González. It's Meghan Walcott." She practiced her deep breathing as she waited to be connected.

"I'm sorry to bother you, Dr. González, but I wanted to discuss the fire set in my office this morning."

"I was about to call you," he said. "The graffiti specialist from the police department gang unit just informed me that the graffiti around your office wasn't done by any known gang. He thinks it's likely that someone deliberately tried to make it look gang-related."

"Why would anyone—"

"Someone appears to be targeting you. My job is to make sure we protect the students and faculty. We don't need any more incidents."

"No we don't." She couldn't help feeling like a student who'd misbehaved.

"Vacation is almost here, and we can get by without you during the summer. I'm confident the matter will be resolved by fall, if not sooner. I know you're on an extended contract now, and you'll be placed on paid leave. It won't be charged against your personal or sick leave."

"There's work I still need to finish."

"Mr. Weiss will be responsible for whatever needs to be done. There's no need to go by the school or administrative offices, assuming you have direct deposit."

"I do."

"I was able to get emergency approval from the board," he added with finality. "I've got to take this next call. Good-bye."

Meghan set the phone back in the receiver and stared into space. Everyone was pressuring her to go into hiding. She stared out the kitchen window, deep in thought.

"I don't see how I could leave Kate and Erin right now."

"Kate has a lot of help," said Bryan. "And after you leave, if Erin's really missing, I'll personally see to it that no stone is left unturned in finding her."

"Hopefully, she'll be back tonight or tomorrow, but I appreciate your offer—very much," said Meghan. "I've got a lot to think about."

She hated to admit it, but she couldn't see herself going back to Central High School. Not tomorrow, the day after tomorrow, or next week. What was worse, the school district couldn't wait for her to disappear. The assaults on her home and office had already brought the school unwanted notoriety, and they probably weren't yet aware of the incident at her church. Everyone around her seemed to be in danger, including her students.

The phone rang, and Bryan passed her the receiver.

"How are you doing?" asked Kate.

"Couldn't be better," she snapped.

"I just got a call from one of Erin's roommates. She's agreed to meet with me tonight at Delectables on Fourth Avenue. She seems to be more concerned about Erin than the others."

"I'll go with you," said Meghan.

"You've got enough to deal with right now, and Rusty will be there with me."

"I hadn't realized you and Rusty were so close."

"This has brought us together, and right now, he's a lifesaver. He's offered to move in with me for a while until things get back to normal."

"Oh, Kate."

"The lease on Rusty's apartment is up at the end of the month, and it just seemed . . . to make sense for both of us. I don't want to be alone right now. Maybe after things settle down."

"It's your decision."

"I *hate* it when you say that. You sound like my mother used to."

"She loved you, and so do I. You can't always depend on some man to get you through every crisis." Meghan flushed, glad Kate couldn't see her there with Bryan's reassuring arm around her shoulder.

"You may be an island, Meghan, but I'm not. And speaking of you, think about what I said this morning. Get away for a while until things cool down. You must have accumulated enough personal leave by now."

"Bryan's offered to send me to Outer Mongolia."

He shook his head with a frown, signaling her to drop the subject.

"So make your own arrangements, but *go*," implored Kate. "I would if I were you. Protect yourself. Anyway, gotta go. Bye."

Meghan sat in silence again. Finally, she turned to Bryan. "Kate agrees that I should go into hiding for a while."

"What do you think?"

"I hate the idea. I don't feel like going anywhere. I've done nothing wrong." She longed to stay right here, her head nestled against his chest. "But I'm a target at the moment, which endangers those around me, including our students."

"That's right. But look at it this way. You'll be paid for the leave, and it could turn into a nice vacation."

"Hardly." She hesitated. "But I'm going to accept your offer. I'll take myself out of the picture for now. Then everyone can focus on finding Erin."

"Good." Bryan headed for the door, with a look of resolve. "I'll come by at a quarter to six to drive you to the airport. That should give you plenty of time to pack. Bring some cold-weather gear and a good book or two. Don't bring your cell phone—it might be tracked. I'll return library books, pick up dry cleaning, tie up whatever loose ends you have, and arrange to have the broken glass removed. Be sure to leave me a list of instructions."

An hour later, she found herself wandering aimlessly through the house, opening and closing bureau drawers, as if in a dream. She ate a few saltines to settle her stomach. Then she sat down and sorted through her mail, placing the bills in her purse. She scrawled out a list of instructions for Bryan.

She rummaged through her closet and drawers, tossing navy slacks and jeans, blouses and tee shirts, a sweater, and a light-blue sweatshirt onto her bed. Then she folded them into her suitcase. She added a light jacket and reached for the gold chain and locket her mother had given her for her fourteenth birthday, along with a well-worn volume of poems by Robert Frost.

"To Meghan Walcott, from her loving father," read the inscription. One of her earliest memories was of sitting on her father's lap as he read poetry to her.

She looked through the bureau for her snapshot of Bryan. He was in his tennis gear, racket ready, with a confident stance and jaw set with determination. He looked every bit the formidable opponent he could be. She wished she'd asked him to take off his sunglasses so she could see his eyes, but she hadn't pushed it because he hated posing for photographs.

Suddenly she remembered her promise to Michael and his mother. She called her contact at the counseling center, then dialed his mom to give her the information. She wished them the best, reiterating how much she thought of Michael and how bright and talented he was. She encouraged them to stay involved with Mr. Orozco, Michael's counselor, but stopped herself before blurting out that she'd be away.

She took a last look around the house, including the living room with its boarded-up window. The holes in her recliner gaped at her, and shards of glass were still strewn all over the floor. Her home was no longer her haven from the world. She tensed up at the sound of each passing car, and was relieved to see Bryan's car pull into the driveway.

CHAPTER 7

They rode in silence to a private airstrip north of Tucson. Bryan still hadn't told Meghan where she was going. As they approached the runway, she saw only a small, single-engine plane and hoped it wasn't the one she'd be flying in, but he pulled up to the single-prop Cessna, opened his trunk, and hoisted her bags out onto the tarmac. He exchanged a few words with the pilot but didn't introduce them.

Bryan took her aside and told her she'd be met at the plane in El Paso and driven to the international airport, where she'd catch a commercial flight. She'd need to use her real name and ID there, of course, but when she arrived at her destination, she was to go by the name of Anne Maxwell. He handed her a prepaid cell phone and a driver's license with her photo and new alias. He'd used her middle name, Anne, along with her mother's maiden name. She couldn't remember sharing it with him, but Anne Maxwell had been her great-grandmother's name.

"Thanks for the phone, but this other name is going too far. How do you even know how to do this kind of thing?" She slipped the phone into her purse and handed the fake ID back to him.

He firmly pressed the driver's license back into her hand. "Keep your voice down. Overkill is better than leaving a trail."

"I'm not the criminal, remember?"

"And you don't want the criminals to find you. We need to hurry."

"How long do you expect me to use this alias?"

"Just a short time, hopefully." Bryan handed her a sealed envelope. "Don't open this until your next stop, and don't use the ID unless you're in a real bind."

She hesitated, setting her tote bag down on the tarmac. "Where am I going?"

"Your boarding passes are in the envelope. The man meeting your plane in El Paso will be driving a white van. Open the envelope at your next stop, and you'll know where to check in. At the end of the third flight, a man named Jeff will meet you in baggage and take you to your destination. He'll find you by what you're wearing and address you by name. He drives a blue Ford pickup. Try to keep a low profile and avoid striking up conversations on the trip." He handed her a copy of Tony Hillerman's *The Dark Wind*. "Reading keeps the talkative types at bay."

She turned back toward the Mercedes. "This doesn't feel right."

"Just trust me." Bryan kissed her on the cheek, his eyes moist. "Now, go!"

She looked at the plane, then turned back to Bryan, her mind racing. She hadn't placed so much trust in anyone since she was a small child, and she was infuriated that he was keeping her in the dark. She could still walk away from this.

If she didn't get aboard this plane, where could she go? Her employer had made it clear that, as a target, her presence endangered students and everyone around her. If she didn't leave now, she'd have to come up with another plan to disappear—fast. She hesitated for an instant longer and made her decision.

"Promise me you'll help Kate find Erin."

"I've already promised," he said gruffly. "If she's not already back by now."

"I sure hope she is." She kissed him good-bye and climbed into the copilot's seat.

The pilot helped her fasten her shoulder harness, closed the doors, took his seat, and prepared for take-off.

The Cessna began to vibrate. The propeller roared.

She watched Bryan turn away and walk quickly back to his car. Through a blur of tears, she caught a last glimpse of him driving off as the Cessna turned and began to taxi down the runway.

A pall of reddish dust rose high into the air as the evening sky blended from carmine to purple. Deep violet shadows fell across the jagged peaks and desert below. As they flew east from Tucson, darkness closed in.

They landed on another small runway near El Paso. As promised, she was met by a man who drove her to the main airport in a white van. Once settled into the van, she opened the envelope containing her boarding passes. She was to depart from El Paso International Airport in an hour and forty-three minutes on an American Airlines flight to Chicago, connecting with a flight to Traverse City, Michigan. She'd be met there by a man name Jeff, who would recognize her by what she was wearing.

She was annoyed with herself for obediently waiting to open the envelope. She'd thought of opening it on the Cessna but had been sitting right next to the pilot. At least now she knew where she was headed.

Until the gunfire into her home two nights ago, she'd never seen this overprotective side of Bryan. She wasn't sure what to make of it, but his compulsive secrecy and elaborate planning would make her harder to track. The pilot who'd flown her to El Paso apparently hadn't been told who she was, so there would be no record of her leaving Arizona. Still, she feared she might have been followed somehow. How easily caution could turn to paranoia.

The driver pulled up to the terminal and helped unload her bags. Aware that security personnel were trained to look for nervous passengers, she did her best to act calm as she processed in. Last to board, she tried to ignore the impatient glares of other passengers as she made her way to the rear of the plane. Once seated, she took out her book, but the humming engines soon lulled her into needed sleep.

At two in the morning, she was awakened by the flight attendant directing passengers to prepare for landing. They circled O'Hare for several minutes before touching down.

Inside the terminal, she began to relax. She had over three hours to get to her gate. She moved through the concourse in a daze, alongside other sleepwalkers. Boys with close-cropped hair in military uniforms drifted past her. Many of them looked younger than her high school students. Harried mothers with strollers and armloads of paraphernalia attempted to comfort crying infants. A slightly wilted flight attendant with dark circles under her eyes maintained her jaunty pace along the moving walkway. They were all in motion, yet somehow suspended in time, in some ill-conceived holding pattern.

Three and a half hours later, she fastened her seatbelt. How could this be happening? She was headed to a place she'd never been so that she could hide from someone who wanted to harm her. It felt surreal.

The lights dimmed and the small commuter jet backed away from the gate, moved into position, taxied down the runway, and lifted off. As they flew over Chicago, she saw skyscrapers and a vast blanket of lights that ended abruptly in a curved edge of unbroken darkness that must be Lake Michigan. Then there was only the inky blackness of the cold water below.

An hour later, as they made their descent, she could see the lights of a small city on a bay. The pilot announced their arrival in Traverse City. As she felt the thud of the wheels on the runway of Cherry Capital Airport, she considered catching the next flight back to Tucson. Yet she'd come this far and was curious about the place where Bryan had decided to send her into hiding—and someone had risen well before dawn to meet her here.

She stepped out into the cool night air and looked across the runway to the small terminal and surrounding woods. She inhaled deeply. It felt like her first full breath since Mother's Day.

At baggage claim, a tall, angular man with gray hair eyed her carefully. "Anne?"

She glanced behind her, then quickly turned back to him. "You must be Jeff."

"Jeff Larsen." He extended his hand. "I'll be taking you the rest of the way. You'll be staying in the cottage behind our house."

"Great." She smiled as if she knew where she was headed. "Thanks for picking me up."

Once they'd retrieved her bags, Jeff loaded them into his pickup camper shell, held open the passenger door, and invited her to hop in. What had Bryan told this man? Probably not much.

As they followed the narrow highway out of town, the woods crowded in, making the night even darker. Finally, darkness began to give way to light, and she could make out rolling hills, rivers, and lakes. They drove through the small town of Honor, then climbed back into the hills. A large expanse of water called Crystal Lake glistened below them in the predawn light. They descended into the Village of Beulah, ascended another steep hill, and drove on.

At the crest of a hill was a gateway arch over the highway topped with a miniature scale-model car ferry, complete with tiny cabin lights. Jeff slowed to a stop. "Welcome to Frankfort. That's Lake Michigan out there."

Below lay the sleepy darkness of a small harbor town before dawn, a sliver of rosy light reflecting off water that extended to the horizon like an ocean. She could make out a ship in the predawn mist. She swallowed hard. It reminded her of the small harbor town where her family had spent summers in Maine.

"It's beautiful," she said. "Sky-blue pink,"

"It's been awhile since I've heard that expression." Jeff's eyes twinkled.

"I must have picked it up from my grandpa." She was about to tell Jeff that he'd recently died, but stopped herself. That had happened to *Meghan*.

They turned left to follow the bay at the base of the hill, then turned onto a narrow dirt lane that led to a white farmhouse.

A sturdy-looking woman with salt-and-pepper hair approached the truck. "You're just in time for breakfast. I'm Joan." The woman smiled warmly and offered a firm handshake. "I bet you could use a good meal."

"I'm Anne Maxwell," she heard herself say. "And yes, I could."

"Then please join us for breakfast, Anne."

A teenage boy already sat at a long oak table in the kitchen, while Joan turned out large blueberry pancakes, mounds of scrambled eggs, and Canadian bacon. "This is our youngest son, Joel. He just turned sixteen. Our other two boys are married now, with kids of their own. Greg's down in Grand Rapids, and Jason is out west, in California."

"I can't believe you two are already grandparents," said Meghan, anxious to dive into the pancakes. She hadn't had a meal since the breakfast she'd lost yesterday morning. She devoured her serving and pronounced it the best breakfast she could remember. Joan responded by dishing her up another portion.

"It's nice to see a woman with a hearty appetite," said Jeff.

Meghan found herself wondering how these friendly, down-to-earth farmers could be connected with Bryan. She couldn't begin to guess and was too tired to try.

"It's a fine time of year to visit these parts," said Jeff. "Downstaters miss the wildflowers and cherry blossoms. The ice melted off last month, so your timing's great."

Joel Larsen was tall like his dad. He spoke little but watched her with sidelong glances. Meghan thanked the Larsens and asked to be shown to her quarters.

Jeff led her to a small white clapboard cottage with dark-green shutters. It was about fifty yards behind the main house, amid a small stand of birch. He unlocked the door and handed her the key. "If you need anything, just let us know."

Overwhelmed with fatigue, she slipped out of her shoes, collapsed onto the bed fully clothed, pulled the heavy comforter up over her chin, and sank appreciatively into the plumpness of the down pillow.

CHAPTER 8

The grease-smeared owner of a remote gas station in northwestern Arizona yanked the nozzle out of the gas tank, carefully wiped the dark tinted windshield of the silver Porsche, and approached the ladies' room. If it weren't for folks traveling through Mohave County on the way to Laughlin or Las Vegas, Zebadiah would have gone out of business years ago.

The girl's face was swollen, with two black eyes. She'd been in the restroom a long time, and the man revved the engine impatiently. Fancy car, young chick to push around. He'd seen the type—a real bastard.

He rapped on the restroom door and rapped again louder. "You okay, miss?" He waited, ignoring the threatening stare of the man in the car.

"If you don't answer, I'll have to send in my wife with the master key. Just let me know if you're all right." Probably pretty without the bruises. She reminded him of his daughter's friend.

"Damn," he cursed, as a pack rat scampered along the wall.

"I'm okay." The girl spoke so softly he could barely hear her voice. He glanced again at the man in the car before returning to the cash register.

When she finally came out, her face was damp and pasty white, and she looked teary-eyed.

"Are you sure you're okay?" Zebadiah asked.

"I'm sure," she mumbled, turning away. She got in the car, collapsed into the seat, and shut the door. The driver of the Porsche cast him a warning glare and screeched off down the highway.

Zebadiah went inside, tore the flyer for last month's church supper off the wall, and scrawled the license number on the back. He picked up the phone, started to dial the sheriff, then thought better of it. He was worried about the girl, but what crime had he witnessed? The girl looked beat-up but would likely deny it. She could have been in an accident, though his gut told him different. The guy in the Porsche was bad news.

If Zebadiah called the sheriff, he'd have to give his name, and he and his wife lived alone in the desert. They didn't need any trouble. He placed the phone back in the receiver, folded the flyer, and slid it under the cash register.

⚘

Erin's ears rang from the buzz of locusts back at the gas station, as if she could still hear them in the moving car. Doubled over with pain, she tried to focus on the distant dust devils and waves of heat rising from the road ahead. Tears streamed silently down her face.

"Take me home, Eddie," she sobbed. "I don't want to go to Vegas. I lost the baby."

She hurt and was still bleeding. She felt a terrible mixture of grief, anger, and fear. She was sure Eddie's blows last night had caused the miscarriage of their baby. He would be overwhelmed with guilt, and she didn't want to make matters worse by saying the wrong thing. Yet in his eyes, she saw nothing.

"Sit on that blanket there, will you? You're going to have to come along for the ride. The last thing I need is more trouble. We're almost there, and I need to take care of some business."

Stunned, she turned to look at him. "I want to go *home!*"

He silenced her with a sharp blow across the mouth. Trembling, she surreptitiously pulled out her cell phone to text her mom.

Eddie screeched to a stop, ripped the phone from her fingers, and struck her again. He pulled the battery from the phone, rolled down the window, and hurled the phone into the desert.

What could she have ever seen in this monster? He was no better than the heartless men her birth mother used to bring home. She curled up against the seat and cried herself to sleep.

When she awoke, they were coming into the city. She tried to distract herself by watching the huge neon signs, but they seemed to flash at her relentlessly. Her head throbbed in pain, like the rest of her body. Even gas stations screamed out their presence with gigantic neon billboards.

Blinking, swirling, surrealistic ads pulsated across the skyline. She'd always wanted to visit Las Vegas, but tonight it seemed unbearable.

Finally, Eddie pulled up to a neatly groomed complex of beige stucco buildings. Dark-red lava rock encircled date palms in a yard of white pea gravel. Near the entrance were clusters of orange and violet lantana. The sign out front read *Ocotillo Center for Girls*.

"What are we doing here?" she asked. "What *is* this place?"

"Relax. I know a doctor here. I want him to take a look at you and make sure you're okay. You don't want me to take you to an ER, do you?"

"No, I guess not."

She was confused by Eddie's sudden concern. Maybe he cared about her after all, but had a serious anger problem. She'd been accused of having a bad temper herself but had never hurt anyone—physically, at least.

She thought of Kate and all that she'd put her through. Her foster mom must be frantic with worry by now. Kate had done everything in her power to provide Erin with whatever she needed to build a good life for herself, even after such a tough start. She loved and believed in Erin, as did her friend, Miss Walcott. She had to find a way to call home.

"I want the doctor to check you out," said Eddie, guiding her into the front lobby.

A short, solid man in a burgundy blazer approached. "So, what have we here?"

"This is Tiffany. Tiffany, say hello to Dr. Fritz."

"Tiffany," the doctor nodded, almost as if he'd been expecting her.

She glared back, saying nothing.

"Tiffany's a sixteen-year-old emancipated minor, and needs to be seen by the doctor." Eddie glared at her in warning not to contradict him. "She just suffered a miscarriage."

Dr. Fritz eyed her, touching her cheek. "Very nice, even with those big shiners."

She shivered. Why was Eddie lying about her name and age? Maybe he gave her a fake name to protect her privacy, and maybe he tried to make her seem three years younger than she was because they only treated minors.

"You can wait over there, Tiffany." Dr. Fritz directed her to a sitting room with deep red carpet, red and gold wallpaper, three leather love-seats, and two large ficus trees. As she gingerly sat down on the worn leather cushion, she caught a glimpse of a wad of cash changing hands. What was going on? This place was giving her the creeps.

She picked up a magazine and glanced through it, but her heart was racing too much to focus. After a few minutes, she slapped the magazine down and returned to the front desk to tell Eddie to forget it. She wanted to go straight home.

But Eddie was gone! She ran to the door and tried to yank it open. It was locked.

A tall, pink-haired girl appeared. She guided Erin firmly by the arm down a hallway. "I'll show you to a room."

"I was told to wait right here for the doctor." Erin felt more alarmed by the minute.

"I'll take you to his examining room."

"I need to make a call, and my cell phone's missing."

"We aren't allowed to call out," said the girl. "Please follow me."

"I'm not staying here!" cried Erin.

Pink opened the door to the room and pulled fresh tissue paper over the examining table. "You can use this restroom if you like. Then wait here. The doctor will be in to see you soon."

CHAPTER 9

The song of a robin greeted Meghan on her first day in northern Michigan. She breathed in the cool, moist air. Spring had already come and gone in Tucson with a burst of yellow palo verde blossoms and cactus flowers. In the Sonoran Desert, even parched saguaros and spiny cholla cacti burst forth with brilliant, waxy blooms. Now she would be granted a second spring, reminiscent of those from her childhood in Maine.

Maybe it was time to make the best of a bad situation and do some exploring. But first, she needed some wheels. With his new driver's license, Joel Larsen jumped at the chance to give her a lift to a small rental car business. Tired of the white, silver, and beige cars in Tucson that reflected heat and showed little dust, Meghan chose a dark-blue Chevrolet Impala.

She paused at the top of the hill to take in the misty harbor town in the light of day, then drove the four-year-old Chevy into Frankfort. She continued on M-115 as it turned into a charming residential neighborhood with Victorian homes; then she got out and walked.

Blue spruce flourished and enormous oaks and maples created a canopy over Forest Avenue. After walking several blocks, she heard a moving version of Beethoven streaming from an open window of a white clapboard house with blue-gray trim. She noticed tulips and daffodils lining the walkway to its front porch.

A large lilac bush extended out over the sidewalk, its blooms within reach. Meghan gently drew a branch toward her, pressed her face into the blossoms, and inhaled. Her eyes stung with tears as she recalled her mother's fragrant lilac bushes.

"Lovely, aren't they?" asked an elderly woman from her porch swing.

Meghan looked up in surprise. Beside the woman was a man wearing faded jeans and a dark-blue tee shirt.

"The lilacs are heavenly, and so is the music," she answered.

The man broke into a broad smile. "Thank you. That's me on the CD," he said in a rich, baritone voice.

"Beethoven's *Für Elise,*" she said. Something about the rendition struck her as familiar. She imagined he must cast a compelling figure at the piano, with his impassioned playing, good looks, and full head of dark-blond hair.

"Are you a fan of classical music?" he asked, disarming her with his steady gaze.

"Yes, I am—especially as you play it." Heat rose up her neck into her cheeks.

"He's a wonderful pianist, don't you think?" asked the woman.

"I certainly do. Have a nice day."

There was a lilt in her step as she headed toward town with the music still running through her mind. He was an amazing pianist, and it was nice to see a man taking time to have tea on the porch with an elderly woman. Maybe he was her grandson.

Meghan was glad to see there were still front porches where people sat and greeted passersby, and it was also great to see lilacs, daffodils, and tulips once again. She'd missed them.

Main Street in Frankfort followed the Betsie Bay. The familiar, plaintive wails of seagulls cried out to her from her past. As she passed a battered dredging barge, she got a strong whiff of someone cleaning fish. From a trawler near shore, an old man laid out his nets in the sun to dry. Tossing tiny fish to the circling gulls, he seemed to be scattering silver dollars across the water. Moored sailboats and cabin cruisers shone bright white against the dark-indigo bay.

Before long, she reached the Lake Michigan shoreline, where there was water as far as the eye could see. She found it difficult to think of this enormous body of water as a lake rather than an ocean. She followed the long boardwalk across the beach and out onto the northern of two piers that reached out into the lake, protecting the harbor like two sheltering arms. When she got to the end, she looked up at the lighthouse, then back toward shore. Enormous dunes jutted from the water's edge to forests high above. She sat down and dangled her legs over the side, lifting her feet when larger swells slapped against the concrete breakwater.

Meghan remembered sitting with her dad on a wharf near a cottage in Maine. He would cast out by the hour, seldom catching fish but entertaining her with stories about historical figures, such as John and Abigail Adams, and Thomas Jefferson. He'd been a history professor and had always been able to make the past come alive. When Meghan's younger brother, Todd, was old enough to join them, father and son began fishing in earnest, and Meghan learned to sail with her grandfather in the Atlantic Ocean.

When a large sloop left the harbor with its sails beginning to fill, the thrill of gliding through the water on a sailboat came back to her. She pictured herself skimming along the surface with sails unfurled, like a great bird in flight. She couldn't wait to get out on the water again.

She noticed a man in a hooded jacket and dark glasses making his way out to the lighthouse. Standing alone on a pier that was a quarter mile from shore, she suddenly felt vulnerable. As the man approached, she saw his fishing pole and stringer.

She chided herself for being nervous. She'd come all this way to elude her stalker. It was bad enough to be forced into hiding. She didn't want to become paranoid and see everyone as a potential threat.

Trying to strike up a conversation with him, she asked, "Do you happen to know the name of these fish that look like big minnows?"

"Alewives," the fisherman said, turning away to cast out again.

Terse and to the point—a quality her New Englander grandfather had valued.

Meghan headed back toward shore. She flipped open her new prepaid cell phone to try again to reach Bryan but got no answer. She'd already left him a brief message that she'd safely arrived and had tried calling again before leaving the cottage. She was anxious to talk with him.

She'd never seen him so upset or domineering as he'd been this past week. She understood that he cared about her and wanted to protect her. Though she was used to handling things on her own, she had to admit that his take-charge personality was part of what had first attracted her to him. She'd liked his handling of details, like making dinner reservations.

Their dates were the old-fashioned kind, where a gentleman brought flowers, helped the woman on with her jacket, and held the door open. After years of caring for her mother, her dad and brother, and then her grandparents, Meghan enjoyed being coddled and looked after. Though Bryan hadn't brought the subject up, she assumed they might one day marry.

She decided to call Kate.

"Where *are* you?" Kate asked.

"I arrived early this morning, and I'm fine. Everything's okay at this end. But have you found Erin yet?"

"I'm afraid not. She didn't return to her apartment last night. I'm getting scared. One of her roommates is starting to get worried too."

"I should be there helping you find her."

"I want you to stay put—*wherever you are*," said Kate with a twinge of irritation." I'm going to file a missing person report, and I'm trying to get the word out any way I can. Rusty and I have friends handing out flyers in places where she hangs out, and friends of hers are putting the word out through all the social media. I can't think of what else you could do right now."

"I'd like to be there to support you."

"You're supporting me right now, over the phone. Hopefully, you're somewhere safe, so I can at least stop worrying about you."

"Don't worry about me. I'm fine. Have you considered accepting some help from Bryan? I know you two aren't crazy about each other, but he promised me that he'd help you find Erin. He knows a lot of people, and he's good at getting things done. I'll remind him to call you as soon as I talk with him."

"As a matter of fact, he's coming over for dinner tonight with me and Rusty."

"Really?" Meghan tried to hide her surprise. "That's great."

"I hadn't expected his call, but I can use his help. In the eyes of the law, I'm just a foster parent of an adult woman—one who often stays over with her boyfriend. I'm having trouble getting the authorities to take her disappearance seriously."

"I told one of the officers who interviewed me that Devrek had gone to prison because of her testimony," Meghan said. "I'd think the police would take *that* seriously."

"There is a police detective who seems very concerned, but somehow I'm starting to get the feeling that finding her may not be a big priority. I hope I'm wrong. Anyway, I've got to go. I've got to straighten the house up a bit."

Later, while Meghan was baking a fresh trout that Joel had given her, Bryan finally called.

"I'm glad you've safely arrived, and I hope your accommodations are satisfactory." He sounded like a hotel desk clerk.

"The cottage is nice, and I like the Larsens. Thank you for arranging all this. How do you know them?"

"Our prison escapee is still on the loose," he said, ignoring her question. "Don't forget, we need to refrain from saying too much over the telephone."

"Yet the phone's all we have right now," she countered. "Maybe you could visit for a weekend. We could talk freely, and there are so many things here we could enjoy together."

"We'll see."

"What's wrong?" Meghan felt like she was talking with a stranger.

"I'm not sure what you're referring to, but I need to go now."

Bryan paced his living room, rearranged books on the coffee table, and straightened cushions on the white leather sofa. He'd been relieved to know Meghan had arrived safely, but was disturbed by her question about his connection to northern Michigan. Sending her there had been the best plan he could put together in a matter of hours, but he was uneasy about her being in the world he'd left behind. He hoped he hadn't opened a Pandora's Box.

He settled into his comfortable Eames chair and glanced at the *Wall Street Journal* headlines, but his thoughts returned to his tense conversation with Meghan. He knew he'd been cautious and reserved, which had upset her. Though she was on a prepaid cell phone, he was concerned that someone might have tapped into *his* phone line.

Now that Meghan was gone, it was time to start pulling away from her. She could never really be his. She had her whole life ahead of her, while his life had effectively ended long ago. Until she'd left, he'd managed to avoid thinking about the future and had actually begun to feel something close to happiness.

The sense of vitality and joy he'd found with Meghan had vanished into the night as the single-engine Cessna disappeared from view. He felt as if he'd lost an arm or leg, the severed nerves raw and exposed—yet he hadn't even told her that he missed her.

He assured himself that she'd be safe there in the small harbor town in northern Michigan, far from Arizona. She was to use an alias and spend only cash, which he could wire to her. It should be almost impossible for someone to track her. He'd arranged for her to live on the grounds of an honest, dependable family. She might even be able to enjoy a brief vacation.

Now he had to prepare for dinner tonight at Kate's. He was in no mood to be around people tonight, let alone Meghan's temperamental friend, but he'd already promised.

He sipped the remainder of his second glass of cabernet sauvignon. Until recently, he'd maintained a self-imposed limit of one glass of wine before dinner, but his thoughts returned to an expensive bottle of Pinot Noir he'd saved.

He reached under the bar, retrieved it, uncorked it, and filled his crystal wine goblet. He took his time, then poured himself another glass. Seated at the hand-hewn mesquite table, he put his head in his hands. Gina approached gingerly. She pressed her head against his thigh and looked up at him with great, sad eyes.

Kate lived west of the university in an older adobe home. Bryan noticed that she'd replaced the window in the front door with stained glass and hung an atrocious, tie-died fabric in the front window. The living room had polished hardwood floors, arched doorways, and walls rounding into the ceiling. It was warm and inviting, but one room was divided from it with strings of colored beads, something he associated with the cloying scent of incense and marijuana. It was as if he'd walked through a time warp back into the early seventies.

"Thanks for coming." Kate's eyes were red, as if she'd been crying. "Rusty's in the kitchen doing stir-fry. Would you care for some wine?"

"That would be nice." Bryan heard loud, frenetic hammering. Either this Rusty character was chopping vegetables, or he was doing demo on the whole kitchen.

Tonight Kate wore a lavender form-fitting tee shirt, a shell necklace, and a long crinkled skirt with an exotic print. He'd never seen a woman with so many freckles or one who wore such flamboyant clothes and wild jewelry. He cringed to think he'd once considered asking her out when they'd served together on a nonprofit board. Later, they'd sat on opposite sides at downtown development meetings. Kate had consistently tried to block a new building because three artists wanted to keep paying artificially low rent for their galleries in an old warehouse. He'd empathized with the artists, but the demolition was already scheduled.

Kate and Meghan were quite a pair. Both were strong-willed and strikingly beautiful, but the similarities ended there. He wouldn't have expected elegant, understated Meghan to have such a free-spirited best friend.

"You must miss Meghan," Kate said. "*I* sure do."

He didn't answer, carefully lowering himself onto a large floor cushion near a low table. He extended his legs out in front of him, crossed them, and leaned on one arm, then another, trying to find a comfortable position, to no avail.

"Did Erin take anything with her when she disappeared?" he asked.

"She had her purse, sketchpad, and paints, but one roommate told us that her travel bag and makeup kit are still at the apartment."

"So you think she planned on returning?"

"I'm sure of it. She'd have taken those things with her for an overnight—like I told the police."

"Did anyone see her the day she disappeared?" Bryan asked.

"Quite a few. I contacted her professors and found out she attended all her classes that day. Her last one got out at three thirty."

"You managed to track down all her professors?"

Kate nodded. "I walked through her entire schedule. While I was talking to her professor of art appreciation, a student chimed in and told me he'd seen Erin walking past Desert Broom's around four o'clock yesterday afternoon. That's the last anyone reported seeing her."

"Does she hang out at places like that—bars around the university?"

"She was seen walking *past* it. And no, I don't think she hangs out at bars." The pitch of Kate's voice was rising. "Despite what you may think, she doesn't abuse alcohol or drugs. She's a very . . . good person."

Bryan reddened. "I didn't say she wasn't, but I can't help unless I have some sense of where she tends to spend her time. And there are a lot of good people, I suspect, who patronize bars." He had better places to be and wished he were home right now, but Kate was Meghan's friend, and he'd promised to help.

"Of course there are, but I don't want anyone to smear her character." Kate's left eye twitched. "There were no ransom calls or anything. As if anyone would waste their time trying to ransom the foster child of a teacher."

"Do you think she's been kidnapped?"

"I don't want to think that, but she didn't take her things, like I said. And headstrong as she could be at times, I don't think she would ever hurt me this way."

"It's that photographer," Rusty chimed in from the kitchen. "We need to find the bastard!"

"That's what I'd like to talk about tonight," said Kate.

"How in hell did she meet up with that guy?"

"I'm not sure, but he offered to do a portrait of her for my Mother's Day gift." Kate showed him the photograph.

"It's very good. It looks professional, but there's no imprint or signature. Do you know his name?"

"I'm afraid not. She told me he gave her photography lessons, but clammed up whenever I asked anything more. As you clearly pointed out the other night, I was a fool for not being on top of this. But she's a freshman in college and a legal adult. I figured I should respect her choices."

"You're still the parent," Bryan said.

"A very *desperate* one, as a matter of fact." Kate glared. "I could use your help, minus the putdowns. Can you help us or not?"

"I'll do my best."

❧

After dinner, Rusty offered to share some weed with Bryan, hoping they could all mellow out. The old guy just shook his head and blinked the smoke away as if it were poison gas, like he was some kind of purist or something. Yet he'd guzzled down all the booze Kate put in front of him, and he'd obviously had a good head start before he got there.

Rusty inhaled deeply, hoping to get into some better vibes. Being in the room with these two was making him feel kind of stressed out.

"Please be sure to let me know Meghan's address," Kate said.

Bryan's jaw tensed. "I'm afraid that's not possible."

Here we go, thought Rusty. This guy's really pushing her buttons.

"Not *possible*?" Kate's face turned scarlet. "We're all friends, aren't we?"

"I hope so." Bryan stood up. "But I need to be getting home. Thank you for the dinner. Let me know if you learn anything new, and I'll do the same."

"I still need Meghan's address."

"Maybe we should just cool it," Rusty said. "Let's not get uptight." He knew Kate was still ticked off that Meghan hadn't told her where she was when they'd spoken on the phone this afternoon. No doubt that this dude was behind all the secrecy.

"*I need her address*," repeated Kate, starting to sound shrill. "What's the big deal? She's my best friend, and I can call and get it the moment you leave."

Rusty put his arm around Kate. "Take it easy, babe. He doesn't want it to get out, so she can stay safe. That's cool."

"Do you think I'll spread it all over town?"

Bryan frowned. "Let's just drop it."

"Trust needs to go both ways if we're going to work together."

Bryan moved with determination toward the front door, his face flushed. "I promised you I'd help, and I will, if you let me."

Rusty saw that Kate was about to blow the whole thing, and she needed all the help she could get. Maybe he could ease things up a bit, if he could just have a few words with the old guy.

He walked Bryan out to his car. Though Rusty hadn't exactly hit it off with Kate's engineer friend, he could see how Kate could really get you going. He understood why Bryan had taken the position he had, but he was off base not to trust Kate, of all people.

"She's a little freaked out right now," Rusty said. "You can't blame her, under the circumstances."

"Of course not," said Bryan. "I'm a bit off myself. We can't afford to let this get in the way of what needs to be done. I'll do everything in my power to help."

CHAPTER 10

Like a great mitten, the Lower Peninsula of Michigan reaches upward into three of the Great Lakes. High, rolling dunes line the western coastline on the windward side of Lake Michigan. Standing sentinel on the storm-battered little finger is the Point Betsie Lighthouse. One of the first cottages built on the point had been left to Will Ashley by his stepfather, a retired ore boat captain.

On Memorial Day weekend, Will stood on the deck of the cottage, looking out across Lake Michigan and breathing in the fresh lake air. He'd always been drawn to Point Betsie, with its vast panoramic view of Lake Michigan in all its moods. At long last, he was home, and today he was going to get out on the lake and fish.

Will had grown up here and knew the harsh winters firsthand. He'd seen forests atop the dunes punished by wind, waves, and ice storms and had witnessed sections of tree-covered dunes break off and crumble into the lake. Still, he couldn't imagine a better place to live.

Out here on the dunes, he hoped to find the solitude and inspiration he needed to finish the symphony he'd begun writing years ago but had never completed while on the concert circuit.

Will had written his first piano concerto in grad school at Julliard, in the stimulating world of serious musicians. After graduation, his career as a concert pianist had taken off, and he'd spent the past eighteen years touring throughout Europe and Asia. In the meantime, his symphony had been on the back burner.

Two months ago, his adoptive mother had called him in Barcelona and asked if he'd consider putting the cottage up for sale. They were losing their main renter, and the upkeep was getting more complicated.

Sell his cottage at Point Betsie? The idea had jolted him like a blow to his solar plexus. Yet why wouldn't his mom want to sell it after dealing with it on her own for all these years? In her eighties, she shouldn't have to do that anymore. He'd like to be there now to help her out. He'd pictured himself composing his symphony to the sound of waves crashing onto the shore. He was forty-four years old, and had decided it was time to go home.

Though he'd already been home for a month, today was the first day calm enough for him to take his fishing boat out onto Lake Michigan. It was overcast, and there was a 20 percent chance of thundershowers predicted, but that was par for the course. Weathermen needed to cover their flanks around here, where weather could turn on a dime.

He hauled his sixteen-foot aluminum fishing boat down to the water's edge. As always, he'd keep a close eye on the sky, but he wasn't going to miss the chance to catch a nice salmon or steelhead for dinner. He cinched up his life jacket, rowed out through the smooth water, and pulled the cord to start his old 9.9 horse Johnson.

Less than a mile from shore, he cast out. He didn't have his downriggers set up yet, but estimated the bigger fish might be suspended well off the bottom at a depth of about twenty or twenty-five feet. He tied a favorite six-inch Rapala lure to the line, along with a sinker, then trolled along, enjoying the hazy afternoon.

When he felt a powerful tug on the line, he set the hook but took his time. He let the line play out before he started reeling it in, aware that the big fish could fight hard and break away. His line was only ten-pound test, and he hoped it would be strong enough to hold. He noticed burgeoning cumulonimbus clouds on the horizon.

Suddenly a beautiful steelhead broke water and leapt into the air.

He continued reeling in the fish, careful to keep the line taut. Then he heard the distant rumble of thunder and saw dark clouds building on the horizon. The wind shifted and was picking up. Time to wrap things up. He started reeling faster, knowing there was no more time to finesse the fish.

The steelhead fought hard and spit the hook when it broke the surface again. Will groaned. At least it wouldn't have to swim around with the hook in its mouth.

He headed toward shore as fast as the small engine would go through waves that were getting bigger by the minute. Once he was close, he turned off the engine and rowed the rest of the way. When the boat hit shore, he leapt out and hauled it up onto the beach. Then he raced to his cottage, grabbed his clothes off the line, and went inside to shut windows.

When he looked back out at the lake, he saw the angry storm moving in fast. Then he spotted a boat heaving broadside in the troughs of big breakers, coming in toward the lighthouse. It was clearly in trouble.

He raced back down to the lake, kicked off his shoes, and ran across the sand. The boat was coming in fast. He took a deep breath and plunged into the icy wall of water, steeling himself as the force of the lake crashed down on him. He struggled to swim out past the first two breakers.

"*Life jackets!*" he shouted, hoping he could be heard against the wind. Only the child seemed to be wearing one. The man rowed for all he was worth, and the woman held the child. The boat bobbed violently near the underwater pilings.

A big breaker washed over Will and slammed him along the lake bottom. He held his breath until he felt he'd explode. Finally, he was tossed to the surface, gasping for air. Still reeling, he had only his internal compass to guide him.

Where was the boat?

He caught sight of it just as it was hurled downward in the trough of a huge wave. It smashed against the rocky bottom. He saw the man grab the boy and heard the woman scream.

Dodging a section of the hull that lurched past, Will swam through the wreckage. He was relieved to see the man struggling toward shore with the boy, who was secured in a life vest.

"Please help my wife!" the man shouted. "I'm not much of a swimmer!"

Will scanned the surf, seeing only wreckage. Then he glimpsed a dark form rolling deeper into the foam. As he reached out, the woman was sucked back under. He struggled to the surface empty-handed, then dove under again. Exhausted and cold to the point of numbness, he was starting to tire. It struck him that they might both drown.

Then she appeared in front of him. With a burst of adrenaline, he swam through the surf with explosive force, dove past her, and came up on her from behind. He locked his right arm across her chest, held her fast in an overhand carry, and headed toward shore, battling against the powerful undertow. Every wave brought them closer to the beach, then dragged them back out. Little by little, they were gaining ground.

A heavyset man broke from a small crowd of bystanders to help pull Will and the woman from the surf. They were followed by the distraught man and the boy from the boat.

The woman looked vaguely familiar. He placed her facedown on the sand and pushed on her back to clear her lungs. Water spewed from her mouth, but she remained grotesquely still. He rolled her onto her back and placed his ear against her mouth. *Nothing.* He held his finger to her carotid artery and thought he felt a weak pulse. He wasn't sure.

"Can someone help with CPR?" asked Will. "I'm pretty winded."

He glanced up to see blank stares and one man shaking his head. He took a deep breath and began resuscitation, gasping for air between breaths.

"Please don't die!" cried the child.

The boy's words shrieked through Will's soul. Light-headed, he pushed himself to keep going. He felt as if he were watching from a distance, kneeling over the woman as if in prayer, his mouth over her cold lips. He pressed on her chest and forced water from her lungs, trying desperately to revive her. He knew what he was doing, yet felt helpless, terrified.

"*Live!*" he demanded, trying to will his own life force into her. He refused to give up on her or to submit to the relentless sense of darkness closing in. Time seemed frozen as he concentrated his entire being on maintaining the rhythm of the CPR.

He finally heard sirens. Suddenly the woman coughed and spit out more water. At last, she started to breathe on her own. Two EMTs ran across the sand and took over. They checked her pulse and vital signs and gave her oxygen.

At last, she opened her eyes and looked up.

"Looks like she's gonna pull through," said Greg Van der Kamp, the medic.

"Thank God." A flood of relief swept through Will. As he stood up, everything went crimson, then black. He sat back down in the wet sand.

"Just lie down a minute, Will," said Greg. "Let's make sure *you're* okay."

"I'm fine. She's the one you need to help."

"She's getting help. We're about to transport her to the hospital."

The blood pressure cuff squeezed his arm.

"Your heart rate's way up and your blood pressure too," said Greg. "You'd better lie here for a few more minutes."

"I'm just a little dizzy."

"Understandable. I know you're a terrific swimmer, but anyone would be exhausted doing a rescue in these waves, then performing CPR. You did a great job."

Will slowly sat up. "I hope she's okay."

The white-haired man from the boat squeezed the woman's hand and leaned down to kiss her on the forehead. Then he turned to embrace Will. "God bless you. You saved my wife, Theresa," he said, tearfully. "How can I ever thank you enough?"

"I'm glad I was here at the right time," Will answered. "How's the boy?"

"My grandson seems fine. The EMTs are checking him out and getting him warmed up. My brother and his wife are over there with them. I feel so bad. I should never have taken them out there today. I didn't see that storm coming up."

"It came up pretty fast. I barely made it off the lake myself." Will placed his hand reassuringly on the man's shoulder.

"We're up here visiting our in-laws, the Larsens. I've got to get back there now."

"I'll be praying for your wife."

"Thank you again."

Will turned toward the small group that had congregated around the ambulance. Jeff and Joan Larsen were watching the EMTs work on Theresa. With them was the beautiful woman who'd stopped to admire his mom's lilacs. As a ray of sun broke through the clouds, her windblown mane of chestnut-colored hair took on a golden cast.

Then he spotted his adoptive mother, Martha, in her black hooded raincoat, leaning on her cane. He took a few more deep breaths, then made his way across the sand toward her.

Martha handed him a blanket she kept in her car. "I'm so proud of you, son. You've saved Theresa Larsen's life. You remember her—Jeff Larsen's sister."

"I just found out who she was." He remembered his stepfather saying that people like the Larsens were the salt of the earth, although Martha had always remained quiet, as if she might have a different opinion.

"You must be exhausted." His mom took his arm. "Let's head back to the cottage."

"A hot shower would be great." Will's teeth chattered. He felt as if the frigid water of Lake Michigan were flowing through his veins. More than that, he felt driven to somehow wash away the cold, hauntingly familiar feel of death that still clung to him. Though Theresa had survived, something terrible had tried to force its way into his consciousness—like it had when his stepdad had died. He'd been free of that feeling for years and was in no mood to deal with it now.

CHAPTER 11

A blaze of crimson sliced along the horizon between the low clouds and dark waves. Some of the most spectacular sunsets came after storms. Martha watched the sun go down from Jake's old rocking chair while Will rested in a guest room on the main floor. The aroma of homemade chicken soup permeated the cottage.

The EMT had told Martha that her son would be fine, and she was sure that he would be. But after battling in the icy waves to save Theresa, then giving CPR for so long in the bitter wind, he had to be cold and exhausted. He hadn't complained but seemed unusually quiet.

She'd encouraged him to lie down while she went to the store to get a chicken, onions, celery, and carrots. Chicken soup had to be made from scratch to get the full benefit.

Her back and hips ached more than usual, probably from being out in the cold wind and standing for so long at the sink chopping vegetables. She'd like to go home and get under a warm blanket for a nap but was too concerned about Will to leave him alone right now. She wanted to make sure he was okay.

Martha picked up *East of Eden* and began to reread it, but phone calls from concerned friends kept interrupting. It hadn't taken long for news of the rescue to get out. She was proud of Will but concerned that he'd rushed out into the storm as if he were still a lifeguard. Thank God he'd survived, and that he'd been able to save Jeff Larsen's sister, Theresa.

The phone rang again. Martha picked it up on the first ring, hoping it wouldn't awaken Will. He needed to rest for a while longer, then eat the healing soup. It was a good thing she was here to answer the phone.

"Hi. It's Joan Larsen. I'm calling from the hospital."

Martha swallowed hard and took a deep breath. After all these years she was still flustered by the sound of Joan's voice—especially tonight when she might be calling with bad news.

"How's your sister-in-law?" Martha asked. "I've been praying for her complete recovery."

"It looks like she's going to make it, thank God—and thanks to your son. They're keeping her here overnight because she has hypothermia, but she's alert and awake."

"That's great news."

"Will was wonderful," said Joan. "My brother-in-law told me how tough the rescue was and how Will refused to give up on her. I can't begin to tell you how grateful we are. You should be very proud."

"I am." Martha's voice caught. "I'd let you speak with him, but he's resting. I'm so relieved to hear Theresa's doing well." She paused, then added, "It's good to hear your voice."

"It's good to hear yours too. I have more calls to make now, but let's talk again soon."

"Let's." She hung up the phone, hand trembling.

Years ago, when Martha had first adopted Will, Joan had peppered her with questions about the adoption whenever they met, making Martha very uncomfortable. She'd assumed that Joan's curiosity was fueled by rumors from Theresa, who'd lived near Will's family in central Michigan. When the questions didn't let up, Martha put as much space between herself and the Larsens as she could. She'd even changed churches.

Maybe the time had come to put her uneasiness about the Larsens behind her. She carefully navigated through stacks of packing boxes on her way to the kitchen to check on the soup.

She couldn't wait to see how the cottage would turn out when Will was finished with his remodeling. She hoped it wouldn't take too long. He'd been sanding the hardwood floors and was about to refinish them. It was too dusty for him to live there now, if you asked her.

Three months ago, she'd gone into the cottage to make sure there hadn't been leaks or damage during the long winter. The windows had been boarded up, a musty smell permeated the air, and there was a fine layer of dust over everything. Two weeks later, she'd learned that the longtime renters had bought a place of their own on Platte Lake.

She'd called Will in Europe. When he'd answered, she could barely hear him over flamenco guitar music. She'd told him about losing the renters and asked if he'd consider selling. There'd been a long silence. He promised he'd figure out something and get back to her.

The next day he called and told her not to sell it. He was coming home.

"But what about your career? I could get a manager to find new renters and tend to the details. That way, your cottage would still be here for you whenever you needed it."

"I'm going to need it very soon," he said with finality. "I don't want you to be saddled with it anymore, and I've been away long enough."

"But how can you leave your concert tour?" Now she'd gone and upset the whole applecart.

"I've been on the road most of my adult life. It's been great, but I don't want to live out of a suitcase forever. I want more than that. I miss you, Mom, and I miss my home."

A few days later, when Martha had called back to try to talk some sense into him, she'd learned that he'd already told his agent not to book any more performances. His current tour would be over in April, and he'd already purchased a one-way ticket home.

Now that he was home, she was thrilled. Her life had taken on a whole new dimension. Nonetheless, it was disturbing to think of him giving up his career when it seemed to be at its peak. He'd invested so much of his time, heart, and soul into it. She couldn't imagine how Will could make a living as a concert pianist in the small town of Frankfort.

She tiptoed in to check on him while he slept. Though Will had always been the type to throw covers off, he was curled up under a down comforter, shivering. Hoping he didn't have hypothermia, like Theresa, Martha drew a wool blanket up over the comforter.

Her son may be a grown man, but after such a heroic rescue, he deserved something special. After dinner, she'd make him popcorn. She'd shake the pan vigorously back and forth over the burner while holding the lid on tight, the old-fashioned way. It wasn't easy, but she wasn't about to resort to microwave popcorn. They could enjoy it later in the wooden bowls, salted, with butter melted over the top.

She thought back to the day he'd come to her, in the arms of a social worker, only days after her nephew had asked if she would consider raising the orphaned boy.

"Why pick me?" Martha had asked. She was a childless woman of a certain age who had long ago given up her dream of raising children, but he'd assured her she would be the best one to raise the child.

She'd always adored the little boy, and he'd seemed happy to see her. Later it dawned on her that it had been a simple process of elimination, rather than a feather in her cap. She was the only other relative still living and healthy enough to raise a two-year-old boy. Still, she felt deeply honored.

In her forties, with no suitor in sight, she had often cried herself to sleep, grieving for the children she would never have. Then suddenly, from tragedy, she was blessed with this precious child. God worked in such incomprehensible ways.

At first, she rocked him to sleep until her arms ached but couldn't get him to take food. He was implacable. It was touch and go for weeks.

She had to put him in the hospital and watch them puncture his tiny veins with all those dreadful needles so he wouldn't starve. When he was released, Martha doted on him and prayed that if she did something wrong, she wouldn't do him any harm.

Existing for weeks on the edge of despair, she listened to him cry out in futility for his mother. At last, the crying diminished, and he became subdued. Too subdued, some of her friends tactlessly suggested.

Martha grew even more frantic. She spent hours on her bony knees kneeling on the bedroom floor, pleading with God to help her find in herself what it would take to raise this child. If only her sister, Sarah, had been alive to help her, she would have known just what to do. Yet if Sarah had lived, she would have been the one raising Will.

Will had started to walk and talk before his first birthday. After the tragic death of his parents, all that had ceased.

Then one day, Will stopped crying and allowed her to minister to him. He started to eat better, and to walk and talk again. He began to explore his new surroundings. In time, her powerful love for him and his desire to live were enough to bring him around. He grew into a strong and active boy who wanted to learn about the world around him, especially as it related to music and the outdoors.

Then she'd been blessed with a second miracle. She smiled at the thought of Jake, her rugged, rough-hewn sea captain and the only man of her life. When Will was five, she'd taken him to the church's annual pancake breakfast. Across the table from them sat Jake Ashley, a widowed ore boat captain. He'd taken to Martha right away and had hit it off with Will. Six months later, they'd married.

For twelve years, until his fatal heart attack, the three of them had been a family. Jake had taken Will camping and fishing and taught him to swim and boat. Those had been wonderful years, and Jake had helped Will grow into a man.

But it was Martha who had nurtured Will's musical nature. She'd always loved music and played the violin, but had never had the chance to go on to college. Will's passion for music and talent as a pianist brought her great joy. By the time he was in third grade, she needed to remind him to stop practicing and come to dinner. She used her nephew's generous funds for piano lessons, summer school at nearby Interlochen Center for the Arts, a Steinway piano, and tuition to the university. Although she was thrilled to have Will back home, Martha feared he might be throwing it all away.

The waves still pounded the shore and the wind moaned softly through invisible cracks in the wood-frame cottage. She'd once enjoyed the sound, feeling cozy there beside her husband. Now she couldn't stand the relentless whine of wind off the lake and the sound of pounding surf. She was glad that Jake had given the cottage to Will and that she'd kept her cozy Victorian home in town.

CHAPTER 12

Meghan had been at the Manitou having dinner with the Larsens when Jeff got a frantic call from his brother-in-law. They'd left their food on the table, promising to catch the bill later. They sped to the point, screeched to a stop at the end of the road, and raced to the beach.

When Meghan saw the limp woman lying on the beach, she could hardly breathe, as if a vise were constricting her chest. The terrible image of her father flashed across her mind.

An EMT was approaching to take over CPR from the man trying desperately to revive Jeff's sister. Meghan thought he might have been the man on the porch with the elderly woman, but it was hard to get a good look at him. She heard cries of relief as the woman suddenly coughed and started breathing on her own.

When the Larsens later followed the ambulance to the hospital, Meghan was offered a ride back to town with Maureen and Gary Lipinski. Warm and friendly, the couple helped get her mind off the haunting images of her dad. They expressed confidence about the EMTs and the hospital, and lifted her spirits with humorous stories about the Larsens.

Meghan asked them about the man who'd done the rescue, wondering if he lived on Forest Avenue. Maureen told her that he lived out on the point, where the near drowning had taken place, but his mother lived on Forest Avenue. His name was Will Ashley, and he'd won swim meets back in high school and had been a lifeguard. He was also a world-renowned concert pianist.

So the brave man who'd done the rescue *was* the handsome pianist who'd spoken to her on her first day in town. His name, Will Ashley, sounded familiar.

She asked the Lipinskis to drop her off in front of the Larsen's farmhouse. As she walked up the driveway to her cottage, tree branches rustled in the wind and metal rings clanged against the flagpole, but the worst of the storm was over.

She looked forward to taking a hot shower and having a glass of wine. Later she could bake a pizza and curl up on the sofa with one of her library books, but she hated being alone tonight. She needed to talk. She was thankful and relieved that Jeff's sister had been saved, yet couldn't push the haunting images of her dad from her mind.

She called Bryan and told him that Jeff Larsen's sister had nearly drowned but had been resuscitated.

He asked her to repeat the name of the victim and sounded upset.

When she asked if he'd known her, he said he hadn't. Then he issued her a stern warning never to go out alone on Lake Michigan.

"I plan to get in some sailing while I'm here," she said.

"There are plenty of inland lakes. Lake Michigan is no place for a novice."

"What makes you think I'm a novice?"

"I've never heard you mention sailing."

"And I've never heard you mention Michigan." After an awkward silence, she added, "Maybe there are a lot of things we still don't know about each other."

"No doubt," he said. "It's the best I could do on short notice. Just be careful. The escaped prisoner . . . is still at large."

He'd completely derailed her attempt to discuss the rescue, much less confide in him about the traumatic memories it had brought back to her. She promised to be careful, and signed off.

She poured herself a glass of wine and paced back and forth in the tiny room. There had to be a way to get through to Bryan other than by phone.

She pulled out a sheet of stationery and dashed off a few lines about the town and her walk on the pier; then she crossed off the part about the pier. She didn't want to hear his reaction to her walking out there alone. She commented on the beautiful flowers and local scenery. Determined to move beyond the superficial, she mentioned that Frankfort reminded her of Maine. She told him about her happy childhood there until she'd lost her parents.

She missed him and hoped they might share their feelings more easily in letters than by phone—but what *were* her feelings? After her grandfather's death, she'd come to care for Bryan and had believed she was falling in love. Now she wondered. His thoughtfulness and sensitivity weren't coming across on the phone, to say the least. Since the drive-by shooting, he'd been so protective that it alarmed her, and he'd never apologized for meddling in her career by talking to her boss. Maybe Kate had been right about the red flags.

She prided herself on being an independent woman who could handle tough situations, but everything had happened so quickly. Bryan had presented her with an escape plan already in place, and she'd made a split-second decision to get on that single-prop plane.

She had to admit that she *did* feel safer here in Michigan, after her surreptitious trip across the country. She would keep encouraging Bryan to visit her here, where they could speak more freely in person. She reread what she'd written so far, crumpled it up, and tossed it into the wastebasket. She'd try again later, when she was in a better frame of mind.

After what had happened today, she couldn't stop thinking about her dad.

Before her mother had become ill, Meghan had enjoyed a good life. She'd grown up in a loving home, and her childhood and early teen years had been happy ones. After dinner, she and her family would often gather around the fireplace eating popcorn while reading their favorite books or playing games. Her father had often read aloud to them. *The Yearling* and *Smoky* had been his favorites, their well-worn covers pulling away from their bindings from overuse. Theirs had been a family rich in tradition and a shared love of learning.

But her mother was the heart of it. After she died, their entire world collapsed. Her dad withdrew into himself, growing pale and thin, and

Meghan's efforts to reach out to him didn't seem to help. Her younger brother, Todd, started having trouble at school.

As the oldest, Meghan grieved briefly, then managed to find the strength her father couldn't muster to see to the household's needs. She took on the role of homemaker and mother to her eight-year-old brother, waking early to make breakfast and send him off to school. She served dinner at 5:30 p.m., just as her mother had done. She even tried to provide intellectual companionship to her father. Once given to stimulating discussions at the dinner table, he ate in silence and picked at his food, and usually withdrew to the den. Though he'd tell her he was going to read, she often found him staring vacantly into space.

When Todd arrived home from school one day with a large rip down the seam of his trousers, Meghan repaired it. She started checking him carefully before he left in the morning. When he started to throw temper tantrums, she took him aside to speak with him gently but firmly, like her mother would have done. She hugged him when he cried and even took him fishing when her father stopped taking him.

She learned quickly about practical things needed to keep a family going. One day a creditor called about an overdue account, and she took over the bills. Though she longed to laugh and joke around once again with her friends, her social calendar was replaced by household responsibilities. She couldn't comprehend why God had taken her mother away from their family who needed her so much.

When she finished high school, she'd been expected to go away to school. Knowing she was needed at home, she informed her dad that she wanted to stay home and attend the local junior college. He wouldn't hear of it, saying she must go to the university as planned and as her mother had wanted. Despite her misgivings, she went off to college.

She threw herself into her studies and campus life, until that fateful day in November. It had been cold and overcast as she'd hurried to her class in the choir room. She'd looked forward to practicing songs from *West Side Story*, hoping for a chance to land the role of Maria.

As soon as she arrived, the professor gave her an urgent message to return at once to her dormitory.

Heart racing, she hurried back across campus. She shivered as the wind whined through the tall pines and carried off the few remaining leaves still clinging to the trees. The carillon bells in the tower chimed one.

Her resident advisor, Andrea, met her inside the large double doors, her expression sober. She guided her gently by the arm to the office, where a gray-haired woman waited. She introduced herself, but Meghan didn't catch her name.

"Please sit down," said the older woman, closing the door. "I'm afraid we have some very bad news."

Meghan wanted to run out the door and leave the news forever unspoken and undone. Instead, she sat quietly, hands folded in her lap.

"There's no easy way . . ."

"What's wrong?"

"Your grandfather called from Maine. He was contacted by the sheriff." The woman paused.

Meghan felt the RA grow still. She could barely catch her breath.

"Your father has drowned," said the woman. "His body was found early this morning, washed up onto the beach. I'm so very sorry, my dear."

"That's impossible! My father *never* would have gone out in the ocean this time of year! They've got the wrong person. I need to use the phone. I'll get a hold of my dad right now and straighten this whole thing out!"

"There was a note."

"A note?"

"In his pocket." The older woman hesitated. "In a plastic baggie, along with his Driver's License. I'm so sorry. Your aunt and uncle are flying in from Seattle. They'll pick you up on their way."

"No!" she cried out. "*No!*"

Her screams were heard out in the lobby.

"I'm so sorry," said the RA, her own eyes red. "I'll walk you to your room, and help in any way I can." She guided Meghan gently to the door.

Meghan would never recall much about the funeral, or the days afterward. But she remembered Uncle Ted telling her that her father had been wearing the brown sweater that her mother had knitted for him and later patched at the elbows.

He'd gone on to explain that he and Aunt Christine would take Todd home with them. Their son had left home to join the military, so Todd could have a room of his own. He was their own flesh and blood, after all. Once things settled down, they would see about adopting him.

Meghan was nineteen and already leading her own life. They would make sure she had the money to complete her studies. There was no mention of a room for her, and she returned to school without a family.

CHAPTER 13

Kate tugged at the jammed drawer, shook the dresser, and gave it one last yank. The drawer crashed to the floor, scraping her knee. Beads from the necklace Erin had made for her rolled along the floor in every direction. She carefully gathered up its broken strands.

She started to cry in deep, gasping sobs. Erin had been missing for over five weeks, and Kate was frantic. She knelt beside the bed and reached under it to retrieve as many beads as she could, but found mostly dust balls. Blood from her scraped knee stained the nightgown she was still wearing at eleven in the morning. She started coughing between sobs.

Cursing, she yanked off her gown, showered, dried herself, and slapped a bandage on her knee. Kate fluffed her hair with her fingers as a prelude to letting her long curls air dry. Swamp coolers didn't work all that well in Tucson once the humid monsoon season began, but she could keep cool for a while with the natural evap-cooling of her drying hair.

She returned to the project of cleaning her bedroom. She'd dreaded the prospect of facing the disarray in her closets and drawers but thought she might as well get something done. Now was the time to cull things out. She'd already cleaned the storage room, hall closet, kitchen cabinets, and guest room. These projects kept her sane and in close proximity to the phones—yet so much of her clutter turned out to be emotional landmines, reminding her of Erin.

This June seemed hotter than ever. Each day was a slow-motion nightmare, and the simple act of reading the morning paper instilled terror. Kate never missed the local news in the *Arizona Daily Star,* or on television, even though phrases like "unidentified body" and "name withheld pending notification of kin" gave her panic attacks.

As the foster parent of a legal adult, she wondered if she would even be contacted by police if Erin were found dead. Twice she'd picked up the phone to find out but had slammed it down before dialing. It was too dark a question to speak aloud.

She was often on the verge of tears. She couldn't concentrate on her reading or yoga meditations. Her cell phone was with her at all times, even when it was being charged; and she kept a wireless landline phone near her whenever she was home, which was most of the time. If Erin tried to call on either one, Kate wanted to be there. Nevertheless, she checked and rechecked her messages, afraid she might have somehow missed a call from her.

She finally managed to clean and separate out the beads that weren't broken, and placed them in a plastic container with a lid. From now on, she'd sweep this room instead of vacuuming it to make sure she didn't suck up beads from the precious necklace. She'd ask Erin to repair the necklace when she got home.

Kate forced herself to look at the photo of Erin that she'd been given for Mother's Day. She cringed to think of what other kind of photographs the unknown photographer might have taken of her daughter. Was he really involved with Erin's disappearance, as Erin's roommates and Rusty believed? The fact that they'd both vanished around the same time made it seem likely. Maybe they'd even eloped.

Yet Kate knew better. Erin would have called her.

What if Erin *wasn't* with the photographer but had been kidnapped by Devrek? She shuddered, as frightening thoughts careened through her mind. She was on the verge of freaking out. She needed to talk to someone.

Rusty would listen politely, but Kate sensed he was starting to burn out on dealing with her panic about her missing foster daughter. Worse, the police seemed to be tiring of her many calls. Meghan was the only one she could count on to listen and encourage her, but she hadn't been able to reach her this morning.

It was too bad she couldn't have combined forces with Erin's natural mother, but the woman had turned out to be a scam artist, as well as a prostitute and drug addict. She'd resurfaced soon after Erin turned up missing and had appeared on the evening news for three nights, pleading for donations to expand the search for Erin. She'd raised thousands of dollars. When it came out that she'd skipped town with the money, local interest in Erin had dropped off. Kate managed to be interviewed by Channel 9, but the story only aired for one night.

Kate loved Erin as much as any natural mother could love a child. She'd done her best to be a good parent, but it hadn't been easy to make up for Erin's formative years when her foster daughter was looking after her addict mother and basically raising herself.

As a free spirit who celebrated individual self-expression, Kate had believed children were like wildflowers who should be allowed to grow freely, unhampered by outdated social mores. Too many restrictions could stifle their budding creativity. But it was clear from the start that Erin was in dire need of structure and guidance. Kate had found herself in the uncomfortable position of needing to impose limits for the first time on a girl who was already fourteen.

It was almost as if Erin had regressed to the terrible twos when she came to live with Kate. When thwarted, she was not beyond screaming, stomping, and running off. She often refused to turn in homework, which created tension between Kate and her fellow teachers.

A school psychologist had recommended counseling to help Erin with anger management, which Kate had arranged. The therapist suggested that Erin seemed very good at managing anger—to her own advantage.

Kate did her best to become a firm and consistent parent. She tried desperately to teach Erin to control her behavior and make good choices. She followed the psychologist's recommendations, though they went against her grain. She kept elaborate charts, complete with grids and stars, until Erin ripped them all to shreds. She reinforced Erin's misbehaviors with *logical consequences.*

She pinched pennies to give Erin voice, guitar, and dance lessons and allowed her to have different pets, hoping to teach her responsibility. Erin didn't take care of the cat, parakeets, or goldfish or stay with anything until her first art lesson.

When she showed a strong interest in art, Kate was delighted. She bought her paints, brushes, canvases, a palette, easel, sketchpads, and pastels. As an art teacher, she taught her as much as she could, then provided her with lessons from other artists.

By the middle of Erin's junior year, Kate's efforts started to show results, and by her senior year, Erin became involved in school activities and made the honor roll. With her artistic talent and letters of recommendation from the principal and several teachers, she was accepted at the University of Arizona.

Erin was a loving, creative, immensely talented girl. There wasn't a blank sheet of paper anywhere in the house that she hadn't graced with one of her sketches, and they were excellent. Kate left them undisturbed, moving them only to dust. But it seemed that all Kate's efforts hadn't been enough to carry Erin through, once she left home.

Kate was getting another headache, and the constant smell of Rusty's weed, mixed with incense wasn't helping. She had to get some fresh air, even if it was over a hundred degrees out.

She yanked open a window and frowned at the gravel yard, with its enormous oleanders that needed trimming and the overgrown prickly pear cacti. Behind her fence were madly proliferating tumbleweeds that needed to go. Hacking them down and getting them hauled off could be her next big project, though some of them were taller than she was. The portable phone worked in the backyard. She'd already tested it.

She could tell she was driving Rusty crazy with her uncharacteristic compulsive cleaning, but this seemed the sanest way to spend time within a few feet of the phone, in terror of what the next call might bring.

Though he'd been supportive at times, Kate regretted letting Rusty move in. He'd spent much of the first month of summer vacation stoned. He tried to be sensitive about what she was going through, but at times seemed more interested in getting high. He wasn't paying his share of the rent or utilities, and she was having trouble keeping the refrigerator stocked with food.

And Rusty wanted her constantly. When he learned she'd been molested as a child and had some serious hang-ups, he seemed to take it upon himself to help. He made a special effort to draw out her feelings and be sensitive to her needs.

She supposed that many women would give their eyeteeth for that kind of attention, but years of therapy hadn't helped Kate, and neither could Rusty. She was frigid and always would be. This was just another failed relationship.

If she ever let another man into her life, which she doubted, she would take her time getting to know him. He would be someone who carried his fair share of the workload and household expenses, and he wouldn't smoke dope. Rusty was a good-hearted person, but it seemed like he'd needed a place to crash and live rent-free for a while.

Tonight, she would broach the subject to him. It wasn't working, and it was time for him to look for another place. She needed to focus all her energy on finding Erin. Kate shoved the drawer back into the bureau.

How she envied women like Meghan, who'd once told her, "It's so beautiful when you're in love." Her best friend seemed to be in love with Bryan, though she'd never said so. Though Bryan was a good-looking man, in great shape for his age, Kate couldn't imagine him allowing someone to touch him, much less making love.

Kate was still angry at Bryan over his remark about her lack of discipline with her foster daughter. She knew she shouldn't allow a put-down from a control freak who knew nothing about raising children to bother her, but it still infuriated her. The bird of paradise flowers he'd sent had gone a long way toward soothing her anger, but his refusal to give her Meghan's address was another sore spot.

He hadn't seemed himself lately. The added flush to his face and his watery eyes reminded her of one of her stepdads when he'd been drinking too much. Stubborn and difficult as Bryan could be, this was the first she'd ever suspected a problem with alcohol. She couldn't recall him drinking at all until a few months ago.

Meghan left the post office with a large manila envelope tucked under her arm. It was addressed to her as *Anne Maxwell*. She knew it was from Bryan, stuffed with her important mail, including the few bills that weren't on auto-pay. Though this was to have been a short-term plan, it would be July soon, and this was her sixth weekly envelope.

She regretted leaving her laptop at home, thinking she'd be away for just a week or two. For now, she was using a computer at the library. She decided to stop by the library again to search online for clues about Erin's whereabouts and any news about Devrek.

So far, she'd found only four-year-old articles about Devrek's trial and conviction, and a few reports dated in May about his escape from prison. There were three articles about Erin being reported missing, and more than a dozen reports about her birth mother scamming generous Tucsonans. The mother's record of convictions for prostitution and drug possession were enumerated, but Kate was never mentioned. After that, news about Erin stopped.

When Meghan tore open the large envelope, she was disappointed once again to find no letter or even a personal note from Bryan. She wrote him a lengthy letter every week, but he never reciprocated. Their phone conversations were strained and brief, and when she brought up their relationship, he would change the subject. Though their love had been unspoken, when they'd been together, she'd been able to read so much from a glance, a touch, or the subtle clench of his jaw. Now that they were apart, she hadn't found another way to connect with him.

Maybe Bryan didn't care for her as much as she'd imagined. Meghan wasn't even sure about her own feelings anymore. She was uneasy about how controlling he'd become after the gunfire into her home and was put off by his cold, detached phone conversations.

He hadn't even told her he was helping Kate search for Erin. She'd found out from Kate, who sounded more distraught with each call. Meghan was anxious to get back to Tucson so she could help in the search, but her friend always advised her to think about her own safety and stay where she was. Kate reassured Meghan that she helped enormously by listening patiently and never giving up hope.

At first, time dragged as Meghan waited in frustration for news of Devrek's capture. Then she began to catch up on her reading and to enjoy her simpler life in Michigan. She decided to make the best of her time in hiding and start treating it as a vacation. She took long walks through town beside the harbor and out to Lake Michigan. She biked the Betsie

Valley Trail through the woods, by streams and ponds, and along the clear, turquoise waters of Crystal Lake. Whether it was the people, great food, beautiful scenery, or the small harbor town that reminded her of Maine, she wasn't sure, but this place was starting to grow on her.

During the long twilight hours, which lingered until almost ten o'clock, she joined the Larsens on their front porch. Jeff was teaching Joel to carve wooden ducks and birds, while Joan hand-stitched traditional quilts. Meghan hadn't touched quilting since her mother's death, but under Joan's supervision, she began a table runner with a simple patch-work pattern.

One evening on the porch, Joel shared his goal of attending a sailing school in Traverse City. In her teens she'd loved sailing off the coast of Maine, and she encouraged his plan.

The next week Joel took her sailing in his daysailer on Lake Michigan, and she enjoyed every moment of the trip. He allowed her to take over the rudder and mainsail, which was exhilarating. On the way back, he invited her to use the boat whenever she wanted.

Maybe she would take him up on the offer. It might be just the thing to help her get her mind off her worries and fears, including her frustrating attempts to get through to Bryan. She'd always felt such freedom and joy out on the water with the wind and the waves.

CHAPTER 14

In the wee hours of the morning, Martha Ashley awoke with a start. She thought she'd heard something amiss, but there was only the sound of crickets and her own heartbeat. She would often awaken in the middle of the night, overcome with anxiety about matters that were quite manageable during the day.

Her back and shoulders ached from the day before, when she'd hauled a large framed oil painting up into the attic. The painting of the dunes had hung over her mantel for as long as she could remember, but she'd replaced it yesterday with a watercolor of a fly fisherman. The way the light filtered through the trees onto the fisherman was magical, and made her think of Jake. Though there hadn't been anywhere else in her home where a painting as large and dramatic as the dunes painting would work, it felt wrong to have it stuffed in her attic.

She tried to go back to sleep, but her stomach churned. Then it came to her. She would give the oil painting to Will as a housewarming gift. He'd always loved it, and someday it might take on a special significance to him.

Unfortunately, she'd have to climb back into the attic and struggle to maneuver it down the narrow steps, taking care not to fall or damage the painting. If Will found out, he'd chide her for not asking for help, as would her neighbors. It seemed an eighty-four-year-old woman wasn't to lift a finger on her own. The neighbor boys would be glad to help, but they never accepted money, and she didn't want to feel like a charity case.

Maybe she could make them molasses cookies again. They wouldn't turn *those* down. Her mind raced on until she drifted back to sleep and dreamed of trying to make cookies with ingredients that kept vanishing.

When she would find the flour, the molasses would be missing, or the butter. As so often was the case in her early-morning dreams, she would rush around in frustration, unable to complete the simplest task.

By 6:30 a.m., she awoke again. She eased her legs over the side of the bed, sat up, stretched, and thanked God for the new day. Martha loved how sunlight streamed through her lace curtains, casting rectangles of light across her white chenille bedspread and blue-and-white floral wallpaper.

She was delighted to see the goldfinches around the bird feeders as she looked down from her second-story window. Through the foliage of her large oak tree, she surveyed the cottages and restored Victorian homes along her street. Hers was one of the few houses with the original wood clapboard and a simple two-tone paint job. One of these years she might get vinyl siding, but she wasn't about to bother with all that extra multi-colored bric-a-brac her neighbors had added to their Victorian homes. It just wasn't practical.

Though her arthritis was acting up, this beautiful July morning would be perfect for a walk to town. She could greet her friends and enjoy the parade of passersby while watching boats out in the bay. Martha felt fortunate to live in the harbor town of Frankfort.

She took a hot shower, then rubbed Aspercreme into her sore knees. For breakfast, she enjoyed a cup of English breakfast tea, a lemon scone, and a bowl of fresh blueberries. Then she headed to town. After walking several blocks, she rested on a favorite bench and watched the charter fishing boats pull up to the docks.

Today she was having dinner with Will at his remodeled cottage and needed to leave time to bake him a pie. This would be her first visit to his place since the rescue, and she couldn't wait to see the improvements he'd made. She hoped he hadn't changed things so much that it would detract from the cottage's special aura, yet a new look might help her get past the sadness that swept through her whenever she entered the cottage. She'd never gotten over being there without Jake. Since Will was living at the cottage now, she needed to feel at home there again.

Her mind drifted back to the painting of the dunes. Several hours remained before dinner at Will's. There was still time to bake him a strawberry-rhubarb pie and to get back up to the attic to retrieve the painting.

Glad that she'd made the pie dough yesterday, she took it from the refrigerator to let it get up to room temperature. She still needed to pick the strawberries and rhubarb from her garden, wash and slice them, and mix in sugar and flour. Finally it was time to roll out the dough. As the oven preheated, she spread the bottom crust gingerly into the pie pan and cut around the edges. She scooped in the fruit mixture, carefully placed on the second crust, trimmed it to size, crimped the edges, and vented the top crust with a knife. She smiled with satisfaction as she put the pie in the oven. It had been a long time since she'd had a chance to make her son his favorite pie.

Then she made her way up the attic steps to get the painting. Neat and orderly, the attic smelled of mothballs. She stepped carefully across the floorboards, stooping to open a small window. The fresh breeze stirred up dust. It made her cough, but she'd come prepared. She reached into her pocket for a mentholated cough drop.

The painting was propped up against the old family cedar chest that held belongings of her sister, Sarah. She'd never felt up to opening it. Maybe today was the day. She wiped it off with a rag, then cautiously raised the heavy lid.

Underneath her sister's old quilt was a silver hand mirror, wrapped in silk and engraved with her grandmother's initials, *MLJ*. Martha caught sight of herself in the mirror and froze. It was as if her grandmother were looking back at her, with her deep wrinkles; light blue, rheumy eyes; and thin white hair pulled back into a bun at the base of her neck. She'd taken on her grandmother's visage without noticing! As a child, she'd thought her grandmother impossibly old, yet she could do worse than look like her beloved grandma. It was an honor to take after her, and it was Martha's good fortune to have lived over eight decades and still be healthy. Even so, it was a shock to see herself as an old woman. She would polish the mirror and place it on her vanity.

Underneath the mirror she found the pastel green blanket she'd lovingly crocheted for the baby shower so many years ago, not knowing there would be twins. To this day she felt the doctor should have known. She took up the blanket in her arms and held it to her face. It was the one she'd given to the first-born twin. She could still smell a hint of baby powder after all these years and could almost feel the little boy there in her arms. The ivory blanket, once yellow, hadn't been completed for the second twin until weeks after their birth.

As a young woman, Martha had helped with the new babies and continued to babysit them as they grew up, when she wasn't working at the post office. She'd always loved the boys as if they were her own.

It didn't seem possible that over forty years had passed since the nightmarish tragedies, starting with the fatal accident that had killed her sister and John. Martha had felt she would never survive all the grief. She still missed them.

At the bottom of the chest, she found an antique silver crucifix that had belonged to her mother, then her sister. Beside it was a small leather-bound book. She opened it and recognized the strong, formal handwriting of her deceased brother-in-law. *Journal belonging to John Jameson* was inscribed on the first page.

Martha stuffed the journal and crucifix into the pockets of her apron and closed the chest. She had to get out of there. The stale attic air was closing in on her, and she felt light-headed. She refolded the blankets and put the mirror aside. She should have gone through the chest long ago but had never felt up to it. She could have used her grandmother's mirror for all these years.

She closed the window, picked up the painting of the dunes, and struggled to hold on to it as she carefully descended the narrow attic stairway. She hoped she wouldn't fall and injure herself on the way down, or she'd never hear the end of it. People loved to talk about an old woman's foolishness and blame her for every little accident.

She made it down in one piece, without so much as a nick on the painting or wall. She waited twelve more minutes until the timer went off, then took the pie out of the oven. Though she was exhausted, she made one more trip up to the attic for the mirror.

Finally she lowered herself into her rocking chair. Hands trembling, she picked up the small journal. She was intrigued, yet uneasy about the prospect of reading it. It was about the size of a small paperback, with its yellowed pages bound in light brown leather. As she thumbed through it, she noticed most of the book was blank. The few entries were written in bold strokes with a fountain pen.

Her sister's husband had majored in English. He'd written poetry and talked of writing screenplays, though he'd wound up working for the newspaper, then managing the local theater. She hoped the book would include some of his poetry.

Journal of John Jameson

May 16, 1950: Sarah undressing. The scent of lilacs wafting through our bedroom window. The sight of her removing her faded housedress makes me despair. Her full breasts, softly rounded stomach, her narrow hips . . . it's been so long.

Her long braid has unraveled, her hair falling across her shoulders. I'm overcome with desire for my own wife of four years. She meets my gaze, flushes, and turns away. I take a deep breath, approach her, and place my hands on her shoulders, taking care to be gentle.

I whisper to her, "It's lilac time again, remember?" During our courtship I'd given her an armful of white lilacs, and she'd cried for joy. Now her body stiffens, pulls away, and I hear that edge to her voice that I've grown to dread. But I'm not giving up. We're young and have a lifetime ahead of us.

I ask her to sit down while I brush her hair. How she loved for me to brush her hair when we were first married. After a while her features would smooth out into a relaxed smile, and then we might make love. Sarah was always tense, but little by little I had guided her into the physical side of things. Now I have to start over again.

I pleaded with her to just let me hold her, but she refused me again.

"What's wrong, for God's sake?" I demanded.

"Don't take the Lord's name in vain." She gave me a cold stare. "And lower your voice—you might wake the twins."

"Don't wake up Stewart—isn't that what you mean? Bryan can sleep through anything. As a matter of fact, it's because of what happened when Stewart was born, isn't it? You're afraid I'll get you pregnant again!"

Once the words were out, it was too late to take them back. Her eyes teared up, and she pleaded with me to be patient for a while longer. I tried to take her in my arms and calm her down, but she pulled away from me and went across the room to stand by the window.

"It's been almost a year," I said.

I stormed down the stairs to the den, where I'll sleep alone again tonight. I've come to detest this room, where I've spent so many lonely nights—and where Sarah almost died giving birth to our second son. Though it's cool, dark, and musty now, it was stifling hot last June when she was in labor. I can't forget the oppressive golden light through the half-drawn shades or the clicking of the fan that seemed unable to move the air. Everything about that day is engraved in my mind.

Sarah hated hospitals and insisted on having the baby at home, as her best friend had done. Her sister, who'd never given birth or helped with one, had agreed to help.

After several hours of labor, Sarah cried out with pain. I could see the baby's head, and by then, I was frantic. The doctor suggested I take a walk outside.

When I returned from my anxious attempt at a walk, there they were—my wife and new son! I'll never forget it. Sarah's face drenched in perspiration, proudly holding our newborn baby, a ruddy-faced, bawling, perfectly formed son.

The doctor cleaned him up, and her sister wiped Sarah's forehead with a cool washcloth. As I held my wife's hand and looked into our baby's tiny face, I felt incredible joy.

Suddenly Sarah moaned, then screamed, her face contorted in pain. Something was wrong!

The young doctor's face paled. He examined her, waiting for the afterbirth. "There's another baby coming," he stammered.

"Then help her!" I shouted.

How could a doctor not know there were two babies? Had he ever done this before?

Sarah screamed while the doctor twisted and tugged, saying he needed to rotate the baby. He reached into his black bag and pulled out steel tongs, rounded at the end to conform to a baby's head. Sarah's eyes were wide with fear, as were those of her sister.

I took the doctor aside and asked him, point-blank, if he knew what he was doing. He answered that he knew what needed to be done. I took that to mean he'd studied what to do in school but had never done it. When he suggested I go for a walk again, it was all I could do to keep from grabbing him and slamming him against the wall. I had to do something, fast!

I told him I was going for Doc Harvey. Doc was our family doctor until he retired the year before, and he'd delivered most of the babies in our town for the past forty years.

"Fine," he said, working on Sarah. "And hurry."

He was in over his head and seemed to know it. My mind raced. I could call the ambulance, but I was afraid that would still leave this inexperienced doctor in charge. I could call Doc Harvey and ask him to meet us at the hospital, but I feared he'd refuse. He'd probably tell me he was retired and had no authority to intervene. I had to find the man who could save my wife and bring him here, bodily.

I backed out of the room, grabbed the car keys, and jumped into my old Pontiac. The engine turned over once, twice, then finally started. Everything seemed like slow motion. My hands were shaking so hard I could barely hang on to the steering wheel. I bounced along the bumpy country lane until I came to a stop in front of Doc Harvey's farmhouse.

He was in his front yard weeding his garden. I blurted out our problem and told him he was urgently needed. I was afraid for my wife and second child.

He reassured me that our new doctor had good credentials and wouldn't appreciate him butting in, but I refused to take no for an answer. I let him know that the doctor had said it would be fine, and to hurry!

He rushed inside, grabbed his black satchel, and followed me out the door. I broke the speed limit all the way home and raced up the steps of our house and into the den, with Doc Harvey right behind me.

There was blood all over the bedding, and Sarah's face had lost all color. I heard her pleading with the doctor to save the baby, never mind about her. I was terrified.

Doc Harvey stopped the bleeding as best he could and told me to call an ambulance. Sarah's sister had already called one, and within minutes we heard sirens pulling up to our house.

We rode along to the hospital, where Doc Harvey delivered our second boy by Caesarian.

He was tiny and bluish in color. When the doctor turned him upside down and spanked him, he let out a loud cry and started to breathe. I was never so thankful to hear crying in my life.

We named the twins Bryan and Stewart. Bryan, the oldest, was named for my father, and Stewart was given the name of his mother's grandfather. The second twin soon gained his color, and his tiny head rounded out. Though the younger twin weighed a bit less, we were told they were identical.

Sarah's recovery has taken a long time. She found a new doctor who told us she was healed and would still be able to conceive. I was overjoyed at the news but saw fear in her eyes instead of joy.

Martha slammed shut the pages of the journal. She would finish it some other time, or better yet, destroy it. The terror, helplessness, and trauma of the twins' birth came back to her with a wave of nausea. It was distressing to be privy to problems in the bedroom of her sister and brother-in-law so many years later. She downed a spoonful of Pepto-Bismol, then made her way to the couch to lie down.

Couldn't John have shown more empathy for her sister, after all she'd been through? Why hadn't Sarah told Martha about her fears? Surely someone could have helped. She hoped she was the only person who'd ever seen the journal—yet here it was in the family cedar chest.

Martha rested her head on an embroidered pillow, pulled a knitted throw over herself, and fell asleep there on the sofa. When she awoke, she was stiff and momentarily confused. It was almost four o'clock, and she was due at Will's in an hour. She put the diary into a dresser drawer. She was glad to be going out and put this journal business out of her mind.

She covered the painting in a well-worn quilt and carefully laid it in the back seat of her car, then she placed the pie in a pie keeper, which she carefully set on the floor of the front seat.

It was hard to believe that Will was back home in Benzie County instead of a continent away. It was such a treat to look forward to dinner with him at his cottage. She only wished she hadn't started reading the disturbing journal this afternoon.

✧

Will saw his mother pull into the sandy drive and emerge from her Olds 88 wearing a blue paisley dress. Her white hair was pulled back into a chignon at the base of her neck, and her strong features crinkled into a smile that softened her prominent nose and jawline.

If he'd stayed in Europe, Will would still be talking with her once a week by phone instead of being able to enjoy time together with her. Now he could be here when she needed him. She'd gone overseas once to see him perform in London and had enjoyed it, but the trip had been an ordeal for her. If he wanted to spend time with her, he needed to be here.

He helped her out of the car and up the steps. His mother entered the living room and looked around. She seemed to take everything in.

Since Will had returned from Europe, he'd torn out floors, added insulation, and installed thermal-pane windows. He'd replaced worn, utilitarian furniture with two brown leather chairs and a cherry coffee table. He'd kept the Shaker rocking chair and grouped Jake's ship-in-a-bottle and old lanterns on the mantel. Will was glad that his stepfather had taught him how to build and fix things and to be fairly self-sufficient.

"This is so warm and cozy," Martha said. "I mean, it always was, but now it's more inviting than ever. Did you use a decorator?"

Will was pleased with the compliment. "I did it all myself, along with the painting, wood-staining, and roof."

"You've done a great job! It's very nice, but I hate to see you up on ladders and roofs."

"I don't mind heights."

"How could I forget? When you were a boy, I always had to keep close tabs on you when there were ladders around."

"I liked being in high places. I still do."

"Just be careful. The Ramseys' son fell off a roof last spring and was paralyzed from the waist down."

Will felt his stomach tighten. It made him uneasy to be fussed over after so many years. It was as if she'd been frightened by tragedies she'd heard about throughout her life and felt obliged to warn him about disaster at every turn.

Martha glanced around the room. "Where's the Steinway?"

"Downstairs."

"I knew you wouldn't get rid of it," she said with obvious relief. "I'm looking forward to seeing the lower level, but first, I need to bring in a couple of things from the car."

As he tended to the dinner, he noticed her struggling with a large, flat object that was covered in a blanket. When a sudden gust of wind threatened to wrench it from her hands, he hurried outside to help.

"I've brought you a housewarming gift. Just set it down there, but don't peek." She returned to the car for the pie, which she set on the counter. "Fresh strawberry-rhubarb pie," she beamed. "Your favorite." Then she lifted the quilt with her thin, arthritic hands, revealing the familiar oil painting of dunes and a stormy sea.

"Mom, are you sure you want to give this away?" asked Will. "I love it, but it's always hung over your mantel."

"I want you to have it. I've already replaced it with a beautiful watercolor. Whenever I look at it, I can picture Jake fly-fishing in the Crystal River on a beautiful summer afternoon." Her eyes teared up. "It's not as if I'll never see this painting again."

"You can see it whenever you like." He reached down to hug her. "Thank you. I'll always treasure it."

"It was painted right out on these dunes."

"Really? For some reason I'd thought it was an ocean scene. Did you know the artist? There are only the initials S. J."

"I was never good with names, but I think it was of this dune. Maybe I'm wrong." She smiled. "Something smells good. What is it?"

"Fresh trout. I caught it this morning. I'd better check on it."

"I've really been looking forward to this. After dinner, maybe you could play me a little Chopin. That is, if you haven't ruined your hands with all that carpentry."

"My hands are fine." Will felt the knot in his gut again but gave her a hug and kissed the top of her head. "Thanks again for the painting. Now let's enjoy our dinner."

CHAPTER 15

Great white cumulus clouds billowed overhead, and a warm breeze formed ripples on the bay. It was humid—the kind of oppressive July day when colors recede and the misty horizon is indistinguishable from the sky.

Meghan decided it would be a good day to solo in Joel's sailboat. She called him to make sure it would be okay. Then she put on her swimsuit, smeared on sunscreen, pulled her hair off her neck with an elastic band, grabbed a light parka and her new life vest, and headed to Elberta.

Joel's boat was a sixteen-foot daysailer with a tiller helm and daggerboard. It was an older model that had been patched and resealed. Meghan found it moored beyond the tall reeds on the east side of Betsie Bay.

The flag fluttered languidly as she hoisted the red-and-white sail, made fast the mainsheet, and adjusted the daggerboard. She hoped there would be enough wind for her to make it through the bay and out onto the open water. She'd hate to get becalmed in the midst of harbor traffic, much less find herself without wind power in the path of a large yacht. She wondered what it had been like to share the harbor with the large car ferries that carried railroad cars.

She cast off. A light breeze caught her sails, and she was able to make headway through the bay, past the Coast Guard station and out through the concrete piers. Once she cleared the harbor, the wind picked up and she headed northwest on a port tack.

It was great to be out on the open water again after so long. She felt herself dancing across the surface, her left hand holding the wind, and her right leading a wet waltz through the waves.

It felt good to lean out over the water as the boat began to heel.

Heady with a newfound sense of freedom, she relished the cold spray on her skin and the warmth of the sun on her back.

Charter fishing boats bobbed in a loose semicircle near the harbor entrance. In the distance, an ore boat neared the horizon, with its long, flat profile and tall pilothouse in the rear. It soon appeared to drop beyond the edge of the earth, with only a thin waft of smoke still visible. Large, forest-crowned dunes lined the coastline as far as she could see.

After a while, she noticed low clouds forming along the horizon. A sudden gust of wind propelled the small boat forward, then died. She studied the cat's-paws rippling across the surface of the water, so she could better take advantage of the next puff of light wind. She pulled the mainsheet in tighter but still couldn't catch enough wind in the mainsail to move forward.

She yanked the mainsheet in, pushed the tiller hard into the sail to come about, and ducked. The boom sped over her head, but the sail luffed back and forth across the deck. The boat was getting pushed backward, and she found herself in the embarrassing predicament of being in irons. She was glad no one could see her. She decided to turn around and head back.

Struggling to gain control again, she eased the sail out, adjusted her course to fall off the wind, then attempted the turn again. Once more the boat moved backward, wobbling through the waves. The wind whined through the sails, and the rigging clanged against the mast as the boat rocked dangerously.

Suddenly a powerful gust of wind filled the sail. She leaned forward and loosened the mainsheet quickly to avoid capsizing, but it burned her palm as it was yanked from her hands. The line controlling the mainsail dragged in the water just beyond reach, and she had to lean precariously over the side to grasp it. Then the wind died again, causing the sail to flap uselessly. Embarrassment was turning to fear.

The thought of beaching the boat crossed her mind, but she dismissed the idea. Taking Joel's boat directly to shore might damage it, and she'd have to find a cottage with someone home who'd let her use their phone, since she hadn't brought her cell phone. She hadn't wanted to get the cheap throwaway phone wet. Then she'd have to find a way to get home. Worse, Joel would need to arrange to pick up his boat—if there was anything left of it after being pounded by huge waves. She needed to make it back into the harbor.

When she'd cast off in light wind and gentle waves less than an hour before, her main concern had been whether there'd be enough wind for her to sail. As much as Meghan had sailed in the Atlantic, she couldn't recall being caught off guard like this by such a sudden shift in weather.

Storm clouds were moving in fast, and her frustration turned to alarm. An anvil-shaped thunderhead boiled upward from the southwest. When she heard the roll of thunder, she knew she had to get off the lake fast. She would beach it wherever she could.

She changed course to head for shore south of the Point Betsie Lighthouse. The wind was now almost directly behind her, and the boat shot forward through the breakers, rocking perilously. Running with the wind, she risked a sudden jibe. If the boom swept across the deck in this wind, she could be capsized.

Will Ashley closed all his windows, then watched from his wooden deck as the angry line of dark clouds swirled in from the southwest. He noticed a small sail fluttering back and forth. He grabbed his binoculars and focused on a sailboat in distress.

The sudden storms off the lake had always fascinated Will, but he was beginning to think twice about watching them. The deck of his cottage was a ringside seat for viewing passing ships, something he and his stepfather had loved doing when he was growing up.

He could still recall the sound of the booming foghorn. The lighthouse had been manned and functional when he was a boy, but back in the eighties, it had been automated. Now it was a historical museum, with its light maintained by the Coast Guard. Lately, he wished there were still a lighthouse keeper. Will was glad he'd been here to save Theresa Larsen's life, but he'd seen another boat in trouble six weeks ago, and now this one. He watched to see if any nearby boats would come to the sailboat's aid, but there were none around.

He heard a chord from Beethoven's Fifth, and answered his cell. It was Joel Larsen.

"Hey, Will. Sorry to bother you, but I loaned out my sailboat to a friend. She's had experience sailing in the Atlantic and knows what she's doing, but there's a big storm coming in. I can't spot her, and wondered if you can see a small sailboat out there?"

"Red-and-white striped sail?"

"Yeah. Sounds like my boat."

"Looks like she's changed course and is heading this way. She might be trying to beach it here."

"Maybe I should call the Coast Guard," said Joel.

"There's not time. I'll just motor out and give her a tow in."

"Be careful."

"I will." Will wondered what it was about the Larsens' friends and relatives that made them oblivious to weather conditions out on the lake. Then he remembered how fast this storm had come up. It had been a calm day an hour earlier.

He put his cell phone in a plastic bag and jammed it into his pocket; then he grabbed life vests, tow lines, a life preserver, and a blanket. He headed for the beach, racing across the sand to the large poplar tree where his two boats were chained. As he unhooked the aluminum fishing boat, he wished he'd finished restoring the more seaworthy wooden boat.

He dragged the boat into the water, jumped in, yanked the starter cord three times, and was off. The old 9.9-horse Johnson sputtered as it propelled the craft out through the breakers. Will negotiated these waters as few could, avoiding sandbars, large rocks, and any obstacles that jutted near the surface.

When a flash of lightning illuminated the distant horizon, his instinct was to turn back. He knew better than to go out on the lake in an electrical storm, but the sail of the small sailboat flapped wildly as if it were about to capsize. He would have to hurry.

"Four seconds," said Meghan aloud to herself, counting the time between the lightning and thunderclaps. She pitted her entire strength against the wind as she held on to the mainsheet. She couldn't afford to capsize now.

She knew she should have already lowered the sail in such high winds, but with the sail down, she'd be adrift, counting on the waves and wind to carry her in. She could be facing a long, cold swim to shore, or worse. If the wind shifted, she could be blown across the lake toward Wisconsin. She was determined to sail toward shore for as long as she could manage.

Then she saw a fishing boat heading toward her. When the driver waved, she gasped. For an instant, she thought it was Bryan, coming to her rescue again. She realized her mistake when he got closer. This was a younger man who looked nothing like Bryan.

She lowered the sail, then clung to the mast to keep from being swept overboard. With waves now more than five feet high, she lost sight of the boat. When she saw it next, it was almost even with the sailboat.

The man at the helm tossed her a towline with hooks on both ends. "Hook it to the bow!"

She grabbed for the line and was able to reach it on the third try. Maneuvering herself to the front of the craft, she secured the hook, jumped into the cold water, and swam with all her might to the fishing boat.

The man held out his hand and she grabbed it. With effortless strength, he pulled her up into the boat. He directed her to sit in the bow as he returned to the outboard motor. Wasn't he the man who'd saved Joan's sister earlier this summer?

His hair was wet and windblown, much as it had been that day. He was adept at handling his boat, even in these conditions, yet her heart sank when she looked back toward land. They'd been blown past Point Betsie, and the shoreline jutted sharply inland. Land was now miles away.

"We can't take these waves broadside!" he shouted over the wind.

Her momentary sense of relief faded as she realized that now there were two lives at stake instead of one. She shivered.

He handed her a blanket, which was soaking wet but still served as a shield against the wind. They rode in silence up and down the mountains of water.

A large wave hurled them up onto its angry crest and back down, crashing over the stern. The tiny engine sputtered, then died.

"Not now, damn it!" He yanked the oars from their holders, jammed them into the oarlocks and began to row furiously. His back was to her now, and she heard him grunt as he dug the oars into the water, pulling them back with tremendous force. She was grateful for his strength and obvious boating experience and couldn't help but notice his lean muscles rippling through his wet shirt.

Booming thunder followed a blinding flash of lightning by less than two seconds. Meghan shuddered. Unfortunately, they were perfect targets in the metal boat.

"Hang on!" he commanded.

She could barely hear him over the shrieking wind. The waves were huge, and chunks of white foam flew through the air. In the distance, she saw a waterspout spin upward into the sky.

It was in that moment that she wondered what it would it be like to drown. How terrible it would be for her brother, who was overseas, to learn she'd died the same way as their father. She thought of Bryan. She'd never told him that she loved him. If they ever found the two of them, he might wonder about the handsome man with her.

She saw an enormous wave surging toward them. Then a wall of water loomed behind the boat, raising them high onto the crest of the wave and down into its trough. The sailboat slammed into the fishing boat and drifted past it, no longer connected. A second wave curled ominously over them and crashed down, capsizing the boat and hurling them into the lake.

Meghan gasped from the shock of the cold water. She held her breath until she bobbed to the surface on the next wave, thanks to her life vest.

Where was the man? *Will Ashley!* That was his name. She couldn't allow the lake to take either of them. When she finally spotted him, his face was covered with blood. She fought back panic, reminding herself that a wound can look much worse in water. Squinting hard, she guessed it came from a gash on his forehead. She began to pray.

Will was praying too. His head throbbed. The boat had struck him as it slammed back down into the water. He willed himself not to slip into darkness. So easy to let go . . . the loosening of a bond. *Lord, help me hold on.*

Fighting to stay conscious, he bobbed to the surface, gasping for air. He scanned the whitecaps, looking for the woman. Everything was a blur at first. Then he saw her swimming toward him.

"Get back to the boat!" he shouted.

He saw her hesitate, then turn back. He labored through the waves and pulled himself up onto the overturned hull of his boat. If the wind didn't change again, they'd eventually be washed up onto the beach. He concentrated on hanging on to the boat, losing all track of time.

Finally he heard her cry, "We're almost to shore!" A moment later, he was jolted off the boat as it slammed into a sandbar. Like a sleepwalker, he felt her hand in his. She looked familiar. The woman who loved lilacs?

He pitted himself against the undertow, placing one foot in front of the other. The woman, thank God, was very strong.

They lost their balance in the pounding surf and were swallowed back into the lake. Then they were tossed shoreward again, smashing along the sand and stones. Clinging to each other, they fought their way through the breakers to shore.

They were north of where he'd hoped to come in, on a remote stretch of dunes. He squinted through the driving rain and spotted his battered fishing boat drifting away in the pounding surf, not far from the hull of the sailboat.

A bolt of lightning struck so close that he felt its heat across his skin. It exploded a nearby poplar, ripping off the bark and charring its trunk to the base.

"We've got to find cover, fast! We'll have to get the boats later. It's too dangerous to stay out here in this storm." As a teen, he'd seen an abandoned cabin near here. He would try to remember the way.

Unaware of how long they'd wandered through the woods, he glanced up and made out the cabin, nearly hidden in a thicket of cedar trees. Some of the windows were broken, and the door hung by a rusty hinge. Just a few more yards. He couldn't fight the crushing fatigue much longer.

Somehow, he reached the cabin. He kicked aside beer cans as he entered and noticed fresh ashes in the hearth.

❧

Meghan felt her blood pounding through her veins. Will was trembling violently, and his face was still covered in blood. She scanned the room for blankets, towels, or fabric of any kind. She shooed a squirrel outside.

"I'm a little shaky," he said. "How about you?"

"I'm okay. That's quite a gash you've got." She touched his forehead gently. "You better sit down, and we'll get this cut cleaned up."

"Thanks."

She helped him out of the life jacket. "Can you get out of your tee shirt and parka?"

He unzipped the front pouch of the parka and handed her a plastic bobber on a key chain. He felt around a moment longer in the pockets, then slipped out of the parka. "Guess my cell phone's gone." He peeled off the tee shirt and dropped it to the floor.

She caught her breath, vowing not to get distracted by the sight of him shedding clothes. She needed to keep her mind on making sure he was okay.

"I don't suppose *you* have a working cell phone on you," he said.

"I sure don't." He was definitely the man from the porch, and Theresa's heroic rescuer. She recognized his voice.

"There's a lighter inside the bobber."

She found the lighter, set it near the fireplace, then tore the shirt into strips and rinsed the pieces outside in rainwater. She pressed one strip against the gash on his forehead, her hands trembling. His neck and upper body seemed to relax at her touch.

She examined the gash. His flesh gaped open across his hairline and brow. Taking a deep breath to calm her queasiness, she bound his forehead with more cloth from the tee shirt. She stomped on the life jacket, squeezing out as much water as she could. She arranged it on the floor as a temporary headrest. "Lie down over here, near the fireplace."

"Whatever you say, Nurse." He gave a weak smile. "Maybe you can get a fire started."

"I'll try. You might need a few stitches when we get to town." She forced herself to sound calm. He might have suffered a concussion. She'd try to keep him awake.

He blinked again, as if struggling to comprehend her words. "I've seen you before, beautiful lady. What's your name?"

"Anne." Meghan flushed, instantly regretting that she'd given him her alias. How could she lie to this man who'd just put his life on the line for her? It seemed so wrong, even though he probably was in no condition to remember what she said.

"I'm Will Ashley." His deep blue eyes looked dilated, and his hair was matted with blood—all because of her foolhardy sailing trip.

"You're the one who saved Theresa Larsen. Very impressive."

"I just happened to be there at the right time."

"So now you just happened to be out in Lake Michigan at the right time . . . to save *me*."

"We're saving each other." He closed his eyes.

Meghan needed to get him help—soon. The wind whined through the walls, but she was cold beyond feeling it. She paced the room, looking for firewood. There were only two broken wooden chairs and an old table. She lifted one chair over her head and slammed it against the table, smashing it into pieces. It was as dry-rotted as she'd hoped and broke easily. Slivers cut through her palms like needles, and her eyes stung with tears. Meghan struck the table again, then broke the second chair apart. She used a stone she found outside the doorway to break the furniture into smaller pieces.

She gathered dry leaves from the corner of the room, placed them around the wood, and flicked the lighter twice. It produced what seemed a tiny, miraculous flame. When the wood finally ignited, she sighed with relief. She tossed the remaining wood into a pile near the fireplace, then hung the strips of cloth near the fire to dry.

Will's eyes blinked open for an instant, then closed again. She curled up beside him, hoping their two cold bodies would generate warmth. She'd read about people who'd stayed warm that way but wondered if it could work when they were sopping wet.

His body was very cold, and her teeth were chattering. It was a long time before she felt the warmth of the fire begin to bake through her flesh and into her bones. At last, Will felt warmer too. She dozed off.

She awoke to a bloodcurdling shout.

"Don't move!" he warned. His arms were locked around her.

She broke from his grip, scanned the room for an intruder, and saw no one. She froze, holding her breath.

"I won't let him hurt you!" he shouted.

His voice had a strange quality, like a sleepwalker's. She saw horror reflected in his eyes. She reached for the jagged chair leg. Armed with it, she searched the cabin, then looked around outside. She couldn't see anyone.

"Tell me what you saw." She had to keep him talking, had to find out if he was delirious or if they were really in danger. She placed her hand on his forehead. It was very warm, and the wound was starting to bleed through the rags. She cleaned and rebandaged his head. Soon, he was sleeping again.

She had to save this courageous man. She didn't hear any more thunder but couldn't afford to wander off into the woods and get lost.

"Can you wake up for a minute? *Please!* Where can I go for help?"

At last he opened his eyes, frowned, and said, "Path behind the cabin, about a mile northeast. There's a big farmhouse." Then he slipped into unconsciousness.

CHAPTER 16

Martha cautiously made her way down the hotel ramp. Her friend, Sandra Gershevski, hated to cancel plans because of bad weather; but for Martha, a cane was challenging enough to manage in the rain without adding an umbrella. She had all she could do to hang on to her purse and grip the railing as she negotiated the slippery incline. She didn't want to wind up like her next-door neighbor, who'd fallen and broken her hip.

When she arrived home, she tugged the rain boots off her shoes, shook water off her pleated, plastic rain bonnet, and hung it up to dry. Then she played back her phone messages.

She was surprised to hear Joan Larsen's voice again; but since Joan's appreciative call about her sister-in-law's rescue by Will, Martha no longer felt uneasy. Maybe it was time to get together and put the tension between them to rest. But Joan sounded upset.

"Martha? This is Joan Larsen. Please call me as soon as you get in."

The second message pierced Martha like a knife. "Call me right away. Our renter borrowed Joel's sailboat this afternoon and was caught in a storm on Lake Michigan. Joel said Will was heading out to tow her in—" The message cut off.

The third call began, "The sheriff found Joel's sailboat and Will's boat washed up on shore a few miles north of the mouth of the Platte River."

Martha grabbed the arms of a nearby chair and collapsed into it as she listened to the rest of the message. "We're out combing the beach and woods with a couple of sheriff's deputies. Call me on my cell phone, or call the sheriff for an update."

She played the messages back, inadvertently erasing the one that gave the cell phone number. The first call had come in at 5:47 p.m. and it was now 7:05. She pulled out the phone book and struggled to find the Larsen's home number without her reading glasses. She was too upset to remember where she'd put them, and her eyes could barely focus.

When she finally found the number, she copied it down, then concentrated on punching it in correctly. Her hands, always a bit shaky, were trembling uncontrollably. When there was no answer, Martha went through the same painstaking process to phone the sheriff.

"I'm Martha Ashley, Will's mother," she told Deputy Yardley. "I just got a message that my son's boat was found washed up on the beach."

"That's right, Mrs. Ashley. We've been searching for them, and so has the Coast Guard rescue boat. Judging from the direction of the wind and waves, and the likelihood they were wearing life jackets, we're hopeful they've already made it to shore."

"Will would have worn a life jacket."

"Good. They may have taken shelter in the woods. First thing in the morning, we're putting a volunteer search party out there with tracking dogs."

"Can't you search *now*?"

"I've got two deputies out there, but I'm not going to put volunteers there in the dark with another electrical storm heading our way. In fact, I'm about to call the deputies in."

"My son would have called me if he'd made it to shore. Please keep up the search—as much as you can without putting people in danger." She began to cry. "Thank you for your time."

Yardley reassured her they were doing everything they could. He suggested she ask a friend to spend the night with her.

Martha hung up and stared out the window at the driving rain. She put her rain gear back on and trudged out to her Olds 88. She headed north with her windshield wipers on high. She disliked driving in the rain but was used to it. Driving in the rain at night was another story.

Just past Miller's Landing, she turned down a narrow road and drove through the woods toward the mouth of the Platte River, where it flowed into Lake Michigan. She parked where tourists dropped off rental canoes during the day, pulling up beside another car. She hoped it belonged to someone searching for Will.

She squinted, trying to make out the low dunes on the other side of the river with her high beam headlights, but there was too much rain. She'd forgotten her cane, but got out and headed off across the wet grass and sand. She had to carefully place one foot ahead of the other, so she wouldn't miss a low spot or trip over something. She knew the risks of walking the shoreline at night in a storm, but her son was out there somewhere. She prayed he'd made it to land.

There was a flicker of light on the other side of the river. "Will!" she cried into the wind.

Lightning flashed, followed by a loud clap of thunder. The rain was coming down harder. Martha stumbled to her knees, got back up, brushed herself off, and hobbled back to the car.

The windshield wipers knocked back and forth, but she couldn't see. Her heart was beating so hard it scared her. She tried to stop shaking. She needed to calm down and think clearly. Maybe she should wait here in case Will was nearby and needed help; or maybe she should drive the back roads, calling out his name. Where would he have gone if he'd made it to shore? Jake and Will had camped and hiked together all through these woods. If only she'd paid more attention to where they'd camped.

Finally, the lightning and thunder moved past. She got back out and walked along the pavement, calling out Will's name. He might hear his mother's voice, even in the wind. "Will?" she cried out. "*Will!*"

Once again, a light flashed toward her from the sandbar. She was sure of it this time. She screamed his name louder, waving her arms.

Jeff Larsen's voice boomed out from across the river. "Is that you, Martha? Get back in the car!"

Thank God. He was still searching for her son. Maybe there were others helping. She returned to the car, eventually dozing off.

She awoke with a start to see a man outside the car knocking on the window. "I'm Joel Larsen!" he shouted. "Jeff's son."

She rolled down the window.

"Sorry if I scared you. Dad sent me over to see if it was you. He thought he heard your voice."

"Get in, Joel. You'll catch your death of cold. Have you found Will?"

"I'm too wet to sit in your car. We found footprints on the sandbar, but with all the rain and so many people here during the day, it's hard to tell. Will and Anne probably washed in on one of the boats or swam in and headed for shelter. The boats were found quite a ways north of here, toward Otter Creek. We have some guys checking around there, too, but Dad and I thought they might have headed toward the outlet, where there tend to be more people."

"Tonight in the storm? I hope and pray you're right. Sit down," said Martha, "and don't worry about the car."

"I've got to get back out there and help my dad and the others," said Joel. "We've got half a dozen men looking for them up and down the beach, along with my mom."

"Your mother's out there too?"

"We told her to stay home, but she wouldn't take no for an answer. Will saved my aunt's life. Mom's real worried about Will and the woman who rents from us, too. So am I. I'm to blame for all this," said Joel, his voice breaking. "I'm the one who loaned her my boat. I took her sailing a couple times. She's an experienced sailor, who's sailed on the Atlantic Ocean."

"My late husband always told me the stretch between here and the Manitou Islands was one of the most dangerous shipping lanes in the world."

"Conditions were fine when she went out," said Joel. "That storm wasn't predicted. I always check the marine weather channel. But I'm the one responsible. She's not that familiar with Lake Michigan—or how suddenly weather can change around here."

"There's no need to cast blame." Martha rested her hand reassuringly on the arm of the distraught boy. "Let's just find them."

But she did wonder at the Larsens' carelessness around the water. Did they think that since her son was a terrific swimmer who lived at Point Betsie, it was his job to rescue any fool who got in trouble out there?

"Maybe I'll drive up and down the back roads to look for them," she said.

"Friends of mine are out in a Jeep doing that," said Joel. "Your car might get stuck in the wet sand. Dad said to tell you to head on home. We'll call you when we find them."

Meghan heard the distant rumble of thunder. The rain had let up, and she felt only sprinkling through the dense crown of leaves above. She'd wandered off the path and couldn't find her way back to it. She stumbled through the thick underbrush of the forest, with only her instincts to guide her through the night. It was too overcast and heavily wooded to seek out the North Star.

She heard rustling in the nearby brush. She froze. Had there really been a prowler back at the cabin, who'd stalked her through the woods? She ducked into a thicket, trembling. Suddenly a large doe and her fawn leapt across her path. She gasped, then laughed with relief.

Meghan had no idea how long she'd been wandering when she finally came to a farmhouse. She rapped on the door. A middle-aged woman cracked the door open and squinted.

"What's going on down there?" called out a man from the upstairs.

The woman opened the door. "We've a visitor—a girl in a wet swimsuit. Get in here, honey, out of that cold rain." The woman pulled a coat from the hall closet and placed it around Meghan's shoulders. "Sit right there, while I heat up some milk and get you a towel and dry clothes. Then you can tell us all about it."

Meghan blinked away tears. This woman was doing what her mother would have done—warming milk and bringing dry clothes.

The man appeared in the doorway, rubbing his eyes. "Why are you running around in a wet bathing suit in the middle of the night?"

"I was out on the lake in the storm. The man who rescued me needs help fast! He has a head injury. He's back at an abandoned cabin between here and Lake Michigan. I think he was struck on the head by the boat when it capsized. We need to call an ambulance!"

"In the old cabin with the windows broken out?"

She nodded. "Sounds like the place."

He dialed 911, gave directions how to get to his farm, then handed her the phone.

"Once I throw on some clothes, I'll pull the truck out front," he said. "When the ambulance gets here, I'll lead the way to the old MacIntyre cabin."

The woman reappeared with thick towels, an oversized flannel shirt, and a pair of slacks with a drawstring, as well as warm milk and toast. She was already dressed. Meghan quickly changed into the dry clothes and gratefully drank the milk and ate the toast.

Soon they heard sirens approaching.

Let's go!" said the man. "I hope the dirt road north of the old orchard is still passable."

CHAPTER 17

Martha fell into an agitated sleep in her recliner-rocker. At 2:34 a.m., she was jolted awake by the ringing of her phone. She reached for it, trembling.

"Hello?" Time froze as she waited for a voice at the other end.

"This is Deputy Watson at the sheriff's department. I'm calling to let you know that your son has been located and is being transported by ambulance to Paul Oliver."

"Why are they taking him to the hospital? What's wrong with him?"

"He sustained a blow to the head and was unconscious when we found him."

"A blow to the head? How bad is it?"

"They'll be able to tell you more at the hospital."

"I'll be right there! Thank you for your call."

Martha grabbed her wet raincoat from the hook. She made her way down the steps and into the car, her legs unsteady. There was no point in imagining what sort of terrible brain injury he might have. She had a million questions, like how he got a head injury while boating, but for now she had to concentrate on driving to the hospital.

Once Will was back on his feet again, she'd try to convince him to move into town. He wasn't one to sit back and ignore people in trouble or to just leave things to the Coast Guard. He had too much confidence in his abilities as a swimmer and boatman, and he always was ready to help. She regretted setting off the chain of events that led him to move to Point Betsie.

Meghan stood in the doorway of the hospital room, trying to slow her breathing and steady her nerves. Will appeared to be asleep. Beside his bed stood a tall, elderly woman. Her sober expression accentuated the frown lines etched in her face as she hovered nervously over Will. Could this be the woman who'd been with him on the porch that day? She looked different, unapproachable.

Meghan ignored her instinct to place her hand soothingly on Will's forehead, and she didn't feel the time was right to ask how he was doing.

"I assume you're the one my son rescued during the storm," snapped the woman.

Meghan bristled at her tone of voice, yet moved toward her with an outstretched hand. "Yes. I'm Anne Maxwell. I was caught out in the—"

"I'm Martha Ashley, Will's mother." Her gnarled hands remained at her sides. "I'd appreciate it if you could kindly explain what happened."

Meghan awkwardly withdrew her hand. His mother? She'd assumed the elderly woman was his grandmother. Something about the angry set of her jaw made her think of Bryan the night he'd found her walking alone in the church parking lot after dark.

She took a deep breath. She'd felt so close to Will yesterday after all they'd been through together, but she was clearly an intruder here. "Your son saved my life. He saw I was in trouble and came out to tow me in. We were in his boat when we were capsized by a huge wave."

Meghan explained how she'd helped Will get to shore, followed him to shelter in an abandoned cabin, and run through the woods to a farmhouse for help. "The Palmers called 911 and led the ambulance to the cabin. I rode along with your son to the hospital."

Once at the hospital, Meghan had been checked to make sure she was okay. When she'd asked how Will was doing, she couldn't find out anything due to privacy laws.

Martha scowled. "Thank you for getting him help. But why is it that people never seem to realize they're putting others in danger when they do reckless things like boating on Lake Michigan in a storm? You both could have died."

"You're right." She blinked away tears. "It wasn't storming when I started out. It looked like a nice day, but that's no excuse. Your son is a very brave man, and I'm so sorry he was hurt rescuing me." Though she'd grown up sailing in the Atlantic Ocean, she'd usually been in more sheltered bays. Her desire to get out on the water and overconfidence in her sailing ability had overcome her normal caution and good sense. She couldn't blame Will's mother for being angry.

Martha turned away and laid her hand on Will's arm. Meghan stood there in silence. Then Martha looked up, her eyes clouded with worry. "How did he get a concussion?"

"The boat must have hit him in the head as we capsized. That's when I noticed his forehead was bleeding."

Martha flinched. "Oh dear." She sat down heavily beside the bed.

"I'd better go now," Meghan said. "I hope we meet again under better circumstances."

Martha frowned, saying nothing.

As Meghan walked down the hospital corridor, she felt sick. She prayed Will hadn't suffered serious injury, but it looked like he had. She had no way of knowing, unless the Larsens could find out.

Last night, Jeff and Joel had been waiting in the hospital lobby to take Meghan home as soon as she was checked out. All they knew was that Will was alive and unconscious. Once home, she'd collapsed into bed, then spent the few hours before dawn tossing and turning.

Tonight, during supper with the Larsens, she brought up her concerns about Will.

"It was my fault for calling him," said Joel.

She turned to the teenager. "What you did helped save my life. I doubt that anyone but Will could have gotten to me in time. I'm sorry I caused all of you so much trouble."

"No problem." Joel blushed.

"You did everything you could, Joel," said his dad. "I'm proud of you."

Joel's eyes filmed over with emotion.

"Joel was looking out for you, and Ashley turned out to be a hero again," said Jeff. "No doubt about it. He saved my sister's life, and now yours. He used to be a lifeguard and won swim meets back in high school. Nobody around here was a better swimmer. But what I can't figure out is why a man who's made a big name for himself as a concert pianist would come back to the states to live alone out on the dunes and work as a handyman."

"I get the idea he's an outstanding pianist," said Meghan.

"He was." Jeff frowned and asked for more potatoes.

"I'm sure he still plays the piano," said Joan. "He's probably just tired of being away from home—and from his adoptive mother."

"He's adopted?" asked Meghan.

"Before he was two years old," answered Joan. "We all need to pray for his recovery. I'll check with Martha later to see how he's doing."

"I'd appreciate that," Meghan said. "I'd really like to be sure he's doing okay."

The next morning, Jeff called out to her as she passed by the shed. He was hosing mud off his tools.

"Got a minute? I could use a little help." Jeff handed her a clean rag to dry the spotless shovels and rakes. "I keep my tools clean enough to eat off."

Meghan admired them, smiling, and dried the tools.

"About Ashley," Jeff began. "I hear there was something a little odd about the adoption. A middle-aged woman suddenly shows up with a baby and no explanation. They say there were some unusual circumstances, but I won't get into that."

"Mr. Ashley saved my life," she said, an angry tremor in her voice.

"Off course he did. He doesn't lack for courage. But there are other good men around here—Ted Allison, down at the hardware store, for one."

She felt her face flush. "I'm not interested in meeting men. I'm sorry if I gave you the wrong impression." Bryan couldn't have told the Larsens much about her. He obviously hadn't clued them in about the nature of their relationship, or Jeff wouldn't have thought she was interested in meeting men.

But then, what *was* the nature of her relationship with Bryan? She'd felt they were in love and had a future together, but he'd given her count-less excuses for why he couldn't come to visit. On top of that, he still hadn't written, and when they spoke by phone, he was reserved and uncommunicative. Yet whenever she asked him if something was bother-ing him, he assured her that everything was fine.

On her morning walk, Meghan noticed the lake was still shrouded in mist. She felt a burst of cool air as an enormous chunk of fog lifted off the surface and sailed over the steep bluffs into the sky. She believed she'd just experienced the birth of a cloud.

Eight days had passed since her disturbing meeting at the hospital with Will Ashley's mother. Though she'd heard from the Larsens that Will had been released to go home the next day and was doing well, she'd lost hours of sleep worrying about him. His mother obviously had thought he might be seriously injured—and Meghan couldn't forget the haunted look in his eyes when he'd awakened her that night.

She decided to pay him a visit and make sure that he was okay. The yellow daffodils she'd sent couldn't possibly convey her gratitude for his courage and seamanship in saving her life.

She planned to walk to the point along the shoreline—something she'd loved to do back in Maine. She was anxious to see Will again and to reimburse him for his damaged boat. It would cost her dearly, but Bryan had already wired money from her savings to reimburse Joel for damage to his sailboat. She hadn't told him why she needed the money or anything about the boating mishap. Now she had to find out how much was needed to cover Will's fishing boat.

As she walked back up the road to her cottage, her shirt clung to her damp skin. She showered, applied makeup, then changed into a favorite pair of white shorts, a navy-and-white striped tee shirt, and red wind-breaker. She debated whether to wear her hair loose or in a ponytail. She wanted him to see her today as a woman in control, rather than as a helpless victim.

She slipped into a pair of well-worn sneakers, placed a jar of Mrs.

Larsen's homemade strawberry jam in a small backpack, and drove to a road that led to the lake. She set out on foot along the shoreline in the direction of Point Betsie. It couldn't be far, she told herself.

She searched along the way for a Petoskey stone to have polished and made into a necklace. Joel had shown her his rock collection, which included many interesting Petoskeys, and she was anxious to find one. Grayish-brown and nondescript when dry and unpolished, these stones displayed their delicately embroidered, lacy patterns of prehistoric coral fossils when bathed in the lake's wet edge. Joel had explained how the coral had inhabited a Devonian sea here about four hundred million years ago.

Meghan trudged through the sand, making her way northward along the beach. Soon the dunes rose sharply from the lake, leaving only a narrow path of stones upon which to walk. When the path disappeared, she plodded through the surf in her old tennis shoes, slipping often on the wet rocks.

A tree had plummeted from the forest above, down the side of the dune and into the water. She had no choice but to climb over it. Other trees lay halfway down, their sand-caked roots jutting out. She'd heard of the harsh winters on the windward side of the lake but was amazed at the effects of the erosion.

In many places, she could barely maintain footing, so sharp was the drop of the dune into the water, but she'd come too far to turn back and wasn't about to return by the same route. Feet aching and exhausted, she realized that if she *did* find Will, she'd need to impose on him for a ride back to her cottage. Once again, she would come across as helpless and inept.

She hoped his mother wouldn't be there. She wasn't up to another tense encounter with Martha Ashley today.

At last, the bluff leveled off onto a beach of gently rolling dunes and tall reeds. Several beachcombers walked slowly along the edge of the gentle surf, now and then stopping to pick up driftwood and interesting stones. She wondered if they were also looking for Petoskeys. She waded along, eyes to the ground, still hoping to discover such a prize.

She heard a splash and glanced up, squinting to be sure her eyes weren't deceiving her. Will was skipping a flat stone across the water, his hair streaked with strands of gold. Lean and muscular, he threw with an easy grace. He looked strong and well, as if nothing had happened, except for a small bandage on his forehead.

"Five! That's pretty good," she called out.

When he turned and saw her, his face lit up with a warm smile. "You've recovered from our little adventure."

She smiled back. "It was a big enough adventure to suit me."

She couldn't help noticing his well-defined physique, broad shoulders, and wet trunks adhering to his tanned legs. He took off his sunglasses and looked at her with laughing blue eyes. The bruising she'd seen around his eyes was almost gone.

"You're a dangerous woman," he joked, surveying her intently, as if for the first time. "But you've got a great smile. Other than getting shipwrecked, how are you enjoying your stay in the North Country?"

"It's beautiful. It kind of reminds me of Maine, where I grew up."

"So you're no stranger to the water."

"Not to the ocean. Lake Michigan is a different matter."

"That's true, and the Manitou Passage has seen its share of shipwrecks."

"Thanks to you, I'm one of the survivors."

"I'm glad," he said. "It's nice to see you again. You're a terrific nurse, and thank you for the daffodils."

She wondered how much he remembered from that night.

"Too bad my mom's lilacs aren't still in bloom," he grinned. "I'd bring you a bouquet."

"Then I wish they still were. I love lilacs."

"I know." He looked into her eyes.

She felt herself blush. "You remember our first meeting."

"Of course."

"You've got a knack for skipping stones," she said. "My little brother was great at it, but I never got the hang of it."

"Want to give it another try?"

"Sure, why not?"

"Okay. Now take this flat stone and hold it like this, between your thumb and forefinger." He took her hand and carefully shaped her fingers around the edges of the stone. Standing behind her, he guided her arm as she threw.

Realizing she'd been holding her breath, she inhaled. She tried to concentrate on the technique and ignore the warm, giddy feeling spreading through her. She recalled the hours she'd spent with her body curled around Will's to help him survive, and was flustered to think that he might also remember.

On her third try, she skipped the stone twice across the top of the smooth swells. She picked up another flat stone to try again.

"Perfect. Three skips in a row and you get a wish." Something in his voice made her believe it.

After six tries, her stone sailed across the surface, bounced three times, and plunked into the water.

"Now make your wish," he said.

"A brand-new fishing boat for you."

"Presto!" Will gestured down the beach, toward a sturdy, wooden, freshly painted rowboat. It was white with gray trim and looked like a lifeboat.

Meghan was speechless.

"Be careful what you wish for," he said, with an unnerving twinkle in his eyes.

"I want to reimburse you for your other boat. That's part of why I'm here today."

"Wishes are free," he said. "If you don't mind my asking, what was the rest of the reason you came?"

She flushed at the intensity of his gaze. "Let me know what I owe you for the boat. I want to make good on it. I want to pay you for your lost cell phone, too."

He continued smiling, as if enjoying her discomfort. "I appreciate your offer, but I'm tired of cell phones—and I already have a fine boat. But I request the honor of your presence on her maiden voyage."

Meghan stiffened with fear at the thought of venturing out onto the big lake again, and for that reason knew that she had no choice. "If you fall off a horse you need to get right back on," her grandfather had always told her.

"Sure." She gave a weak smile. "That would be nice"

The small engine propelled the wooden boat out into Lake Michigan; then they turned and followed the shoreline north. The blue-green water and clear sky were calm and hospitable today, and the rocking motion of the gentle waves filled her with delight.

"To the north is the Sleeping Bear Dune, called Mishe Makwas by the Chippewa Indians," said Will. "A long time ago a mother bear and her two cubs were forced to leave the shore of Wisconsin because of a forest fire. They swam for a long time, but the cubs became exhausted and lagged behind. The mother bear reached land and climbed a high bluff to wait for them on the Michigan shore, but they never made it. Finally she died, waiting for them." He paused. "The Great Spirit Manitou raised the mother bear to be seen forever as the Sleeping Bear Dune, that enormous mountain of sand. The cubs became the North and South Manitou Islands."

"What a sad but beautiful story."

"An old Native American legend." He watched her. "Off to the right is the mouth of the Platte River, south of where we came in during the storm.

"It sure looks better today."

"You're right about that," He chuckled. "This is where Coho salmon and steelheads swim upstream to spawn in the fall. Right now, it's perfect for canoeing."

"I love to canoe," she blurted out. This man was throwing her off kilter.

"We could go sometime while you're here." He paused. "Are you free Thursday?"

"What time Thursday? I'm expecting a call that afternoon from my fiancé." There. She'd signaled her unavailability, tactfully but directly. She hadn't meant to exaggerate by calling Bryan her fiancé, yet she'd let Will know up front that she was in a committed relationship and was only open to a platonic friendship.

He eyed her intently until she averted her glance. "Nine o'clock sharp, then," he said, with a wry smile. "So you can get your phone call."

CHAPTER 18

Will led Anne down a wooded path beside the Platte River. Their hikes together were the highlights of his week. Anne had made it clear she was involved with someone, but she had at least left the door open for friendship.

When he wasn't with her or working on his symphony, he could think of little else but the next time they'd be together. He was drawn to her warmth, intelligence, and unaffected beauty and had been impressed by her strength and courage during the storm. He'd met fascinating women across the world but couldn't recall being so drawn to any of them.

He would never forget that day several weeks ago when he'd seen her coming down the beach toward him, her windblown hair shimmering in the sunlight, and her long, tanned legs glistening in the wet surf. He'd been touched that she'd walked all that way along the shoreline to check on his recovery, bring him strawberry jam, and reimburse him for his boat and phone. When she'd flashed her warm smile, he'd been lost.

On their first boat ride after the storm, he'd felt energized by her passion for the natural beauty around her. She'd shown genuine interest in the Legend of the Sleeping Bear Dunes, the formation of the Great Lakes during the glacial age, and the local flora and fauna. He'd even confided to her his closely guarded secret of how to find white morels in the spring, when they grew in the rich loam of abandoned orchards near the stumps of old apple trees. She seemed to devour everything he shared with her and didn't accuse him of sounding like a tour guide, as one woman had done.

As they followed the path around a bend in the river toward the fish hatchery, he pointed out a box turtle sunning itself on a log and waved back at a couple in a passing canoe.

"Imagine what it must have been like back in the 1600s, when Étienne Brûlé explored the Great Lakes by canoe," he said.

"I would have loved to see it. Wasn't Brûlé the first of the coureurs des bois?"

Will turned to her in surprise, nearly tripping on a log that had fallen across the sandy path. "That's right. So you're a history buff too?"

"You could say that. I love the way you make it come alive, kind of like my father."

"Your dad loves history?"

"He was a history professor."

"Is he retired?" asked Will, encouraged that she'd finally shared something about herself.

She swallowed. "My parents are both deceased."

He put his hand on her shoulder, fighting an urge to gather her into his arms and comfort her. "I'm really sorry. When did it happen?"

"My mother passed away when I was sixteen. My dad died about three years later." Her voice quavered. "I was in my first semester in college."

"That's tough."

"I don't want you to get the wrong idea. I had a happy childhood and a wonderful life before my mom got sick."

"But not after that?" he gently asked.

"Not so much." Her voice fell.

"Where did you grow up?"

She hesitated. "I don't quite know how to say this, but it's better right now if I don't talk much about myself or why I'm here."

"A woman with secrets." He made light of it, though he felt as if she'd thrown cold water in his face.

"Just for a little while longer."

They continued walking in silence. Then Will asked, "Are you in some kind of trouble?"

"Not exactly. I've already said more than I should have."

"Do you have an abusive ex-husband or something?"

"I'd rather not get into the details."

"An abusive *husband?*" He had to ask.

"I'm not married."

Relieved, he pushed on. "If I knew who was bothering you, maybe I could help."

"I appreciate it, but my best protection for now is being here, below the radar."

"How long is 'for now'?"

"I honestly don't know, but I've got a life somewhere else and have to return to it."

"You trust me with your life when we go out onto the lake, but not enough to tell me who, or what, you're hiding from."

"It's not about trust. I don't want to put you in the position of having to keep my secrets and deceive your mother and friends about me."

"If you told me, you'd have to kill me," he joked.

"Right." She smiled.

His clear blue eyes bore into hers, his smile fading. "But just remember—it *is* about trust."

Her face reddened. "Soon, I'll be able to tell you everything."

"Then I'll wait." He squeezed her hand. Maybe the man in her life back home was the one she feared. If Will knew what kind of threat she faced, or who was after her, he'd have a much better chance of protecting her. Yet he'd waited a long time to meet someone like Anne and could wait a while longer.

He shifted gears, not wanting to get her more upset. "What attracts you to history, other than your dad's influence?"

She thought for a moment. "I love learning about how people who came before us lived, though I get frustrated that history focuses mainly on battles and wars."

"That's what is best documented."

"I know. But wouldn't it be interesting to know more about how average people lived and survived in the past—how they dressed, ate, and played?"

"Ordinary people don't tend to get their stories told."

True, but that's about to change," she said. "Think of the massive amount of information that's going to be available about everyone, because of the Internet."

"More than anyone will ever care to know."

"That's for sure," she agreed. "I know it's not fair to ask you a personal question after what I said. But I was wondering—did you study history in college?"

"Ask away. I don't mind. I did take several history courses, but picked up most of this through my own reading and travels. I majored in music—piano."

"I was a music major too, in voice."

"So you sing!"

"I can carry a tune," she said.

"Maybe sometime I could accompany you on the piano."

"I'd love that."

They came to a fork in the trail. Will headed to the left, where the trail passed under a canopy of tall maples, oaks, and beech trees.

"What type of music do you like to sing?"

"Just about everything, but I love musicals most of all—especially the old classics, like *South Pacific*."

Will walked several hundred feet in silence, then turned to face her. He cleared his throat and began to sing "Some Enchanted Evening." He sang it in its entirety, in full voice, as he'd done years ago in a college musical. He was encouraged when the blood raced to her cheeks and her eyes misted over.

She applauded, blinking back tears. "But I thought . . . that you were a pianist," she stammered. "You've got a *wonderful* voice!"

He gave her his warmest smile and bowed. Maybe there *was* a way to connect with the mysterious Anne after all.

Music. He could do that.

Meghan was quiet as Will drove her back to her car at Miller's Landing. After he dropped her off, she watched him pull out onto M-22 in his red Jeep. She'd never forget this afternoon, when he'd unexpectedly turned to her and sung one of the most romantic songs ever written. His baritone voice was powerful and in perfect pitch, but what had left her flustered was the way he'd looked into her eyes and sang as if he meant every word of the song.

Yet she couldn't allow herself to be carried away by a superbly performed love song. Though her relationship with Bryan wasn't going well at the moment, she was sure things would get back to normal soon. There could only be one man in her life, and that man was Bryan.

Determined to get her mind off Will, she stopped off at the beach on the way home. Walking along the shore, she enjoyed the fresh breeze and steady rhythm of the pounding surf. As she reached down to pick up a smooth, flat stone, she felt a wave of heat at the memory of Will's arm guiding hers as he taught her to skip stones. She tossed it into the lake. It bounced twice.

She walked on through the surf, saw an interesting piece of driftwood, and picked it up. It brought to mind happy memories of beachcombing with her dad. They'd often collected shells and interesting driftwood, and he'd taught her and her brother about the sea and its varied life forms. Many of their best times had been at the ocean.

The breeze this afternoon was balmy and gentle, and there was an ethereal quality to the late-afternoon sunlight across the water. It reminded her of one July afternoon in Maine—the summer after her mother had died.

She'd just turned seventeen and had spent the afternoon on the beach of a tiny barrier island with her dad and younger brother. She could still remember the squeak of sand beneath her bare feet and the breeze against her skin as she climbed a small dune and raced back down into the water. They'd played in the surf and rested on blankets, enjoying the ham sandwiches, lemonade and oatmeal cookies she'd packed for their lunch. It had been good to be together again at the ocean.

That was the day she'd felt a glimmer of hope that maybe she'd find a way to save her family. It was her only happy memory of her family after her mother's death.

CHAPTER 19

"You heard me right. I'm issuing a stop order on the job!" Bryan enunciated his words into his office speakerphone.

From her station in the reception area outside his office, Lois flinched at the anger in his voice. The office manager continued working on a letter about soil compaction for a new subdivision northwest of town and tried not to be distracted by the heated conversation.

"And I won't issue a start order until the contractor decides to follow all state and federal specs to a T! He's skimping on the percentage of asphalt in the bituminous mix, and the gradations in the stockpiles don't pass, as you must be aware."

He lowered his voice. "Let me explain something. You've got three alternatives. First, you and the sponsor can fire us and put another engineer on the job, because I will *not* proceed until the requirements are met. Second, you can send me a directive, in your name, to go ahead although the tests didn't pass, *you* taking full responsibility for any problems that might arise. Your third choice is to hang up. Get out of our way and don't call us again. We'll get the job done as fast as we can, in the correct manner."

"He hung up," said Bryan. "If they don't want it done right, they've come to the wrong firm."

"That's for sure, Mr. James."

"I'd like a cup of coffee, when you get a chance—and bring me those Exhibit A's for our Albuquerque job. Then get me the FAA on the line. After that, I need to get in touch with Kate O'Neil. I'll give you her number."

Lois retrieved the plans he wanted and stepped into his office. It made her uneasy to see his face so red, with a vein bulging over his left temple. "Here are the Exhibit A's, and I'll ring the Federal Aviation Administration. I've a fresh pot of coffee brewing for you. Wouldn't you like some orange juice too?"

"Sounds good. Here's Miss O'Neil's phone number. And thank you."

Mr. James was a demanding and difficult man to have as a boss, but she wouldn't want to work for anyone else. She valued his integrity and high standards, but these past few weeks he seemed strung too tight.

He'd been dating a much younger woman since last winter and had seemed as happy as she'd seen him in years. But there had been some kind of shooting at the woman's home, then a fire set in her office at the high school. Though he'd said nothing about it to Lois, she'd seen it on the news. The report had stated that no one was hurt, but since then, it was as if the woman had dropped off the face of the earth. She didn't come by the office anymore, and he never spoke of her. The news media had even dropped the story, and Lois knew better than to bring it up. Her boss had become noticeably agitated, and she feared for his health. She decided to suggest that he take a few days off.

Just then, a beautiful redhead burst into the office wearing tight jeans and a skimpy top. She had lots of freckles and a figure as slender as a teenage girl. She looked vaguely familiar. Lois took an instant dislike to her.

"Hi. I'm Kate O'Neil, and I'd like to speak with Mr. James."

"Miss O'Neil is here to see you," Lois announced into the intercom. At least she wouldn't have to track the woman down. Did he have no sense of discretion? She couldn't help wondering why men her age chose women young enough to be their daughters. Apparently, they couldn't picture any woman with as many crow's feet as *they* had in a romantic way.

Then Lois remembered why she looked familiar. A few months ago, she'd seen this woman on TV too. She'd appeared on a local news show, pleading for the return of her daughter. Lois's initial hostility was eclipsed by a rush of sympathy and concern. She wondered how Mr. James was involved.

Bryan looked up in surprise. Kate wore faded jeans, a revealing halter top, and a jade choker necklace that was the same shade of green as her eyes. He'd never seen anyone with such a great mass of red hair. And for once, her timing was perfect.

"I came by to thank you for the flowers," she said.

"Have a seat," he said, rising to pull out her chair. He closed the door to the outer office.

He squinted, trying to remember. "The Birds of Paradise, back in May?"

"I should have thanked you sooner, but every time we talked, I was so focused on Erin."

"Of course. And no need for thanks. They were given as a thank-you for the dinner. Glad you liked them."

"I'd taken them as an apology."

"That's fine too." He carefully measured his words. "As an apology, then."

"So, you *are* apologizing?"

"Sure, why not?" He wondered how Kate had escaped the effects of the unforgiving Arizona sun. Her skin was as smooth as that of a younger woman. "I was about to call you."

"Seems we're on the same wavelength."

"Maybe." He could tell by her expression that she was still hopeful. But days had turned to weeks, and for each hour gone by without word of her daughter, the chances of finding the girl alive diminished. At some point, he would have to tell Kate he had nothing more to offer, as the police had essentially done.

"She's alive," Kate said fervently, as if she'd read his mind. "I know it!"

"Good." What else could he say?

"So why were you going to call me? Have you heard something?"

"I've made a lot of calls and used all the clout I can muster. Nothing has surfaced yet. But I called an old friend, with a . . . different group of contacts. He's meeting me tonight."

Once an attorney for a couple of high-ranking members in the Mafia, Sarducci no longer worked as a DA. Bryan had heard he took occasional cases as a private investigator, and Sarducci owed him a favor. Bryan had once bailed him out of a big real estate deal that was going sour.

"You and your mysterious contacts," said Kate. "If it's about Erin, I should be there."

"Not this time. I just need to know if you've thought of anything else related to her disappearance that I could pass on to him. Maybe a letter or address found among her belongings?"

"That's why I'm here. Her roommates found someone to take Erin's place next semester, and they emptied out her room." She blinked back tears. "While they were cleaning, they found something the police had missed."

She handed Bryan a copy of a business card that said, "Eduardo Maldonado, Photographer," and listed a phone number. No address, website, or email address. "One of the girls found this between the mattress and box spring, took it to the police, and gave me a copy. Unfortunately, that phone number's been disconnected."

"Is that the man she was seeing?"

"Her roommates are pretty sure he is, though they never met him or heard her mention his name."

"But at least now there could be something to go on."

"I sure hope so. And I've brought along some more pictures." Kate reached into her purse and retrieved an envelope with photographs of Erin, including another senior picture and a photo taken on her birthday in March.

Bryan's heart sank when he saw Meghan sitting beside Erin in the birthday photo, her radiant smile ripping at his heart. Until now, he'd managed not to think of her all morning.

"There'll be questions you can't answer. I'd like to go along," said Kate.

Bryan pocketed the photographs, determined not to say something he'd later regret. "I'm not even sure if this person could be of any help at all. If I find anything out, I'll let you know, but I need to go alone."

"There's something else—at least there *might* be. I have a feeling she could be pregnant."

"Pregnant?" He reddened. "Why didn't you tell me before? Damn it, Kate."

"Please lower your voice. Last night I was looking through a box of photographs again. I dumped them out onto the table, and two snapshots of Erin in the same bathing suit ended up beside each other. They were taken three months apart. Side by side, I spotted a slight change in her figure I hadn't noticed before. Then I dreamed about it."

Kate showed him the photos, then put them back in her purse. "She could have put on a little weight, and it's a subtle difference. If she were pregnant in the picture, she couldn't have been far along. That last picture was taken in early May."

"I'll share this with my contact."

"How do we know this is someone who can be trusted?" asked Kate.

"Trusted to do what? If you're asking if I trust him to do what I'm going to ask of him in complete confidence, the answer is yes."

"Yet you don't even trust me."

"To do what, specifically?"

"To keep Meghan's address in confidence, *specifically.*"

He stared her in the eye, making her shift in her seat. "As a matter of fact, I don't. In fact, I'd be willing to venture that she's already given you her address and that you've already told at least one other person of her whereabouts."

She flushed. "Well, of course, Rusty—"

"Who may have ties that you're quite unaware of and who could have already told someone else—but let's not reopen that can of worms."

She glared at him. "How can we work together without some basic trust?"

"To tell you the truth, Kate, I made a commitment to help you find your foster daughter, and I have every intention of doing what I can. That's all I can offer."

"It's obvious we both have strong feelings that we need to bring out in the open."

"What we *need* is to end this conversation with as much civility as we can manage."

"We wouldn't want to lose control now, would we?"

"No." His features hardened. "We wouldn't. And if you had exercised a bit more control back when it was needed, maybe we wouldn't need to be here having this conversation." Instantly, he regretted his words. He saw the blood rush to her face again.

"Sorry. I shouldn't have said that. You've only had her for a few years. No doubt they let her run wild before that."

Kate's stood abruptly and stormed out of the office, slamming the door so hard a picture fell off the wall. Bryan shook his head, wondering why he'd allowed her to goad him once again into saying something rash.

The sun descended beneath the towering blue-black thunderheads, and for a moment, streaks of fiery red lit up the dark underside of the clouds. Bryan opened the sliding glass door to the balcony, a tall goblet of Chablis in hand. To the east, he saw a violent electrical storm in progress, with angry cumulonimbus clouds billowing upward above the rounded peaks of the Rincons. Silent bursts of light exploded deep within the icy core of the cloudbank.

Bryan found the monsoons fascinating. Living high in the foothills of the Catalinas, he relished the changing moods of the massive mountain range. This time of year, he could often bask in the sun while watching sheets of rain deluge another part of the valley. He smelled the unmistakable, pungent scent of the creosote bushes reaching for water. Rain couldn't be far behind.

He felt agitated and unsettled. He shouldn't have let Kate get to him the way she had this afternoon. He couldn't repress a disturbing vision of her sitting across from him, her green eyes flashing with anger.

Then he imagined Meghan gazing at him with the warmth he'd found necessary to his very existence. In his fantasies, she understood him without having to ask; yet in the short time they'd been apart, he'd pushed her away. The prison of his own mind was starting to close in on him. Much as he wanted to pick up the phone and ask her to return, he'd heard reports from the police that Devrek might be back in Arizona.

Though Bryan dreaded returning to Michigan, it looked like he'd have to go there if he wanted to see her. Lately he couldn't stop thinking about the kind of life the two of them might have had together—a life of quiet elegance, perhaps somewhere far from Arizona or Michigan. He could afford to retire, yet had avoided thinking about it. The idea of free time had always struck him as an alarming prospect.

He could make a decision later about whether to visit her in Frankfort. By then he'd have met with Sarducci and might have a better handle on things. In the meantime, he would do his best to avoid any more confrontations with Kate. For some reason the woman threw him off balance.

He finished his glass of Chablis, placed the crystal goblet on the table, studied it, then refilled it. All these years of self-discipline had at least provided him with a semblance of order and stability, which now seemed to be coming undone.

There had been other women after Susan. Sheila, lovely Sheila, had so desperately tried to win his love. She'd been determined to break through the so-called "shell" she claimed surrounded him. One day, in despair, she'd resorted to screaming at him and pounding on his chest, as if she could break through to him using physical force.

"What an unnecessary display." He'd turned away and walked out of her life.

Then there was Jane, a kind and sophisticated woman of the local elite who was a big fund-raiser for worthy causes. As board members on two of the same nonprofits, he and Jane appeared to have much in common. Friends had encouraged the match, but Jane had gone so far as to suggest he get therapy. Not long after that, he'd gone his separate way.

He'd always felt Meghan cared for him as he presented himself, never trying to penetrate the privacy of his world or tap feelings best left permanently buried. And yet by leaving, she'd done just that. Now that she was gone, he was a raw wound.

Her mere presence had somehow made him feel alive again. At times he'd even felt himself reeling with a heady sense of well-being—even happiness. Yet he viewed happiness as a dangerous illusion.

Lately, Meghan had been pressing him to discuss their feelings for each other. Though he loved her now more than ever, he knew he shouldn't allow himself to continue in their relationship. He couldn't bring himself to discuss it with her, for what could he say? That it was easier to distance himself from her now, while they were apart?

He was determined to regain control. He poured himself a refill and sipped slowly, savoring the bouquet. He would need to exercise exceptional care in following his routines. He would get things back to normal.

He tried not to think of Meghan, but he suddenly smelled a wisp of her perfume that seemed so real, he turned, expecting to see her standing there. He crushed the goblet in his hand.

While clearing up shattered fragments of glass mixed with wine and his blood, his cell phone chimed, reminding him that he had to leave the house in ten minutes. He cursed, knowing that he should have allowed more time to make his way through flooded roads. On top of that, he had to tend to his hand and the broken glass.

Once en route, Bryan carefully navigated the slippery roads, slowing before entering low spots where water flowed across the road. A sudden shower in Tucson could quickly flood streets, many of which served as conduits of water when needed. Not long ago, cars had to drive along the steeper sides of these roads, with someone invariably marooned in the middle. Flash floods had even caused a few tragic drownings. Bryan had encouraged the local leadership to invest in some well-placed bridges, culverts, and storm sewers.

Over the years, more drainage was added—some by his engineering firm. Yet each year, some drivers ignored the warning barricades and wound up stranded in low spots on flooded streets. Due to Arizona's Stupid Motorist Law, they could be held responsible for paying their rescue expenses. Assuming the rescue had been successful, a front-page photo of a motorist sitting sheepishly on top of their car in the middle of a roaring wash seemed to tweak the offbeat humor of many locals.

Twenty minutes later, he pulled up to the Manzanita Lounge, a dimly lit, low-profile bar where neither he nor Sarducci should be recognized. Once inside, he squinted in the dark room, locating Don Sarducci at a secluded table near the back. He still sported his Magnum PI mustache and dark eyebrows, but was heavier than before, and balding.

They'd done a lot of business together over the years, and when the recession hit the construction industry, Bryan had been there to help. Sarducci had let it be known he wanted to return the favor.

"What the hell happened to your hand?" asked Sarducci. "Get a little too fresh with one of your lady friends?"

"I was hoping to play on the sympathies of some gorgeous woman," said Bryan, "but the only one interested was some guy who looks like a balding Tom Selleck."

They both roared with laughter.

"Make that two more of the same," ordered Sarducci.

"I'll have orange juice this time. Thanks."

"Two screwdrivers," called out Sarducci.

Bryan didn't protest.

The two men exchanged old stories, then discussed the latest on the big mall going up northwest of town. After the second round, Sarducci leaned toward Bryan and said in a low voice, "You said there's something important. Money? A woman? What's going on?"

"I need information about a missing girl."

Sarducci frowned. "I don't have a hotline anymore."

"I understand," said Bryan, "but I heard you're a PI now. Maybe somebody out there knows something we don't. Anyway, here's the story."

Bryan reached into his pocket and drew out a photograph of a beautiful young girl, looking wholesome and sweet in her senior picture. "Erin O'Neil disappeared from her apartment west of the university almost two months ago. A so-called photographer she was seeing—we think he went by the name of Eduardo Maldonado—disappeared around the same time. Bryan handed Sarducci a copy of Maldonado's card. "And she might have been pregnant."

"A pregnant runaway takes off with her boyfriend. Dime a dozen. Was she on drugs?"

"Don't get the wrong idea," said Bryan. "I doubt she does drugs, and her foster mother is a respected schoolteacher who really cares about her. She studies art at the U of A, and was doing very well until recently. I need to find out whatever I can about this Maldonado character. Who is he and where is he? Is his photography business on the up and up?"

"What else?" asked Sarducci.

"Four years ago, Erin testified in court against Dr. Karl Devrek, a psychiatrist. He went to prison for molesting her but escaped in May. She disappeared within days of his escape."

Sarducci frowned. "Which agency is handling the case?"

"The Missing Person's Unit at TPD."

"The US Marshalls are probably involved too, since there's an escaped convict," said Sarducci. "What about the FBI?

"I don't think so," said Bryan.

"If the FBI's not involved, there's probably no evidence yet that she's been kidnapped or taken across state lines. What have the police found out so far, that you know of?"

"She's classified as a missing person," answered Bryan, "but I get the feeling maybe she isn't a top priority. A nineteen-year-old girl runs away with a boyfriend, like you said. One officer told me there are so many young people that are missing, it's impossible to track them all down— especially when a good percentage of them don't want to be found."

"What did her foster mom think of the photographer?" asked Sarducci.

"Her daughter didn't bring him home to meet mom. It was all very secretive."

Sarducci frowned, stirring his drink. "How are *you* involved?"

"Friend of a friend."

"She's jailbait." Sarducci winked.

Bryan shook his head, frowning. "I may be an SOB, but not like that."

"Just kidding. Bet she's got a pretty mama, though."

Color crept up Bryan's neck and into his cheeks and forehead.

Sarducci smiled. "You can never fool an old friend. There's at least one beautiful woman at the bottom of all this."

"At least one," Bryan chuckled. They arose and shook hands, right to left, Bryan's bandaged hand at his side.

Sarducci's features sobered. "I'll find out what I can. If anyone's heard of the photographer, or the girl, I'll let you know."

"Thank you."

"Sarducci never forgets a friend."

CHAPTER 20

Time flowed through her in waves and currents, and Meghan had forgotten to wear her watch. She was no longer in a hurry to return to Tucson before summer's end. Occupying her time in unexpected ways, she found herself helping Joan Larsen put up jams and vegetables for the winter ahead.

This far north, along the western edge of the Eastern Time Zone, precious daylight lingered until almost ten o'clock. In the twilight hours, she would often sit with Joan on the porch of the big house, stitching tiny cloth hexagons for a quilt with a bright floral pattern called Grand-mother's Garden. As she quilted, she felt not only a sense of connection to her mother, who'd taught her to quilt, but to women throughout the ages who'd quilted together in comforting cocoons of friendship.

Jeff and Joel would join them on the porch in time for the sunset. On overcast days, a brief burst of scarlet light beneath the clouds might be the only glimpse of sun for the day. Relaxed conversation about fishing, church suppers, and day-to-day events reminded Meghan of small town life in Maine, while the rhythm of their voices over the steady squeak of the porch swing created a kind of peaceful background music. At times like these, the frightening events that had brought her here seemed far removed.

She was falling in love with this beautiful North Country, as well as growing attached to her self-appointed guide. She treasured her growing friendship with Will, and appreciated that he honored her request to avoid personal topics and keep their relationship platonic. She found herself spending more of her time with him.

It was difficult to think of Will without smiling, and she would awaken early in anticipation of their outings. He was comfortable to be with, and his enthusiasm about everyday things was contagious. It was a delight just to watch him rowing his boat, swimming, or simply walking toward her. When they talked, he really listened. Instead of trying to control her conversations and limit the topics, he tried to draw her out, to the extent she would allow. In truth, she was the one keeping him out.

Yet she felt a deep sense of loyalty to Bryan, despite the fact that they'd never made a formal commitment to each other. More than two weeks had passed since her last conversation with him.

She disliked seeing herself as someone in hiding. She began to redefine her stay in Michigan as a summer vacation and told herself she could go home whenever it suited her. She wasn't going to wait anymore for Bryan's go-ahead to return home. She'd felt he was carrying things too far, yet had to admit that he'd probably been right about the need for secrecy. Arranging for her to leave town quickly from a small private runway, under an alias, must have made her tough to trace. The threats had stopped as soon as she'd left Tucson. Had she departed on one of the regular airlines under her real name, she might not even be here to talk about it.

Still, her stomach churned every time she used the alias here with her new friends. Most of all, she hated deceiving Will.

At times, Will reminded her of Bryan—something in his posture or the intensity of his eyes—but in most ways, they were polar opposites. Will was creative, while Bryan was the logical engineer. Will was talkative, open, and comfortable in his own skin, while Bryan seemed increasingly aloof and inaccessible.

She'd been diligent about writing to Bryan, but he never wrote back, and their phone conversations were flat, like champagne without the fizz. He spoke cautiously on the phone, as if it were bugged. She hoped that the separation would be over soon and that they could talk in person about their feelings for each other. Until then, awkward calls and letters to him would have to do. So much of what had passed between them had been unspoken. Practiced as Bryan was in masking his feelings, Meghan had learned to read volumes from a telltale squint or a subtle change of complexion. She hadn't been drawn to the image that Bryan presented to the world but to a deeper presence she only sensed.

She still wondered about his connection to this area. He'd never discussed his past or his life before Tucson. She'd never heard him refer to his family or his childhood friends, but if this region wasn't familiar to him, why had he sent her here?

Lake Michigan glistened deep blue against the tall bluffs as Meghan and Will sat on the end of the pier in the harbor at Ludington, about sixty-five miles south of Frankfort. They watched cars, RV's and semi-trucks being loaded onto the car ferry, soon to depart for Manitowoc, Wisconsin. Then the passengers boarded.

When Will had told her about the big car ferries that once docked in Elberta, across the bay from Frankfort, she'd asked him if there were any still in operation. The car ferries had once hauled railroad cars, automobiles, and passengers across Lake Michigan and into the other Great Lakes as an extension of the Ann Arbor Railroad. Will missed them and had jumped at the chance to bring her to see the remaining car ferry, the SS Badger.

The Badger cast off, creaking and groaning away from the wharf. The deep blast of its horn resounded through the harbor as it sailed between the two piers. Like the lumbering train cars it was built to carry, it was a vestige of another time.

Meghan waved at the passengers on deck, goose bumps rising on her arms as the blare of the horn echoed through the harbor a second time. The large boat parted the water with its nearly vertical black prow, building up speed as it passed through the piers. She turned to Will to ask him how far it was across the lake.

"Over sixty miles," he said, smiling. "You remind me of a little girl right now."

"That's how I feel."

"Annie, listen to me."

"I'm listening."

He looked into her eyes. "I don't want you to leave." For an instant, the sunlight seemed trapped in his gaze.

She held her breath, sensing he was about to take her in his arms and kiss her. She turned away quickly, in time to see the giant propellers of the car ferry churning the water and creating a great wake. Like a duckling behind its mother, a small motorboat fell in behind it. A cloud obscured the sun, changing the sparkling indigo waves to a dark, steel-gray.

"Every vacation comes to an end," she said. "But let's not talk about that right now."

His features darkened. He drove back in silence, coming to an abrupt stop in front of her cottage. He opened the Jeep door for her, walked her to her porch, and turned to leave.

Twenty minutes later, Meghan poured herself a cup of Earl Grey tea. She concentrated on steadying her hand as she lifted the delicate china cup to her lips, trying to make sense of the feelings that swirled through her.

What was it in Will's change of expression this afternoon that had so disturbed her? What feeling had been betrayed in the translucence of his gaze? What essence of his soul had been revealed, and why had it upset her so much? She wondered how she could even talk with him about it, when there had merely been an indefinable change of mood. How might he react if she tried to discuss what had, or had not, taken place? Would he stare at her in that unnerving way of his, or would a chilling darkness come over him, as it had this afternoon?

If she tried to discuss their friendship, he would likely smile and make light of it. She chided herself for making so much of a mere glance, but when he'd told her he didn't want her to leave, he'd said it with such disarming intensity.

There could not—*would* not—be two men in her life. Sadly, she realized she couldn't continue to spend all her free time with Will. Maybe she should stop seeing him altogether. But that would mean ending their friendship, and Meghan abhorred endings. In the event a relationship must end, she invested as much of herself in the undoing as in the doing. Her friends took seed within her, winding their roots and tendrils through her bones and flesh. Ending a relationship felt like major surgery that could result in permanent crippling. She assumed the other person must undergo the same risk, and for that reason had to extricate Will from her life at once, before he was hurt, no matter how hard it might be.

But saying good-bye to Will would be devastating. She couldn't imagine losing his friendship, or even going through one day without his company.

⚹

Meghan turned the old Mercury Sable off M-22 onto the sandy road to Will's cottage. Since the beginning of the month, the Larsens had let her use the car that had belonged to Jeff's mother, as long as she covered the insurance and kept up with oil changes and maintenance.

She stopped in the driveway. She'd made a point of meeting Will at different places, never going to his cottage or inviting him to hers. But today his Jeep wouldn't start and she'd agreed to pick him up.

It was a clear day, and she could make out a cluster of fishing boats about a mile out on Lake Michigan, near where she'd been caught in the storm. She saw Will, disturbingly handsome in his faded jeans and navy-blue tee shirt, leaning up against the cottage beside his canoe. When he showed no sign of getting in, she turned off the ignition.

"I hope you're hungry," he said. "I'm about to whip us up some breakfast."

"I *am* hungry, and could use another cup of coffee. I didn't sleep too well," she said uneasily. "But don't go to any trouble."

"No trouble. And I didn't sleep that well either." He smiled, gesturing for her to enter.

As soon as she stepped across the threshold, she felt at home. His cottage felt warm and comfortable. The ceiling was cedar, rising to a peak high above, and a large laminated beam ran the length of the cottage. On the oak floor was a traditional braided rug. Over the fireplace hung a painting of the dunes and lake in one of its more stormy moods; and on the mantel was a replica of an ore boat. An oak table was set for two, with woven place mats, rustic stoneware plates, and blue-gray napkins. Beyond the table were sliding glass doors that opened to the dunes and lake beyond. Will seemed to have an eye for harmony and beauty.

"I love your place."

He grinned. "Thanks. I'm very fortunate to have inherited this from my stepdad. It would be hard to afford something like this now."

The aroma of freshly brewed coffee permeated the air. He poured her a cup, leaving room for cream. With the Larsens, she'd started using fresh cream.

"I like the miniature ore boat on your mantel. The detail is amazing."

"One of my stepdad's first mates made it for him. It's a perfect replica of his ship."

"Did he work on an ore boat?"

"He was captain of that one for nine years, but he piloted a lot of vessels during his career. Unfortunately, when I was seventeen, he died of a stroke."

"I'm so sorry. That's around the age I was when I lost my parents. I still miss them too."

"At least he was with us for twelve years."

"So you and your stepdad got along well?"

"Very much so. He was the only father I ever knew."

"Is that a picture of the two of you, holding that big fish?" Meghan was intrigued to see a photograph of Will as a boy, with a distinguished, rugged-looking gentleman with a gray beard. He looked every bit a ship's captain.

"Right. That's Jake and me with my first big salmon. He taught me how to fish and just about everything else."

Will invited Meghan to have a seat at the table, and just relax with her coffee while he chopped the vegetables. Adept in wielding the cleaver, he diced the potatoes, peppers and onions. He filled a large bowl with cold water before adding raspberries, and with great care, gently rinsed the delicate berries with the tips of his fingers, taking care not to smash them with a direct stream of water. Then he served them in cream. He whipped up a veggie omelet, ham, and cottage-fried potatoes, then took sourdough biscuits out of the oven. It was mesmerizing to watch him at work in the kitchen, and she couldn't wait to eat.

"It's delicious," she said after a few bites, in increasing dread of her mission. It was the most marvelous breakfast she'd ever had, but her stomach was starting to churn.

Breaking off any friendship could never be easy, but telling him her unhappy decision now would be more like deliberately smashing a child's sandcastle—a castle the two of them had built together. Meghan's throat was dry, and she could barely swallow. She wanted to continue their friendship more than anything, but knew she shouldn't.

"Do you always cook like this?" she asked, stalling for time.

"Whenever I can."

"I like your home very much. Sorry. I keep repeating myself."

"That's okay. I love to hear it." He beamed with pride. "I put a lot of myself into getting this place the way I want it." As he reached for the biscuits, his left arm brushed against hers, sending a shock of heat through her.

After an awkward silence, she managed, "Your stepfather must have been quite an interesting man."

He looked out across the water. "He was terrific. He knew the Great Lakes like the back of his hand. The storms Jake described would make your hair stand on end. He was quite the storyteller."

"Is Jake the one who taught you so much about boating?"

"Boating, fishing, swimming . . . you name it. He insisted I had to be an excellent swimmer if I wanted to go out on the lake. It's come in handy over the years."

"So I noticed."

"Working as a lifeguard helped put me through school. Jake was trained as a lifeguard too, as well as to captain ships."

"He sounds like he could do almost anything."

"He could. I was very lucky to have him. My parents were killed in a car accident before I was two. Martha's my adoptive mother."

"So you're an orphan, like me. I'm sorry."

"Thanks. But I haven't felt like one. Not only did I have a great stepdad, but my adoptive mom has always been a mother to me. She's still there for me."

"I had both parents, and yet I guess I have felt like an orphan, for a long time," she said quietly. "Even though I was grown and off to college by the time I lost my dad."

He took her hand and squeezed it. "I'm really sorry."

Fighting her desire to leave her hand in his, she drew it away. "My parents were great, and I had wonderful grandparents, too. I lived with my grandpa up until his death last winter so he could stay at home."

"I never knew any of my natural family, but Jake's people in upstate New York have opened their hearts to me."

"How did Martha and Jake meet?" She couldn't imagine the woman she'd encountered at the hospital being swept up in a romance.

Jake came into our lives when I was about five years old, and Martha was in her forties. He met us both at a pancake breakfast in the basement of a church. He 'took a real fancy to her,' as he used to say."

After a long pause, as if picking up the thread of a conversation in progress, he asked, "How long will you be staying here, in Michigan?"

"I hate to say it, but I should get back before school starts, which is in August." *There.* She'd made her intentions clear without having to be unkind. Their time together would soon have to come to an end. She'd finally shared something real about her other life. Now he knew that she was an educator and that she'd be leaving soon.

"That doesn't give me very long."

"Long for what?"

Will took her chin in his right hand, turning it gently toward him until her eyes met his. "I'm in love with you, Annie."

She felt her face burning. "You don't even know me."

"Then why not start by telling me about that other man in your life. You've already said you're not married. Are you engaged to him?"

"Not really. It's just that—"

"That's good enough for me. I'm not playing by your rules anymore. You say there's someone else. Fine! Then where *is* he? You've been here over two months, and he's obviously never come for a visit. Going two days without seeing you is too long for me."

"It's not so simple. There are complications."

"Life's full of complications. You're warm, kind, strong, and intelligent. I love you, Annie, and I can't help believing that you care for me too."

"Of course I do. But from the beginning, I let you know we needed to keep things platonic—"

"How can I duel with a phantom?" He smiled, boldly handsome, his blue eyes daring her to resist.

"What are you saying? That he's a figment of my imagination?"

"What I'm afraid of," he said quietly, "is that *you're* a figment of *mine*." He squeezed her hand tighter as she pulled away.

"Can't you understand?" Her voice broke. "There's someone else, and you know that. And now you've gone and spoiled the best friendship I've ever had. Now I can't go on seeing you anymore."

Will looked stricken. "Don't say that, Annie."

Her eyes filled with tears. He didn't even know her real name. The *Annie* he loved *was* a figment of his imagination, for he certainly didn't know Meghan Walcott. She pushed herself away from the table, feeling sick.

"You haven't finished your breakfast."

"It's the most delicious breakfast I've ever had, but I can't eat another bite." Tears streamed down her cheeks. "I'm so sorry . . . about everything. Good-bye, Will."

CHAPTER 21

The days had lost their lustrous sheen and a heavy mist crept through the Betsie Valley. The Larsens had gone to a wedding downstate, and the unaccustomed quiet at twilight made Meghan uneasy. Nine days had passed since she'd broken off her relationship with Will, and she missed him more than she cared to admit.

To keep busy, she alternated between long walks, bike riding, and weeding the Larsens' garden. She forced herself to keep moving yet seemed to accomplish little. She was plagued by doubts about her decision to end her friendship with Will. She tried to put a dent in the stack of library books she'd checked out but couldn't keep her mind on reading.

The mist nearly obscured the Larsens' farmhouse from view as she creaked back and forth in the rocking chair on the tiny porch. If Will were here with her now, the fog might have seemed romantic or could have led to interesting stories. He always was able to enliven the world around him. Instead, the evening felt oppressive, even ominous.

It didn't help that Bryan hadn't been in touch since she'd brought up the topic of their relationship. She wondered if her loyalty to him was misplaced.

She decided to work on her quilt but soon pricked her finger. A drop of blood fell onto one of the small white octagons of fabric she was stitching into one section of the quilt. Fuming, she used the seam ripper to tear the piece free, then threw it out.

As she washed her hands, she couldn't get the tip of her index finger to stop bleeding or coax a bandage to stay on it. She put the quilting away in frustration and picked up her latest mystery novel. Though she'd started to get caught up in it yesterday at the beach, she soon put it aside. Tonight the dark tale wasn't what she needed.

Then the phone rang. It was Bryan.

"It's good to hear your voice," she said. "I've been looking forward to talking with you. I hope everything's okay at your end." Maybe she could better reconnect with him now that Will was no longer in her life.

"The situation here is unchanged," he said.

"What do you mean? Are you saying Devrek is still at large?"

"Please don't refer to certain people by name over the phone. But yes, that individual is still unaccounted for."

"You act as if someone's listening in. Don't you think you're being a bit too cautious?

"Not at all. He may be back in this area, according to the police."

"I hope they're wrong." She felt as if she'd been kicked in the stomach. She'd almost convinced herself that Devrek must have moved out of the country, since he'd escaped capture for so long. She wanted to believe it would be safe for her to return home to start the school year.

"I hope they're wrong too," he said. "I'm still working behind the scenes to help your friend locate a certain person."

"I've been doing some searches for Erin on the Web," said Meghan. "No luck so far, but I'm trying to help as much as I can from this end. I've also tried to find out more about Devrek—I mean, the escaped convict—but I haven't found out anything new yet."

"Bad idea," he warned. "You need to stay off the Web, especially when it comes to . . . the convict. You never know how computer savvy someone might be."

"I use a computer at the library and change the screen whenever anyone walks by. I found out he'd once been licensed in New Mexico."

"Again, I don't want to talk about sensitive information on the phone."

"Then why don't you fly up here for a week, or at least a weekend? It would give us a chance to talk and to enjoy some time together."

"We're talking now."

"Are we? You can't even tell me what's going on back there." She hesitated, then ventured, "And it would be nice to sit down together and talk about . . . the two of us."

There was an awkward silence. She wondered if the call had been cut off. Finally, he said, "It's hard for me to get away right now. Maybe later. Anyway, I've got to leave the house in a few minutes to make it to the club for a tennis match. We'll have to put this conversation on hold."

"Then you'd better get going," she snapped. "Good-bye."

She was tired of his excuses and cryptic conversations, and frustrated that her efforts to talk about their relationship met with such resistance. The comfortable companionship and growing romance between them wasn't working across the miles. They hadn't had a meaningful conversation since she'd left Arizona. Maybe they'd never had one.

She couldn't help wondering if she'd made a terrible mistake in coming here. When she'd first called Bryan to tell him she'd arrived safely in Michigan, she'd sensed a kind of wall between them; and during the past two months, she hadn't been able to break through it.

Meghan was also haunted by thoughts that if she'd stayed in Tucson, she might have made a difference in the search for Erin. When her father had most needed her, she'd been away at college. Like Kate, he'd reassured her things were fine without her—but they hadn't been fine at all. Now that Kate and Erin needed her, she was hiding out across the country. Once again, she wasn't around to help those she cared about when they needed her most.

Agitated, she swept the floors and reorganized the kitchen cupboards. Too bad she couldn't channel her excess energy into reorganizing her house in Tucson, which actually needed it. She had so few belongings here that it didn't take long to whip things into shape.

Finally, she made herself hot cocoa, settled down on the couch, and picked up an old favorite of hers, the novel *Rebecca* by Daphne du Maurier. Much as she loved the story, she soon dozed off.

She sees her father, walking into the ocean. She's in a rowboat, trying to reach him. Suddenly Devrek is holding her dad under the water. She tries to scream, but is mute. She tries to strike Devrek with an oar, but can't move. Why is a dog barking so far out at sea?

Bryan appears on the beach, a gray wolf at his side. Will has a large pistol in his hand. He cocks it, takes aim, and fires. The fur of the wolf turns scarlet with blood. Again, she can't move or cry out. Bryan brandishes a knife in Will's face, his eyes filled with rage.

The bark of a distant dog had forced its way into her dreams and finally awakened her. *Rebecca* was still open across her lap, and it was 2:10 in the morning. She headed straight for bed, dispensing with her usual routine. When she finally fell back to sleep, she had a nightmare about gunfire through her window.

She awoke with a start, thinking of Will. She got up, paced the small cottage, and picked up her book of poetry by Robert Frost. Then she followed her mother's remedy against sleeplessness and heated up a saucepan of milk. After downing the warm milk, she slid between the cool sheets and pulled the comforter up to her chin. All too soon, the sun would peek through the curtains, and she was determined to take a trip today. At last, she drifted into a more peaceful sleep.

She's walking through a beautiful forest. There's a rustle in the bushes, and a red fox frisks off into the woods. She kneels to gather a cluster of morel mushrooms at the base of an apple tree, then follows a brook to a clear pool of water. A beautiful doe and her spotted fawns are drinking from the pond. They approach her gingerly, and she feeds them flowers. She is overcome with a sense of peace. Will emerges from the pool, his broad shoulders and strong chest glistening in the sunlight. He comes to her, and they make love in the soft grass.

When she awoke, she still felt Will's touch. Her dream was so vivid that she found herself aching to return to his embrace. As she climbed out of bed and headed to the kitchen, her lips were still warmed by his kiss in the dream. She was overwhelmed with emotion.

She was falling in love with Will and could no longer pretend otherwise, even to herself. But that didn't mean she had to act on it.

She'd studied a brochure Will had given her on the Arts and Crafts Trail through northwestern Michigan. Today was a crisp August day, perfect for the trip. The fog was gone, and there was a fresh breeze out of the northwest. Colors were brilliant, and details were unusually distinct— as if nature had gone high definition.

She downed a hearty bowl of oatmeal with fresh blueberries and washed them down with two cups of coffee. Despite her lack of sleep, she decided to go ahead with her plans for a trip north. She needed time away from here and the compelling world of Will, so she could think more clearly. She hoped that, like the scenery, a vision of her future could come into sharper focus. If the trip tired her, so much the better. Maybe tonight she could get a full night's sleep.

She packed a few snacks and set the brochure with its tour map on the seat beside her. Her first stop was to a cabin, deep in the woods. Enchanting carvings of woodland animals and elves were displayed on rough-hewn shelves. Further north, she stopped at Leland, a quaint fishing village with small art galleries and souvenir shops. In some ways, it reminded her of seaport villages in Maine.

She walked the docks of the marina, admiring the yachts and cabin cruisers, while she waited for the mail boat to South Manitou Island to begin boarding. She found a seat in the back, beside an elderly gentleman. Once they were underway, he began to tell her about his life there on the island. He'd grown up on a farm with a small cherry orchard. His family had struggled to make it despite high winds, sandy soil, and a shorter growing season than on the mainland. They'd managed to raise much of their own food, including delicious peas, beans, and rye that were only grown on the island. He wished he'd saved some of the heirloom seeds.

He explained how South Manitou Island had thrived in the days of wood-burning steam ships that needed to stop there to refuel. His eyes glistened with tears as he told her about his family and the small group of people who'd lived there. He'd always thought that one day he would move back; but the park service had taken over the island and the town was gone, along with its people. He could never move back home again.

His story almost brought her to tears. As they approached the island, she spotted the lighthouse. Once on land, she saw that it had gone back to its natural state. On another day, she would have been intrigued with the interesting flora and fauna, and the chance to be away from civilization, but today she was overcome with melancholy for the bereaved gentleman and the lost community that had held so many of his happy boyhood memories.

She thought back to her terrifying sailing trip, when she'd first noticed the island looming off in the distance. Later, Will had told her the Native American Legend of the Sleeping Bear and how the Manitou Islands had been raised to mark the mother bear's drowned bear cubs by the Great Spirit Manitou.

So far, she was failing miserably in her efforts not to think of Will. She was not the first woman to fall for a handsome stranger in a romantic, faraway place, but she couldn't let her emotions override her own sense of logic and morality. Yet what was the moral thing to do? She had no idea where she stood with Bryan anymore. He might even be dating other women in her absence. Maybe she was naïve to assume he wasn't. Though she'd thought that she and Bryan were in a committed relationship, it had never been put into words. After their phone conversation last night, she wasn't so sure. Maybe Will was right about her phantom lover.

Meghan hated ambiguity. She liked things to be crystal clear, but they never seemed to be with Bryan. She made up her mind that when they talked again, she would ask him, point-blank, how he felt about her and where he thought their relationship was going.

When she left Leland, she headed toward Northport, near the northern tip of the Leelanau Peninsula. Lake Michigan shone a sapphire-blue, and once again, she was drawn to the marina before exploring the town. She squinted in the brilliant sunlight at the white sailboats that glistened against the deep-blue water.

In town she discovered a small shop that was devoted to quilting and bought material for a second quilt. Her grandmother would have disapproved of such extravagance, as she'd seen quilting as a way to put discarded remnants to good use. But her mother would have understood.

Somehow, she sensed her mother's presence in the shop. It was as if her mom were guiding her selection of fabrics or trying to tell her something. Goosebumps ran across her skin. Definitely not enough sleep, she thought, lingering in the small boutique. She hated to leave, and sever the warm, unexpected feeling of closeness to her mother, however irrational. When she left, tears welled in her eyes as the bell on the shop door tinkled farewell.

She headed south, down the east side of the peninsula, through Sutton's Bay. Cherry orchards and picturesque old barns framed breathtaking views of Lake Michigan.

She longed to share the scenery with Will and to hear him make it come alive for her with his stories. She often caught herself wanting to point out a cloud formation to him, or to ask him the name of a certain tree.

An art studio near home was her final stop. The artist's home and studio nestled in wooded hills that overlooked Crystal Lake. Enamored by his work, Meghan purchased a watercolor of sunlight filtered through trees in the fall. It captured the elusive spirit of autumn that she'd missed so much in her years in the desert.

She wished she could stay into the fall and see if it compared to autumn in New England, but knew she must return home, get back to work, and reestablish the ties to her world. If she stayed much longer, she might not want to leave at all.

As she headed toward Frankfort, the sun was low in the sky, glaring in her eyes. She reached the Gateway Arch as the tiny lights of its miniature car ferry blinked on. In the harbor below, a flicker of sunlight was reflected off the window of a cabin cruiser. If she hurried, there was a spot on the lake near the steep dunes of Arcadia where she could enjoy the sunset from atop a high bluff. It was an isolated, magical spot that Will had once shown her. Perhaps there she could regain her sense of perspective.

It was almost sundown when she pulled off the road into the parking area. She was delighted to have the lookout to herself. She hurried down the weathered, broken steps to the third landing and sat down to watch the show.

The unusual sunset resembled an enormous, fiery egg yolk breaking over a misty sea in a kaleidoscope of shifting colors. Then it was gone. She shivered as the last brilliant rays reached across the water. Deep crimson gave way to violet, then to the blackness of night, and she was encompassed in peaceful darkness.

Then she heard a car engine. Her heart began to beat faster, something that happened all too often lately. What if her stalker had tracked her to this spot? Once again she'd put herself in a bad position. She had nowhere to run except down the cliff into the pounding surf.

A car door slammed. She held her breath as the sound of heavy footsteps descended the stairway toward her. Who would come down here in the dark? She felt in her pocket for her cell phone, wondering if she'd be able to pick up a signal, and remembered she'd left it in the car.

Bryan had been right. She could be careless about her own safety. Here she was, alone after dark, miles from the nearest house. Yet why shouldn't she be able to enjoy a beautiful sunset alone? A man could enjoy his solitude in nature, but a woman needed to do that in the confines of her home. She hadn't even been safe in her home, she thought angrily.

She needed to think fast. Was there real danger, or had her imagination run wild again? She could calmly, quickly, head back to the car, casually greeting whoever was heading down the wooden steps; she could slink off into the dunes and try to disappear in the undergrowth and tall reeds until he was gone—or she could make her way down the dunes to the lake, swim out into the dark waves, and hide in the rolling surf.

Though the last option was chilling, especially after her recent misadventure in Lake Michigan, it might be the best plan.

The heavy footsteps were getting closer. If, by some remote chance, Devrek had managed to follow her to this isolated spot to kill her, it was already too late. Even if it wasn't Devrek, or whoever had been stalking her, a woman out alone like this was an easy mark.

She shuddered as she saw a dark silhouette of a man coming toward her. He stopped on the first landing, then continued down. She held her breath, not moving.

CHAPTER 22

"**A**nne!"

"Will," she whispered hoarsely. "I'm sorry. I . . . I thought—"

"You're trembling," he said gently. "I didn't mean to scare you," He held her in his arms, reassuring her. Then he drew away, watching her carefully. "We were on the same wavelength tonight, Annie. No doubt about it."

"Maybe so," she said in a faltering voice.

"Where were you? I was worried."

"Remember that brochure you gave me? I took the Arts and Crafts Tour today. Then I came here to watch the sunset."

"I'd meant for us to take the tour together," he said with disappointment.

"I needed some time to myself."

"That makes sense. But fate's thrown us back together again, wouldn't you say? When I saw your car, I realized what had driven me to come here. But I'm sorry I frightened you."

"I shouldn't be so jumpy." She recalled the night Bryan had come up on her in the dark in the church parking lot. Though she'd had good reason that night to be afraid, she'd been edgy and nervous ever since the gunfire into her home. "I shouldn't have been out here alone."

"Who's the bastard you're running from?"

Tears streamed from her eyes.

"I'm right here, Annie," he said tenderly. "When you're ready to tell me about it, I'll be here for you." He took her gently in his arms.

She felt Will's heart beating against hers. The poplars rustled softly in the night wind, and the surf broke against the beach far below. All her fears, loneliness, and guilt seemed to spill over in a flow of salty tears onto his dark sweatshirt.

"Come home with me, Annie," he said softly.

She nodded, wordlessly, ascending the wooden steps beside him. He got into his Jeep and she followed. She reminded herself aloud that it wasn't too late to change her mind. She could still turn off the highway and head home. Yet she continued to follow him north on M-22 through Elberta, Frankfort, and past Pilgrim. She turned off onto the sandy road leading to his home.

As they entered his cottage, the sight of the oil painting of dunes on a stormy day made her shiver. It struck her as the loneliest, most haunting painting she'd ever seen.

Will took her by the hand and led her down the stairs to the lower level of his home, which consisted of one large room. He drew the drapes and opened the sliding glass door, allowing a fresh breeze to permeate the room. She'd never wanted any man as she wanted him now.

A loveseat and overstuffed chair faced the lake, along with a magnificent Steinway piano that looked like it belonged in a concert hall. On the opposite side of the room was a hand-carved oak bed covered with a blue-and-white Lady of the Lake pattern quilt. A painting of a sailboat on a windy, blue day hung over the bed.

Then she saw the CD, *Will Ashley Plays Beethoven*. There was a photograph of Will at the piano. She grabbed it and turned it over. "Moonlight Sonata" was one of the songs.

"Now I remember!"

"Remember what?"

"This CD! I heard it one night on my radio, before I ever came here. I was so moved by your rendition that I was going to buy your album. I even wrote down your name. That's why your name sounded so familiar!"

He beamed with pleasure, then took her hand in his and placed it over his heart. "One more sign that we were meant to be."

Her eyes shone with tears. "Maybe you're right. Your music reached out to me. That's a favorite piece of mine, and I'd never heard it played before with such depth of feeling. It was as if it flowed straight into my soul."

"But you didn't buy it?"

She hesitated. She'd heard the song just moments before shots were fired into her home. "Something bad happened, and the note with your name on it was lost. I forgot about it until now."

He took her in his arms. "Want to tell me about it?"

"Not now. What I'd love right now is to hear you play 'Moonlight Sonata.'"

"I'm sorry something bad happened to you, and I hope you'll tell me about it one day. But think about it, Annie. Somehow I was able to reach out to you before we ever met."

"It's true. Somehow you did. Then you reached out to me again with your music, and with your friendly greeting, on my first day here. You helped lift me from a pretty dark place."

"Sit here beside me." He began to play "Moonlight Sonata."

She smiled through tears of joy. Why had she fought this for so long, when everything about it seemed right?

When the sonata was over, they sat quietly for a moment. Then he took her in his arms and kissed her with the fervor of an embrace long denied.

He carried her tenderly to the bed, carefully undressing her as he lightly kissed her bare skin. He caressed her gently and at great leisure, until she could bear no more.

Will made love to her slowly, with infuriating restraint. With agonized impatience, she tried to hold back. Slowly, he drove her to more maddening heights until she could no longer endure. She held him tight, as if to keep from spiraling into fragments. She heard herself cry out. Only then did he give himself to her fully, and with abandon.

Never in her life could she recall having felt so completely joined to any man. For the second time that night, her salty tears bathed his chest, now merging in tiny rivulets into the sea of his perspiration. His eyes were moist too.

Meghan and Will listened for a time to the soft rain on the roof. Later, they walked through the gentle rain to the lake and waded along the edge of the surf, hand in hand.

Genesis 4:3–5

In the course of time, Cain brought to the Lord an offering of the fruit of the ground, and Abel brought of the firstlings of his flock and of their fat portions. And the Lord had regard for Abel and his offering, but for Cain and his offering, he had no regard. So Cain was very angry, and his countenance fell.

CHAPTER 23

While July brought hazy, humid days and warm nights, August was vivid, with a bite to it. If July had cast a misty spell, the fresh winds of August seemed to force their way into forgotten corridors of her soul.

She and Will looked forward to their times together. Some mornings, they would bike over to a favorite coffee shop, where they could look out across the bay as they drank lattes and ate apricot scones to the soft strains of Norah Jones. They rented a speedboat on Crystal Lake, fished in the Manistee River, and broke in Will's new two-person kayak in the Platte River. Will took her back to the Arcadia lookout, high above Lake Michigan, where she filled her lungs with cool, fresh air. Then they kissed while waves broke against the sand below. One night they caught a double feature at the Cherry Bowl Drive-In.

Meghan now understood the meaning of the phrase "swept off your feet." Strangers and acquaintances seemed unusually warm and friendly, as if drawn to her; yet sometimes she felt strangely vulnerable to their deepest, unspoken pain. Her favorite foods were more delicious than she could remember, yet she often forgot to eat. Colors were brighter, and music moved her more than ever. Songs on the radio seemed directed to her, and she felt energy and joy she'd never felt before. This morning in her car when she heard Beethoven on the classical station from Interlochen, she pulled over to the side of the road and wept like a fool.

But she grew more and more distraught about Bryan. She needed to tell him she'd met someone else, and break up with him, but she couldn't reach him. For over ten days, she'd tried to call him at home, on his cell, and on his direct line at work. She'd left numerous messages, but he wouldn't return her calls.

It occurred to her again that he might be seeing another woman. Kate said she didn't think so but wasn't sure. As a last resort, she decided to write him a letter. As much as she wanted to break the news to him directly, it didn't seem to be an option anymore. He obviously didn't want to talk with her.

She carefully selected a delicate woodgrain-patterned sheet of stationery that she'd purchased at the Gwen Frostic studio along the Betsie River. A print of a fawn in tall grass graced the upper left-hand corner. She began writing furiously on a yellow legal pad, scratching out words and sentences and inserting others in a futile attempt to soften the harsh message. She reread what she'd written, then tore it to shreds. After three more tries, she had a letter that was as kind, caring, and honest as she could manage under the circumstances.

She sealed the letter, headed for the post office, opened the mailbox, and released it into the mail chute. Instantly, she was seized by a pang of regret. She wished she'd spent even more time trying to contact him and talk things over. It even crossed her mind to plead with the postmaster to open the box, retrieve the letter, and give it back to her.

She continued trying to call Bryan, rotating between his different numbers, in hopes of reaching him before the letter did. After a week, she knew it was too late.

Sedona was a place where Bryan could relax and gather his thoughts. The cool, thin mountain air had never failed him. He looked out over the spires of red rock formations in Oak Creek Canyon, taking in the changing moods of the valley under the roiling cumulus clouds. He felt as if he could actually see the entire spectrum in their white intensity as they billowed high into the cerulean sky.

Years ago, he'd vowed never to get seriously involved with any woman again. As soon as he realized he was falling in love with Meghan, he knew he should end it. While they were apart, he'd vowed to break it off, but he hadn't had the fortitude to follow through. Instead, he'd acted cold and aloof, essentially driving her away. Yet her Dear John letter had left him reeling.

Lois had suggested he consider taking a few days off, but he hadn't wanted to leave until Erin was found, and the Albuquerque job was completed. Yet the New Mexico job could drag on for weeks—and he was coming to the terrible conclusion that Erin might never be found. He needed to pull himself back together now and was taking Lois up on her suggestion.

Rather than fish in Oak Creek as planned, he decided to enjoy a leisurely lunch in town and visit a few art galleries. As he wandered from one to another, he grew more agitated. Many of the paintings lacked vitality, and their use of light and shadow was ineffective. Now he remembered why he avoided art museums.

One small gallery stocked a limited quantity of art supplies. He found himself purchasing a sketchpad and charcoal pencils and heading back to his rented cabin. He stopped along the way to pick up a couple bottles of vodka and wine.

He settled into a wooden chair by the rushing water of the creek. He began to sketch a twisted juniper growing from a craggy rock. At first, his hand felt clumsy and stiff. Then it began to move forcefully across the rough paper as the charcoal pencil became a familiar extension of his fingers. His eyes again discerned texture and form, and the long-forgotten thrill of creation electrified his being.

Time passed unnoticed until the chill of dusk enveloped him. The great, surrealistic rock monoliths of the narrow valley glowed crimson in the setting sun.

Bryan set the pad aside and examined his three sketches, the last of which was much better than the first. He'd come to Oak Creek Canyon hoping to regain a sense of normalcy but was finding quite the opposite. It was as if someone else's hand had created the drawings.

Once inside the rented cabin, Bryan propped the sketches up against the wall on top of the bureau. He removed the cellophane from a plastic cup and filled it with wine. Lying back against the pillows, he stared vacantly at his sketches while he drank the wine, then the vodka. The walls were yellow, reminding him of those in another room, in another time. Suddenly bile rose in his throat, and he had trouble catching his breath.

※

Stewart was alone in Milan on his twenty-first birthday. He looked down from his window at the busy piazza below, then back at the yellow walls of his hotel room and his unopened suitcases. He'd just completed his summer classes and was set to begin a weeklong tour to Paris.

He and Susan had both agreed he should seize the opportunity to study architecture in Milan, Italy during the summer session, but it had turned into the longest summer of his life. Hopefully, it would help him decide once and for all whether to switch his major from fine arts to architecture. He'd already taken several architecture studio classes, as well as calculus and physics, but had also completed coursework in art history and oil painting.

Though oil painting was his passion, he was also drawn to the field of architecture, which should help him better provide for his beautiful young wife and son. Rather than throwing all his energy into becoming a serious artist, he was considering a more lucrative career in architecture, while painting in his spare time. Susan deserved more than a life on the edge of poverty, especially now that they had a child.

She and his art teachers were the only ones who'd thought his art was worth pursuing. His father had ignored his artistic inclinations, denying him the praise he so freely lavished on his twin brother, and his mother's words of encouragement somehow had seemed to lack conviction.

He'd never been able to please his parents or compete with his brother, who excelled in everything; yet in the one important thing in life, he'd won. He'd been favored in the area of love, which was all that mattered.

His twin brother could also draw but preferred to perfect his drafting skills for a career in civil engineering. Someday, when Stewart became a great artist, or architect, he might at last gain the respect of others, but it was too late to earn his parents' respect.

He was still reeling from the shock of their tragic deaths two years before. He'd first heard about the accident on the car radio. He'd thought he must have heard the names wrong, and had frantically gone up and down the dial, trying to find more news—*different* news. He'd heard Simon & Garfunkel singing "Mrs. Robinson" as if nothing had happened. Then the announcer had broken in with the same horrible news. His parents had been in a fatal accident. They would never see their grandchild, and he would never see them again.

With summer classes in Milan now over, Stewart decided to cut short his stay in Europe and return home as soon as he could book another flight, skipping the planned excursion to Paris. He missed Susan and his son desperately and wanted to spend a few more days with them before he headed back to school in the fall.

He smiled to himself as he pictured her surprise to see him walk through the doorway of their small farmhouse a week ahead of schedule. He thought of her dancing blue eyes and blonde hair against her sun-kissed cheeks. Never had he seen eyes as blue as Susan's. He pictured the scene over and over in his mind, each time more anxious for their reunion. Maybe she would burst into tears of joy, like she had last Christmas when he'd come home early from school.

Stewart glanced out the window at the endless water below, trying to ignore the turbulence and roar of the jet engines. He clenched the arms of his seat as they made a sudden drop in altitude. He'd never liked flying, and a big jet had crashed last month. He couldn't bear to think how it must have felt to plummet into the sea.

He thought of how terrified his parents must have been as they saw the train bearing down on them. He knew they'd seen it coming, because their car had left long skid marks.

There'd been a steady flow of wine in Milan, but after his most recent blackout, he'd abstained, until now. He found his resolve to arrive home sober diminishing with each round of Manhattans. He'd vowed to start fresh with Susan, *and he would*—as soon as he landed.

The plane hit another air pocket. It was like a bad carnival ride. He managed to get to the tiny restroom in time to lose his lunch—and hope-fully, several drinks. He doused his face with cold water, and considered spending his first night at a motel sobering up. Yet he couldn't bear another night without Susan. He'd tell her he'd just had a couple of drinks. She'd look at him dubiously, but as the days and weeks wore on, she'd realize he'd really changed and that he no longer had a drinking problem.

Once, after drinking too much, they'd argued about the power being shut off because he'd forgotten to pay the bill. "Why can't you be responsible, like your brother?" she'd blurted out, covering her mouth at once as if to muffle the words, but they'd flown through her lips like arrows in irreversible flight toward their mark.

His hand had shot across her face like a whip, leaving a red mark on her cheek. He would never forget the shock and hurt in her eyes. He'd prayed to God that the deed could somehow be undone. He'd begged her forgiveness, and she'd accepted his apology. She had instantly regretted her cruel comparison to his twin, given the relationship between them, but she'd made it clear that a man shouldn't give up his self-control to alcohol. He told her not to worry. He'd never to lay a hand on her again, and he promised to get his drinking under control. They'd held each other for a long time in silent embrace.

That had been the day he'd started to fear the power of his monstrous envy of his brother. Since childhood, he'd fought to control his jealousy, and had held it in check, until that day.

Logic told him his skills should be similar to those of his identical twin, but somehow *his* gifts had always seemed slightly inferior. He'd felt that his brother had been inexplicably blessed by God. Stewart had read and reread the story of Cain and Abel, trying to understand why God had not appreciated Cain's offerings.

His twin could run faster, throw a ball further, and even had a better smile, judging by its effect on people. Sometimes when he was alone, he could throw as far and run as fast as his brother, but when his brother was around, he'd choke.

He'd heard his parents talk about him in low voices. He was sure he'd done something to upset his mother and make his father angry. He'd somehow ruined things by being born—and kept on disappointing them.

Things were even worse at school, where the differences between them were measured and documented for everyone to see. In the primary grades, he was a good student, but his brother was always head of the class. Their mother believed twins did their best when they were together, and had insisted they be placed in the same classrooms. Some teachers tried to play down the subtle and not-so-subtle differences, and others called attention to them in a misguided attempt to motivate him.

By fourth grade, he'd begun to slip from near the top of his class to the bottom. He could tell that his parents and teachers had given up on him, and he began to accept the role of a failure. He started having tantrums that left him feeling humiliated and out of control. He prayed each night to stop getting so mad, and he followed the counselor's advice to count to twenty while taking deep breaths, and to punch pillows to release anger.

The tantrums subsided, but he despaired of ever making his parents proud. His mother gravitated more toward him than to his twin, yet there was an invisible wall around her that kept him from getting close to her. She often seemed sad and distant.

He drew pictures in the margins of his notebooks, gaining minor acclaim from classmates for his drawings of popular icons like Superman, Roy Rogers, and Wyatt Earp. Later he did realistic portrayals of his classmates and teachers. His mother bought him a complete set of oil paints when he was twelve. He assumed the role of sensitive artist—a small bone his brother allowed him to keep. Math had always been a favorite subject, though in school he'd left it mainly to his twin. In grade school, he came home with Cs and Ds in arithmetic, but in junior high, he was placed in different classes than his brother and began to excel in math. He enjoyed its pure logic, which provided an interesting balance to his art. His parents didn't seem to notice the improvement.

When the boys had to shower in their freshman year, Stewart died inside each time they had PE class, for Bryan was first to hit puberty. Stewart began to mature physically a few months later, but still felt boyish and unmanly next to his brother.

Both boys did well in high school sports, especially tennis. Stewart played aggressively and was starting to win matches; but his nerves would get the best of him, and he'd miss key shots when he played against his brother. He quit tennis and took up long jump, something the family didn't find of particular interest. Though he often won, they rarely attended his track meets.

Over the years, his twin developed an easy confidence and an air of authority that Stewart longed to have. He grew more popular with class-mates and teachers and was elected class president. Though Stewart was now as tall and good-looking as his brother, his peers seemed to sense vulnerability and targeted him for cruel teasing.

When Bryan came upon such a scene, he would step forward and magnanimously tell the offenders that they'd be sorry if they ever talked that way again to his twin. But Stewart didn't miss the condescending gleam of superiority in his brother's eyes.

One day, he overheard his English teacher addressing his art teacher. "Isn't it interesting how different Bryan and Stewart are, though they're identical twins?"

"If you ask me," said his art teacher, "Stewart can do anything Bryan can, and he's the more creative of the two. He just lacks confidence."

"Maybe so, but I think we ought to get the school psychologist involved."

He turned around and walked briskly away, burning with humiliation.

At fifteen, he learned that alcohol could help deaden a gnawing pain inside him, making him temporarily indifferent to how far short he fell in the overall scheme of things. By sixteen, the boys were indistinguish-able except for stance and demeanor, but the die had been cast: Stewart, the vulnerable artist, and Bryan, all-around leader, top student, and star athlete.

There was one advantage to Stewart's resemblance to Bryan. A guy could only date so many girls at one time, and Bryan preferred cheerlead-ers and members of the most popular clique, so there was a spillover of girls available to Stewart.

But Susan had not been part of his brother's entourage. Bryan hadn't even noticed her at first. She belonged to 4-H and Future Homemakers instead of Blue Triangle and the Pep Squad. On the fringes of high school reality, she was a farm girl who helped her parents milk cows and can fruits and vegetables instead of cheerleading.

Susan sat behind Stewart in math and often asked him for help. She had earnest blue eyes and sun-streaked blonde hair and emanated a wholesome beauty he found irresistible. She smiled at him and seemed to want him to notice her. He was drawn to her warmth and radiance.

He offered to help her with homework, leading to long spring evenings in the screened-in porch of her family's farmhouse. The scent of apple blossoms drifting through open windows in the cool spring air would always be intertwined in his mind with the heady urgency of lust and young love. Flyaway wisps of fine blonde hair framed her sweet face like a halo. Susan, with her laughing blue eyes.

Then one day he saw her in the hall talking with his brother. She'd been appointed by the dean to serve on the prom committee, and Bryan was the committee chair. They must be discussing plans for the big dance, he told himself.

Bryan glared coldly at Stewart as he approached, his forced smile and possessive stance warning more clearly than words could, *you've had your fun; now back off.*

The prom committee had brought Susan into Bryan's realm, where she was worthy of conquest after all. As his brother grinned with fierce determination, Susan smiled brightly, oblivious to what was going on. He felt like choking his brother with his bare hands.

Stewart never doubted his twin would win her over, but as he sat through his fifth-period class clenching his jaw, he made up his mind to stand up to his brother this time. He would fight for her. By bedtime, his resolve had hardened to stone. For once, he wouldn't step aside. Stewart cared deeply for Susan and would do everything in his power to keep her.

For several weeks, Susan was courted by both twins. Bryan escorted her to the best parties and dazzled her with his winning smile and self-assurance. For the first time, she was welcomed into the in-crowd. Stewart lavished her with unexpected gifts, regaled her with flowers, and even arranged for her to be serenaded by the Boy's Quartet, which he paid for with a week's income bagging groceries.

He learned to dance to please her and became her best friend. He even listened to her agonize about being the subject of the rivalry. While

Bryan overwhelmed her with his brilliance, Stewart reflected back her own strengths and inner beauty. He wrote poetry for her and painted her portrait, which he presented to her parents as a gift.

"That's our Susan, alright," her father said proudly. Stewart's portrait of her captured her very essence. The competition of the handsome twins for his daughter provided Susan's father with considerable amusement.

By May, she faced up to the fact that she could no longer delay making a choice. She could only walk with one brother at the graduation ceremony.

One day in math class, Stewart received a note from her. "Would you please walk with me at graduation?" He read the note a second time. A wide grin broke across his face that didn't seem related to logarithms.

She had decided Stewart was more important and necessary to her happiness than Bryan, dashing and impressive as he was. She treasured Stewart's understanding and support and felt she could be herself with him, while Bryan had been pressing her to "go all the way" to prove her love. "Bryan is more in love with himself than with me," she'd told Stewart. "Sometimes I feel like he wants to win me as a prize."

Bryan had smiled with confidence as he'd escorted the homecoming queen in the graduation march, but Stewart could tell his brother still seethed with anger and humiliation on the night when he should have been in his glory, as valedictorian of their high school class.

Six weeks later, Stewart and Susan were married.

As the wheels of the plane hit the runway in Lansing, Michigan, Stewart still felt like a newlywed, though they'd been married for two years. Through his fog of alcohol, he again pictured how thrilled Susan would be to see him.

He wondered if he should have asked her to meet him at the airport. But that would ruin the surprise. He caught a Greyhound bus to his hometown, then hitchhiked out to the farm. A man from Canada didn't mind going a little out of his way on his trip back to Ontario.

It was almost sundown when he was dropped off near the farmhouse. It was a good time of day to arrive, with fields of ripening corn bathed in rich, golden light. He had the driver stop far from the house so the sound of the engine wouldn't spoil the surprise.

Stewart walked quietly toward the house, suitcase in hand. Susan's car was in the driveway, so she was home. He opened the screen door, his heart pounding with anticipation. He didn't see his wife or son in the front room or kitchen. They must be napping, which was better yet. He opened the bedroom door.

Susan didn't smile, or rush to embrace him. She sat up in bed, her eyes wide with terror. Her nude body glistened in perspiration, as did that of his brother, Bryan, who was naked beside her. Then everything went black.

CHAPTER 24

Stewart heard loud pounding on the door. Led Zeppelin blasted from the stereo. Disoriented, he stumbled out of bed and crashed into a dresser. It took him a moment to grasp that he was in his brother's apartment. The clock said 5:15 a.m. He threw on a pair of Bryan's shorts and one of his tee shirts and headed for the door.

He was too drunk to remember how he got there, but when he looked out the window of the small studio apartment, he noticed his brother's red Corvette parked out front. He felt a wave of nausea as the vision of his brother in bed with Susan flashed across his mind. Bryan must have driven him home last night, hoping to apologize.

When he opened the door and saw the sheriff's deputies, their expressions were grim. Something was terribly wrong.

One of the men swallowed hard, then asked if he was Bryan Jameson. He heard himself answer *yes*. He was *Bryan*.

"You'd better sit down, sir. Your brother, Stewart, and his wife have been found dead. They were both shot."

"No!" he cried. "That can't be true!" He felt cold all over and couldn't catch his breath. He was dizzy, light-headed.

The deputies helped him to a chair and got him a glass of water. They seemed very sympathetic, but told him he'd need to answer questions later.

Of course there would be questions. He must have killed them.

After the deputies left, Stewart showered and changed into a pair of his brother's khaki pants and a cotton shirt. He finally ventured into the hallway, heading out to buy more booze. He ran into a woman who looked vaguely familiar, and very angry.

"Hey, Bryan," she snapped. "I asked you three times to turn down your stereo last night. Thanks for nothing. I should have called the police, but apparently somebody else did. I could barely hear myself think, much less fall asleep. And I *hate* that music."

"Sorry," he stammered. "I guess you're not into heavy metal. I'm afraid I had a few drinks and crashed for the night. I promise to keep it down from now on." He was appalled to hear himself glibly feed into her misperception that he was Bryan, and had been there all night. Who *was* he?

Stewart watched in horror as the coffin was closed. Through layers of sedation and alcohol, he tried to grasp the enormity of what had just happened. There had been a terrible mistake. The second funeral had been his own.

The violent deaths of his wife and brother had brought an outpouring of love and support for him and his in-laws. At Susan's funeral the day before, he thought he would die of grief and despair as one person after another stood to praise her short life, sharing what she'd meant to them and how much they'd miss her.

Today he sat through his twin brother's service in horror and shame. It tormented him to hear all the undeserved praise that was heaped upon *him—Stewart—*now that he was believed to be dead. Under different circumstances, he'd have been comforted to realize how much people cared for him. But no one had uttered one word in honor of his deceased identical twin. They all believed Bryan was the survivor and that Stewart had been murdered, along with his wife.

When it was over, he felt his aunt's reassuring hand on his arm, propelling him up the aisle and out onto the street behind the pallbearers, followed by Sheriff Haggerty, his father's best friend. Susan's grief-stricken parents trailed behind.

How could this be happening? Had he really murdered his wife and twin brother?

After Bryan's funeral, he stumbled back into his brother's apartment in East Lansing, near the campus, and drank vodka until he fell asleep.

He woke up the next morning nearly drowned in his own vomit. A gut-wrenching ache ran the length of his body. He saw a full bottle of sleeping pills beside Bryan's bed. Trembling, he picked it up. He poured himself a glass of vodka and struggled to open the bottle of pills. Half the pills flew out onto the floor, jarring him back to reality.

He prayed for the strength not to scrape them off the floor and swallow them. Right now, he needed to focus on making plans for the care of his little son. He swept up the fallen pills and threw them in the wastebasket. He started to put the bottle into the medicine cabinet, then threw it out too.

He was famished. He found a clean dish in the crowded dish drainer and poured himself a bowl of Shredded Wheat with milk. Afterward, he washed and dried the bowl and spoon, nervously opening and closing drawers, trying to find where his brother kept his dishes and silverware. He found the silverware jumbled together in one drawer, along with spatulas, can openers, matches, and potholders.

Stewart began a frenzied reorganization of the kitchen drawers but couldn't block out the terrible thoughts that screamed through his mind. He should be behind bars—and would be, soon.

It was hard to believe that a week ago he'd thought of himself as a happily married, good man—a decent father with a bright future. He dialed the sheriff's department and asked for a deputy to stop by his apartment.

Hours later he heard knocking at the door. Sheriff Haggerty gave Stewart a somber nod, then a bear hug. Again, the officer told him how sorry he was. He reminded him that he and his dad had been best friends, and that he'd always felt like an uncle to Bryan and his brother. In a voice filled with emotion, Haggerty confided how his dad had once pulled Haggerty's sister from a burning car. He would always be indebted to him.

Stewart nodded. "I've heard about that." He wished they'd sent a stranger. Haggerty's sympathy and love for him and the family made things so much worse.

"It took a lot of courage, and he was burned in the process. I never got to repay him." Haggerty glanced around at the empty bottles. "Drinking just makes it worse, son. I tried to drown my misery with beer after I lost a buddy of mine in the war. It didn't help. I don't suppose there's anything tougher than losing a twin."

Stewart looked him in the eye and swallowed hard. "Losing a twin . . . *and a wife.*"

The blood drained from Haggerty's face. He lowered himself heavily into an armchair, rubbed his hands together, and cracked his knuckles. Finally he spoke. "Don't forget my official role here. I'm the investigative supervisor on this case."

"It was Bryan who was buried yesterday. I'm *Stewart.*"

Haggerty looked down at the floor, then back at Stewart. He shook his head. "So that's what you came home to—the two of them in bed together."

"Afraid so."

"Your wife with your twin brother." Haggerty shook his head. "I'd thought the world of Susan. I never dreamed she was that kind of woman."

Stewart's face turned crimson. "No, she wasn't like that! I don't want you to get the wrong idea. She was a wonderful person—like everyone said at the funeral."

"Well, son, it looks pretty bad. Not too long ago, some would have called it justifiable. You might want to stop and think about that for a moment." After another long pause, Haggerty added, "Something like this would tarnish her good name and that of your brother as well. Your families would be hurt even more than they are now."

"She was a *good woman,*" he insisted. In his confusion and despair, it hadn't occurred to him how his confession would make his deceased wife and brother look.

How long do you think it was going on?"

"I was studying in Milan this summer. I came home early, as a surprise." His voice broke. "I walked in on them."

Haggerty frowned. "You flew home from Europe with a gun?"

"I had Susan get a gun for self-defense while I was overseas. She kept it in the nightstand."

"Do you remember holding the gun in your hand and pulling the trigger?"

He cast his eyes downward. "Not really."

"Why not?"

"I'm not sure. I was pretty drunk—or maybe I've been too upset to remember."

Haggerty glanced at one of the empty bottles lined up on the coffee table. "Have you ever had a blackout from drinking too much?"

He nodded. "A couple times."

"I've always known you to be a good person and a levelheaded guy, but you've got yourself a serious drinking problem there. You'd better leave the stuff alone and get some help. Throw out all this booze. I'll help you do it right now. Get yourself to an AA meeting. But you'd better dry out. Make sure you remember exactly what happened before you make an official confession."

Haggerty stood up and walked to the kitchen. He opened one cupboard after another, grabbed every bottle of wine and liquor he could find, and poured them down the drain. "I can make a few calls, get you admitted to a treatment center."

"I can't do that," said Stewart. "I have to get things arranged for my son. That's the most important thing right now—before I go to prison. Do you know where he is?"

"He's with Susan's parents." Haggerty shook his head. "I just can't believe she'd do something like that."

"My wife was the one of the finest people I've ever known."

Haggerty stood up. "If that's what you really believe, then you might not want to repeat what you just said to anyone else."

"I can't think right now. This is such a nightmare."

"Yes, it is—but you *need* to think, long and hard."

"I need to pay for what I've done."

"It doesn't sound like you really know what you've done. But you'll pay, alright—one way or another—whether you actually did it or not. Nothing we can do about that."

"No, nothing." Stewart's head pounded with pain.

Haggerty looked him in the eye. "And stay off the booze, *Bryan.*"

Stewart watched Haggerty head out the door, then collapsed into a chair, gazing at the wastebasket full of empty bottles. He went into the bathroom, reached back into the cabinet beneath the sink, pulled out a bottle of vodka, and took a deep swig.

Haggerty had a point. The publicity would be ugly, forever staining his wife's memory. She would become Susan, an adulteress found nude in her marital bed with her husband's twin brother, killed by her betrayed husband in an act of passion. She would no longer be Susan, devoted daughter, mother, wife, and Sunday school teacher—an innocent victim everyone had loved and admired.

To confess would destroy her memory. Disgrace would be added to her parents' grief, and his brother's memory would be destroyed as well. If Haggerty was right, some might even think they got what they deserved. When he was old enough, his son would be ashamed of both parents, as well as of his uncle.

The day after Haggerty's interview, two other sheriff's deputies arrived to question him. He told them he'd been home listening to heavy metal music. He'd drunk too much and fallen asleep with the stereo turned up loud. His alibi checked out with the neighbors.

With Haggerty calling the shots, it wasn't pursued in depth.

The following day his attorney called to notify him that he was to be named as executor of his brother's estate and would need to look into plans for his nephew.

"Executor?" he stammered.

"You'll be in charge of both your brother and your sister-in-law's estates."

"Right. I remember now." Both he and Susan had listed his twin brother as executor of their wills, and the attorney thought he was Bryan.

"The reason I didn't wait a few days to call is that you're also listed as guardian of your nephew. Susan's mother was just admitted to the hospital for another heart attack, and the little boy is about to be placed in temporary foster care."

"Foster care? Thanks for letting me know." His voice trembled. "Is

Susan's mother going to be alright?" He must be to blame for her heart attack too.

"You'll have to contact your father-in-law or the hospital about that."

After the call, he collapsed onto the bed sobbing. Then he was sick again.

For a fleeting moment, he'd been relieved at the prospect of getting his son back. He wanted to rush to him, take him from the shelter, and bring him home. Then he remembered who he was now—a drunken murderer. He was the kind of man he'd never want to raise his son. He might wind up spending the rest of his life behind bars. Even worse, he no longer trusted himself.

But who could he find to care for his little boy? His parents were deceased, and Susan's mother wasn't well enough. His mind was spinning. Susan was an only child and there was no one else. He got on his knees and prayed.

Then it came to him. His aunt had been like a second mother to him. She was warm, caring, intelligent, and loving. She'd never had children of her own, but she was great with them. She'd doted on his son since he was born, and the little boy clearly adored her.

That evening, he paid her a visit. "I've been named executor of Stewart's will, and need to make plans for my . . . my *nephew*." His voice broke. "I can't handle him right now."

"Of course you can. You're a capable man. You need to be strong and trust in the Lord."

"I really need your help." His eyes glistened with tears. "My nephew . . . has his whole life ahead of him, and I want him to have a good home. Could you help me . . . make a plan for him?"

She looked him in the eye. "For a moment there, I thought you were Stewart."

He paled, saying nothing.

"I'm sorry." She studied his face. "I miss your brother so much. My mind's playing tricks on me."

When he didn't reply she said, "Why don't you think about this for a week or two? Pray over it. If you still feel you can't do this at the end of two weeks, I'll help you make arrangements to find him a good home. I adore that little guy."

"I was pretty sure you did."

"Of course I do."

"I don't need two weeks . . . and I have prayed about this." He hesitated. "To be honest, I feel that *you* would be the best one to raise him, though I know that's too much to ask."

Her lips quivered. "It's not too much to ask. But you're his uncle and his dad's twin. You're his next of kin, and the one person in the world most like his father. When you marry, he'll have two young parents who are the perfect age to raise him."

"Right age, but the wrong person," said Stewart. "I feel you'd be the best possible person to bring him up. I don't want to pressure you, though. It would be a huge responsibility."

She sat down, clutching the wooden arms of the kitchen chair. "I've always dreamed of having a child. But are you *sure* about this?"

"Very sure."

"Then I would be honored."

A week later, the phone rang. "This is Snyder Hall. I need to speak to Bryan Jameson."

"Speaking," he heard himself respond.

"We've been trying to reach you. You're on dinners every night and breakfasts Mondays and Fridays."

"I'm afraid that I—"

"You need to report to the cafeteria this afternoon at 4:15," said the woman. "If you don't want to keep the job, just say so, because there are plenty who'd like to have it."

"I understand." He hung up, surprised Bryan would have taken such a mundane job. It wasn't like him. Maybe he needed extra money to keep up the Corvette.

Hours later, Stewart found himself in the cafeteria of Snyder Hall. He bussed tables a little slowly at first, but many students had heard the news that his brother and sister-in-law had been tragically murdered. He couldn't be expected to be himself.

He moved from table to table, clearing away the dishes and silverware as if in a trance. It seemed that everyone had a kind word, and the woman who'd been so abrupt over the phone apologized. She hadn't known.

It turned out to be a relief to be occupied for several hours a day gathering up dirty glasses and silverware, and he was strangely gratified by the warmth showered on him by other students, even though it was meant for his twin.

People should be turning from him in revulsion, yet for what seemed the first time in his life, they were glad to see him—rather, glad to see the man they *thought* he was. Several girls smiled or waved. One rushed over to embrace him. "So sorry, babe."

He'd forced a smile, but soon he let her and his brother's other close friends know that he needed his space right now. It was going to take him some time.

Though he wore Bryan's clothes, used his cologne, and even wore his shoes, he needed to avoid Susan's family and those who'd been closest to Bryan. They were bound to catch on.

Back at the apartment, he tried to avoid looking at Bryan's newly purchased textbooks, which were neatly lined up on his desk, along with the receipts. Stewart felt queasy whenever he saw them. He couldn't bring himself to move the books, or to return them. Finally, he thumbed through them, hands trembling. Stuck between the pages of a math textbook was Bryan's class schedule. He'd signed up for courses in science, math, and engineering.

Unlike his brother, Stewart hadn't enrolled yet for fall classes. He wondered if he still had time. Then he remembered. *He was dead.*

His heart raced, and he couldn't catch his breath. All his credits in art and architecture, including the coursework he'd worked so hard on abroad, would vanish. For all intents and purposes, he no longer existed, and nothing he'd ever done had any further relevance. Once again, Stewart drank himself into a stupor.

The following Monday morning, he found himself moving across campus in a daze, attending Bryan's classes. When Bryan's name was called, he raised his hand as present. He continued to wear his brother's clothes, study his books, and greet his classmates, who were surprisingly understanding and patient. They remained friendly and helpful, but after a while, they stopped trying to include him in their plans.

It was turning out to be the most perfect retribution: attending his own funeral, burying his beloved wife and brother, and walking in the shoes of his murdered twin. Sergeant Haggerty had been right. He would pay.

Three weeks into the term, Stewart cleared out his and Susan's home. He took an axe from the shed, chopped his paintings to pieces, and tossed them into the fireplace. He hurled brushes and paints on top of them, creating a terrible-smelling fire. Then, one by one, he threw all their photos into the blaze.

Stewart no longer existed. Dead and buried, his sentence in hell was to go through the motions of his envied brother's life.

He stopped attending Mass, stopped feeling and being, and donned the mask of being Bryan. In order to pass the semester, he hired a tutor and immersed himself in his engineering studies. Though he'd taken several of the math prerequisites, switching from architecture to civil engineering required intense effort and concentration, along with the help of the tutor.

Sometimes while he was absorbed in mathematic equations, the relentless anguish would temporarily fade, and he could lose himself for a while in his lessons. There were even nights when he stayed up so late studying he would drift off into real sleep.

He passed his finals, eking out four Cs and one B. He stared in consternation at the report card, with his brother's name on it.

There were nights when he spent long hours on his knees, praying for God to strike him dead. The only response was always the sound of his continued breathing. He began to accept that he was to remain very much alive, in this unique torment for which he was perfectly suited. He wouldn't be able to watch his son grow up. He even came to despise the cowardly sound of his own voice and began to emulate Bryan's more confident speech pattern. He was surprised how naturally it came to him. But he started to develop stomach pains.

Two months later, a doctor at the campus infirmary diagnosed bleeding ulcers. Once the problem was pinpointed, counseling was recommended, along with medication and a bland diet. He longed to talk with someone, but knew he could never confide in a counselor, priest—or anyone. He would always need to hide the truth. It could never be any other way.

At the end of the semester, he transferred to a university in the southwest and managed to drop a couple letters off his name and secure a new Social Security number. Still playing the part of his brother, thousands of miles from Bryan's world and friends, he was surprised to find he was still well received by new classmates—better than he'd ever been accepted as Stewart.

He started playing tennis again. He needed the exercise, enjoyed it, and found it was a good way to blow off steam. He was pleased to discover how much his game was improving and how competitive he was getting. Back in high school, he'd pulled away from the sport after losing once too often to his brother.

For the first time in his life, he felt driven to become strong and successful. He would become everything Bryan was meant to have been and all that Stewart never had been. He worked obsessively hard to excel, both in academics and in his revived sport. The hard work, change of scene, and rigidity of his schedule began to deaden some of the pain, but he never stopped missing his son or hating himself for giving him up.

At times, he looked in the mirror and felt he was actually seeing Bryan. It was oddly reassuring, for he despised Stewart—weak, inadequate, murderous Stewart, who hadn't been able to handle life, drank too much, and had let himself be overpowered by a terrible envy.

Blackouts and hangovers didn't work in his new lifestyle. One day he stopped drinking, cold turkey. He felt rotten for a while, but lost days and nights became a thing of the past.

Though he'd been self-centered and inconsiderate, Bryan had possessed many positive attributes. It wasn't hard to see how he'd seduced Susan.

Once in a while, he still considered turning himself in. He longed to rid himself of his terrible burden and take what was coming to him, but he was always stopped by his duty to provide financially for his aunt and son, along with his fear of hurting them even more.

He was haunted by the thought that someone might be falsely accused of the murders. He rented a post office box under an assumed name to get his hometown newspaper. After three years with no news about the crime, he canceled his subscription.

Thoughts of his own death still haunted him from time to time, but he came to the conclusion that God's punishment would not be so easy or so quick. He would always have to live with his ugly secret. Eventually a saving numbness took hold, deadening the pain and walling off feelings and memories.

After graduation, he found a job with a civil engineering firm in Tucson. When the owner retired, he took over the company, expanded into airport planning, and made several well-timed business moves. The firm's reputation and profits soared. At first, he plowed everything back into the business but later began to invest in vacant land and developments on the outskirts of Tucson. He was beginning to enjoy his life as Bryan.

Once he'd turned his life around, he started thinking about getting his son back. He visited him twice in Michigan, but the visits went badly. His son had clearly bonded with his adoptive mother and stepfather. They adored each other, while the boy seemed to shy away from Bryan. At times, he even seemed afraid of him. After the second visit, he realized that the right thing to do was to leave well enough alone. He never went back for another visit.

When a group that gave temporary haven to battered children approached him for a donation, he gave them a piece of land to build their shelter. Later that year, he was offered a seat on their board, and before long, he was a familiar face on several nonprofit boards. The president of one organization told him that he admired how he could get things done.

He really *had* taken on the persona of Bryan, and by now, it felt more natural to him than being Stewart. In time, he sought out the pleasure of female company, for he was a passionate man. But he'd vowed to himself to never let any woman get close to him again—until Meghan.

He heard someone talking, as if through layers of gauze. He had a pounding headache.

"Bryan?"

He opened his eyes to Kate O'Neil. Where was he? His secretary, Lois, and Kate were staring down at him with worried frowns. What were the two of them doing here? He blinked again, trying to focus.

He was lying on a cot, covered with a white blanket, in a tiny space bound by a white curtain. He hurt all over. "Where in the hell am I?"

"You're in a medical center in Sedona, drying out," said Kate.

"Damn." He wished it had all been just a nightmare. Unfortunately, his ugly past as Stewart was real and had come roaring back to him during his drunken binge. He hoped it would never happen again.

"When you didn't check out, the manager went into your cabin and found you passed out, surrounded by empty bottles," said Kate. "He called 911 when he couldn't get you to wake up."

"Spare me the details." Leave it to Kate to elaborate. It was bad enough for Lois to see him like this, but Kate would undoubtedly share everything with Meghan.

"The hospital got the office number from your business card," said Lois. "We came as soon as we could."

"That's nice of you, but unnecessary. Why did you bring *her*?" He glared, at Kate.

"Back to your old charming self, I see." Kate's green eyes snapped.

"I'm sorry, Mr. James. I'd assumed that she was . . ."

Suddenly it hit him. Lois thought Kate was his latest flame. Why else would she have dragged her all this way? And Kate, out of some warped sense of being helpful, had come along.

"Ladies, you need to leave," he commanded, suddenly aware of the scant hospital gown, held together with mere strings. "I need to get dressed and out of here."

CHAPTER 25

Bryan and Kate barely spoke on the way back from Sedona as Kate sped down the mountains behind the wheel of his Mercedes. What was there to say? Kate, Lois and the doctor had ganged up on him, informing him he wasn't ready to drive home. Since the two women had driven up together in Lois's car, Kate was stuck being his chauffeur.

As Kate negotiated the Phoenix freeways and drove on through the desert, Bryan tried to think about his work, his tennis game, fund-raising—anything but the nightmarish memories just dredged up from his past. He vowed not to touch a paint brush again, and to try to cut back on his drinking.

On the northern outskirts of Tucson, Kate turned off the freeway and headed toward Bryan's gated community. After being waved through the security gate, she followed the twists and turns of the meandering *avenidas* until she reached his home.

Once inside the garage, Bryan activated the car alarm, unlocked the door between his garage and utility room, and then carefully relocked it, including the deadbolt.

"Why all the locks?" Kate asked. "Are you trying to keep something out? Or in?"

Blood rushed to his face. "Thanks for the ride. Sorry to have inconvenienced you." Quite an understatement, he knew. He ought to offer her something to eat or drink, but more than anything, he wanted her to leave. It had been a long day, and he cringed at the image of Kate and Lois finding him in a skimpy hospital gown, coming out of a drunken stupor.

When she didn't move, he said, "Would you like some herbal tea? I don't have any pot."

"I don't smoke pot."

"My mistake." Then why in hell had she allowed Rusty to smoke up her house with it?

He switched on the answering machine without thinking. There were two calls from the club to schedule tennis matches; one from the dog groomer, who said Gina was doing great and was getting so spoiled she might not want to come home; and three calls from Lois, each one sounding more worried that she couldn't reach him on his cell phone. The last message was from Sarducci. "Give me a call. I've got a question for you."

"Who's that?" asked Kate.

"A friend."

"Is this the guy who's helping us find Erin?"

"If he can help, you'll be the first to know." Bryan regretted playing back his messages in front of her. Unfortunately, Kate seemed to have a sixth sense about things.

"I would expect to be the first to know. I know you're a very self-contained person. I get that. But please don't keep anything from me that relates to Erin."

"Understood. So what'll it be? Green tea? Sparkling water?"

"Green tea's fine." Kate sat down cross-legged on the carpet.

"Would you be offended if I used the furniture?"

"Let's call a truce." Kate smiled, waving a white tissue. "I'm too tired to keep this up, and you can't feel too great yourself."

"I didn't realize we were at war," he said, in a carefully modulated voice.

"Let's stop playing games. Try to relax and be yourself."

He managed a bitter smile. "What kind of world do you think it would be if everyone suddenly decided to 'be themselves'?"

"A lot better than it is now."

"That's where you're wrong. Without this thin veneer of civilization, the human race would probably have destroyed itself a long time ago."

Kate looked him in the eye. "I get the feeling *your* veneer is wearing pretty thin."

He tightened his jaw. He wasn't up to a confrontation with Kate right now. "I just remembered. I'm out of tea, and I'm tired. Thanks again for the ride. See you later."

She didn't budge. "I know you're only helping me because I'm Meghan's friend. I'm well aware that you can't stand me. Even the way I look, eat, walk, and talk are offensive to you, but if you don't mind—"

"You're mistaken," he interrupted. "I *do* like the way you look—and walk."

She flushed a deep red. "Let's be straight with each other, just this once."

"Let it all hang out?"

She stood up and looked down at him, standing far too close. "That's your whole problem. You put everyone into little cubbyholes, including yourself. You're afraid I'm some neo-hippie, but I don't play games and don't care about your *veneer of civilization*. I care about who you really are. I may not be much, but I'm neither more nor less than who I seem to be. I'm too honest, and I think that's what bothers you."

She took a deep breath and went on. "I need your help to find Erin. You're the only one who's still willing to help, and I believe that you can. Meghan's a very lucky woman to have a man who'd spend all this time with someone he detests, just as a favor. That's real devotion."

His face reddened. "I don't detest you. I'm sorry if that's the impression I've given."

"Apology accepted," she said quietly.

"Make yourself at home," he said. "I was just teasing about you sitting on the floor."

Kate moved across the room to join him on the sofa. "I'm in no mood at the moment to sit on the floor, looking up at you."

"You just . . . set me off sometimes."

Kate looked him in the eye. "I get the feeling you're like a keg of dynamite, ready to go off at any moment. But you always stop yourself in the nick of time, don't you?"

His eyes misted over. "If only that were true."

"We've all done things we regret." said Kate. "Do you want to talk about it?"

"No."

She took his hand, gave it a warm squeeze, then stood up again. "I always carry a couple of tea bags with me. No one ever seems to have the kind I want. I'll boil up some water and make toast. And don't ask me to fix you a drink, because I won't."

"The bread and jam are in the refrigerator. I prefer blackberry. And if I'd wanted a drink, I would have fixed one." He did want one—desperately, as a matter of fact.

"I can help you get in touch with some good people about your drinking." She kneaded the fabric of her long skirt, then smoothed it out. "There are some good treatment programs here, not to mention AA."

"I don't expect you to understand, but I need to go it alone."

"I might understand more than you think, and you don't have to go it alone. Not with the drinking or with that . . . dark secret of yours. You'd be surprised how much better you might feel to get things off your chest. I know I talk a lot, but I'm also willing to listen."

"Let's just drop it." It was uncanny, the way this woman cut to the heart of things. She threw him completely off guard. He'd never come this close to blurting out the truth to anyone since he'd confessed to Sergeant Haggerty over four decades ago. He was actually tempted to spill out the whole sordid tale to Kate.

But that wasn't going to happen. He reached into his pocket for a handkerchief. He never cried anymore, not even when he was alone. But sometimes when he was holding back tears, his nose would start to run.

❧

"Hold on," said Meghan. "This is a bad connection. I'll hang up and dial again."

A minute later, Kate picked up. "The line seems okay now. How's it going?"

"I'm fine." She took a deep breath. "Any news on Erin?"

We're trying something new. I'm offering a reward of a hundred thousand dollars to anyone who has information about her, and Bryan's helping me finance it. Two TV stations are willing to run public service ads on her again as a missing person. They're encouraging people to call 88CRIME. Anyone can make an anonymous call and still get the reward if their report leads to finding her. Someone must know something. Now they'll be motivated to call."

"That's a great idea!" Meghan said. "Put me down for another hundred thousand."

"You can't afford that!"

"I inherited some money from my grandfather, and that's how I want to spend it."

"Are you sure?"

"Very sure. I'm sorry I didn't come up with the idea sooner. I'm glad Bryan's there to help, and wish I could be there supporting you too."

"Like I've said, I don't want to worry about both you and Erin. At least I feel you're a lot safer now than you were before. And from a selfish point of view, if you *were* here, Bryan would be spending his time with you instead of helping me find Erin."

"I'm not so sure about that." She wanted to reach Bryan before confiding in Kate about the breakup.

"Thank you *so much* for helping me double the reward. Two hundred thousand dollars will really get people's attention!"

"You've no idea how good it feels to find some way to help."

"I really appreciate it," said Kate. "But there's another reason I'm calling. I heard a rumor over the weekend about the school district. They want to give Rhonda Allen a promotion, of all things. Everyone knows she's done a lousy job as principal and can't handle discipline over at the junior high. Of course, she has this *special* relationship with one of the higher-ups."

"I can't deal with district gossip right now," said Meghan.

"But it's *your* position they're planning to give her."

Meghan felt as if she'd been slapped across the face. "The district hasn't notified me about changing my assignment."

"Yet."

"So let me get this straight." She tried to control the tremor in her voice. "According to the grapevine, they're replacing me with someone's mistress?"

"I heard it from two good sources," said Kate.

"*Unbelievable*. I've put off calling Human Resources, hoping the authorities would capture whoever was stalking me first—but who knows when *that* will happen?"

"Maybe you'd better call now."

"I will, as soon as I hang up. If it turns out the rumors are true, I need to move fast. I can't afford to sit here on the other side of the country while my career goes up in smoke. No pun intended."

Kate chuckled. "At least you still have your sense of humor. It must be tough having to hide out all this time in some godforsaken place."

"It's not like that," said Meghan. "In fact, this has turned out to be a pretty nice place. In a way, I'm not all that anxious to leave."

"Really? But what about Bryan?"

"What about him?"

"He doesn't quite seem himself," said Kate.

"What do you mean?"

Kate hesitated. "It's hard to say. Just give him a call, but don't mention we've talked."

"I've haven't been able to reach him."

"He's been . . . out of town for a few days. He was in Sedona."

"I see *you've* had no trouble reaching him," answered Meghan. "I get the feeling you're not telling me everything."

"He's still helping me look for Erin, so he stays in touch. Promise me you'll try to call him again."

"He won't take my calls." Meghan hesitated. "I finally had to explain everything in a letter. The next step is in his hands."

"What do you mean?"

"It was a very tough letter to write."

"You wrote him a Dear John?"

"I guess you could call it that."

"Are you seeing someone else?" asked Kate.

"I *have* met someone, as a matter of fact. But things broke down between me and Bryan as soon as I left town. I feel like he shut me out."

"So you decided to break it off in a letter?"

"I know it sounds bad, but I must have tried to call him at least twenty times. I've met a man I really care about. He's the one who rescued me when I was caught out in that storm on Lake Michigan. I doubt it matters to Bryan anymore, or he would have been in touch."

"You couldn't be more wrong."

"Jack?" Meghan knew the director of Human Resources from his days as a teacher at Central High. "This is Meghan Walcott. I'm calling to check on the date when I need to be back at work. I'm out of state and may not be getting all my mail. I was placed on a temporary personal leave of absence at the end of the school year."

"I'm aware of that. It's good to hear your voice." Jack Robbins sounded tense. "There've been a few changes. Hold on a minute. This computer's slow."

She waited. Maybe something *was* wrong.

After a long pause, he said, "Okay. It says here that you're to be reassigned to a position as assistant principal over at Jacobs Middle School."

"So I'm being demoted?"

"You'd still be an assistant principal—but there would be an adjustment in salary."

"An adjustment down, I take it."

"Well, the salary schedule for a middle school—"

"There must be documentation as to why I'm getting a demotion," said Meghan. "There's something that's not quite right here, Jack. I know you can't tell me, but I think we both have an idea what it is. I'm out of town, and I need you to follow up on this. Otherwise, you'll be hearing from my attorney."

There was a deafening silence at the other end of the line. Finally Jack asked, "Would you *really* want to go back to Central High?"

Meghan hesitated. "I love that school. I've worked there ever since I started out with the district, but I'm open to change. I'm just *not* open to a demotion I don't deserve. If they try to hurt my career because an arsonist torched my office or for any reason other than my job performance, I'd be forced to take the school district to court. My career is very important to me. And I was put on leave, not *demoted*."

"I hear you," said Jack.

"I know you'll do what you can," she said. "Good-bye."

Four days later, the phone rang. "It's Jack Robbins, from HR. The principal of Lincoln High School just notified us that he plans to retire at the end of the semester. We could place you there as interim principal. You'd have to reapply at the end of the year, but I think the board might go for this. You'd be going from interim assistant principal to interim principal of a high school. That would be a promotion. Lincoln's one of the largest high schools in the district."

"And the dropout rate is the highest, with test scores near rock bottom."

"That's why I'd like to get you over there," he said. "I think you could turn it around."

"So do I. But don't play games with me, Jack."

"It's always a game. It's hard to get somebody good right now, since everyone's under contract. And you're out there on leave, without a school. This could be a win-win, especially for the kids at Lincoln High."

"I can do the job. That I'm sure of." She needed to get her life back on track, and no criminal was going to have the power to prevent her from returning home.

"That's what I was hoping you'd say. But this doesn't open up until the first of January. We'd need to extend your leave, and I'm not sure all of it could still be paid."

She hesitated, then thought of five more months with Will. She could manage for a while longer with what she'd inherited from her grandfather, even allowing for the money she was putting up for the reward. Her expenses were low here, and she could try to find some temporary work in Frankfort.

But she had to be sure the offer was solid. "Would I get a contract?"

"I'll run it by the superintendent and the board."

"I'd need to have a written contract."

"Understood. I'll get back to you again in the next few days."

Meghan called Kate back to thank her for tipping her off.

Kate was glad to hear about her possible promotion. Then she brought Meghan up to date on the latest news about Erin. She'd just talked to the detective on Erin's missing persons case. They suspected that Devrek was still at large and might be headed north.

"*North?* Where in the north?"

"That's all the information I could get. I don't think the police know much more than that. The US Marshalls are probably handling it."

Meghan shivered as she hung up. *North!* Had he tracked her down?

✑

Encouraged by Kate, Meghan dialed Bryan's number several more times. As before, she kept getting his machine. She left three messages and hung around in case he called back. Considering Lois's recent unwillingness to put Meghan's calls through to him, she didn't want to call his office again; but at 5:25 p.m. Arizona time, she dialed the number. That was usually the best time to reach him at his desk.

Her voice cold, Lois reported that Mr. James was on another call. She offered to take a message, but Meghan asked to be put on hold. After four minutes she heard the line go dead.

She redialed.

"James Engineering."

"Bryan?"

"We've nothing to say to each other." The line went dead again.

Her eyes welled with tears. She slammed down the phone, grabbed her parka, and stormed out to her car to drive to the beach.

It was time to move on. It was really over between her and Bryan. He'd made it painfully clear. She would make no more calls or attempts to reach out to him. She had cared deeply for him, and still did, but not in the same way. It was time to admit to herself that he'd never expressed any intention to marry her and start a family. Maybe she'd never really known him.

But then, how well did she know Will? Though he'd often told her how much he loved her, he hadn't brought up the idea of marriage either. And she still hadn't told him the truth about who she was. She needed to level with Will and let him know she had a life in Tucson. Though it no longer involved another man, she had just committed herself to returning home to head up one of the biggest and toughest high schools in the Southwest.

Deep down, she almost hoped the school board wouldn't approve her for the position. She'd fallen in love with this beautiful lake country and its small-town lifestyle, and she couldn't imagine being away from Will.

The wind picked up as Meghan walked through the town, across the beach, and out onto the breakwater, a favorite spot of hers to gain perspective. At the end of the pier, she noticed the waves were getting big enough to splash over the breakwater. She needed to head back.

Then she saw a man heading out toward her and remembered Kate's comment that Devrek might be heading north. Could he have followed her out into the fog, a quarter mile from shore? Her pulse raced, but she told herself she couldn't allow herself to react with fear every time some man headed out onto the pier when she was out there alone. She loved walking out on piers, as she'd often done while growing up in Maine. She wasn't about to give it up.

But the lake was getting too rough, and she needed to get back to shore. With waves getting big enough to sweep her off onto huge boulders and into dangerous undertow, she tried to make her way toward land between the big breakers. There was lifesaving equipment spaced along the pier, but no one else was there to help. And if someone meant her harm, no one would even suspect foul play if she were found washed up on the shore.

Twice she slipped on the wet surface. She should have paid more attention to the waves and slippery concrete and shouldn't have ventured out onto the pier today. At last she made it to the elbow of the breakwater, where it widened and changed direction. Now the waves angled along the side, slurping at her feet, but no longer washed over the walkway. The man was nowhere to be seen. Once again, she'd given that bastard who'd disrupted her life too much power over her mind.

CHAPTER 26

Meghan and Will huddled together on an isolated stretch of dunes along Lake Michigan, waiting for their bonfire to ignite. It was a chilly, crystal-clear August evening—ideal for viewing the predicted meteor shower.

"We couldn't have picked a better spot or a more perfect evening to celebrate you staying through the fall," Will said. His easy smile warmed her to the core of her being. He'd been trying for weeks to convince her to delay her return home. He'd even promised fall colors as vibrant as any she'd experienced in New England.

The fire took time to get started, as the wood was slightly damp. She watched the kindling slowly ignite the driftwood logs, the flames growing hungrier by the minute. When the fire was ready, they roasted hot dogs, which they devoured with baked beans and potato chips. After dark they roasted marshmallows and ate s'mores. She couldn't recall food tasting more delicious.

Suddenly it crossed her mind that Bryan might have once roasted marshmallows around a bonfire here on Lake Michigan. Though he wouldn't take her calls, Meghan still felt very uneasy about the lack of closure between them. Kate clearly disapproved of the way she'd handled the breakup, implying that he still cared. But she couldn't allow it to cloud this wonderful evening.

"Look out there, toward the Manitou Islands," Will said. "We're getting our own private light show—the Northern Lights!"

Curtains of red, green, and white light danced across the sky, casting shimmering rivers across the dark water.

"Amazing!" Meghan had never seen the Northern Lights before. Now she was watching them with Will, and it felt like another sign of good things to come. Peaceful in the crook of his arm, she was overcome with an unfamiliar feeling of bliss.

Driftwood logs sparked and crackled in the cold night air. She'd never felt so at one with the universe.

She noticed an ore boat moving across the horizon. "This reminds me of the ocean. Wouldn't it be fun to take a cruise in the Great Lakes?"

"Funny you should mention it," he said. "I used to entertain a fantasy about getting a Great Lakes cruise ship going. Maybe I could name it *City of Milwaukee II*, after one of the old car ferries. It could travel around the Great Lakes."

"Sounds interesting."

"Frankfort was once a resort for wealthy people from Chicago, but the Royal Frontenac Hotel burned down in 1912. Up until the early 1980s, the Ann Arbor Railroad and its car ferries operated across the bay in Elberta. With our harbor, marina, and great beaches, this place is a very popular attraction. A small Great Lakes cruise ship might be a fun addition."

"Dinner and dancing, with a live band—you on piano, and me, singing." She laughed. "Or we could reverse it. I could play, and you could sing."

He looked at her in surprise. "You play the piano too?"

"Enough to accompany a choir."

He smiled. "Let's try a duet sometime."

"I'd love to."

"If the tracks hadn't been pulled out, maybe we could have gotten a hold of an old steam engine and an antique passenger car so we could revive the *Ping Pong*. That was the passenger train that once carried tourists back and forth between Frankfort and the Crystal Lake Pavilion in Beulah."

"You sound as if you remember it."

"I was born about seventy years too late for that; but as a kid, I did get to watch the train come around the south shore of Crystal Lake at night. First you'd hear the whistle as it crossed the highway; then its powerful headlights would beam out across the lake, just before the engine made the sharp curve around Railroad Point. As it rumbled its way into Beulah, the blast of its horn would echo across the water. I learned about the *Ping Pong* from an older friend of Martha's. She told us about the old days when everybody seemed to know each other. It sounded like they had some great times."

"That kind of sense of community is rare nowadays," she said.

"Not so rare in small towns."

"I grew up in a small town in New England, and I've missed that." She'd almost let the name of the town slip out. It seemed innocuous, but what if he did an online search and found out that the only Anne Maxwell from her hometown was her great-grandmother, born in 1898?

She longed to tell Will everything. Without Bryan to chide her about the importance of remaining below the radar, it was harder to remember why she shouldn't. It was also getting tough to recall what she should and shouldn't share with Will.

"That log looks like a fire-breathing dragon," she said, changing the subject.

"You're right." He pulled her closer. "I love the way you help me see things from a different angle."

"Tell me more about your plans for a Great Lakes cruise ship."

"The final cruise of the season would be a fall color tour. We'd go from Frankfort to Leland, then on to Northport, Traverse City, Petoskey, and Harbor Springs. We could end up at Mackinac Island."

"Why don't you do it?"

"It's just a fantasy. In the real world, I don't have the patience to deal with the details and logistics that would be involved. We creative types don't thrive on that sort of thing."

"You've got a point." Meghan looked out across the water. Was she a creative person trying to force herself into a career that involved too many administrative details and logistics? Being choir director had felt like an extension of her being, but adapting to her new role as assistant principal had been a struggle. Now she'd be a school principal.

Will took her hand. "The cruise ship idea may be a fantasy—but I *do* want to take you on a color tour."

"That would be great. I've missed the fall colors so much all these years."

"Then we'll do it. Look! Our first falling star! The meteor shower has officially begun."

Meghan made a wish: to enjoy many more evenings like this with Will.

"Let's lie back and watch for a while." He helped her down to the blanket.

She lay against his chest, dazzled by the falling stars and the brilliance of the Milky Way. After a long, peaceful silence, she asked, "What is your *real* dream, if you don't mind my asking?"

"To finish my symphony and perform it with the Boston Symphony Orchestra."

"And you will." She loved his passion for music.

"I hope you're right. I started composing music when I was in grad school and even wrote a piano concerto, but I never got much done while I was on the concert tour circuit. Now that I'm back home, I've reconnected with my creative side, and I'm making real headway. I know it may look like I've dropped out of the music world, but music will always be central in my life."

"Maybe your world of music is right here for now."

"I'm exactly where I need to be—here with you." He looked into her eyes. "When I perform it, Anne, I want you to be there in the front row."

Her eyes stung with tears. He'd placed her into the middle of his fondest dream, as well as squarely into his future, but he didn't even know her real name.

"What's wrong?"

"There's so much I haven't told you yet, and I know it's not fair."

He stroked the inside of her palm. "You trust me, don't you, Anne?"

"Of course I do." She was on the verge of telling him everything—yet it didn't seem fair to expect him to become a part of her deception. That could create problems in his own relationships, especially with his mother.

Her life was on hold until her stalker was captured. It was infuriating that it had driven her to keep a wall between herself and Will, and her new friends. She'd always been an open, honest person, and deception grated on her spirit. If Devrek weren't captured soon, she was going to throw caution to the wind and drop all the secrecy, along with the alias.

"It's not like I'd betray your confidence."

"I know. Believe me, I'm anxious to tell you everything, but I need to lay low for a little while longer."

"Okay, I'll keep waiting. But how about sharing some of your dreams with me, Annie, like I did with you. That might mean more than the details of your 'real' life in helping us get to know each other better. Plus, it's your turn." He gave her a crooked smile, eyes twinkling,

"Fair enough." She thought for a moment. "For as long as I can remember, I've dreamed of being a teacher, though my mother encouraged me to consider other careers. She told me that when she was young, most girls who did well in school were advised to become teachers or nurses. She did teach for a few years, before I was born. She loved it but wanted me to know I could be anything I wanted to be. She told me girls in her day got the message they should keep their dreams nebulous so they could blend nicely into a future husband's plans, yet they were encouraged to prepare for a career, in case they never married or their husbands died young." Her expression darkened. "As it turned out, my mother died young. They both did."

He hugged her tighter, kissing the top of her head. "I'm so sorry."

"My dad was a history professor, and my grandparents were also teachers. I always loved education and wanted to be involved in it. I had this fantasy of teaching enthusiastic students. In one daydream, I was leading my kids in an amazing rendition of *West Side Story*. That one actually came true. It's still such a joy to recall them singing and dancing with such passion and energy. I remember the entire performance. I'm afraid I'm a bit of a romanticist."

"You're idealistic, Anne. I admire that."

"That means a lot to me." Others had poked fun at her idealism as unrealistic, and Bryan seemed to view it as dangerously naïve. "My mom was idealistic," she said. "She wrote letters about issues she cared about to everyone, from the mayor to the president, and was planning to run for town council when she found out she had cancer. She'd always wanted to make a difference in the world. Now it's up to me."

"Maybe it's up to you to make a difference in your own way."

"I've always seen myself as a teacher."

"It's great to be so clear about your goals."

"My friends used to say that. Most of them were music majors who got their teaching certificates as a backup plan in case they didn't make it as performers. Funniest thing, most of them are teaching now, and I'm not."

"You're not?"

"Not anymore. I'm assistant principal of a high school, soon to be a principal, if all goes according to plan."

"You don't sound too thrilled about it."

"Maybe not right now, but as I move up in the ranks, I'll be able to develop programs, set policy, and maybe even become a superintendent one day. It may not be as much fun, but I could have a greater impact on more students."

"Are you sure about that? I don't even remember who our superintendent was. An orchestra conductor had the biggest effect on me. Who influenced *you* most, your favorite teacher or the school superintendent?"

"A superintendent can set the tone and influence the success of an entire school district. But you're right. My high school choir director made the biggest impression on me. She was my main supporter when my mother died. Sometimes the only thing I looked forward to was choir practice. I even wound up becoming a choir director." It felt great to share something about her real life with Will and to have her dreams taken seriously.

"Where did you teach choir?"

She felt her body tense. "In the Southwest."

"Who are you hiding from, Anne?"

"I'm not sure. But the best way to help me now is to be patient for a while longer."

"I could help, if you'd let me," he said with an edge to his voice.

"I can't expect you to fight my battles."

"You could do worse. I'm a brown belt in karate."

"When did you find time for *that*?" Somehow karate and being a concert pianist seemed like an odd combination to her, but so was working as a handyman while composing a symphony.

"I first got involved in martial arts when I was in grade school. Martha wasn't happy about it, but Jake encouraged it. I could help protect you better if I knew what you're up against."

"I'm fine right now because a certain person doesn't know where to find me." At least she hoped not. "Let's get back to sharing our dreams. I don't want to spoil this magical evening."

Will gently brushed her hair from her eyes. "This *is* a magical night."

"Another shooting star! Did you make a wish?"

His eyes glistened in the light of the bonfire. "I sure did."

As they lay back on the blanket watching meteors streak across the sky, he pulled her to him and kissed her. Lost in his kiss, a wave of desire ran through her. She longed to make love with him right there on the beach and knew that was what he wanted too.

Suddenly she heard something. She held her breath.

"What's wrong?"

"Did you hear that rustle? Over there," she whispered, pointing to the low, rolling dunes behind them. She sensed they were being watched.

"It's only the wind through the reeds." He held her closer.

She shivered. "I definitely heard something."

"If it makes you feel better, I'll go check." Will stood up and headed toward the reeds.

Meghan huddled alone in the blanket beside the fire, hearing only the waves quietly lapping the shore. It was a clear, moonless night, and the temperature was dropping fast.

Her teeth chattered. She listened, willing her heart to stop beating so hard. She still felt someone watching her. She wished she'd gone with Will.

When she heard footsteps approaching, she sat perfectly still.

"It's me, Annie," called out Will. "I don't want to give you another scare. All I could find was tall grass blowing in the wind."

He nestled in beside her again, warming her shivering body against the cold night air. She recalled their first night together in the abandoned cabin and how his teeth had chattered. Terrified that he might die, she'd tried to warm him with her body heat, though they'd been little more than strangers to each other.

"I still hear something."

"It's just reeds rubbing against each other, Annie. They can make a lot of noise. You're safe here with me." He paused. "And if you're uncomfortable being alone at your place, you're welcome to move in with me. Then you wouldn't have to live alone on the edge of the woods."

She turned to him in surprise. "I really appreciate the offer, but I think it's a little soon for that." The idea held a strong appeal, but she wasn't about to move in with a man unless she was married. She didn't dare say that, though. Will just might propose.

She needed to stay rational. They were just getting to know each other, and they needed more time. "I feel pretty safe there at the cottage, so close to the Larsens. No one can drive to my place without going right past them."

"Do the Larsens know about your situation?"

"No, I don't think so. Not from me, anyway."

"So they wouldn't be on the lookout for you. And they couldn't see someone coming down the bike trail back in the woods behind your place."

"It's not all that close to my cottage is it?" She'd never seen the farm while biking the trail through the woods, and hadn't thought of it as close to her cottage. She'd felt quite safe there.

"Close enough. Do you know how to use a gun?" he asked.

"Not really."

"I could teach you. I inherited a couple of pistols from my stepdad. We could find one you're comfortable with, and I could loan it to you."

"I've resisted getting a gun, but maybe you're right."

"I could teach you how to use one."

"I'll think about it. But I feel pretty safe there." It was nice that he felt protective of her, but he was starting to remind her of Bryan.

He kissed the back of her neck. "When you're ready to tell me more, I'll be here for you."

"Thank you. I'll never forget our night together, watching the Northern Lights."

Will's eyes shone in the starlight. "I love you."

"And I love you," she said.

"Oh, Annie. That's what I've been waiting to hear."

Their words hung suspended in the cold August night, drifting upward into the silent dance of the Aurora Borealis as they embraced.

Annie, a common diminutive of her middle name, Anne. When Will said it, it became one of the most moving words in the English language. Right after the words "I love you."

The fire dwindled down to flickering embers, and darkness closed in around them.

CHAPTER 27

The first day of August wasn't off to a good start at the Last Chance gas station. There'd been no customers all morning, but tomorrow was a Friday. He hoped business would pick up as folks filled up on their way into Las Vegas.

Zebadiah wiped oil off his hands and took a break from overhauling an old big-block, V8 engine. He turned on the small Magnavox TV on top of the file cabinet and sat on a stool behind the cash register as he watched the twelve o'clock news. He wolfed down his ham sandwich, apple, and chips, and saved his wife's homemade molasses cookies for later.

The newscaster reported that Lake Mead was getting low, and there was still no rain in the forecast. Forty-seven malnourished cats were rescued from a woman's trailer in Phoenix. Then a public service ad for a missing girl flashed on the screen.

His heart nearly stopped. *It was her*—the girl in the silver Porsche. She was a *missing person*. They gave her name, age, height, weight, hair and eye color, and stated that she'd been missing from her apartment near the University of Arizona in Tucson since May 13.

"Oh my God," he moaned, holding his stomach as if he'd been kicked in the gut. Wasn't that about the time he'd seen her?

He'd known something was wrong. He'd even taken down the license number but had done *nothing* to help the girl. The ad said she was from Tucson, where she was a student at the University of Arizona, like his daughter.

The bastard had probably killed the girl. He grabbed a pencil and scrawled down the numbers to call. Then he raced to the bathroom and threw up.

Where had he put that note with the license number? He rifled through the drawers, then scanned the bulletin board. He checked the safe. Finally, he tilted up the cash register and spotted a slip of paper underneath. That was it—the license number and date. *May 13!*

As before, he was flooded with fears of negative fallout if he made a call to the police. He could wind up testifying in court against the Mob, a drug cartel, a murderer, or at the very least, a man who battered and kidnapped women. He'd seen the girl so long ago it was probably too late, but he knew he had to try. And hadn't the ad said he could dial the 800-88CRIME number and make an anonymous report?

He dialed the number and reported that on May 13 he'd seen the girl in the missing person ad at a gas station. He gave the location and license number, but didn't mention he was the owner of the station. He reported that the girl had been with a dark-haired man in his late twenties or early thirties, and he was driving a silver-colored Porsche. Though her face had been swollen and bruised, he was sure she was the one in the ad. He got a good look at her but not at the man with her, who'd been wearing reflective sunglasses. He'd had a gut feeling something was wrong and had considered calling the sheriff but had nothing specific to report except that the girl had bruises on her face and stayed a long time in the restroom. He'd been concerned enough to make a note of the plate number and date and put it in a safe place. He was very sorry he hadn't called at the time and hoped it wasn't too late.

❧

Meghan was jolted awake from a disturbing dream in the middle of the night. She'd been in a meeting with Devrek in a casino on the Las Vegas strip.

Then she remembered that yesterday Kate had told her there'd just been a report that a girl of Erin's description had been sighted in May, heading in the direction of Las Vegas. That must have triggered the dream.

She laid her head back on the pillow, then heard a strange sound. Something was scraping against her cottage. Maybe it was tree branches, but she'd never heard the sound before. She got up, heated some milk, and sipped it while she read. Then she went back to bed and lay on her back with her eyes closed.

As she started to drift off to sleep, the words *Las Vegas* flashed in her mind like a neon sign. She sat up with a jolt. Las Vegas! There was something about Devrek and Las Vegas—but *what?* She needed to remember.

She got out of bed again and sat in a chair in the corner of the bedroom. She closed her eyes and tried to meditate about the dream, breathing slowly, in and out. She visualized the name of the city, and then pictured the strip and the inside of a casino. Nothing. She pictured Devrek at the trial and still drew a blank.

In the dream, she'd been in a meeting. She thought back. There had been a few staff meetings with Devrek at his halfway houses before she'd known Erin. She closed her eyes, trying to relax. Eventually one meeting started coming back to her.

She saw herself in a small conference room. She'd been an administrative intern, there to observe, rather than participate. She recalled a school social worker with a bright smile, and a young, mustached school psychologist named Mark. She vaguely recalled two or three members of the halfway house team. Devrek, a bearded, pipe-smoking psychiatrist, had come across as arrogant and abrasive. It was probably the first time she'd met him.

She opened her eyes, sat up, reached for her notebook, and started jotting down notes. She noted that Devrek had done most of the talking, painting a picture of a very disturbed adolescent girl. He'd pushed hard to get the girl into a self-contained classroom for the emotionally disturbed, but according to the school team, the girl was doing well at school in a less restrictive learning disability resource program. The school social worker had carefully explained the girl's academic and social progress at school.

The positive report clearly hadn't been what the psychiatrist had wanted to hear, which had struck her as odd. Devrek had encouraged one of his psych techs to elaborate on the girl's deviant behaviors, but the school psychologist had held his ground. He'd explained that the girl not only didn't meet requirements to be labeled ED, but that she was almost ready to progress out of the learning disability program.

Devrek had stood up, thanked everyone for coming, and with a tight smile, apologized for taking up their time. He'd mumbled something about how it had slipped his mind that the girl was to be transferred to another of his treatment centers.

That was it! Devrek had said he had a treatment center out of state that would better meet the girl's needs. The social worker had asked where it was located. Hadn't Devrek replied that it was in Las Vegas, Nevada? *Las Vegas!* She was almost sure of it.

The school team had been uneasy and concerned about the girl's welfare, but was probably not as worried as they should have been. Meghan remembered that the social worker had followed up to make sure the girl had actually arrived at the treatment center and enrolled in the new school. She cringed to think of what might have happened to her.

Despite the trial four years ago, Devrek's reference to having a program in Las Vegas had slipped her mind until tonight. In retrospect, it occurred to her that Devrek might have been trying to get the girl labeled as emotionally disturbed to make her a less credible witness. Maybe she'd threatened to report him for molesting her. Meghan shuddered. When he'd run up against a school team who knew their students well, cared about them, and followed legal requirements for special education placements, he'd yanked the girl out of the school district.

She shivered. The sun was finally starting to come up, but because of the three-hour time difference, she forced herself to wait until eleven to call Kate.

At eleven o'clock sharp, she dialed her friend's number. "I just remembered something, Kate. When you told me yesterday that some man had been seen driving a girl that looked like Erin toward Las Vegas, it must have jogged a forgotten memory. I woke up in the middle of the night dreaming about a meeting with Devrek in a Las Vegas casino."

"And?"

"I tried to meditate on it and finally remembered a staff meeting years ago at one of Devrek's halfway houses, years before we'd ever met Erin. At the end of the meeting he'd said he was sending a girl to another of his residential treatment programs—*in Las Vegas.*"

"Are you sure Devrek said it was *his* center?"

"Pretty sure. It didn't strike me as important at the time, especially since the case was being handled by the special ed. team. I was just there as an observer. Even after testifying in court against him, his mention of Las Vegas hadn't crossed my mind again until my dream last night."

"Do you remember the name or address of the treatment center?" asked Kate.

"Sorry, I don't. I only attended that one meeting about this girl and don't even remember her name. This might not be such a great clue after all. It felt like a big deal in the middle of the night. I was tempted to notify the police about it, but I guess it's pretty vague."

"And quite a few years ago. But I'll see that it gets passed on to Bryan's PI, who's trying to help us connect the dots. It gives me the chills to think of Devrek having a treatment center in Vegas, after that report that someone had seen Erin get in a car that was headed that way. I'll call Bryan about this as soon as I hang up."

"Bryan's got a PI involved in the search for Erin?"

"I thought I'd told you," said Kate. "It's an old friend of his."

"Good. You need all the help you can get." Meghan was starting to realize just how out of the loop she was.

❧

As Bryan stepped out of his car into the bright sunlight at the Silver Saddle Steakhouse, he noticed storm clouds building up northwest of the city. Each day during the monsoons, enormous cumulonimbus clouds would churn upward into towering formations, and some fortunate neighborhoods might receive the precious gift of rain. This morning as he'd left for work he'd noticed his ten-foot-high stand of prickly pears drooping. They were crying out for water. If his place didn't get rain today, he'd give them a good soaking tonight.

Their new missing person ads on Erin's disappearance had started airing a week ago, with photos, dates last seen, and other pertinent information, and there'd already been an important tip. Bryan kicked himself for not offering a reward sooner. He hated to think what could have happened to Erin in the ten weeks she'd been missing.

Bryan had notified Sarducci about the reported sighting of Erin en route to Las Vegas, as well as Meghan's recent recollection that Devrek had once run a treatment center in Las Vegas. Sarducci had Vegas connections, and Bryan hoped he could help them put the pieces together. Sarducci had called this morning to set up a lunch meeting so he could bring Bryan up to date.

Bryan found his old friend settled into a private booth in the back of the restaurant, away from other customers. It was a comfortable ranch-style restaurant with Western decor. The smell of mesquite-broiled steaks wafted through the air, reminding him that he was famished.

They both ordered the Kansas City steak with cowboy beans and ranch fries. A bowl of homemade tortilla chips and two small bowls of salsa were placed in front of them, along with a large, mouthwatering frozen margarita for Sarducci. There was an iced tea for Bryan, who'd recently decided to drink alcohol only after 5 p.m.

"Have you come up with anything new?"

Sarducci nodded, taking a deep swig of his margarita. "Some interesting stuff."

"Let's hear it." Bryan squeezed lemon into his iced tea. Sarducci had gone way beyond returning a favor for a friend and was now working in his professional capacity as a private investigator. Bryan would insist on being billed for all his work.

"I was able to pull a few strings and get the license plate number that was reported to the police. It was registered to the photographer whose card turned up in our missing girl's room."

"So she was with the photographer. At least it wasn't the escaped convict."

"Not so fast. Maldonado has a connection to the shrink."

Bryan put down his fork. "Tell me I'm hearing you wrong."

"You're not." Sarducci dipped another corn chip into the hot salsa.

"So he wasn't really a photographer?"

"Actually, he *is* a professional photographer. His photographs of desert flowers were good enough to be shown in local galleries and published in *Arizona Highways*."

"Why didn't the police find that out?"

"He'd submitted his work under the name of Edward Costino, another name he goes by. A few years ago, he started getting into porn, stepped on some toes. A couple of months ago, he dropped out of sight under either name."

Bryan's jaw tensed. "Do you think he could be working for Devrek now?"

"It's possible. Since a witness placed the girl at a gas station near Las Vegas, and your friend recalled the shrink running a treatment program there several years back, I've been checking in Vegas and Clark County.

"And?"

"Devrek did run an adolescent drug rehab program in Las Vegas. It was over ten years ago, and Maldonado was on the staff. There were rumors of girls being abused there—even disappearing."

Bryan put his head in his hands. "My God."

"No one knows for sure what's been going on, or if the center still exists. It probably started out as a legitimate treatment center, but at some point it seemed to have gone off the tracks."

"Probably when that perverted shrink got involved."

"Could be."

"Can you give me the name of the place?" asked Bryan.

"A year ago it was known as New Horizon, but that building's empty now, and the phones are disconnected. Unfortunately, I don't have the new name or location—if there is one."

"What if I were to contact some treatment centers in Vegas?" asked Bryan.

"It probably would be a dead end. A place like that would be operating under the radar, calling itself anything—a rehab program, retreat, private school, maybe a wilderness program. I'll get in touch with you as soon as I have more information."

"I need to do something *now*," said Bryan.

"Too risky. Wait until I get back to you."

"We may not have time to wait. I want to do some checking myself, now that I have an idea where she could be. Call me any time, day or night, if you find out anything more."

"Will do," said Sarducci. "You know, it's hard to find a good steak like this anymore."

"You're right. But I'm going to get mine boxed up and take it with me. I want to get right on this. Don't worry. I'll be discreet."

Sarducci shook his head, frowning. "Be careful."

Bryan slid out of the booth, picking up the tab on the way out.

Back at his office, he went online to check out adolescent treatment and drug rehab centers in Las Vegas, as well as schools for girls with behavior problems. Under the guise of seeking help for a daughter, he painstakingly contacted each one.

Intake workers inquired about his imaginary daughter's diagnosis, then requested psychiatric evaluations, school transcripts and information about insurance. Several of them even encouraged him to tour the facilities, once he filled out some preliminary paperwork. He crossed each one of them off his list.

He was looking for a place that showed no interest in psychiatric evaluations or giving tours. He worked his way through the lists with growing frustration. Sarducci was right about the futility of this approach. The kind of place he'd described probably wouldn't be listed along with legitimate treatment centers. What in hell could he do now?

CHAPTER 28

"Want some tuna?" asked Wendy. She passed the half-eaten can to Erin, who made a face but ate it, scraping the sides of the container with her fingers.

"Eat up, princess. You've got to keep up your good looks. Otherwise they won't let you go to any of their *parties*." Tanya could always be counted on for sarcasm.

Erin glared at her. "Why don't you just shut up?"

"She's getting well, wouldn't you say, Wendy?"

Wendy sat on the bed, staring vacantly into space. "Hey, Wendy! *You're* the one who don't look so good," said Tanya.

Erin had noticed. Wendy's color was sallow and her eyes glassy. If she didn't know better, she'd think Wendy was getting drugs here on the inside, but that wasn't allowed.

With bars on the windows and no way to call out, the place was a nightmare. At first, there were annoying group sessions where Erin was supposed to share her innermost feelings about coping with her non-existent addiction. During the first two weeks, she'd been honest and explained that she wasn't an addict, but that had only made matters worse. They'd accused her of being *in denial.* She'd wound up with more group sessions and the worst jobs, like scrubbing the floor on her hands and knees, and cleaning toilets.

She soon got the message that it was better to participate actively in the groups and pretend to struggle with addiction. She shared some of her mother's disastrous experiences as if they'd been her own. *That*, they believed.

Yet not long after that, they inexplicably dropped her from group counseling. Some girls seemed to be involved in treatment programs, but others, like Erin, were largely ignored as far as treatment.

She wished she'd run back out the front door that first day, before it was too late. She vowed never to ignore her gut instincts again.

What a fool she'd been to believe Eddie had cared for her. He'd deliberately misled her from the beginning, then had pressured her to distance herself from those who loved her. She'd believed his lies, ignoring the many warning signs. He was a real bastard. She hoped she wasn't going to be like her birth mother, always attracting despicable men.

Erin couldn't believe she'd gotten herself into this mess, after such a long battle to get her life back on track. Her life had started to turn around when Miss Walcott believed in her and stood up for her in court; then the world had opened up for her when her teacher, Kate, had cared enough to become her foster mother.

Erin had fought Kate's rules at first, but deep down, she'd known that her foster mom really cared. With her love and guidance, Erin had started getting good grades and had been accepted into the University of Arizona. She regretted shutting Kate out these past few months and hoped she'd be able to make it up to her.

Many of the girls at Ocotillo were runaways. Her friend, Wendy, called herself a throwaway, and it fit. Abused at home, with nowhere to go but the streets, she'd once felt this place was her best option, with its three square meals a day and a roof over her head.

Erin wanted to keep her distance from the other girls. To help her, Wendy had spread the rumor that "Tiffany" had a highly contagious, incurable skin disease. It had worked like a charm. None of the girls would get near her. Wendy had also told them that Erin had a violent, unpredictable temper and should never be crossed. Erin had confirmed the rumor by flying into a rage when no staff members were around.

The staff basically stayed away from her too. She couldn't imagine why Eddie had dumped her here. He knew she never took drugs except for smoking a little weed with him once in a while. And why were they keeping her here?

Wendy was Erin's only friend at the center, and she was probably

Wendy's last ray of hope. They vowed to help each other get out. They watched and waited, determined to find a way to escape.

At least Erin was allowed to have a sketchpad and pencil. She'd convinced a therapist it helped calm her down. That's how she'd kept sane so far. She sketched the girls, coffee cups, and even palm trees through the barred windows.

"The bars aren't as decorative as they look," Wendy had told her when she'd arrived. "They serve a purpose." Erin hadn't believed her at first.

Her latest sketches of the girls were done with heavy, dark strokes and possessed a frenetic energy that contrasted with the tired, dull faces of her subjects. A disturbing emptiness in their eyes came through in her drawings. She had to get out of here soon, before her *own* eyes took on that same vacant stare.

She sketched Wendy, arms curled around her pillow as if it were a teddy bear. The angle of her legs and arms offset the mass of hair across the pillow. She was sleeping with her eyes wide open, which gave a disturbing quality to the portrait. Once finished, Erin held the sketch away from her for perspective. She shuddered.

At 3:00 a.m., she awoke with a start. Wendy's haunting eyes had penetrated her nightmare, and Erin thought she'd heard her friend call out to her for help.

She flicked on the light. Tanya cursed as Erin stumbled to Wendy's bed and took her hand. Her friend's skin was disturbingly cool to the touch. Erin shook her. "Wendy! Wendy, are you okay? *Wendy, please wake up!*"

"Shut up and go back to sleep!" snapped Tanya.

"I think she's OD'd or something," cried Erin. "She needs help!"

Cursing, Tanya stumbled out of bed and knelt beside Wendy. She put her palm on Wendy's forehead. She took out a small mirror from a dresser and placed it in front of Wendy's lips. "She's not breathing. Looks like she's dead."

Erin ran out the door, screaming hysterically for help. Sergio, one of the staff, appeared. He put his hand over her mouth and firmly guided her back into the room. She kicked and punched, fighting to get to her friend.

"Cool it, sweetheart! She's gone."

"Give her CPR!" Erin shouted.

She heard Sergio call for backup, then felt herself being impaled with a large needle. Through a haze, she saw a large, full laundry bag being wheeled from the room. Struggling unsuccessfully to remain awake, she heard bits and pieces of conversation.

"Got to get rid of her . . . too risky to have around . . ."

She awoke late the next day to see Sergio's dark brown eyes staring down at her as he sat on her bed. "You're not like the rest of them."

She looked into his eyes, forcing herself not to scream. With surprising intensity, he added, "You don't belong here."

"Neither did Wendy, and now she's dead!" She started to cry. Without Wendy, no one at Ocotillo cared about her in the least.

Sergio looked away. "She's in a better place."

Erin shielded her eyes from the morning light as Danny yanked open the blinds. Why was he waking her up? No one seemed to care anymore if she skipped group therapy, and since Wendy's death, Erin had been left alone to read and sketch. She hadn't been able to sleep much since the cooler broke down, finally falling asleep just before sunrise. Her skin was damp with perspiration, and she was on edge. At eight in the morning, the room was already stifling hot.

Something had happened yesterday. She'd overheard that someone had seen a picture of her on TV. Though she'd prayed that Kate hadn't given up searching for her, she also feared that her survival here might depend on staying below the radar.

"Dr. Randolph needs to see you now." Danny's voice was low and threatening. He called himself a psychologist and seemed to have authority at the center, but he was callous and uncaring. The entire staff of Ocotillo seemed like automatons, impervious to the girls' humanity.

"What for?" Erin felt blood rush through her entire body, as her muscles tensed in readiness to run away as fast as she could, though she knew there was nowhere to run.

"You'll find out when you see him."

✌

Dr. Randolph's wall was plastered with degrees and certificates. Erin wondered if they were real. He could talk the talk, but didn't seem the least bit interested in helping the girls. He was a coldhearted man, like Dr. D.

She'd heard the staff refer to some of the girls as "bipolar" and others as "conduct disorder." Some of his diagnoses might hold a grain of truth, but she suspected most were fabrications. She wondered which label they'd stuck on her.

"You have an appointment tonight, my dear," the doctor said coldly. "You'll be meeting with an important colleague."

"I don't want to meet anyone," she snapped.

"Oh, it's mandatory." Dr. Randolph stared through her with cruel, blue-gray eyes. He turned to Sergio, who waited in the doorway, staring coldly at the doctor.

Erin felt Sergio undress her with his eyes. So they weren't *all* robots. She sensed Sergio's anger at the doctor. Growing up in the dangerous world of her mother, she'd learned at an early age how to read moods, especially anger. She had an uncanny ability to please dangerous people, which had helped her survive. Unfortunately, she also seemed to attract them.

Sergio still gazed at her, almost as if with regret. She keyed in to his reactions, turned toward him, and caught his eye. When he reddened, she saw her one chance.

Dr. Randolph handed Sergio a sealed envelope and dismissed her. As she left, she overheard the doctor saying, "Make sure that she has whatever she needs to get fixed up. She looks like a size eight. I'll get someone to repair the damn cooler. The girls look like hell." She couldn't hear the rest, as the doctor closed the door.

That afternoon Erin sucked in while Lori zipped her into a skin-tight jade-green blouse and black mini skirt they'd given her. Lori held a pair of gaudy earrings up to her face and told Erin that the outfit looked great with her hair. But what Erin saw in the mirror made her sick.

She noticed Sergio peering at her through the open door. She looked every bit a hooker, like her birth mother, but seeing herself in full attire gave her the courage to make her move. She didn't have much time. She looked into his eyes and smiled, her gaze moving slowly up and down his body, like she'd seen her mother do.

He blushed, bolstering her confidence.

"So you guys never . . . hang out with patients?" She smiled shyly, seating herself carelessly on the bed, her skirt slightly askew. She felt ashamed, but Sergio was the only staff member who'd ever shown any interest in her.

"It's against the rules. But your dress . . . definitely fits," he said, raising an eyebrow. Better take it back off so it doesn't get wrinkled. You can put it in this garment bag."

"A lot of rules get broken around here," she said in a whispery voice she hoped was sexy. "Maybe we could get away from here for a little while. Doesn't anyone owe you a favor?"

"Everyone owes me favors," he said with a leer. "Maybe it's time to collect."

⁂

Erin hadn't expected the long drive through the desert. She'd thought they were going to a local motel and had planned to escape from there. She panicked as Sergio kept driving away from town. Was he taking her out into the desert to kill her? But why had they been so anxious to dress her up? What was the appointment Dr. Randolph had told her about?

When they crossed the huge bridge that bypassed the Hoover Dam, she figured they were back in Arizona. Pulling into a small gas station reminded her of that horrible stop on the way to Las Vegas with Eddie, when she'd lost her baby. She should have tried to escape back then. The man at the gas station had been concerned about her and might have helped, but she'd been too weak and devastated after the miscarriage to even contemplate escaping.

Any thought of escape at *this* gas station was dashed, because Sergio planted himself right outside the restroom door.

Once back on the road, Erin dozed off. When she awoke, it was dark. Sergio was speeding through an even more desolate part of the desert and was drinking tequila, straight from the bottle. Terrified, she pleaded with him to stop drinking while he was driving.

Her mind raced to come up with an alternative escape plan. She'd have to be ready to run at the drop of a hat.

"I thought we were going to a motel," she complained. If they were really headed to a motel somewhere, he would need to sign in and get a room key. That might be her only chance to get away. She would run to the closest place and ask them to call the police.

"Don't worry," he said. "We're almost there. We'll have a good time. Then you can wait there for the man you're scheduled to meet."

"What man?" she cried. She saw lights in the distance.

"Forget it."

"Please don't leave me there with some stranger. Take me with you!"

"I can't do that."

Erin choked back tears but knew she had to fight off her rising hysteria at all costs. They were coming into a town. As Sergio slowed to a stop at a traffic light, she yanked on the door handle, trying to jump out of the car. Nothing happened. He must have set the kiddy lock.

"Cool it! You're not going anywhere."

"I just don't want to be left alone there with some creep."

"Shut up!"

Minutes later, he pulled into the parking lot of an older, single-story motel on the outskirts of some desert town. She spotted a metal sign that said "Route 66," but she'd been so intent on jumping out of the car that she'd missed the town's name.

She was ready to dash from the car the minute he went to the front desk to sign in. Instead, he drove right up to a ground-floor room, parked at the door, took a keycard from an envelope, and unlocked the door.

She hadn't counted on that. This was well planned and coordinated. Maybe the motel even had ties to Ocotillo. She couldn't depend on anyone here to help.

Once inside, she scanned the tiny motel room for the phone, but there wasn't one. She had to get Sergio's cell phone without his knowing it. Then she needed to get him out of the room.

"Irish Cream would be *so* great, right now!" she blurted out.

"Don't worry. I brought tequila."

"I noticed. But I hate that stuff. Couldn't you *please* get me some Irish Cream? I'm kind of nervous, and it would help me relax." She smiled and embraced him, while slipping his cell phone from his pocket.

He pushed himself away from her. "Don't run out on me, or you'll be very sorry."

She smiled as seductively as she could manage. "And miss the fun?"

"You're something else, but I'll get you your Irish Cream." He stormed out the door.

Before she ran, she wanted Kate to know she was alive and needed help. She considered calling 911, but there wasn't time for her to explain everything, and she didn't know where she was. Even if the police could trace her, what if they pulled up with sirens blaring? Maybe Sergio would use her as a hostage, like bad guys did on TV.

She would call home. Then she remembered that Kate never seemed to have her cell phone turned on and rarely checked for messages. Meghan kept her phone with her and would know what to do. Her fingers trembled as she dialed her godmother's cell phone. Her heart sank at the words, "This phone has been temporarily disconnected at the customer's request." She punched in Meghan's home number and got the same message.

She could grab the phone and run, but feared they could somehow trace her that way.

Mr. James! He'd given her his business card the day she started the drawing of his office building. She'd memorized it, along with his home number written on the back, before she'd flushed it down the toilet. Wendy had warned her that they'd confiscate everything.

Since it was after working hours, she called his home number. She got his voice mail. The pause between the end of his message and the beep seemed to take forever.

Finally, she began. "This is Erin. I'm at the Sunset Motel, off Route 66—" She heard the sound of the keycard in the door. She hung up, jammed the phone between the mattress and box spring, and willed herself to stop trembling.

Her chance to escape was gone. She should have run, instead of wasting precious time trying to call home. She'd figured Sergio would be gone at least ten or fifteen minutes but only five had passed. Mr. James would have no idea where she was. There must be hundreds of Sunset Motels in the country.

She smiled at Sergio, gulping back tears.

"You're in luck," he said, eyes burning with desire. "There's a liquor store right next door. Let's hope this will calm you down."

"I hope so. I *am* pretty nervous. So thank you." She hadn't noticed the store. How could she have been so blind? She could have asked for ice cream, a hamburger, or *anything* that would have taken longer. Even a few more seconds would have given her time to say she was in a town in Arizona, somewhere south of the Hoover Dam.

She sipped the drink slowly, stifling the urge to gag, and then passed the bottle to him. She'd never tasted it before, but the name, Irish Cream, had sounded appealing. Instead, it made her feel like throwing up. Yet she had to keep drinking it, and pretend to like it.

He looked at her with smoldering eyes. She knew she couldn't stall much longer. He took another drink, then pulled her to him and kissed her.

Maybe there *was* another way. She took a deep swig, then another. This time she didn't fight it. She started gagging and covered her mouth. "I'm sorry," she said. "I think I'm . . . gonna to be sick."

He pushed her away. "Get away from me, damn it!"

She ran into the bathroom and threw up, loudly. From the corner of her eye, she spotted a small ground-floor window.

"I've got it all over me!" she cried. "I've got to rinse off in the shower. I guess I'm not that used to drinking." That much was true.

She closed the door and turned the shower on full blast. She stood on the edge of the tub, shoved herself through the small opening, and dropped to the ground, as silently as she could. She dashed away from the window in her stocking feet.

Minutes later she heard a door slam. Sergio was yelling her name.

She scanned the vacant lot behind the motel for a place to hide. She was afraid to go to the front desk, in case it had ties to the Ocotillo Center. The tall oleander hedge was too well trimmed to hide her, and the scraggly desert bushes in the vacant lot behind the motel weren't big enough. She raced to an old pickup truck with a camper shell and yanked frantically at the passenger doors and the back door. They were locked.

That left the two large garbage bins. She heard Sergio shouting her name again, his voice ragged with rage. She took a deep breath, clamored into the second bin, and burrowed deep into the vile mound of garbage until she was completely covered. She heard footsteps getting closer.

What a fool she was. The bins were too obvious, but she'd run out of time. He opened the door to the first bin and slammed it shut. She held her breath. He opened the bin she was in and stood there, cursing. Then he slammed the metal door and stormed off.

She had to get out of this disgusting bin but didn't dare raise her head to see if the coast was clear. Finally, she peeked out but saw only darkness. She feared that Sergio was lying in wait.

She tried to think of what to do next. Sooner or later, someone would throw out some trash, and she could tell them to call the police, but that probably wouldn't happen until morning.

A car door slammed; then she heard a car speed off. She hoped it was Sergio leaving but couldn't be sure. She came up for air and waited for what seemed like hours. She decided to wait a few minutes longer. If she heard nothing more, she'd run off through the desert.

Once in a while, a car came to a stop, and car doors and trunks slammed shut. Finally, she heard footsteps again. Was someone bringing out their trash in the dark? Maybe they could help.

The heavy, determined steps grew closer. Someone was so close she could hear them breathing. Had Sergio come back for her?

"When I get my hands on you, I'll kill you, you little bitch."

She froze. *Dr. Devrek!* She'd recognize his voice anywhere.

Erin held her breath for as long as she could. Her heart was pounding so hard she was afraid he might hear it. She gritted her teeth at the odor of foul meat and the feel of evil slime against her skin. Something was crawling in her hair. It took all her will not to scream.

CHAPTER 29

Bryan followed a rigid routine. When he arrived home from work, he'd carry things in from the car, put them in their proper place, feed the dog, check the answering machine, and then relax on his deck with a glass or two of wine. Since he'd wound up in a drunken blackout on his disastrous trip to Sedona, he'd limited himself to a couple of glasses of wine each evening—or at the most, a bottle.

Tonight he arrived home to a scene of cold cereal, cereal boxes, and a half-eaten banana strewn across the kitchen floor. Gina, his golden retriever, was evidently miffed that she wasn't getting enough attention lately.

As he swept up the mess, he mulled over what to do about Sarducci's bombshell news that Maldonado, AKA Costino, and Devrek had once worked together at some sort of a sinister treatment center in Las Vegas. If the place was still in operation, they needed to find it. It might be a matter for the FBI, but that could take time—and there wasn't time.

When he finished mopping and sweeping up, he turned on his answering machine and played back the partial message, twenty-two minutes after it had been recorded: "This is Erin. I'm at the Sunset Motel, off Route 66—"

Stunned, he played it again, hoping to hear more, but there was no more. His caller ID showed only "Private Caller."

Erin had said she was at a Sunset Motel off Route 66, but where? A blocked number meant he couldn't call her back. He wouldn't have, anyway. Something had caused her to hang up midsentence and not call back. She could be in serious danger.

He thought about Sarducci's disturbing news that Maldonado had once worked at a drug rehabilitation center run by Devrek in Vegas, and Meghan's sudden recollection that Devrek had once mentioned that he planned to send a girl to a treatment center of his in Las Vegas. Back in May, there'd been a sighting of Erin at a gas station near the Arizona-Nevada border. The driver had been headed in the direction of Las Vegas.

Heart slamming against his chest, he dialed the Tucson Police Department detective assigned to the case, reported Erin's call, and shared why he thought she might be in Las Vegas. The detective said he'd run it through the Communications Department, which could contact other law enforcement agencies and coordinate any response.

He hung up, punched in the cell phone number of Greg Gillespie, the pilot who flew him to remote engineering jobs. Bryan asked him to meet them at the Marana Regional Airport as soon as possible and to charter a fast plane to get him to Las Vegas. He'd pay whatever it cost. Time was of the essence.

Then he called Kate. "I hope you're sitting down. Your daughter left a message on my answering machine about a half hour ago! I just played it back."

"Oh my God! *She's alive!*" cried Kate. "Where is she?"

"She said she's at a Sunset Motel on Route 66 but was cut off, midsentence. The caller ID said Private Caller. The call was blocked, and she never called back."

"I don't like the sound of that," said Kate. "She must be afraid of something. I wonder why she didn't call me. I'll check my messages, in case I missed it somehow."

"I don't like it either. Go ahead and check your messages and let me know, but hurry. I've chartered a plane at the Marana Airport to get us to Las Vegas as soon as possible."

"You're sure she's in Vegas?"

"Not really, but the few clues we have point there, and I don't have a better plan. Can you meet me at the Manzanita Motel at Cortaro and I-10?"

"I'm on my way, as soon as I notify TPD."

"I already did."

Seventeen minutes later, Bryan pulled up to the motel, parked near the entrance, and went to the front desk to arrange for Kate to leave her VW.

Minutes later, Kate sped into the parking lot, screeched to a stop beside Bryan's Mercedes, leapt out of her car, and got into his. "Let's go!"

Bryan merged onto the freeway, heading toward the Marana Airport, northwest of Tucson.

Kate's hands trembled as she did a search for the motel on her cell phone. "Are you sure you got the name right? I can't bring up any Sunset Motel in Vegas or anywhere in Nevada."

"That's all she had time to say. Try Arizona or California!" said Bryan. Then he brought her up to date about Devrek and Maldonado once working together at a treatment center for girls near Las Vegas.

Kate gasped. "Maldonado and Devrek worked together?"

"At one time, anyway. I just heard that a couple of hours ago. I was going to tell you about it when you got home from work."

"Never wait to call me on news about Erin," snapped Kate.

"I didn't want to pull you out of the classroom to give you background information from years ago. You can get mad at me later, but don't stop your search!"

"Nothing could stop my search." Kate worked diligently as they drove, her hands shaking worse than before. "I'm searching now for any kind of lodging on Route 66 that has the word *sunset* in the name."

He slammed his hand against the dashboard. "Damn! Route 66 doesn't go through Vegas!"

"Cool it!" she snapped. "Just get us to the airport in one piece! I'll find the motel."

"What the hell was I thinking? We've got a plane waiting to take us to the wrong place!"

Several minutes later Kate cried out, "I've got something! There's a Sunset Vista Motel in Kingman, which *is* on Route 66. That's not far from where Erin was last seen."

"Or from Vegas."

As they drove out onto the runway, the pilot waved from a sleek-looking, four-passenger turboprop plane. "You said you were willing to pay for speed," said Gillespie. He looked a bit like a young and dashing Howard Hughes. "I hope you meant it."

"I did. Good work. But there's a change of plan. Can you get permission to land this thing in Kingman?"

"That's where you want to go now, Kingman?"

Bryan looked at Kate, who nodded in agreement.

The pilot radioed the Kingman Airport.

"Can we get a rental car there?" asked Bryan.

"They'll probably be closed by the time we land," said Gillespie.

While he was getting clearance to land in Kingman, Kate was able to contact a car rental agent who agreed to stay open late and meet them at the airport.

"You'll have to turn off your cell phones now. We're about to take off."

Once they were airborne, Kate asked if she could contact the police in Kingman.

"I could radio the airport and they could contact the police or sheriff," said Gillespie.

Kate's face was damp with perspiration in the dim light of the cabin. "I'm afraid our message could get garbled, going through different parties. Too many things could go wrong."

Bryan turned to the pilot. "How long before we land?"

"Less than an hour."

"It's your call, Kate," said Bryan. He could hear her teeth chattering.

After a long pause she said, "Let's call 911 when we land."

Finally, they saw lights below and made their descent. Minutes later, they taxied onto the runway. The pilot pulled up to the small terminal building, slowed to a stop, exited, and hurried around to open the door for them.

"I'll call you when we know something," Bryan told Gillespie. He rushed down the steps, checking a new cell phone message. It was from TPD, informing him there was no Sunset Motel listed in Las Vegas or Clark County, Nevada.

They raced toward the terminal, where the car rental agent waited. He drove them to the rental office he'd held open for them and did a rush job on the paperwork.

"Do you have a city map?" asked Bryan, as the agent ran his credit card. He didn't want to depend solely on some damn GPS.

The agent handed him the car keys. "Where are you headed?"

"To the Sunset Vista Motel," said Kate.

"It's not far." The agent opened the map and highlighted the route with a yellow marker. They thanked him, grabbed the map, and rushed out to the car.

Bryan drove while Kate read the map. From the airport, they turned onto a road that led to old Route 66. Then they started looking for the motel.

Kate was first to see the sign, partially obscured by a tall Joshua tree. The words *Sunset Motel* were lit up in neon, but there was a large space in between the two words, which contained the neon letter *s*.

"This has to be it!" shouted Kate. "The *s* must be from the word *Vista*. She'd have read this as *Sunset Motel!*"

Bryan veered into the parking lot, stopping in front of the office. "Time to call 911."

"You call them! Explain what's happened and tell them to hurry but not to use sirens. I'm going to try to get the room number." Kate leapt from the car and headed for the office.

"May I help you?" The front desk clerk was a short, thin man with wiry, gray hair and eyes that glanced around nervously.

"I hope so. My daughter and her boyfriend are staying here. She's nineteen years old, tall and slender, and has long strawberry-blonde hair. She wanted me to . . . bring her insulin right away. Could you direct me to her room?"

"What's the last name?"

"Good question." Kate felt her face get hot. She was a poor liar. "Her name's Erin O'Neil, but they just eloped . . . and I don't remember the jerk's last name."

The clerk scanned the computer, shaking his head. "Hold on," he finally said. "What's *your* name? I'll buzz them."

"Just tell me the room number. Don't buzz the room!" Kate's voice was shrill.

"Don't worry. I couldn't if I wanted to. My mistake." He remembered they were in one of the rooms without a phone.

"Just call 911!" cried Kate. "I think she's being held hostage."

The clerk's darting eyes locked into hers. "What happened to her diabetes? You'd better get your story straight before we bring the police into this."

"I'm sorry. Let's start over. My friend's outside calling 911, but I'm sure they'd take it more seriously if a local businessman like you called too. But please give me the room number! We might already be too late."

"Calm down, lady. I'll call the sheriff, and give *them* the room number." He punched in the digits. "It's Gus, down at the Sunset Vista Motel. I might have a hostage situation in room sixteen. I've got a hysterical mother here in the front office and need somebody out here, fast!" He put down the phone. "They're already on their way."

⚹

Bryan called 911. Then he called the TPD to ask them to clue in the Kingman police that Erin was a missing person. He kept his eye on the three rooms with cars parked out front, one of which had the door slightly ajar.

Kate rushed outside and leaned into the driver's window. "Room sixteen, and the police are on their way!"

"Get in the car," he directed. "We'll wait for them to get here."

But Kate was already out of earshot, headed toward the room.

"Damn." Bryan yanked open the car door and caught up with her as she approached the room. He signaled her to stop several yards from the open door.

"Wait here," he whispered.

He heard a sound inside the room and moved quietly toward the door. He craned his neck to look inside and was able to make out a pair of women's green pumps on the floor. He cracked the door open a little wider.

Suddenly he felt cold metal against the back of his head. "Stop right there!"

Bryan raised his hands. "Sorry! I thought this was my daughter's room. I must have got turned around. Take it easy."

"Too late for that—and for Red."

A chill ran across Bryan's flesh. The man reeked of alcohol.

"She was a nice kid." He gave a harsh laugh. Bryan spun around with all his force and knocked him to the ground. The gun flew from the drunk's hand. Bryan managed to kick it away.

"Get the gun, Kate!" Bryan struggled to keep him pinned to the ground. He knew he couldn't hold down the stronger, younger man much longer, no matter how drunk the guy was.

Kate dove for the gun, picked it up, and cocked it. "I've got you covered," she said, fiercely. "You, on the ground. Don't move! Where's my daughter?"

"You got the wrong guy. I came back here because I forgot my cell phone. This man broke into my room."

At the sound of approaching sirens, Bryan summoned another burst of energy. The wailing grew louder until it stopped beside them. Red lights flashed against the pavement. He'd forgotten to ask them to avoid sirens and was glad to hear them.

"Put down the gun, lady!" the officer ordered.

Kate lowered the gun to the pavement. "Thank God you're here!"

"Let him go," a second officer commanded Bryan. "Get up very slowly with your hands in the air. You on the ground—don't move!"

Bryan loosened his grip and rose from the pavement with difficulty, his hands up. "My name is Bryan James," he said, breathing hard. "I'm the one who made the 911 call for help."

"The man on the ground had a gun aimed at my friend's head!" said Kate. "My friend knocked it out of his hands, so I got the gun and held it on this guy until you could get here. I think he's abducted my daughter."

"We'll get all your stories, ma'am. You'll have plenty of time to explain everything."

"We *don't* have time!" cried Kate. "My daughter, Erin O'Neil, has been missing from Tucson since May, and she called us tonight for help.

We think she's being held somewhere at this motel! She's on the missing persons list. You can check with the Tucson Police Department."

"We will."

"You might want to ask this gentleman about someone he referred to as Red, Officer," said Bryan. "He seems to know something about her."

"Please help us!" cried Kate, illuminated by the flashing red lights. She spat out the pertinent facts as fast as she could, doing her best to get the police to focus on finding Erin and to convince them that she and Bryan weren't the bad guys. "Mr. James, in the navy shirt, has been helping me find my daughter. We think this guy knows where she is."

Bryan broke in, his voice carefully modulated but forceful. "We've reason to believe that Erin is close by, Officer, and that she's in extreme danger." He didn't add that, according to the bastard on the ground, it was already too late.

CHAPTER 30

Through the darkness came the sound of bare feet slapping against the concrete. Pale, disheveled, and streaked with filth, she suddenly appeared from behind the motel.

"Mom!" cried Erin, not stopping until she reached Kate.

Kate locked her daughter in a fierce embrace, while they both sobbed. Bryan stood off to the side, answering questions.

Then an officer turned to Kate. "I'm going to have to take you all in for questioning."

"The bitch propositioned me, then ran off," growled Sergio from the back of a squad car. "I never did anything to her. I just came back for my cell phone."

❧

We need to get her to a shower," said Kate to the officer.

"Sorry, but there are a few things we need to take care of first."

"The poor thing. Look at her!" said a heavyset red-haired woman who was on the cleaning crew at the police station.

"I need to interview her and get her checked out at the hospital." The officer took Kate aside and quietly explained that they might need to use a rape kit.

"Can't she just shower?" implored Kate. "She was hiding for hours in a filthy garbage dumpster."

"I'm sorry, ma'am. We need to follow procedure. I know it's hard to understand, but there could be evidence destroyed. After we're finished, we'll get her to a shower right away. One of our female officers is meeting us over at the hospital."

Erin was led away. Another officer showed Bryan and Kate into different rooms and questioned them separately.

Kate told the officer the whole story, and asked him to contact the Tucson Police Department to verify what had taken place so far. He told her they already had.

Then they waited for Erin. To Kate, it seemed like forever. When Erin finally returned, her hair and clothes still reeked of garbage.

"Are you okay, honey?" asked Kate.

Erin nodded, her eyes teary.

"She didn't want to shower at the hospital," said the female officer. "She wanted to get back here with you. We're taking her to shower now. I'll be right outside, in case she needs anything. She said she didn't need the rape kit," she said quietly.

"Thank God," said Kate.

"I went home and got her something to wear," said the night custodian. "I live only three doors down." She handed the plastic bag to the officer. "She can keep the clothes."

"Thank you so much. You're very kind." Kate hugged the woman.

Erin finally reappeared, freshly scrubbed, with damp hair, and wearing a loose-fitting Hawaiian muumuu. Her freckled skin was ghostly white and her eyes red under the florescent lights. She was the most precious sight Kate had ever seen.

The officer took in the scene. "I'd like to get to the bottom of this."

"Can we go home now, Mom?" asked Erin, in the voice of a little girl.

"Have we answered all your questions?" asked Kate.

"I think we're all set for now. We've checked out your story with the Tucson Police Department. They confirmed that you are who you say you are and that you've been looking for Erin since May, when you filed a missing person report. We have your statements. You held the assailant at gunpoint with his own weapon to keep him from fleeing and defend your friend before we got there. You didn't fire the gun, and no one was injured."

"That's right," said Kate.

"You're free to go. Just make sure we know how to reach you."

Kate and Bryan thanked the officers. It was after 2:00 a.m. as they left the station. Bryan put in a call to Gillespie that they were on their way back to the plane.

Kate hugged Erin. "You're safe with us now."

Erin beamed. "I can't believe I'm free! How did you ever figure out where I was? I only gave the name of the motel—the *wrong* name—before that jerk came back into the room."

"It's a long story," said Kate, "and we'll have all the time in the world to talk later. But there's a call I need to make right now, before we're airborne. Meghan's been terribly worried about you."

"No offense, Mom, but she was the first one I tried to call. You don't keep your phone on."

"That's all changed since you went missing. Now I can be reached anytime, anywhere. My cell phone is on day and night, and it's always with me."

✍

At 5:15 a.m., Meghan was jolted awake by her cell phone. When she saw Kate's number, she froze. Every time Kate called, Meghan feared bad news about Erin. At 2:15 in the morning in Arizona, she *knew* it was bad news.

Her hands trembled as she reached for the phone. "Kate?" she cried in alarm.

"Hi, Miss Walcott! It's me, Erin!"

Meghan covered her mouth, unable to speak. Her lips trembled and tears came to her eyes.

"Miss Walcott?"

"Erin?" she finally managed to say. "Is it really you?"

"It's me, alright. I'm on my way home with Mom and Mr. James."

Meghan broke down, sobbing. "I've never heard such wonderful news in my entire life! Thank God you're safe."

"I was held captive in some horrid, phony treatment center near Las Vegas. Mr. James and my mom rescued me tonight."

"Good heavens! Are you really alright?" So her dream about Devrek in Vegas, and her nearly forgotten memory about his Nevada treatment center *had* been important.

"I'm okay," said Erin. The police asked me a million questions, but now I'm all cleaned up, and we're headed to the airport to fly home in an airplane Mr. James rented."

"We all love you so much," said Meghan, her voice breaking.

"I'm sorry for all the worries I've caused," said Erin.

"You're not to blame. All that matters is that you're safe! I can't wait to give you a great big hug!"

"Me too. Here's Mom."

"I'm the happiest woman alive," said Kate.

"This is the best news ever!"

"I know! Thank you for your tip about Devrek having a treatment center in Las Vegas! It turned out to be very important."

"I'm so glad I could help!" said Meghan.

"Bryan planned the rescue and arranged for a private flight to get us to Kingman." Kate was talking faster by the minute. "He fought the guy who'd brought her to the motel. I held his gun on him while Bryan held him down until the police arrived. Can you believe it?"

"Not the part about you with a gun. I'm glad Bryan was such a big help." Meghan was amazed he'd thrown himself so completely into the rescue, to the point of wrestling an armed gunman to the ground and holding him there. Maybe she'd never really known him.

"I should finally be able to get a good night's sleep," said Kate.

"Me too." Meghan paused. "When they capture Devrek, we'll sleep better yet."

"True. But I'm too happy right now to think of anything except that Erin's safe with me. I have Bryan to thank for it."

"I'd like to thank him myself," said Meghan.

The phone went silent, as if it were muffled. "He's tied up on another call right now," said Kate. "Maybe later."

"Okay. Thank you for calling me. This is a miracle."

Meghan had never expected to hear Erin's voice again. When the call was over, she did something she hadn't done in a long time. She got down on her knees and thanked God.

Will and Meghan hiked the Betsie Valley Trail along the south shore of Crystal Lake. It was a cool, blue morning, with wind from the northwest. Colors were brilliant, and the trees and cottages on the opposite shoreline looked closer than usual, and more vivid.

Will signaled her to stop and pointed to an enormous woodpecker—black, with bold white striping and a flaming red crest. It was perched on a nearby birch tree. They silently admired the magnificent bird until it flew off.

"What a stunning bird!" she said.

"It was a pileated woodpecker."

"I had no idea woodpeckers could be so big."

"Maybe this is a good sign," he said. "I've always wanted to see one, and when I turned, there he was. This may sound nuts, but I feel like he had some kind of positive message for me."

"I don't know about the woodpecker, but I have some great news! My nineteen-year-old goddaughter has been missing for several months, and last night she was rescued! I got to talk with her on the phone!"

"What great news!" Will took her in his arms. "I'm so happy for all of you. Is this what you've been so upset about?"

"It's the main thing, yes. Her foster mom is my best friend. Deep down, I doubted she'd ever be found alive."

"That's a heavy load to carry alone. I wish you'd have shared it with me sooner."

"I should be able to tell you the rest soon."

"I hope so." He squeezed her hand.

Bryan, Kate, and Erin arrived at Kate's home as the first rays of sunlight radiated from behind the Rincon Mountains. Bryan stayed in the guest room and tried to grab a few hours of sleep. He didn't wake up until about ten in the morning.

Kate whipped up a hearty breakfast while Erin slept in.

"Great hash browns. Everything's delicious," commented Bryan. Kate had remembered to leave the sprouts off his plate.

"Thanks," said Kate. "I hope you enjoy it. And before I forget, here's that number I mentioned. You should be able to get an appointment within the week."

"Damn it, Kate. When I want your help I'll ask for it," he said, crumpling up the number of a local alcoholism treatment center.

"I appreciate all you've done for us, and I'd like to do something nice for you in return."

"Like telling me how to live my life?" Blood rushed to his face.

"I thought you might need to talk to someone," said Kate, with measured calm.

"I heard your offer the first time, after the Sedona fiasco. Let's enjoy this outstanding breakfast, shall we? This is a celebration."

He saw Erin standing in the doorway, pale and thin, with dark circles under her eyes.

"It was so great being in my own bed that I could barely sleep." Erin hugged them both. "I love that my room is just the same as I left it when I went off to college. I'm so sorry, Mom, for all you've gone through because of me. I promise I'll make it up to you."

"That you're alive and well is all I need—and I love it when you call me 'Mom.'"

Erin turned to Bryan. "I can't imagine what you must think of me."

"I think you look like you could use a few more hours of sleep," he said with a warm smile. "And one of these days, when you get rested up, I'd like you to finish that drawing you started of my office."

The kindness was not lost on Erin. She knew her mother had thought Mr. James was cold and aloof, but she knew better. By changing the subject, he'd conveyed to Erin that he thought no less of her, despite all that had happened. He'd laid his life on the line for her, and as far as she was concerned, he was the most wonderful man in the world.

"The drawing's finished, and I want you to have it as a gift." She leaned over and kissed him on the top of the head.

His eyes filmed over with tears. "Thank you."

"Thank *you*—and you, Mom!" She hugged them both. "You two saved my life."

"You saved your own life by calling Bryan and then hiding until we came."

"I don't see how you found me."

"A lot of things came together," said Bryan.

"At least we've got a couple of weeks before school starts." Kate served up two more slices of ham.

"I thought you were a vegetarian," said Bryan.

"Erin's not, and neither are you. I was up early and decided to pick up a few things at the grocery store."

"Thanks. I appreciate that." Bryan cut up the ham. "I know school's about to start, but I'll bet you both could use a vacation."

"There's something I've got to tell you," said Erin, her voice nearly too soft to hear. "I already reported it to the deputy, along with where to find Sergio's cell phone, but I didn't want to get you any more upset last night."

Kate placed her arm around Erin's shoulder. "What is it, honey?"

"Dr. Devrek was there last night by the dumpster, looking for me. He threatened to kill me once he got hold of me."

Bryan slammed down his mug. "Are you sure it was him?"

"I'd know his voice anywhere."

"Oh my God." Kate cried. "How could that be? I thought he'd fled the country."

"We've got to get you somewhere safe," said Bryan.

Erin tilted her head, frowning. "I thought he was in prison."

"He escaped in May," said Bryan. "The same week you turned up missing."

"The very same week?"

"Just days before."

"You're not saying we should go into hiding, like Meghan, are you?" asked Kate. "I have to report back to work in two weeks."

"If Devrek tracked her to a garbage bin in Kingman, Arizona, I guess he'd be able to find her at her home."

Kate and Erin fell silent.

"I just wanted to enjoy our first few hours together," Kate said quietly.

"I wish I never had to think of scum like Dr. D. or Eddie ever again," said Erin.

"Did you know Maldonado may have worked for Dr. Devrek?" asked Bryan.

"What do you mean?" Erin's voice was shrill.

"I was told by a detective that Eddie once worked at a treatment center run by Devrek."

"That bastard!" cried Erin. "But it makes sense! How else could Dr. D. have found me there in Kingman? He must have hired Eddie to win me over with lies and then drag me off to that horrible place. I can't believe I ever thought that Eddie cared about me!"

"Kate took her daughter's hand and squeezed it.

"I'm such a fool! I'd actually thought he might be in love with me." She began to cry. "But he beat me so hard—"

"He *beat* you?" Kate paled.

"He beat me so hard," sobbed Erin, "that he killed our unborn baby. I lost it the next day, on the way to Las Vegas."

"Oh my poor, poor girl!" Kate put her arms around Erin and rocked her back and forth, as they wept in each other's arms. "I'm so sorry."

"He killed our baby . . . and didn't even care."

"I kind of had a feeling that you might have been pregnant," said Kate, softly.

"And to think, he was just a pawn of Dr. D! That makes it even more terrible!"

"I'd love to get my hands on the two of them," said Bryan.

"So would I," said Kate, her voice cold.

"I was trying to outsmart them and come up with an escape plan," said Erin. "Instead, I headed right into a trap set by Dr. Devrek. I've been such an idiot!"

"But you did outsmart them. You got away, thank God. You're brave, and you kept your wits about you," said Kate. "Now you're safe from those evil men."

"She'd be a lot safer out of the country," Bryan said. "This whole thing will probably get picked up by the media soon, and your place will be crawling with reporters and TV cameras. Everyone will know where she is, including those predators. We need to move fast."

"What makes you think the sheriff in Mohave County would let us leave the country?"

"Neither of you were charged with anything," said Bryan. "I'm pretty sure if there's a trial, it's going to involve the FBI, TPD, the Kingman Sheriff's Department and a lot of other law enforcement agencies. Plus they'd need to track down the ringleaders of that operation at the center. Any trial will probably be a long way down the road. In the meantime, you need to get away until Devrek's recaptured. Don't you have people abroad?"

"I've a distant third cousin in Ireland, but have never met her." Kate said. "I bet the last thing she needs is for a couple of shirttail relatives from the States showing up on her doorstep. Besides, I don't want to send her out of this country." She paused, thinking. "I do have a great aunt who lives in a remote part of Appalachia, in the Blue Ridge Mountains. She said her son and his wife are just a stone's throw away."

"She'd probably love to see you," he said. "Then I could check out a few more things without worrying about your safety."

"What about *your* safety? Sergio saw you," said Kate, "and your name must be in the records at the Mohave Sheriff's Department. It'll get out, if it hasn't already."

"That can't be helped."

Kate's mind raced. It *would* be too dangerous for Erin to stay home or to return to the university, where she'd be an easy target.

"I'd like to help fund your trip," said Bryan. "I'll be back in a few hours."

"I appreciate your kind offer, but no thank you," said Kate. "You've done so much already. I'll handle this."

At one in the afternoon, Bryan appeared at the door, handed Erin an envelope addressed to Kate and Erin, then departed. When Erin opened it, she found a stack of fifty-dollar bills totaling two thousand dollars.

"Mom, come quick!"

Kate looked at the money. "This is ridiculous. We have to give it back."

Erin turned to Kate. "Don't be offended, Mom, but I was wondering . . . Are you and Bryan . . . I mean, I thought that he and Meghan—"

"We've gotten to know each other better over the summer, while he helped me search for you. That's *all*. He did it as a favor to Meghan and because you're one of his favorite people."

"Seriously?"

"Seriously. He thinks you're a wonderful girl and a very talented artist. He's been a terrific help in finding you, but there's nothing romantic between us—that's for sure. In fact, he can barely tolerate me."

"Yeah, right. So why would he give you all this money?"

"He must be convinced we really need to get you away from here. He got very protective about Meghan, too, when he found out she was in danger. He helped her go into hiding."

"Why was she in danger, Mom? What happened?"

"Somebody fired gunshots into her living room, tried to tamper with her car at choir practice, and set her office at school on fire. This happened about the same time you turned up missing and when Devrek had just broken out of prison."

"So Dr. D is out for revenge, and Eddie's helping him!" Erin trembled with anger.

"And you're still in danger. We need to get you away from here. I'm going to make some calls."

At ten thirty that evening, Kate knocked on Erin's bedroom door and told her to pack enough for a month. "Aunt Cora Jean seemed thrilled at the prospect of a visit from us. We're catching a midnight flight out, so hurry. They'll pick us up tomorrow at the airport."

"Mom, I don't feel like going anywhere, now that I'm finally home."

"I know. But you need to be somewhere safer. I'll stay with you until you're settled, then head back in time to start the school year."

Erin rubbed her eyes and arose to pack, as if she were sleepwalking. She hadn't had a good night's sleep since before Eddie had beaten her and made her lose her baby. It had felt so good to be home in her own bed for a few hours, between her mother's cool, percale sheets.

CHAPTER 31

Autumn blew in overnight with the north wind. It whistled through cracks, rustling the curtains through closed windows. Meghan paced back and forth in her cottage, making a mental note to buy a heavy wool sweater and a warm jacket.

For family-filled homes with warm hearths and friendly bodies to curl up next to, fall in the colder climes was a social time—a turning inward to family and friends. But after more than a decade of blue skies and sunshine in Arizona, she suddenly dreaded the dark, cold days that stretched out before her, with steel-gray sky, and wind whining through the walls.

Just two weeks ago, she and Will had spent Labor Day hiking and kayaking on Crystal Lake. The summer people had reappeared in full force, boating, swimming, biking, and having barbeques. It was like the Fourth of July all over again, except that by Monday afternoon, lawn furniture and many boats and docks were gone, as well as most of the people. The sight of school buses the next morning had jolted her back to the reality that she hadn't been at work in Tucson to help coordinate the first day back to school.

She was glad she'd accepted Will's invitation to meet with Martha's friend, Sandra, about managing her gift shop while she was abroad. The woman who'd promised to fill in for her had experienced a sudden change of plans. A job could help Meghan supplement her income, keep busy, and get a chance to be around more people on the long, gray days that loomed ahead.

There was barely time to shower and dry her hair. All summer it had fallen freely over her shoulders or been tied back with a scarf. She'd had no reason to tame it, and her thick mane was more unruly than ever, giving her a look that was edgy and all wrong for today. She did a careful blow-dry and even spritzed on hair spray to tame it down. She was anxious to get off on the right foot with Will's mother this time, after the bad start they'd had at the hospital. She chose a simple lavender sundress, then filed her nails and applied two coats of Raspberry Sorbet polish. Once outside in the wind, her hair was hopelessly fixed into a wild, windblown look.

Most of the luncheon crowd had dispersed. She easily spotted Martha and Sandra already settled at a table overlooking the marina. She glanced nervously at her watch and was relieved to see she was four minutes early.

Both women smiled and rose to shake her hand. Martha introduced her to Sandra as Will's friend, Anne Maxwell. Meghan felt her cheeks burn as the falsehood meant to protect her was repeated once again— this time, by the mother of the man she loved. To make matters worse, now that a potential employer was involved, she'd have to explain her situation or tell more lies.

"We certainly need the rain after such a dry summer," Sandra commented, filling the awkwardness of the moment.

Meghan nodded, wondering how anyone could consider this harbor town to be dry. She hoped her ability to carry on small talk hadn't diminished during a summer of neglect.

"A lovely dress, my dear," Martha said. "That's a good color on you."

"How nice of you to say that." Meghan breathed in and out slowly, trying to relax. She should have corrected Jeff about her name when she first got off the plane, but her mind hadn't been as alert as it could have been, and Bryan had been so insistent that she use the alias until her stalker was captured.

"My sister once had a prom dress that color," Martha added.

"I bet she looked beautiful," said Meghan.

"Oh yes." Martha smiled, her eyes misting over.

Meghan ordered a turkey lettuce wrap and iced tea, but could barely eat. The conversation eventually wended its way around to the reason for the meeting—the management of the Candlestick Gift Shop during Sandra's trip to Europe.

Since Will had recommended her, the deception about her identity would also reflect badly on him. She should tell them the truth, but how could she confide in Martha and Sandra before she told Will that she'd been going by her great-grandmother's maiden name?

"Have you managed a business before?" Sandra asked.

"I ran a coffee shop while I was in school back in Maine, but I've been an educator ever since." She twisted her napkin nervously in her lap, preparing for the moment when Sandra would request a reference. What would Martha think when she found out that her son was involved with a woman using a false identity?

Sandra would need Meghan's Social Security number, and then it would be out in the open. She should never have come here today. She couldn't possibly take this temporary position. Her mouth was so dry she could barely swallow.

"You went to school in Maine?" Martha sounded pleased. "I'd like to visit Maine someday. I hear it's very picturesque."

"Yes, it really is." Meghan tried to recall if she'd ever told Will she was from Maine. "I'm sure you'd find it a worthwhile trip. In some ways, it reminds me of northern Michigan. This is such a nice area to have a gift shop," she said, steering the conversation away from her past.

As Sandra enthusiastically described the Candlestick, Meghan grew anxious to finish lunch and meet with her at the store. Later, when they were alone, she'd find some way to explain her alias as part of an informal witness protection program—although that would defeat the purpose of keeping her identity secret.

"Since no one cares for dessert, we'll be on our way," Sandra said.

Meghan pushed herself away from the table. "It's been lovely."

"Yes, it has." Martha reached for the check. "I'd like to call you soon to invite you to tea." Martha and Sandra exchanged a knowing glance.

"That would be nice. And thank you for the lunch." Meghan smiled. Whether or not the job worked out, she'd passed inspection with Will's mom.

❧

As Martha shook out her umbrella and hung up her raincoat, she thought about Maine. She loved to hear about places to visit, though she rarely ventured outside of Benzie County.

Her throat tightened as she recalled her trip to Europe to visit Will and see him in concert. Martha wondered if she'd ever comprehend why her son had suddenly come home, cutting off a brilliant future in music at the peak of his career.

This Anne Maxwell seemed to be a lovely girl, charming yet reserved. She was the first woman Will had introduced to her since high school, and Martha could see in his eyes how much he cared for her. Though he'd been seeing her for almost two months, Martha knew almost nothing about her. She found herself wondering about Anne's religion. She'd never seen her at church, but perhaps she was Catholic, or Methodist.

She could understand why Will would be drawn to her. She admired Anne's radiance and vitality. Although Anne had seemed a bit nervous at lunch, there was something warm and alive about her. Will's new friend possessed a keen intelligence and an understated elegance that was natural and unaffected. Martha had no use for affectation.

As for Anne's religion, if she wasn't affiliated with a church, so much the better. She might be more open to an invitation to attend church with Martha. Will had mentioned she had a beautiful singing voice, and they could always use someone new in the choir.

❧

Candles made of sand were displayed in the Candlestick's window, along with a magnificent star quilt that Meghan had admired as she'd passed by. Tiny bells jingled as she and Sandra entered. The gift shop was paneled in rough barn wood and was redolent with the aromas of sandalwood and cinnamon from burning candles.

"I took this place over from my aunt. It's been in our family since the 1950s." Sandra proudly pointed out cheerful displays of coffee mugs, wall hangings of sailboats and seagulls, and a showcase of jewelry made from Petoskey stones and bright pebbles. In the back was a wheelbarrow of damp sand, small blocks of wax arranged in stacks, wicks, dyes, and incense. Perhaps she would have a chance to try her own hand at making candles.

It reminded Meghan of shops in seaside towns when she was a girl. She remembered a treasured bracelet of shells that her father had given her.

Sandra expressed relief to find someone reliable to run her store on such short notice. Now she wouldn't have to close the shop while she was away. She showed Meghan the books and the safe. She would still be in town for two more weeks and would help her get acclimated and make sure that she felt comfortable running the store by the time she left.

Sandra hesitated. "Do you mind if I pay you in cash? It would be less complicated."

That would be fine," said Meghan with relief. Apparently, there would be no request for references. Will's recommendation was enough. She wouldn't need to show ID or get into the details of her situation.

She glanced at a calendar on a linen wall hanging, noting that school in Tucson had already been in session for weeks. As she listened to the rain drumming against the roof, her life in the West seemed as remote as the baking desert heat.

༈

Late September was turning out to be beautiful, and Meghan had never been happier. She'd rediscovered long-forgotten pleasures with Will and took new delight in even the most ordinary activities, such as shopping together for ingredients for an evening meal. Somehow, she'd never had occasion to do such mundane chores with Bryan. She couldn't recall ever having felt such joy in being with a man as she did with Will.

He made good on his promise to play the piano for her, and it took her breath away, especially when he played Rachmaninoff's Piano Concerto no. 2 or Brahms. He also played Broadway hits, including several classics she loved. When she sang along with him to "Somewhere," from *West Side Story*, her own voice sounded better to her than ever before.

"You have a beautiful vibrato," Will said. One day he played a deeply moving rendition of "Rhapsody in Blue" that gave her goose bumps.

But one afternoon, Will stopped by Meghan's cottage to explain that he wouldn't be spending the evening with her as planned.

"Is something wrong?" When she tenderly encircled him with her arms, he stiffened and drew away.

"I'd just like to be alone tonight. I hope you can understand. I'm feeling a bit down." He closed the door on the way out, without waiting for an answer.

Staring in surprise at the closed door, she wondered if Will was struggling with depression. She'd always tried to avoid getting involved with men given to mood swings or depression. Her father's suicide had made it clear she had nothing to offer them.

Her early memories of her father were filled with fun and adventure. He'd always had something new to share—a conch shell with the ocean roaring inside, a treasure map, or a bottle holding a miniature ship. Yet it had all been so fragile. After her mother's death he'd slipped into a deep depression, and despite her desperate efforts, she'd been unable to help him. Bryan had pushed her away too. He'd apparently been upset about something, but instead of letting her help, he'd shut her out. She couldn't bear to go through that with Will.

She told herself she was imagining things and that everyone felt blue once in a while. She needed to get herself in a better frame of mind, because tomorrow she'd been invited to visit Martha at her home.

※

As Meghan approached Martha's immaculate Folk Victorian home, she recalled the first time she'd seen it. When she'd stopped to admire the lilacs, Will's smile and kind words had lifted her spirits and dissipated her anger and frustration at being sent into hiding.

Now bright-yellow chrysanthemums and blue delphiniums lined the walkway to the porch, and a few maple trees were starting to turn red and orange.

Martha greeted her warmly at the door and invited her in. "Welcome to my home. It isn't fancy, but I'm very comfortable here."

"It's charming," said Meghan.

A needlepoint of a shepherd with a lamb over his shoulders hung prominently in the entryway over a collection of china figurines. "The Lord Is My Shepherd" was stitched into the pattern. The lace curtains and crocheted doilies pinned on the arms of overstuffed chairs reminded her of her maternal grandmother's home. Faded chains of pink and violet flowers with pale-green leaves adorned the wallpaper, and over the sofa hung a watercolor of a fisherman in a stream.

The far wall of the living room was crowded with photographs of Will at every age—Will as a babe in arms with a much younger Martha, Will as a small boy proudly displaying a large bass, a slightly older Will seated at the piano, Will as a lifeguard, and as a dashing young man in a karate uniform. There were pictures of Jake and Will, and one striking photo of Jake taken on his ship. He looked very much the rugged sea captain. Meghan longed to be left alone to absorb the essence of each frozen slice of Will's life.

"Let's go out on the porch," said Martha. "It's a bit stuffy in here. And how about some iced tea?"

Moments later, she was having tea with Martha on the very same porch where she'd first seen Will. She'd thought front porches, as she remembered them, had pretty much vanished. Most of her neighbors in Tucson would arrive home with their car windows up, pull into their garages or carports, and disappear into their homes and back patios; yet here they sat on a front porch, on a street that seemed untouched by time.

Martha chatted leisurely with passersby, and Meghan began to chime in. The delphiniums and chrysanthemums were the subject of much discussion, but the real focus was on Meghan, whom they referred to as Anne. She felt her face grow warm when a heavyset, blonde woman from across the street shared that she was glad to meet the beautiful woman who'd captivated the town's most elusive bachelor.

A kind-looking gentleman with horn-rimmed glasses and gray hair approached with his wife, whose face was crinkled with laugh lines. After being introduced as the minister and his wife, they spoke with Martha about their gardens, then speculated about when the fall colors might peak this year. After they left, Martha asked her what she thought of them.

Meghan liked them and said so.

"They're very caring people, and he gives a meaningful sermon. It's a congenial parish." Martha hesitated. "Would you care to join me this Sunday? We're having a soloist from Interlochen. Will is going to play the organ at another church, so he won't be coming with me this week." She seemed nervous, coloring slightly as she extended the invitation.

Meghan had been active in church as a girl, but after her father had taken his own life, she hadn't gone back to church for years. At first, she'd been too hurt and angry to even pray; but five years ago, she'd finally gone back to church and joined the choir.

"I'd be happy to come along."

Martha beamed, unable to conceal her pleasure. "I'll pick you up at ten fifteen."

As they entered the old stone church five days later, she admired the beautiful stained-glass windows. She followed Martha down the aisle to a straight-backed wooden pew. The soloist was excellent, the sermon meaningful, and the congregation friendly.

After church, Martha invited her to brunch. Whenever Martha brought up questions about Anne's past, she shifted the topic to her life in Frankfort, or to Martha.

"Will went to grade school near here," Martha said, after they'd placed their orders.

At last, they could discuss the matter at hand: *Will.*

"Later, I sent him to private schools, including nearby Interlochen, an international school for music and the arts. I imagine Will has already taken you there."

"No, not yet."

Martha's smile momentarily faded. "I'm sure he will soon. His gift has always been piano, of course. After graduation, he went on to study at Julliard. He's been very successful as an international concert pianist."

"Why did he stop giving concerts?"

Martha flinched visibly at her unexpected directness. "Who can say? Whatever he does is fine with me so long as it makes him happy." She dabbed at her mouth with her napkin, then left the table to replenish her plate. Upon returning, she carefully situated herself back in the booth.

"I'm not sure how much I should tell you, Anne, but you do seem to care for my son."

"Yes, I do," said Meghan uneasily.

"He's a very private person, so if you please, let's keep this little conversation between the two of us."

"Of course."

"Like so many men of genius, he can be rather . . . intense. He feels things very deeply. After his stepfather died, there was a time when I had to get him help."

"Psychiatric help?"

"Counseling. He lost his parents as a babe. I've done what I could to make it up to him, but . . . it wasn't always easy." Martha looked at her plate, cutting her chicken into smaller and smaller pieces. "He can get . . . a bit down in the dumps at times."

"He's so fortunate to have you." Meghan forced herself to keep chewing her meal, and swallowing, as Martha seemed to confirm her deepest fears about Will. "Anyone can experience a difficult time. It's nothing to be ashamed of."

"You're right," Martha agreed.

"Are there still problems?"

"Not really," said Martha unconvincingly as she smoothed and refolded her napkin. "It was normal to be depressed after he lost his stepfather, and he responded nicely to the help. I just thought you might want to know. We all get a little down once in a while, don't you think?" Not waiting for a reply, she steered the conversation to Will's awards in music, swimming, and karate.

"He's gifted in so many different areas," commented Meghan, truly impressed.

"You're so right." Martha beamed.

She remembered how her father's depression had swallowed their home in darkness, foreshadowing the tragedy to come. She felt helpless in the face of chronic depression, yet feared Martha had touched on the subject to warn her.

"What's really depressing is the effect of all this marvelous pastry on my waistline," Meghan joked, successfully distracting Martha from her discomfort about the subject of Will's moods.

"I can't see why it would concern you," Martha remarked, with a hint of annoyance. "You could actually stand to put on a little weight."

⚹

Will was delighted that Meghan was staying longer and that she'd met with his mother and Sandra about filling in at the gift shop. It would give him more time to win her over.

But right now, when he should be happiest, a cold, dark stone had lodged itself in the pit of his stomach, along with a growing sense of dread that something terrible was about to happen. It had started in again while he was resuscitating Theresa from drowning.

The recurring nightmare that used to haunt him in his youth was tormenting him once again. There was always the sight of blood, a sensation of death, and the frightening face of an angry man. When he awoke, he could never recall the face, but always felt helpless and terrified.

After Jake's death, when Will was a teenager, he'd slipped deeper and deeper into all-encompassing darkness. Martha had seen to it that he got help, and he'd come out of it but had gained no insight about what was wrong.

Will could tell it was starting to drive a wedge between him and Anne. He was determined to get to the bottom of it before it destroyed everything. He had too much to lose.

CHAPTER 32

Breakers pounded the beach, and Meghan heard the rumble of distant thunder as she stood on Will's deck, agonizing about what to do. Her secret identity was creating tension between them, and it was possible that whoever had threatened her life might never be captured. She couldn't wait much longer to take Will into her confidence and tell him who she was and why she was in hiding.

Will closed the slider behind him, catching the curtain's edge in the door. "Damn!"

"What's wrong?" she asked. "You seem upset."

"I guess I'm a little off tonight."

"Have I done something to upset you?"

"Not at all." Will grabbed his parka from the closet. "I just need to go for a walk."

"It's about to storm, so be careful. And if you want to talk, I can listen."

"I need some space right now." He headed to the door.

"Should I leave?" She tried not to sound offended.

"It's up to you. Stay, if you like. I'm going out." He closed the door behind him.

Through the window she saw Will walking toward Lake Michigan, where a wall of rain advanced across the lake like an army. She gathered up her purse and jacket to leave, then set them back down and started pacing.

Why in the world was Will heading straight into the storm? Just how upset *was* he? When the rain hit land, he disappeared from view. Suddenly she couldn't catch her breath. She focused on inhaling and exhaling deeply to stave off rising panic. She needed to get hold of herself and honor his request to be alone. She should get in the car and drive off—yet she couldn't shake the image of her father walking out into the ocean alone for the last time.

She grabbed her parka and headed toward the beach. Lightning flashed along the horizon, and great white-capped breakers crashed relentlessly against the shore. Will was nowhere in sight.

"Will!" she cried as she ran toward the lighthouse. Could she be too late?

Finally she saw him heading toward her. She broke down sobbing.

"What happened?" He embraced her, holding her close.

"I was afraid that you . . ."

He stepped back to study her face. "Afraid that I *what?*"

"That you were so upset—"

"Sometimes I need to be alone for a while. I went down to the old boathouse and sat there, looking out at the water. Why would that bother you?"

"It's just that my father . . ." She swallowed hard and tried to steady her voice. "I never told you how he died."

"Then tell me," he said tenderly. "How did he die?"

Rain pelted her head and back. She pulled the hood of her parka tighter around her face.

"My dad went into a deep depression after my mother died. If he had that tendency before, I'd never noticed it as I was growing up. Three years later, I went away to college." She swallowed hard. "One day he walked out into the ocean—and drowned himself."

"Oh, Annie. I'm so sorry." Will embraced her and stroked her hair as if she were a small, hurt child. "No wonder you're upset."

"I'm sorry. I totally overreacted." She hugged him more tightly.

"Look at me." He took her chin and turned her face gently toward him, looking into her eyes. "You don't need to worry about me. I'd never take my own life. I take good care of myself. I don't have a self-destructive bone in my body. There *is* something that's really bothering me, and I'm trying to figure it out. But I'll keep a better handle on things and not bother you with my problems. I don't want to upset you."

"What bothers me is feeling shut out. I guess I never got past the trauma of not being able to help my father, but that's not your problem."

"At least now I understand. But what your dad did wasn't your fault."

"That's what they say."

"I know it's easy to say, but I'm sure there was nothing you could have done."

"I begged him to let me stay home and attend our local community college. He wouldn't hear of it; yet I blame myself for going away to school when I knew he wasn't doing well."

"What a terrible burden to carry all this time. I wish I could say something that would help." He kissed the top of her head.

"Thanks. I just wanted you to know why I got so nervous tonight."

Arm in arm, they walked back to the cottage through the rain.

"I'm glad you told me. It's better to get things out in the open."

"That's true," she said. "Maybe it would help if you told me what's been worrying *you*."

Will opened the door for her, stomping water off his feet. "I've got to warn you, it's pretty dark. Are you sure you want me to lay this on you tonight, when you're so upset?"

"Of course I'm sure." But she wasn't sure at all. She pictured herself getting into her car and heading back to her cozy cabin to spend the rest of the night reading.

Will put a log in the fireplace, added kindling wood and newspapers, and lit the fire. He plumped up cushions on the loveseat and asked her to join him.

"It's weird," he finally began. "This all started in again after I rescued Theresa Larsen. Something about it really got to me. When I was giving her CPR, I felt this cold darkness closing in. That night, I started having terrible nightmares again . . . someone dying, and me helpless to save them. Lately they're even more vivid than those I'd had in my teens after Jake died. When I wake up I feel like I'm in a black hole, with a chill of death around me."

She shivered. "That *is* dark. Is there a certain person in the nightmare?"

"There's always this same angry face . . . my personal demon, you might say. Then everything goes dark, cold. Once I'm awake, I can never remember the face."

Locked in the fierceness of his gaze, she understood more than she cared to. "Could something have happened when you were small, before you were adopted?"

He paused. "I don't know. I had some counseling back in high school because of the nightmares. Nothing specific turned up. Then I threw myself into karate and swimming and got back in the swing of things with my schoolwork, friends, and music. The nightmares finally stopped, until this summer. Now that they've started up again, I need to get to the bottom of it."

"Do you remember your natural parents?" she ventured.

He shook his head. "I was less than two when they were killed. Martha's told me their car was struck by a train, and they were killed instantly. She said they didn't suffer, but that's all she would ever say. I got the idea that the accident was too painful for her to talk about."

"How terrible. I'm so sorry." She reached over and took his hand into both of hers. "So Martha never told you much about your parents?"

"Not even their names. But one time when I was about twelve, we were driving by a farmhouse downstate, and she mentioned that I'd lived there as a baby. I memorized the address on the mailbox."

"Do you still remember it?"

He nodded. "I asked Martha about my parents several more times, but she always changed the subject. I should have gone back to that old farmhouse to see if anyone could remember them. I guess I didn't really want to find out."

"Maybe you were right not to go back."

"Maybe so, at the time. But I'm going back now. I want to find that house."

"Are you sure you want to do that?" Her stomach started to hurt.

"I'm sure. Maybe you could go with me, if you could break away from the gift shop for a day or two. My mom might fill in for you. She's done it many times in the past for Sandra."

Meghan nodded, regretting she'd brought it up.

The air was humid and close. Martha took in short, shallow breaths, struggling to exhale. Will was planning to go downstate to his birthplace to dig into his past, and this time, nothing she'd said could dissuade him. Her hands and knees ached worse than ever, and she had a miserable headache.

She put a fan in the window, attempting to get some air moving. She tried to focus on her novel, *The Shell Seekers,* by Rosamunde Pilcher. She set it down, then picked up a magazine on gardening. Even that couldn't hold her interest.

She suspected Anne had instigated this trip to look into her son's past. He'd brought up the idea when he was younger, but Martha had always been able to steer him away from it. She'd warned him it would serve no purpose to delve into the tragic details. It would just be upsetting. She'd even gone so far as to ask, "Haven't I been a good mother to you, and Jake a good father, God rest his soul?"

The truth could only bring pain and questions that Martha couldn't answer. She felt ashamed. She should have told him a long time ago.

On the morning of Will's planned trip downstate, thick fog blanketed the low-lying areas, and Martha worried about him driving on the two-lane, heavily wooded M-115. She prayed for their safety.

As she began to get ready for her day at the Candlestick, she couldn't stop agonizing about Will's trip into his past. She hated to imagine what might happen if he found out the truth. She started to dial his number but remembered he'd lost his cell phone in the lake.

She considered calling the Comstock Inn and a few motels near Owosso until she tracked him down, but what could she say now? It was too late.

She rubbed Aspercreme into her hands, frowning at the sight of her bony fingers and prominent blue veins that showed through thin skin covered with liver spots. When had her pretty hands with slender fingers become the hands of an old woman? She sometimes wished she could wear gloves when she went out, as some ladies had done when she was a girl. She and her sister, Sarah, had worn them on special occasions, such as Easter.

She could still remember Sarah posing with John on the night of their senior prom, wearing her beautiful lavender gown and long white gloves. Martha had thought they were the most perfect couple. She'd always believed that, until she'd started to read John's journal. She hoped Sarah had never read it, as its contents would have devastated her.

She went to her bedroom, reached into the cedar chest, and pulled out the leather-bound journal, wrapped in a silk scarf. Its pages were yellowed, but the musty smell had given way to the aroma of cedar. She sat on the chair beside her bed and opened the journal to where she'd left off.

June 19, 1950: Sarah has painted one of Stewart's toes with nail polish to keep the twins straight. I can't comprehend why, since he lags behind on everything except his fits of temper. Bryan sleeps through the night, while Stewart cries incessantly, his entire body crimson with rage.

September 7, 1950: Things are a bit better at home. Bryan runs up to greet me from work with an impish smile and sparkling blue eyes. He calls me Dada. His brother waddles along behind. At least he's finally walking.

December 16, 1950: Stewart is starting to catch up with his brother, and most people can't tell the boys apart anymore—but when he reaches a new milestone weeks or even days after his brother, I don't feel the pride I do with Bryan. Just relief.

Suddenly it came back to Martha. She remembered Stewart's first steps. "About time," his father had mumbled. Her sister had glared at John in strained silence. Stewart rarely got to be the one showered with praise, while his older brother sliced boldly through the waters of life with a jaunty air of expectation.

How could her brother-in-law have been so insensitive? Surely, the younger twin had realized that he wasn't measuring up.

She needed to make sure Will never saw the journal. Maybe it was time to break down and get a shredder. Better yet, she could rip out the pages and toss them into the fireplace, one by one. It was up to Martha to destroy it before it hurt anyone else.

CHAPTER 33

Meghan and Will sat facing each other on two double beds in a small motel room between Owosso and Flint. It was the kind of humid autumn day that can envelop a person in an oppressive layer of tired gray mist.

"Sorry about the motel," Will said.

"We just need a place to sleep." What else could she say? Will had told her they wouldn't need reservations, but with two class reunions and a big conference at the same time, this was the only place they found with a vacancy.

Meghan leaned back against two pillows she'd propped against the imitation walnut headboard and stared vacantly at the framed painting of a covered bridge, rendered in the same rust and gold colors as the patterned bedspread. She glanced absentmindedly at a cigarette burn in the brown carpet. The fan pushed out cool, stale air in a steady hum. Today it was warm enough in Lower Michigan to warrant air conditioning. In the background, a Tigers baseball game droned in and out on the radio.

Will's shoulders slumped. "I don't know what I expected to find out without my birth name. I guess I assumed they could locate my records under Martha's name."

"Maybe your adoption wasn't done in Shiawassee County."

"Maybe not." Will paced back and forth in the tiny room. Tomorrow, I'd like to find the house on Harville Road that Martha pointed out to me years ago, if it's still standing."

"Do you think there might still be any of the same neighbors around?"

"I doubt it. It's been over forty years. I need to go home and talk to Martha again and insist that she tell me my birth name."

"We can't afford to get discouraged now, just when we're getting started." She tried to sound upbeat, despite a growing sense of dread.

"You're right. What would I do without you?"

"I hope you won't need to find out." She reached out to him, and they embraced.

He brushed a strand of hair off her forehead, held her face to his, and kissed her. "Thanks for the encouragement," he said.

✧

Though Will had told Meghan he remembered the house as a sturdy white farmhouse with green trim, it now looked abandoned and in disrepair. Local children might tell each other it was haunted. Behind the house was a building that had been a garage and an old barn that looked as if it might blow over in the next windstorm.

Next door was a clapboard farmhouse with faded blue shutters, a large front porch, and a gabled roof. It was in dire need of a coat of paint. On the mailbox was the name, Connors.

Will and Meghan parked on the road near the mailbox and made their way up a dirt driveway flanked by two hickory trees. An old black dog with milky eyes sniffed them halfheartedly, then curled up under a large shade tree. The ground beneath it was strewn with shiny chestnuts, like those Meghan had loved to gather as a child. They stepped carefully over a rotted porch step.

Will knocked several times, while Meghan fought the urge to rush down the steps and head back to the car.

At last, an elderly woman appeared at the door. "May I help you?"

"Are you Mrs. Connors?" Will asked.

"Are you selling something?"

"No. I'm Will Ashley, and this is my friend, Anne. I'm sorry to disturb you, but I think we might have once been next-door neighbors." He pointed toward the house next door.

"There hasn't been anyone there for years."

"Have you lived here for quite a while, then?" asked Will.

"All my life. I was born in this house."

"Back in the early seventies, I believe a young couple with a baby lived there," said Will.

The woman eyed him suspiciously. "That was a long time ago."

A wiry man with a few tufts of white hair appeared behind her. His baggy pants were held up by suspenders, and he walked with a cane.

"Hello, sir," began Will. "I wondered if either of you remembered a family who used to live next door."

The man glanced at his wife and frowned. "We keep pretty much to ourselves."

Will pushed on. "I think the parents were killed when a train collided with their car."

The woman frowned, shaking her head. "I don't recall that."

"So you don't remember anything about them . . . or their baby?"

"If it's the Jamesons you're talking about, you've got your facts mixed up," said the woman. "They weren't killed in a—"

"That's enough questions," snapped the man, glaring at his wife.

"The *Jamesons*?" asked Will, perspiring.

"Are you a detective or something?" asked the man.

"No. I was once told I was born in that house. I wasn't quite two years old when—"

"Well, I'll be!" The woman stepped back and studied Will's features. "You do take after her . . . your mother. She was a lovely person."

The man extended his thin, calloused hand to Will. "You seem like a fine young man, but we don't know anything about what happened, like we told the sheriff at the time. Sorry."

"The sheriff?" Will grasped the porch railing, his knuckles white.

"Sorry we can't help, but best of luck to you," the man said as he shut the door on them.

Will and Meghan stood there, facing the closed door. They turned and made their way down the rotting steps and headed back to the Jeep.

"That was a pretty weird reaction," said Will, wiping sweat from his forehead. "Why do you think he brought up the sheriff and asked if I were a detective?"

"They seemed pretty suspicious of us, but we were asking a lot of questions. Maybe we should drive over to the house where you think you were born and look around. It looks like no one's living there."

"I'm as close as I want to get to that house, but I think I might have what I need to get started. My last name. Let's get some lunch. Then you can shop in town while I head back to the county seat to see if I have any better luck tracking down my adoption records, now that I have a last name. I might also check with a few more neighbors. I'll handle things from here on out. There's no reason to put you through all this."

"I don't mind. That's why I came."

After lunch, Will dropped Meghan off near Main and Washington Streets in Owosso. "I'll meet you at 4:30 at that cafe over there."

Meghan set off exploring. Trees and bright flowers adorned the decorative sidewalks, with benches for shoppers to rest and chat with their friends. An old-fashioned dime store piped upbeat oldies out into the street. She went inside and bought bright potholders to match the kitchen curtains, kitchen utensils she needed for the cottage, and a jar of her favorite hand cream. She wandered through a flower shop, then a small bakery, where she had an amazing, cream-filled pastry that was shaped like a triangle.

In another store, she purchased fabric for a quilt she planned to make for Erin. She hoped her goddaughter was safe in Appalachia, in a home where she could begin healing and reconnect with who she was. Erin was resilient, and Meghan had faith that she could come out of all this stronger than ever.

As she left the downtown, she wandered along quiet residential streets with boughs of oaks and maples arched overhead in tunnels of foliage. Victorian and Italianate homes lined the streets on lush, green lawns, much as they must have a century ago.

Sunlight flickered through the leaves, drawing Meghan back into her childhood in New England. She inhaled deeply of the autumn air. Suddenly she longed to jump into a pile of fallen leaves. She was overcome with a desire to go back in time and be the happy, young girl she'd once been.

She turned back toward town. Even though Will had told her he would handle things himself, she was here to help him. The neighbors had mentioned the sheriff and acted as if there were something they wanted to avoid talking about.

On the way into town she'd noticed a stately library. She decided to stop there to look through old newspapers from the time Will said the accident had taken place. Surely, a young couple killed by a train would have made headlines.

The library was within walking distance, and minutes later, she climbed the concrete steps and entered through the large double doors. She felt right at home amid the tall oak bookshelves, two-story windows, and overhead fans that stirred the air with the intoxicating scent of books.

When she asked to see old newspapers from July through October of 1969, she was shown to the collection of microfilms. She skimmed through them using a microfilm reader until her vision blurred. She paused to look at an ad with a man in sideburns and bell-bottoms standing in front of a long, sleek, '69 Chevy Impala convertible. In July, Neil Armstrong was the first human to set foot on the moon, and in August, there was an article about Woodstock.

Then she saw it.

"Tragic Murder of Young Couple: Toddler Found Clinging to Mother."

At first Meghan skimmed the article: *Jameson . . . Harville Road . . . both found murdered at home in their bed . . .*

Her heart pounded furiously as she reread the article.

> *"The bodies of Stewart and Susan Delong Jameson, a young local couple married two years ago, were discovered last night follow-ing an anonymous call to the sheriff's department. The husband and wife had been fatally shot. Their crying toddler was found with his murdered parents. The community is shocked and outraged. There are no suspects at this time, but the authorities are determined to find the killer."*

There was one of those painfully sweet graduation pictures of the slain wife, a lovely young woman with a radiant smile—the kind that tears one's heart out when accompanying such an article. Meghan could see a resemblance to Will.

There was no mention of the child's name or picture of the father, but there was little doubt in her mind that the baby was Will. The paternal grandparents had been tragically killed the year before when a train had struck their car. That's what Will thought had happened to *his parents!*

The library was suddenly oppressive, its silence broken only by a clicking sound from overhead fans. She made her way to the main desk and requested a copy of the article. It seemed to take forever for the elderly librarian to produce the copy, yet only three minutes had elapsed.

"Susan was such a bright girl. Very pleasant, and an avid reader. Long ago as it was, I still can't forget. Nowadays there's something terrible in the paper every day. I can hardly bear to read the news anymore."

"Do you remember what happened to the little boy?"

"I believe he was adopted. Dreadful, positively dreadful. The poor thing found crying, with his dead parents."

"That *is* dreadful." Meghan was suddenly queasy and needed to get some fresh air.

"Are you okay, miss?" asked the librarian. "I'm sorry if I've upset you."

"I'm fine. And thank you for your help."

She glanced at her watch as she left the library. It was already 4:15. She had just enough time to meet Will by 4:30, but what could she possibly tell him?

She hurried to the cafe, feeling nauseous. She rushed to the restroom and was sick.

Will was already seated when she returned. "You look as if you've seen a ghost."

"What in the world are those green drinks?"

"Lime phosphates. Carbonated soda water with lime syrup, which is tough to find anymore. I think you'll like it."

"I'm not that thirsty right now."

"What's wrong? Aren't you feeling well?"

"I think I got a little too warm," she said.

"It *is* a pretty hot, muggy day. But I've got good news," he smiled. "I found my birth certificate! My given name was William L. Jameson. The court assigned me to Martha when I was almost two years old. Then I drove by the house again. Some neighbors on the other side of the road have a vegetable stand. I bought a dozen ears of sweet corn, passed the time of day, and casually mentioned I was born out that way. Tomorrow I'll go back and see if they'll open up a bit more."

"That's nice." She couldn't look him in the eye.

He studied her face intently. "Something *is* wrong."

"I met a librarian who said she'd known your mother."

"What did she say?"

"She told me that your mother loved to read."

"You're not telling me everything."

Meghan looked away.

"You're not upset about my mother's reading. Let's get out of here." He rose, slapped five dollars on the table, and escorted her out the door.

Once at the motel, he closed the door behind them. He grasped her gently by the upper arms and looked into her eyes. "Tell me what you found out."

"I'm not sure that I want to. It's not something I'd want to know, if I were you."

"You can't protect me from the truth. I'll find out, one way or another."

"You don't have to." Her voice trembled. "It's your choice. Let's just turn around and go back up north and never talk about this again."

"*No way.*" He waited for her to begin.

At last, she opened her perspiring palm and handed him the damp, crumpled copy of the newspaper article.

Will sat on the foot of the bed, reading and rereading it. Then he folded it with trembling hands and stuffed it into his pocket. He felt like he was suffocating. Finally, he arose and walked to the window. He opened the drapes to reveal the rain, which had finally come.

"Of course," he grimaced. "It makes sense."

Rain oozed down the sliding glass door, with its double locks and safety bar. The heavy sky had released its burden, and the rain would have to serve as tears, for his eyes were hot and dry. He could hardly catch his breath. Cold, he felt so cold. He could almost taste blood. Horror was turning to rage. He had to get out of here!

⚶

Meghan sat alone in the dismal room with its orange-and-harvest-gold theme and the odor of stale cigarette smoke. She felt Will's anguish in every molecule of her being. There must be a place, she thought, where the violence and horrors of the human spirit couldn't find her. Her courage to wage this battle alongside Will was starting to falter.

She decided to lie down on the bed for a few minutes. She thought of her parents—her mother's lingering death and her father's terrible, self-chosen end at sea. She remembered the shotgun blast into her home, the fire at her office, and the months of helpless fear until her goddaughter was found. Finally, she dozed off into a tormented sleep, blasted by the air-conditioner. Its cold, damp air chilled her deep inside.

Shivering and stiff, she awoke to the sound of a key in the door. Will was soaking wet, and the rosy color was back in his cheeks. As she grasped his hand, a surge of energy seared though her, as if his rage were a palpable force.

"You're sopping wet. Let me help you get dried off."

Will crushed her against his cold, wet body. Then he pushed himself away, his eyes wild and haunted.

She shuddered. She'd never brought up the frantic look in his eyes or the warnings he'd cried out to her on the night of their boating disaster. She'd assumed he was delirious.

"Wouldn't you like a hot shower right now?" She tried to sound calm.

"That face. I need to remember that face, so I can put an end to this, once and for all!"

"Stop it!" she cried. "You're scaring me."

"My *demon* is a real man—and the murderer of my parents! I just need to find the son of a bitch!"

CHAPTER 34

Martha closed her front door against the driving rain and turned anxiously to Will. He stomped his feet and hung his sopping wet coat on a hook.

"I found out the truth," he said, his face pale with anger.

"I'm sorry to hear it." Martha clutched the stairway banister to steady herself. Then she sat down heavily in the chair beside the telephone stand in the vestibule. "I did everything I could to protect you from it."

"Even when I was in therapy? I can't believe you lied about my history to the counselor."

"I just didn't tell him *everything*. Are you happier now that you know?" She wanted to go out the door into the rain, but her feet felt frozen to the floor.

"At least I know what's been bothering me. Something horrible did happen. My parents were murdered in their bed by some monster, and I was found there between them, holding on to my dead mother."

"Who would tell a child such a terrible thing?" Her voice broke. "I couldn't see how the truth could do anything but cause you pain." Will was her life, and he was furious with her.

"After Jake died, I had terrible nightmares and dark feelings I couldn't understand, and now they're back."

"I'm sorry to hear your nightmares are back—and so very sorry that I've made you angry." Her voice broke. "I did what I thought was best."

"Did Jake know?"

"No."

"So is this all? Or is there more?"

Martha felt her face flush. "What do you mean by *more?*"

"More secrets. There are, aren't there?"

"Probably. They kept secrets from me too. But all I've ever wanted was for you to have a loving family and a happy childhood."

"You can't change reality."

"I didn't want to poison your life with needless grief. Instead, I've ruined everything." She began to weep.

He leaned over to embrace her. "I love you, Mom. I always will. Just promise me that you'll tell me the truth from now on. I'm strong enough to take it."

"I know you are. You're everything to me, son. I love you more than life itself and never meant to hurt you."

They held each other and cried.

Will finally stepped away from her, taking both her hands in his. "Let's move on from here, Mom—but we have to be honest. You can't protect me from being hurt."

"I wish I could have. But I'll do my best to be honest to you."

"Good."

"But, Will . . ."

"What?"

"Please don't run off before you try that peach pie I baked for you. It's hot out of the oven."

He shook his head in frustration, unable to repress a smile. "Sounds like another blatant attempt to change the subject, but it works for me. I smelled that pie the minute I walked in the house."

"I need you to help scoop the ice cream," she said, wiping her eyes. "It's hard as a rock." She headed to the kitchen, set out two china plates, cloth napkins, and her best silver. Hands trembling, she sliced an extra-large piece of pie for Will.

Martha sat motionless in her chair for close to an hour. She opened her Bible and read the Twenty-third Psalm. Then she went into the bedroom and took John's journal from the cedar chest. She carefully removed it from the silk scarf. She would finish it now, then decide what to do with it. If she were going to be completely honest, maybe she should start by sharing the journal with Will.

October 17, 1950: The main source of entertainment around here is the theater. Big stars like Grace Kelly and Jimmy Stewart bring people to the movies in droves. As the manager, I make a decent living. But lately the young widow who works at the ticket window has become increasingly direct, giving me long looks and standing closer than need be when she addresses me.

I spend extra time on my knees each night before retiring, but the strength I pray for hasn't been forthcoming. I've always viewed myself as a good Catholic and a family man. There has never been anyone but my Sarah, but she's banished me from her bed and turned a cold shoulder to me. I think she's fearful of getting pregnant again. The months have worn on, and I'm in sore need of a woman's touch.

November 14, 1950: One day in the darkness of the empty theater, she took me in her arms, the whole length of her body pressing against mine. I'm ashamed to say I didn't resist, and things got out of hand.

December 22, 1950: I've stopped going to Confession. How can I repeat the same confession again and again? I'm not ready to give her up. She has a kind of hold on me. But sometimes when I see Sarah smiling at me, it's all I can do to keep from crying. I wanted things to be so different.

January 19, 1951: I got home late last night, after being with her. After I went to bed, Sarah came down to the den. She'd summoned up her courage and slid beneath the covers in the sofa bed. She took my hand and drew it to her breast.

I pulled my hand away, rolled over, and turned my back to her. I knew it was the wrong thing to do the minute I did it.

She went to the window and tried to open it, but it was frozen shut. I went to her and placed my hands on her shoulders. She looked out at the snow-covered earth in the moonlight, with tears streaming down her cheeks.

"Never for a moment did I believe the rumors about you and that woman. Until now."

I dropped my hands to my sides and turned away. I saw the painting of the Virgin Mary staring down at me disapprovingly.

Then a cry pierced the night like a falling icicle, and I made my way mechanically up the stairs to the twins' room. Sarah followed behind.

Bryan was in a deep sleep, his tiny arm curled contentedly around a tiny, stuffed bear, but Stewart was inconsolable. Sarah came into their room and took him in her arms and rocked him. I watched her tears fall silently onto his forehead.

It was the final entry. Martha closed the journal and let it slip to the floor. It had been over half a century since she'd helped with the twins after their difficult birth. She'd lived with the family for several months, then rented an apartment down the street. She'd looked after them whenever their parents went out and had been included in most family gatherings. She'd often envied her sister, with her sensitive husband and wonderful sons. All these years she'd believed that Sarah had enjoyed a happy marriage.

Martha put her head in her hands and sobbed for the second time that day.

CHAPTER 35

Anne knew his darkest secrets, though Will knew so little about her. Unfortunately, it had fallen to her to break the terrible truth to him about his parents. Now it was his turn to be supportive of her. She'd become very upset that night when he'd returned to the motel saying he had to find the son of a bitch who'd killed his parents. She'd told him he was scaring her, and that was the last thing he wanted.

Terrible as the truth had been, an inexplicable darkness had lifted from his life to be replaced by anger and grief. He was sure that if he could recall the face of the killer, he would be able to excise his "demon" forever.

He needed to recall that hideous face. Then, and only then, would he find a way to drive it from his life. He hoped to have the nightmare again, in more detail than before. He was determined to mentally reconstruct the eyes, nose, and hair—every feature until it assumed the proportion of a man. Though Will had been less than two years old when his parents were murdered, his recurrent nightmares made him think that, at some level, he remembered.

Anne had tried to encourage him to talk about his traumatic discovery, but he was determined to avoid burdening her with any more discussion about it. He wished he hadn't gotten her involved with it in the first place.

Now it was time for them to relax and enjoy each other's company. He'd been hoping for a few perfect fall days so he could take her on the promised color tour. After the traumatic journey to Shiawassee County, he and Anne needed a real vacation together—time strictly for fun and romance. Unfortunately, September and early October were rainy and dismal, with none of the extravagant beauty he'd promised.

Then a brisk northerly wind blew in the vibrant glory of a crisp October day. Whitecaps pounded the beach. Scarlet and orange maples, yellow beech and birch, and golden-brown oaks contrasted with the evergreens of the surrounding hills, and the aroma of drying leaves hung in silent suspension. The visibility was so breathtakingly clear that the distant dunes seemed to have moved closer during the night. Now the color tours would begin, and he and Anne would be part of them.

His mom had agreed to fill in again at the Candlestick. She seemed relieved for a chance to do him a favor, as if that might help atone for all the years of deception. He felt bad that he'd upset her so much, but he'd never been so angry with her. He knew she'd been trying to protect him, but how could he completely trust her anymore? Though they'd made up, he suspected there was something she was keeping from him, even now.

On the day of the trip Meghan was as excited as Will seemed to be. He picked her up at eight and they headed north past Miller's Landing. They turned off onto Esch Road, where they followed a path to the beach at Lake Michigan. They ate the picnic breakfast she'd packed with hard-boiled eggs, plums, and prune kolaches, a Czech pastry Joan had taught her to make. Later, they strolled along the beach to Otter Creek, a crystalline stream flowing into the lake.

They could see the Manitou Islands and the Sleeping Bear Dunes to the north. Will pointed out to her where they'd come to shore during the storm.

"I was such a fool to go out that day," she said.

"And yet it was meant to be." Will squeezed her hand. "Maybe we'd have never gotten to know each other if it weren't for that storm."

She laughed and squeezed back. "I could have used a less dramatic first date."

"We'll always have something to tell our kids," he said.

She turned to him in surprise.

He winked.

She brushed her hair from her eyes. "Isn't it kind of soon to be talking that way?"

"If you think so, then it is. We'll just relax and enjoy this beautiful day together." He started packing up the remains of their breakfast. "But we'd better get going again, so we can climb the dunes before lunch."

Forty-five minutes later, she stood at the base of the Sleeping Bear Dunes, looking up. "It's a lot higher than I'd thought." She kicked off her shoes and started to climb up the mountain of sand with Will. She seemed to have more energy lately, and before long, they reached the crest of the first dune. Stopping to catch their breath, they gazed out at Glen Lake, deep turquoise against hills of dark-green, red, and yellow. Then they raced each other to the bottom.

After a concerted effort to brush all the sand from their clothes and feet, they took the Pierce-Stocking Drive. She was amazed by the sharp angle of the dunes as they jutted into Lake Michigan far below. Will took her picture, and a bystander took one of them together.

They drove on to Leland where they ate whitefish at the Bluebird. Afterward, they browsed through several shops in town and on Fishermen's Wharf. She couldn't forget how distraught she'd been the first time she'd been there to catch the mail boat to Manitou Island. She'd just broken up with Will. Fortunately, it had only been for nine days, which was long enough for her to realize that she'd made a huge mistake.

They continued up to Northport, where she'd bought material and supplies for her quilt a few months earlier. The store had closed for the season and the crowds were gone, along with most of the yachts. Gone too, was the sense of her mother's presence she'd felt that day.

They headed down the east side of the Leelanau Peninsula, through Peshawbestown, Sutton's Bay, and on to Traverse City, where they spent the first night of their tour.

The next morning, there was a steady breeze out of the northwest, and they chartered a thirty-two foot sailboat for a half day of sailing in West Grand Traverse Bay. Meghan was happy to get out on the water and start building confidence in her sailing again. It felt good to be sailing with Will in a larger boat, similar to the ones she'd learned to sail in.

After turning in the boat, they headed north, stopping at a shoreline park in Elk Rapids to picnic as the late-afternoon sunlight danced across the waves. Across the water they could see the wooded hills of the Mission Peninsula that divided West and East Bays.

She took a deep breath. "This must be the freshest air on earth."

"You're probably right." Will put his arm around her shoulder and pulled her closer.

They spent the night at a bed and breakfast in Charlevoix. That night as they caressed, only a thin wall separated them from guests in the next room. When her desire for him grew unbearable she did her best not to cry out.

After a hearty breakfast the next morning, they continued up the coast to Petoskey. There were several upscale shops, and for some reason, Will was determined to buy her an elegant evening gown, matching heels, and all the accessories. She couldn't talk him out of it.

At Bay View, they strolled past Victorian summer homes nestled along walkways through the wooded grounds. He informed her that in the 1800s a group of Methodists had decided to gather there to engage in Chautauqua-type literary and scientific circles. Letting her mind drift backward in time, she imagined herself in a long dress on the porch of one of the charming Victorian cottages, with Will seated beside her. She felt as if she'd somehow known him a hundred years before.

She wished she'd met him in high school or college. They could have strolled together across campus as falling leaves drifted to the ground. They could have gone to football games together, with Meghan wearing a wool coat and knit scarf, and Will carrying a warm blanket over one arm. He could have escorted her to the homecoming dance and held her hand through woolen gloves as their boots crunched through fresh-fallen snow.

She stood on her tiptoes to kiss him.

He returned the kiss with a gentle restraint that inflamed her to her fingertips. "So you like the color tour?"

"I love it, especially the guide. But where I grew up, we called it a fall foliage tour."

"Really? So does this measure up to the *fall foliage* . . . wherever you grew up?"

She nodded, smiling. "Definitely. I just wish I'd met you sooner."

"Maybe you did."

"It does feel like I've always known you." She felt a giddy sense of joy that almost scared her. Though she'd been a cheerful and optimistic child until her mother became ill, she'd never known this kind of happiness.

From Bay View, they followed the curve of the lake to Harbor Springs, then on to Mackinaw City. Like a true Michigander, Will held up the palm of his right hand to represent Lower Michigan. "This is where we are right now," he said, pointing to the tip of his middle finger.

She couldn't help but admire his strong, angular pianist's hands.

He'd saved the best for last. He'd made reservations at the Grand Hotel on Mackinac Island. The ferry sped through the converging waters of Lake Michigan and Lake Huron. As they approached the island, she spotted the white colonial-style hotel perched majestically on the hill, overlooking the harbor. According to the guide on the loudspeaker, the hotel's pillared colonnade was the world's longest front porch.

At the docks they were met by the hotel's horse and carriage, which transported them in style through the main streets of the nineteenth-century village, then up into the hills to the Grand Hotel. By the time they checked in, it was nearly dinnertime. As she passed people heading to the dining room, it dawned on her why Will had purchased an expensive dress and gown for her and why he had packed a dress suit, navy blazer, silk tie, and dress shoes for himself. At the Grand Hotel, guests were required to dress for dinner, and Will had gone all out to make this a wonderful experience for her.

After dinner, they danced together in one of the ballrooms. She felt herself floating weightlessly around the room in his arms as the band played classic romantic songs. When they played "When I Fall in Love," nothing mattered to her except the warmth of his arms as he guided her around the ballroom. Gliding across the floor together, they were transported into another reality, where they were safe from her stalker and Will's dark past.

He looked into her eyes. "This can be our song."

But moments later they played "Unforgettable," and the spell was broken. She was reminded of her first dance with Bryan, and a sense of uneasiness forced its way into her consciousness.

The next morning, she took a leisurely stroll through the grounds, past the large, serpentine pool once made famous by the legendary swimming, diving, water-skiing film star, Esther Williams. They spent much of the day bicycling around the island. In the late afternoon, they enjoyed cocktails on the great porch of the Grand Hotel.

"You've outdone yourself this time." Meghan beamed.

He answered with a courtly bow and kissed her hand. Had the mood of the island captured him as well, or had one of them casually drifted into the other's fantasy?

The tour had come just in time. Two days later the shoreline was dominated by dark, angry skies, and most of the remaining leaves were blown off the trees by a biting wind that was a prelude to winter.

CHAPTER 36

Though nights in Tucson were starting to cool off, the heat was relentless, with ninety-degree days pushing into October. Bryan couldn't recall the heat bothering him like this before. He'd made an effort to cut back on his drinking, but decided to deal with it later, once things settled down. He wasn't about to attend AA or enlist the help of a therapist. He still couldn't afford to be trapped in a situation where he'd be expected to share his deepest feelings. He would always need to keep everything stuffed inside.

He felt more alone now than ever. He knew he had no right to the feelings of abandonment and betrayal that had gripped him ever since he'd read Meghan's letter. He'd never made any commitment to her or told her that he loved her. He'd eventually walled her out, as he'd done with every other woman he'd grown to care for.

He didn't feel worthy of having a woman love him, much less Meghan, who deserved only the best. She shouldn't be expected to make a commitment to a man who was but a pale imitation of the man his brother might have become—yet the thought of her with someone else pushed him to the edge of despair.

He was also agitated that Devrek and Maldonado were still at large, and that the missing girls from the vanished treatment center seemed to be a low priority. Though it wasn't his problem, there seemed to be no one else to advocate for them, and he often tossed and turned at night wondering what had become of them. He tried to prod Nevada authorities to intensify their investigation but was told in so many words to back off. He was reassured that everyone involved was doing their best to locate the missing girls, and that the FBI would be calling the shots.

He turned to Sarducci, but once Erin was rescued, the detective bowed out. "Time to move on," Sarducci warned. "We found your friend's daughter."

Bryan was working near peak capacity and sensed he was close to his limit. He was out of ideas and was getting tired—bone-tired.

Working together with Kate had helped bolster his spirits for a while, but he'd pulled away from her when she'd returned from her short trip to Virginia. As he lay on his back, staring into the darkness, he still ached for Meghan.

One night as he tried to fall asleep, he grew increasingly agitated. Shortly after midnight, he went online and reserved a seat on a flight to Traverse City for the next day. He left a message for Lois to shift his appointments for the following week to his chief engineer, or to postpone them. He didn't tell her where he was going. He reached over and stroked Gina's head. In the morning, he'd call the groomer who adored her and drop her off.

He'd never planned to return to Michigan, but at the moment, it seemed to be the only option. Meghan had often implored him to come so they could talk face-to-face. Deep down, he hoped she might want him back. If not, why had she kept trying to call him for so many weeks after she'd sent him the Dear John letter?

As Bryan looked out the window at the ground below, he remembered the flight home from Europe, decades earlier, and how excited he'd been to return home early to Susan. He could never forget the shocking sight of his wife in bed with his brother or her horrified expression as she saw him standing there. Yet whatever had happened next was still a complete blank.

One of them must have said something. But *what*? He must have taken the gun from the nightstand drawer. Had they tried to stop him? Who had he shot first? Whether it was due to an alcoholic blackout or the trauma—maybe both—his mind had managed to blot out all the ugly details of his evil deed for over four decades. He figured it was nature's way of protecting him from the darkness of his own soul.

Bryan picked up an in-flight magazine. His hands trembled. He accepted the flight attendant's offer of a drink, then had several more.

Will stoked the fire in a fruitless attempt to cut the chill wind that whistled through the cracks in Anne's cottage. "I'll be glad to do some caulking for you tomorrow, if it's okay with the Larsens."

"I'd appreciate it. I'll check with Jeff."

He handed her a well-worn copy of *Waiting for the Morning Train.* "You might want to read this to get a deeper sense of Benzie County. Bruce Catton describes growing up here in the early 1900s. He pulls you right into his world at that time."

"Thanks. It sounds interesting." She took the book from him and began to leaf through it. Suddenly she stiffened. "I think I hear something."

"Of course you do." He drew her closer. "Everything movable from Lake Michigan to Lake Huron is banging against something else in the wind."

Will was worried about Anne. Lately she'd been imagining strange sounds and had become downright jumpy. While he'd been doing battle with some internal demon, she always seemed afraid of someone or something *out there.* He'd even seen her cast furtive glances in her rearview mirror, as if she were being followed. He hoped she'd tell him soon what was going on.

Not knowing was starting to get to him, but he stayed focused on projecting calm reassurance. For now, that seemed to be what she needed most. He took her tenderly into his arms, kissed her, then held her in a lingering embrace.

Suddenly there was a loud pounding on the door. The knob turned, and the door flew open. A tall man with gray hair barged into the room. When the intruder spotted the two of them in each other's arms, he froze.

"Sorry to interrupt this cozy rendezvous!" he snapped.

"Bryan!" she cried. "What are you doing here?"

This must be the man who'd terrorized Anne—and he was coming at her!

Will planted himself in front of her. "Go right back out the door where you came in!"

"Why don't *you* leave?" demanded the older man. "I need to speak with her, in private."

"Let's talk some other time, when you're in a better frame of mind," she said.

Will lunged toward the man, his arms raised instinctively in an offensive karate stance.

The intruder's face seemed familiar, and Anne had called him Bryan. His blood ran cold. Could the man whose face was contorted with rage be his *uncle* Bryan? He wasn't sure, since he'd last seen him when he was a small boy.

The man drew back his fist, taking aim at Will. Will raised his arm and blocked the punch, then landed a blow to his solar plexus, knocking the wind out of him. He doubled over and fell to the floor. Will struck him again across the face, and blood rushed from the guy's nose.

"Will! Stop!" she cried.

"Will?" Grabbing his nose in pain, the older man squinted at his opponent. "Will *Ashley?*"

"The same," frowned Will. So it *was* his uncle Bryan! But how could Anne know his name? No time to figure it out. He had to protect her.

"Just as before," his uncle rasped. "First my brother—now my son."

Will tried to comprehend. His uncle was still fighting him, his face a fiery red, eyes ablaze, and breath reeking of alcohol. That *face*!

"It's *you!*" Will shouted. "You're the monster who killed my parents! I ought to choke you with my bare hands! I won't let you hurt Anne!" Bryan was turning redder, and a vein pulsed from his left temple as Will held him down.

"Take your hands off him, Will." Her voice was low and fierce. "Bryan, I know you're upset, but you should have called first. Later, when you've calmed down, we can talk." She placed her hand firmly on his arm.

"You're so right, Susan," he said bitterly. "*If only I'd called first!*"

"I'm not *Susan!*"

"Meghan," he corrected.

Will jerked his head toward her in confusion.

"Let him go!" she screamed.

Will looked up at her, then down at Bryan's gasping, bloody features. "My God! What am I doing?" He loosened his grip on Bryan but didn't let go. "Call the police. He's dangerous."

"He's just upset, finding us here . . . together."

"Why should he be? Who *is* he to you, Anne?"

"He's the man I told you about."

"The one who's stalking you?"

"No. He's the man I told you I was seeing."

Blood raced to Will's face. "You and my uncle were *lovers?*"

"Call an ambulance!" she cried. "He needs help right now. I'll explain later."

Will dialed, leaving bloody prints on the white receiver.

"Bryan, can you hear me?" Meghan whispered. She knelt at his side, wiping blood from his face with a wet towel. "You're going to be alright."

She couldn't comprehend what was going on between Will and Bryan, but somehow this whole ugly mess was because of her.

The paramedics moved in efficiently, took vitals, noted facial lacerations, possible broken nose, and elevated blood pressure.

A sheriff's deputy arrived moments later and took in the scene. "Can someone please tell me what happened here?"

"I was sitting here in the living room with my friend, Will," stammered Meghan. "We heard a loud pounding at the door—"

Bryan broke in, struggling to talk. "There was an intruder. I made the mistake of going after him."

The deputy frowned. "An intruder? What is your name, sir? I need all your names.

"I'm Bryan James. This guy who broke in hit me in the face and stomach. He was holding me down, and Will pulled him off me and chased him out the door."

"Can anyone describe this . . . *intruder?*" The deputy turned toward Meghan.

"It all happened so fast," she mumbled.

"And what is your name?" asked the deputy.

She flushed, then turned to Will, looking directly into his eyes. "My name is Meghan Walcott. I'm from Tucson, Arizona."

Will turned ashen. He sank heavily into a nearby chair.

The officer watched Will and glanced at the blood on his hands, then at the bloody prints on the white telephone. He looked back at Meghan, then at Bryan.

"Will called 911 for me," Bryan offered.

"Whatever you say, pal." The deputy shook his head in disbelief. He shoved his notepad into his pocket, gave Will a dark look, and muttered, "Domestic quarrels—they're the worst. And no one ever wants to press charges."

The EMTs placed Bryan on a stretcher, took his vitals, and moved him to the ambulance.

Hadn't she heard Bryan refer to Will as *son?* But that was impossible. Will's father and mother had been murdered!

CHAPTER 37

Will watched in stunned silence as Anne followed his Uncle Bryan to the ambulance. He saw her lean over and speak tenderly to him as he lay on the stretcher. His uncle whispered something in her ear. She rushed back into the house, looking upset.

The Larsens were watching from across the yard. They must have been alarmed by the police and ambulance racing up their driveway, sirens wailing. He wondered how much they'd seen and heard.

Will stormed back inside. He couldn't look at Anne—or Meghan, whoever she was. How could he ever think of her as *Meghan*, let alone absorb the rest of it?

"Bryan didn't want me to go with him to the hospital. He told me to stay with you."

"How thoughtful of him." His face felt hot. "Looks like you're not too happy about it."

"I'm so sorry about how this happened. I had no idea who he was to you."

"Nor could I ever have imagined who he was to *you!*"

"There's so much I need to tell you," she said. "I'm not sure how to begin."

"Then don't!" Will's voice trembled with rage. He headed for the door.

"Please don't leave now," she pleaded. "This isn't what you think."

"*Isn't* it?"

"I broke up with Bryan back in August, as soon as you and I . . . became more than friends. He never told me he was coming—in fact, we haven't spoken in over two months. I honestly don't understand what's come over him. You and I really need to talk."

"I don't think so."

"Then let's get together after things calm down a bit. If you decide to stop by the hospital later to check on him, could you let me know? Maybe we could go over there together."

"Are you serious?"

"I'd feel a lot better going over there if you were with me," she said.

Will glared at her. "Somehow I get the idea the sight of the two of us together isn't what he wants to see right now."

"I guess not," she stammered. "Maybe we could take turns going in."

Will's eyes blazed with fury. "Just have a little man-to-man talk, is that it . . . *Meghan*? Have a chat about a lifetime of lies? Decide over his hospital bed who gets the girl?"

Meghan turned crimson. "He says he's your father. What's he talking about?"

"My father's dead."

Will had to get out. He headed for the door without turning to look at her. He couldn't. He didn't even know her anymore, and probably never had.

⚹

Before work the next morning, Meghan drove to the end of Main Street, parked on Father Marquette Circle, and gazed out at the harbor and two piers. The horizon was obscured by haze, and the grayness of the lake reached into the sky.

As she opened the door to the Candlestick, a beam of sunlight glanced off hanging crystals and a bright copper kettle. By now she was familiar with each item and knew who might be interested in it.

She felt overcome with sadness. Sandra was scheduled to fly home on Saturday, and by Monday the shop would be back in its owner's hands. It had been peaceful, enjoyable work, and she would miss it, along with the new friends she'd made. These past five weeks had flown by, and now her time as a shopkeeper was coming to an end. So was everything else that mattered. Yesterday her world had come crashing down around her.

Two women came in to stock up on candle-making supplies and to see if the store would take some of their candles on consignment. While she waited on them, tinkling bells announced another customer.

Will stepped inside, his hair tousled by the wind and his eyes swollen and puffy. He looked as if he hadn't slept. She longed to take him in her arms and never let go, even as Bryan lay in a hospital bed because of her. Without meaning to, she'd brought so much pain to those she loved.

"I'll be right with you in a moment," she managed. She turned back to the women, who were staring at Will. They glanced at each other, then back at her. Could they have already heard about the incident yesterday at her cottage?

"I'll be happy to display your candles here," she told them. "I like the way they're made from sand and pebbles from your own beaches."

"Thanks." The heavyset blonde broke into a smile. "We appreciate your support."

His back to her, Will appeared to be absorbed in selecting a ceramic mug.

After the customers stepped outside, he continued to examine the mugs. "Looks like rain," he said, his eyes focused on a point miles away. "I can't work outside today and don't feel like composing. If you still want to go over to the hospital after work, I might as well go with you."

Relief flooded through her. "That would be nice."

"I'll pick you up."

As Meghan rode with Will in silence up the steep, wooded road to the hospital, a large doe stood on the edge of the road and stared directly into her eyes. She commented on the deer, trying to break the ice. He didn't respond.

From the high bluff where the hospital perched above the small harbor town, she felt she could almost make out Lake Michigan through the bare-armed trees.

Once in the lobby, she approached the front desk and asked for Bryan's room number. As she and Will headed down the corridor, they saw a nurse leaving his room. "Can you tell us how he's doing?" Meghan asked.

"Are you his daughter?" asked the nurse.

She felt the heat moving up her neck. "I'm Meghan Walcott, a close friend."

The nurse opened Bryan's chart, glanced at Will, and hesitated. "Mr. James has you down as an emergency contact, Ms. Walcott, along with Mrs. Ashley."

Will moved away to a discreet distance.

"Mr. James has facial lacerations, but his nose wasn't broken. His blood pressure was significantly elevated. So was his blood alcohol level. We decided to keep him here last night to help stabilize him and start the detox."

"Detox?" Meghan was stunned. Though she'd smelled alcohol on his breath yesterday, she'd never thought Bryan had a drinking problem.

"The doctor recommended he spend some time in an alcohol rehabilitation center. We can keep him here a day or two more, until a bed opens up at one of the centers in Traverse City. He's agreed to check himself in."

"Thanks for the update," she said, unable to think of what else to say. She headed back toward the lobby, where she saw Will sitting in a corner, looking angry and unapproachable. She wished she were anywhere else but in this hospital waiting room.

"You can go in first," she said.

She needed a few moments to pull herself together and gather her thoughts. How could she have missed a serious drinking problem? Could it have developed since she'd left Arizona? Kate had seemed worried about Bryan but hadn't been willing to say why.

She told Will what the nurse had said.

"I'm not surprised. I got a big enough whiff of it, and he was acting like an angry drunk."

"I never saw any sign that he drank too much."

"And who better than you to know?" He stood up. "Either I go in now, or I'm out of here."

"Good luck. And tell him I'm here, if you don't mind," she said. "If he doesn't want to see me, let me know."

"I don't get it," said Will.

"What don't you get?"

"He wouldn't let you ride in the ambulance, yet you're his emergency contact. You told me you'd broken up with the other man in your life, but he said he was betrayed."

"I broke up with him over two months ago, like I told you."

"So why did he act like he'd caught you cheating on him. And you're acting guilty! What the hell is going on?"

"I wish I knew." Her voice quavered. "He wasn't himself, and didn't even remember my name. Remember?"

"How can I forget? He was coming at you, calling you *Susan*—my mother's name!"

She winced. "I didn't . . . make the connection."

"And how can I forget you corrected him, saying you were *Meghan*?"

Her face reddened. "I was planning to tell you everything, as soon as they captured whoever was stalking me."

"Guess I found out the hard way," snapped Will. "So tell me. Why is my uncle so angry?"

"I honestly don't know. He stopped taking my calls weeks before I broke up with him, and I never had the chance to talk with him about it. Finally, I had to resort to a letter."

"A Dear John? That's how you broke up with him?"

"He wouldn't answer my calls—"

"Spare me the details. I'm sorry I asked." Will turned abruptly and headed down the corridor, footsteps echoing in the hallway. He couldn't picture himself being alone with Bryan. Sterile hospital smells and ominous beeping sounds only increased the darkness of his mood. His heartbeat thudded in his ears.

Then he saw his uncle hooked to an IV, his face swollen and bruised.

Suddenly he remembered his own words on the night he'd discovered his parents had been murdered. "*That face. I need to remember that face, so I can put an end to it once and for all.*"

Will stood numbly in the doorway until the older man finally looked up.

"Come in," Bryan commanded.

Will ventured across the room to the bedside. "I'm sorry."

"Sorry you didn't finish the job?"

"If you say so."

"Like father, like son," Bryan said.

"Don't call me son, you murdering bastard!"

Bryan felt a current of shock jolt through his body. No one had ever called him a murderer, and here was the only possible witness doing just that! Deep down, he'd held on to a small shred of hope that he hadn't done it. Had his twenty-month-old son witnessed the crime, and *remembered*?

After a long silence, Will spoke again. "You said it was just like before. You were betrayed, like before. By whom?"

"It's gone this far. I might as well tell you everything." Bryan took a deep, labored breath. "When you were twenty months old, I was betrayed by my twin brother . . . your uncle Bryan."

"What in the hell are you talking about? *You're* my uncle Bryan!"

Bryan shook his head, coughed, then continued. "I'm your father, Stewart. Your uncle Bryan was my identical twin brother. He was murdered that night."

Will turned red in the face. "You killed him, didn't you? And my mother too?"

"It sure looks that way, though I can't remember what happened."

"How convenient to forget."

"I'm not so sure about that."

"And I'm supposed to believe you took over your twin's identity?"

"Afraid so." Bryan coughed again, then struggled to go on.

"So you became Bryan." Will frowned. "But my father was listed on my birth certificate as Stewart *Jameson*. Your last name is *James*."

"Guess I dropped off a couple letters."

"Sure, why not?" Will shook his head in disbelief. "Might as well add to the deception."

Bryan didn't respond.

"Why did you give me away?" demanded Will.

"I wanted you to have a good life. I chose Martha, the most loving person I knew, to raise you. I didn't want you to be brought up by a dangerous drunk like me."

"You know my mom?"

Bryan nodded. "She's my aunt Martha, and one of the finest women I've ever met."

Will had to get some air. There was ringing in his ears. His mother was still keeping secrets from him. Everyone had deceived him about who they were and even about who *he* was. And the woman he loved had been with his *father*?

"Why did you send Meghan here, into my world?"

Bryan clenched his jaw. "I needed to get her away from a dangerous predator. I thought you were living abroad. It never occurred to me—"

"That she'd go for the son, too?" Will pushed hard against the window frame and forced it open. He filled his lungs with the damp, chill air. As he turned back, he found himself face-to-face with the sad, dignified, broken features of the man who'd been his demon, but what he saw was a mirror of his own pain.

With a flood of shame, he wondered how different he was from the man lying in the bed—the man who claimed to be his father.

"Why didn't you come back to see me again?" Will dimly recalled one visit through the eyes of a small boy. According to Martha, his uncle Bryan had supported Will for years and had helped send him to the best schools. Will had often wondered about his distant uncle's generosity, considering that he didn't call or visit.

"I didn't feel I could face you again," said Bryan.

"I'm not so sure I can face *you* right now. I need to get out of here."

He found Meghan just where he'd left her in the lobby, hands clenched in her lap. He'd been so absorbed in his own private battle that he'd given little thought to hers. Her eyes pleaded with him to tell her how it had gone.

What must it be like for her to wait while the two men she loved, father and son, met face-to-face? Never trying to deceive anyone, she'd found herself in a most compromising situation. He had almost killed his father over her—at least that was how she must have seen it. Will could only guess how distressing this was to her. His first thought was to protect her and keep her from being hurt. He considered reaching out to embrace her and tell her everything was going to be alright, but he'd said too much already and was too upset to talk right now.

When he'd seen Bryan coming at her, his features distorted with rage, he'd recognized his demon, and his own rage had nearly gotten the best of him. Or had he been overcome by his fear of helplessly standing by again, while the one he loved was killed by the same monster that had killed his mother?

Will turned away from Meghan and walked out of the hospital alone.

Meghan rose from her seat in the waiting room and moved down the hallway as if she were slogging through a bad dream. She found Bryan resting with his eyes closed, his strong, proud face swollen and bruised.

When she took his hand, he squeezed hers so tightly that she flinched. She feared Will might reappear at any moment and observe this small intimacy. Bryan had such a hopeless look—a look she remembered all too well from her father. How could she abandon him now?

His eyelids fluttered. "Darling." He touched her cheek. "I've put you right in the middle of this ugly mess. I'm so sorry. But why? Out of all the men in the world, why my son?"

"That's not fair. You never even told me you had a son! Then you sent me here to live, right in the middle of his world. If you hadn't been so secretive, this *never* would have happened."

"This was the only safe place I could think of on such short notice."

"But didn't you think about your family living here? I was bound to meet them in such a small town."

"I was afraid that you might stumble on someone or something from my past." Bryan frowned. "But I didn't have time to check out other places. I wanted to get you out of danger fast and was willing to take that chance. As for Will, I thought he was living abroad. The last time I saw him, he was a little boy. It never crossed my mind that you and he—"

"You haven't visited him since he was a small boy?"

"Afraid not."

"I almost feel like you set me up. You sent me here, then started shutting me out as soon as I arrived. You wouldn't visit me here, though I kept trying to convince you to come. And you refused to write or take my calls. It felt like you wanted to end our relationship."

"I vowed years ago that I'd never allow myself to be in another serious relationship, after what I'd done. I didn't deserve to be with *anyone*, much less someone as wonderful as you. But I loved you too much. I couldn't bring myself to start . . . distancing from you, until we were apart. Once you left, I decided it was time to start pulling away. Long past time."

Meghan's eyes stung with tears of anger. "Why didn't you tell me you wanted to end it? I asked you how you felt about us, and you refused to discuss it. Then you burst into my cottage without warning. At least you could have knocked! It's as if something came over you, and you weren't yourself."

"It seemed to be happening all over again, just like before."

"What do you mean, 'like before'?"

"I found them together—my brother and my wife. The next thing I remember is that they were dead. Murdered."

"What are you saying?" Meghan cried. "That *you* killed Will's parents?"

"His mother and my twin brother—Will's uncle. He looked directly into her eyes. "I came home from abroad to find my wife, Will's mother, and my twin brother in bed together."

"My God." Meghan grasped the arms of the chair beside the hospital bed and lowered herself into the seat. She was finally starting to catch on. Bryan was Will's "demon"!

"Last night, I might have killed you both," he said. "Thank God Will stopped me."

"For a minute, I was afraid that Will might kill you."

"He'd have been within his rights. I was a threat, and he defended you. Whatever he did to me, I deserved."

"That's not true." After a long silence, she spoke again. "It wasn't supposed to be like this. I'd imagined we would sit down and talk things over, face-to-face. I'd hoped you'd understand, and that we could still be friends."

"I don't know what I thought I could accomplish here. I guess that, at some level . . . I hoped you still had feelings for me. Maybe once you saw me . . ." His voice trailed off.

"You're one of the most important people in my life."

"But not on top of your list." His eyes glistened with tears. He turned away from her and closed his eyes.

※

Martha saw Will storm through the lobby as if he didn't see her. She'd followed him outside, hoping to calm him down, but by the time she reached the exit, he was on a trail heading into the woods.

She returned to the lobby, trying to figure out what sort of disaster had happened yesterday afternoon between Will and his uncle that had landed her nephew in the hospital. She had a feeling it had something to do with Anne.

About ten minutes later, Martha saw Anne hurry through the lobby, obviously distraught. She recalled the first time she and Anne had met, here at this same hospital. Her first reaction had been to blame Anne for what had happened to Will in the storm. Over time, she'd put those thoughts and feelings aside, but maybe her first impression had been right. This woman she'd grown to care about seemed to have driven her nephew and son into some sort of ugly conflict.

Martha headed down the corridor to her nephew's private room with a sober expression. At first glance, he looked older than she could have imagined, and broken. But then, it had been decades since she'd last seen him.

"You didn't have to come, Aunt Martha. I'm sorry to have dragged you into this mess."

"Never mind about that. We'll have plenty of time to talk when you're feeling better. Have they brought you your dinner?"

Bryan shook his head. "I don't feel much like eating."

"Maybe not, but try to eat what you can." Martha ran her hand soothingly over his forehead. "I don't understand it. Will has never raised a hand to anyone in his life. Except in karate, of course."

"I guess this is what he's been practicing for."

"I can't believe he'd do this to you."

"I burst in to her cottage angry and unannounced, and he didn't recognize me after so many years. He was trying to protect her."

"One or two well-placed blows could have accomplished that."

"They were well-placed, all right. Did I help pay for the karate lessons?"

"I'm afraid so. It wasn't my idea, but at least I held out for an instructor who didn't teach his students to break wooden boards and bricks with their hands. Will was a pianist, first and foremost, even at thirteen."

Martha turned to look him in the eye. "The fine arts seem to run in the family."

Bryan gave a crooked smile from the side of his mouth that he could still move. He took her hand and looked into her eyes. "You know, don't you, Aunt Martha?"

"Know what?"

"That it's me, Stewart?"

Her eyes welled up with tears and she embraced him. "I didn't know. But there've been times when I suspected. Your *eyes*. That's how I used to tell the difference between you two when you were little boys. I always saw so much sensitivity and kindness in your eyes."

"For God's sake, Aunt Martha." He had a fit of coughing. "*Kindness*! I killed Bryan—and Susan, too! "

She sat down heavily. For a while she said nothing. Then she turned toward him and touched his face gently, careful to avoid the bandages. "I can't believe that. Look at me, Stewart. Darling nephew, you were the most considerate, gentle boy I ever knew. When I told you about the boy in my Sunday school class everyone made fun of because he stuttered, you went out of your way to befriend him, even though you were teased more after that. You carried crickets and other bugs outdoors to spare their lives. I don't believe you could have hurt anyone."

"Guess I treat bugs better than people. You can't recreate reality just by calling it something else—though I've tried."

"Okay. Then just what *is* the reality? What happened that night when you found them there together? Did you arrive home fully armed?"

He squinted. "I think there was a gun in the nightstand, but let's not talk about that now."

"Why not?"

"Those damned blackouts . . . I could never remember. And with all the pain killers right now, it's even harder to think straight." He rubbed his forehead.

"So you'd had a blackout that night. I take it that you'd had too much to drink."

"Right."

"Then you're not really sure what happened."

"It's pretty obvious, isn't it?"

Martha frowned. "Not to me."

"I found them in bed together. The next thing I knew, the sheriff was at the door of Bryan's apartment, telling me they'd been shot to death. I should have turned myself in. I didn't want to ruin Susan's good name, or Bryan's—and I was a coward."

"Dear God." Martha's face crumpled into tears.

"So now you know," he said. "And when I saw Meghan with Will . . ."

"Who's Meghan?"

"You know her as Anne, which is her middle name. When I saw her with Will, I got upset."

"So she *did* cause the blow-up between you and Will."

"*I* caused it with my own stupidity."

"Are you saying you were involved with Anne . . . romantically?"

"Once upon a time, but she'd broken up with me."

"What's she doing here?"

"She needed to go into hiding. Someone was stalking her and tried to kill her. I sent her here and gave her an alias to use so he couldn't find her. She's still in danger, so please keep this to yourself."

"I understand. But you sent her here, into our part of the world, where we could grow to care for her—and I think she cared about us, too. You should have told me. I can keep secrets."

"That's true."

"Did she know Will was your son?" demanded Martha.

"She didn't even know I had a son."

"If you'd only told me, this would *never* have happened. I'd have made sure of it."

"There are a lot of things I should have done, and more that I shouldn't have done. But it's too late now, isn't it?"

"It's never too late in God's eyes." Martha reached into her purse and carefully unwrapped a small object from an embroidered handkerchief. "I recently came across this in a cedar chest I was cleaning out." She took out an antique silver crucifix. "This belonged to your mother and your grandmother before her. I know they'd want you to have it."

"I wouldn't feel right taking it from you."

"Please. You're meant to have it." Martha gently pressed it into the palm of his hand and folded his fingers around it.

He gripped it tightly. "Thank you. You're the one person in my life I could always count on, Aunt Martha. I want you to know that. And I want you to know how grateful I am to you for doing such an outstanding job of raising my son."

"He's been the light of my life."

"Tell him I love him."

"Tell him yourself."

Martha looked into his eyes and was alarmed by the despair reflected back. She remembered his father's comment in his journal that the older twin's eyes had more of a sparkle to them. She could never forget Bryan's bright eyes and impish smile, which had always projected confidence and joy in being alive, while Stewart's could be brooding and sad, as they were now.

"I hear the cart with the dinner trays coming, so I'll leave you. Try to eat. You've got to get some nourishment."

❧

When Martha arrived home, she watered her plants, made herself a grilled cheese sandwich, and read the weekly newspaper. Then she went into her bottom drawer and retrieved her brother-in-law's journal. She decided to reread it in its entirety.

She thought back to Stewart's funeral, when she'd experienced a chilling sense that she was sitting beside Stewart, instead of Bryan. At the time, she'd thought that she was so grief-stricken that she was starting to lose it.

Later she'd managed to convince herself that Stewart had indeed been the murder victim. Otherwise, it was too terrible to imagine what might have taken place. She'd refused to follow that train of thought.

When he'd gone on to become a successful engineer who excelled at tennis, she'd been convinced that he was Bryan. His emotional distance from her had been further evidence. While Stewart had been very close to her and enjoyed going with her to the library and to movies, the older twin had preferred spending time with his friends. After the funeral, Bryan had become even more distant than she could ever recall him being. Somehow, Stewart appeared to have assumed his brother's personality in almost every way.

He had always sent a generous sum of money to them each month, which was enough to send Will to the best private music tutors, to the Interlochen Fine Arts School, and later to Julliard. He'd told her that as executor of his brother's estate, he'd put Stewart's life insurance policy into a trust fund that was doing very well. She'd been surprised that a struggling young art student had purchased such a large life insurance policy. After the first ten years, Martha felt certain that any life insurance money must be gone, and that Bryan, with no children of his own, was providing for his nephew from his own personal funds.

When Will became independent, Bryan continued to send a check each month for Martha to use as she wished. She'd protested repeatedly and sent the check back several months in a row, but he always added the amount of the returned checks to the current check, which arrived like clockwork every month. She'd finally given in and accepted the money.

She thought back to the last time she'd seen Bryan, over three decades ago. There had been a moment during the visit when she'd once again been gripped by a feeling that she was looking at Stewart. She'd even gone so far as to ask him if he'd ever developed any interest in art.

"He was the artist, not me," he snapped.

"Sometimes when I look at you, I feel I'm looking at him."

Bryan walked to the window, his back to her. "We were identical twins."

"Of course. I shouldn't have said that."

Bryan turned back to her, his eyes moist. "I know that you and Stewart . . . were very close. He loved you very much . . . and so do I."

She put her arms around him and broke down in tears. "I've always loved you both so much."

He returned her embrace, then turned back to the window. "Before I forget, I've noticed that you have quite a few shingles on the garage that are curling up at the ends. If you have any extras, I'd like to get up there and replace them for you before I leave."

"Jake can do it when he gets back from taking a load of iron ore from Duluth through the St. Lawrence Seaway."

"I can get at them right away."

Bryan had replaced all the bad shingles but had never returned to see her or Will again.

CHAPTER 38

Martha had tossed and turned most of the night, trying to figure out what to do. By dawn, she'd formulated her plan. At seven in the morning, it was too early to call Anne, or Meghan, whoever she was. It was going to be quite a while before she'd be able to think of her as anyone but Anne.

At eight o'clock, she dialed Meghan's number and was relieved to get her recording. Martha was in no mood to speak to her, but Bryan had listed Meghan as his number two emergency contact person, and she couldn't think of anyone else she could ask to check on him. Though she didn't want to involve anyone in the family's private business, she wasn't about to ask Will to do it. He would probably need a lot more time before he could face the father he'd long thought dead.

"This is Martha Ashley," she recited after the beep. "I'm sorry to call so early. I'm going to be away until tomorrow afternoon and would appreciate it if you would please look in on my nephew at the hospital again, just to make sure he doesn't need anything. I should be back by dinnertime tomorrow. Thank you."

Martha hated leaving town while Bryan was in the hospital but figured she had to act fast, before he was discharged. The doctor had told her they planned on keeping him in the hospital a couple more days before releasing him, hopefully, to an alcohol rehabilitation program. She'd done her best to avoid thinking about the tragedy for most of her life. Now she only had one or two days to get to the bottom of it.

She called the Comstock Inn in Owosso to reserve a room for the night and taped a carefully worded note to the back door.

Will,
I'll be out of town for a day or two. I'll call you when I get back.
Mom

Will might think she was visiting one of her friends in nearby Traverse City, which was as far as she ever drove these days. If she told him what she had up her sleeve, he'd insist on going along or put the kibosh on the whole plan. She needed to do this alone.

Her nephew needed her help, and she was afraid for him. He sounded like he was ready to give up and confess to a crime he couldn't remember committing. He'd apparently been tormented by guilt about the murder of his wife and brother all these years, yet what little he recalled was mired in confusion. He'd never been arrested, and as far as she knew, no one had ever been charged with the crime. Now it was time to look at the records on the case, if they were still available. It was time for her to find out the ugly truth and face up to it.

A sharp pain shot through her shoulder as she hoisted her overnight bag into the trunk. She painstakingly lowered herself into the driver's seat, fastened her seatbelt, and turned the key in the ignition. She hoped the car was up to snuff. It had been a while since she'd driven her Olds 88 any further than to church or the store, and there wasn't time for a trip-check.

She unfolded her well-worn map of the state of Michigan. With trembling hands, she traced her planned route from Frankfort to Owosso with a yellow highlighter. From Owosso, she'd drive the extra mile to Corunna, the county seat.

Soon she was heading southeast, down heavily wooded M-115. It was too bad that the colors had already peaked, and most of the trees had lost their leaves. She hadn't been back to Owosso for years. She was afraid to think how much things might have changed. She thought of the theater her brother-in-law had managed over sixty years ago and wondered if it was still there.

She wished she'd destroyed his journal without reading it. It was disturbing to discover that her sister and her husband had not had the happy marriage she'd believed, and that a deep resentment between Sarah and John had been focused on the younger twin.

It was dreadful how history had repeated itself. First Stewart's brother had betrayed him with his young bride. Now, in his eyes, his own son had betrayed him with Anne—though that's not how it had really happened.

Martha had always loved both twins dearly and helped her sister with their care when they were young. In retrospect, she could recall her sister often sticking up for Stewart, possibly to make up for his father's preference for the older twin. Martha herself might have been overprotective of Stewart. Maybe she still was.

She probably should have checked out the official records on the murders a long time ago, but hadn't wanted to draw attention to the crime or delve into the details of the terrible tragedy. She'd even stopped following the case in the news. She had done whatever she could to close the door on that part of the past—and to keep it closed.

That was why she'd tried to avoid Joan Larsen for all these years. Back when Bryan and Stewart were boys, Jeff Larsen's parents had helped the Jamesons open and close their cottages when they were downstate. The families had known each other well, so the Larsens' curiosity was understandable, but worrisome. Martha had never told her nephew that Joan's sister-in-law had lived in Shiawassee County at the time of the murders or that Joan had asked a lot of prying questions related to Will's adoption. If he'd known about that, he probably wouldn't have arranged for Meghan to stay on the Larsens' property.

Martha had become very fond of Will's new friend. She seemed to be a lovely person, and it was easy to see how both men had fallen for her. What she *couldn't* understand was why her nephew had tempted fate by sending the woman he cared for into their world without telling Martha who Anne was to him. He'd created this disaster by being so secretive.

As she approached M-127, she was starting to get drowsy. She rolled down the windows and popped a mint into her mouth. Her shoulder was still bothering her, and her right leg was starting to cramp up. She pulled over at a rest stop to get out and walk for a bit. By the time she got back to her car, dark clouds were moving in, and a cold wind was starting to kick up. A few large drops of rain splattered off her windshield.

She turned off onto M-57. She'd miss Uncle John's Cider Mill but could catch it on the way home. Hot apple cider with a fresh buttermilk donut could serve as a little reward when she was done with the whole ordeal. It would be something to look forward to.

She passed several farms and turned south onto M-52. In Owosso, it became Shiawassee Street, where she stopped to gas up at an old familiar station at the corner of King and Shiawassee Streets. She wondered if it was still operated by the same family who'd always been so friendly and helpful. She saw the old bell in front of Central School and blinked back tears at memories of her family and friends as she passed by their old homes. The houses had been well maintained and looked pretty much the same, for the most part, but her loved ones were all gone.

She decided to go straight to the hotel and get settled in before the weather got nastier. She was exhausted and needed to take a nap. Then she'd get a bite to eat before venturing out in search of the truth. Whatever had taken place four decades ago should be in the records at the Shiawassee County Courthouse.

Martha slowly ascended the steep marble staircase. Her arthritic knees ached in the penetrating cold of the late October afternoon that seemed as dark as any December day. Her raincoat, even with the liner, was no match for the icy sleet.

She hurried through the large double doors of the courthouse, not taking time to stop and admire the stained glass of the dome above. She made her way up the staircase only to be told to return to a lower floor. Laboriously, she went back down the stairway.

She entered an office, took a deep breath, and approached the woman at the desk. "I'm writing a book that touches on some unsolved crimes that took place several decades ago."

The young woman behind the counter gave her a blank stare.

"I believe there was a couple murdered in their own home," she continued, trying to steady her voice. She gave the exact date, adding, "I don't think the crime was ever solved."

"You're writing a book on unsolved crimes?"

"That's right." Martha nodded, ashamed at her unabashed lie. "I'd like to start out with that case, if I may. I believe the last name of the victims was Jameson. I'd like to review the public records pertaining to that, if it's at all possible."

The girl disappeared into the back for what seemed like a very long time. Finally a white-haired woman emerged from behind the counter. She regarded Martha carefully, gave her a nervous smile, and offered her a cup of coffee.

Martha declined the coffee, folded and unfolded her gnarled hands, and waited. Her hands were cold, painfully so. She had no business being here, prying into her nephew's tragic past and telling lies in the process. This wasn't the sort of thing she would do—yet here she was, doing it. Something had compelled her to come all this way, and now she was determined to follow through. She had to know, once and for all, what the records showed.

She was deeply worried about both her nephew and her son, but at least Will was reacting with a healthy dose of anger. His father seemed like he was giving up.

Finally the clerk returned, empty-handed. "I can't find any record of that case. I'm sorry."

"Nothing?" Martha couldn't think of what to say next.

"Nothing under the name you gave me or the date. Would you like me to look for one of the other cases?"

Martha frowned, then managed, "I'd appreciate that . . . but not today. Thank you for your time." Crestfallen, she rose to leave.

As she reached the door, the elderly clerk stepped around the counter and followed her into the hallway. "My name is Ruth. Maybe I can help."

"I'd appreciate that."

"Call this number." Ruth handed her a name and phone number written on neatly folded pink memo paper. "It belongs to a retired sheriff's deputy."

Martha thanked her, placed the note in her wallet, and ventured back out into the cold, damp air. She carefully negotiated the steep steps back down to the slippery sidewalk. Then she noticed a sign directing traffic to a handicapped entrance in back and realized she probably could have taken an elevator.

She braced herself against the penetrating wind and rain. Across the street was a rare find—a pay phone. She wished she'd listened to her friend Sandra and gotten herself a cell phone. On the other hand, a pay phone was anonymous.

Martha turned her back to the wind to shield herself from the elements, holding the slip of paper with care to keep it dry. Her hand trembled as she dialed the number.

The phone was ringing . . . five, six rings. Her heart was beating fast. She could hang up now, and no one would ever know about her dangerous meddling.

A gruff male voice answered, jolting her back to reality. "Hello?"

"Hello. Sergeant Haggerty?"

"Sergeant Haggerty, retired."

"I'm sorry to bother you, but Ruth, down at the courthouse, gave me your number."

"Ruth Thompson?"

"I didn't catch her last name." Martha forced herself to continue.

"And I didn't catch yours. But how can I help you? We need to make it fast. I'm heading out for a doctor's appointment."

"I'm writing a book on cold cases," she stammered. "I plan to . . . touch on a few unsolved crimes that took place in Michigan . . . in the early 1970s."

"I'm no longer employed by the sheriff's department."

"I understand. But Ruth seemed to think you might know something about the murder of a young couple years ago. I believe their name was Jameson. No records could be found, and Ruth thought perhaps you might . . . that you might be able to help me with some information."

"About the Jameson case?" asked Haggerty.

"Yes. Do you remember it?"

"A young couple killed in their home. Baby found crying between them. I could never forget."

Martha had to hold on to the sides of the phone booth to keep her balance. Her voice nearly failed her. "I believe that's the one."

"I need to ask you one question before we go on," said Haggerty.

"What's that?"

"Are you personally involved?"

"Personally involved?"

"Let's get right to the point. I'm asking if you're related in some way to the Jamesons. If your interest is only in getting research for a book, then I'm retired and can't be bothered."

After a long pause, Martha finally answered. "Alright then, Sergeant Haggerty. You've made yourself perfectly clear. And I do have a personal involvement with the family."

"Do you know Stewart Jameson?"

Martha's throat constricted. Stewart? No one except for her, Will, and Meghan could know he was still alive—and none of them had known that until yesterday!

"Just a simple yes or no," he said.

Her mind raced. Her nephew could be arrested because of her. She was calling from a pay phone and hadn't given her name, so there was still time to walk away from the call.

"Could you give me an idea what this is about?" she asked.

"Well, ma'am, let me put it this way. If he's still alive, and you and Mr. Jameson were to cross paths in the next day or two, please have him call me at this number. Let's see . . . today's Wednesday. I'll be waiting for his call at noon this Saturday."

CHAPTER 39

The eerie howl of the north wind made Meghan uneasy. The trees outside were bare, but no snow had fallen yet to soften the stark, desolate landscape. She decided to have another cup of coffee and take a hot shower. Then she'd have oatmeal with cinnamon while reading *Waiting for the Morning Train,* the book Will had loaned her just before the disastrous altercation with Bryan.

The phone rang while she was in the shower. Her neck and shoulders tightened as she played back Martha's message. She dreaded another visit to the hospital to see Bryan, yet that's exactly what she'd been asked to do. What more could she possibly say to him?

Moments later the phone rang again.

"This is Jack, from HR. There's been a change of plans. The principal at Lincoln decided not to wait until the end of the semester to retire. He's leaving as soon as he gets his points."

"When's that?" asked Meghan.

"On his birthday, this Friday."

"This Friday? What happened?" She was aware that early retirement could be taken when an employee's age plus years of service reached a certain number, but this was ridiculous.

"Normally I can't say much because of HIPPA, but it's public information now. It's all over the news. You can go online and find several versions of what happened. One student's parents are up in arms that their son, a star soccer player, got suspended for the third time this year. They convinced one of the TV stations to do an investigative story, and he wound up getting raked across the coals by the media."

"One battle too many," said Meghan.

"So it seems. We'll have a school with no principal in less than a week."

"This is all very sudden. I've got important obligations here too." She couldn't leave town with Bryan still in the hospital, especially after Martha's call. Most of all, she needed time to work things out with Will.

"I know this is short notice, but I'm afraid the offer depends on you being able to start next week."

"I see. Is there anything else?" She'd read online about some problems at the school.

"There have been a few issues with the community."

"Such as?"

"Several parents were angry about suspensions, demanding that all discipline be handled on campus. You know how it goes. Don't bother me at work, and clamp down on those other bad actors, but not *my* kid."

"I saw online that some of those kids were suspended for selling drugs on campus. If the district wants things swept under the carpet, I'm not the one for the job." Her instinct was to decline the offer and hang up. She wasn't about to take on a leadership role, only to let the school be overrun by drug dealers.

"The board wants an active problem-solver, someone who really cares about the kids and has a strong background in community relations. I told them that they were describing you."

"That means a lot coming from you, Jack. I appreciate your going to bat for me."

"I'm going to bat for the kids and the school district, too."

But what about putting students in danger, she wondered. Devrek was still at large, as far as she knew. "I hate to bring this up, but what about the fire incident? Is the superintendent ready to bring me back on board?"

"He signed off on it. You can't stay on leave forever. The crisis period has passed, and we have to move on."

Meghan didn't want to draw violence to a school just by being there, but she needed to get back to work. Her savings were dwindling down, and her career was at stake. Devrek was probably living it up somewhere abroad. If he'd been in the country, she figured the US Marshalls would have tracked him down by now, especially after he'd slipped and let Erin hear his voice.

"Can you give me three days to get back to you?" she asked. "I'm in the midst of a crisis that I need to deal with at this end."

"Forty-eight hours," he countered. "If you don't want this, we've got to get someone else."

"Okay. I'll call you the day after tomorrow."

She set down the phone, trying to think clearly. This was the opportunity she'd been looking for, yet the timing was terrible.

A week ago she'd been happier than she'd ever felt in her life. She'd been confident that her relationship with Will was solid and that their love for each other would continue to grow stronger every day. Now she was being pushed to uproot herself again and to leave Will behind—along with Bryan, Martha, the Larsens, and the small town she'd come to love.

Before she made her decision, she needed to talk things over with Will, but he clearly wasn't ready to talk with her. Telling him about her directive to return at once to Tucson could bring their relationship to a head at the worst possible time. It would probably come across as an ultimatum: make a commitment to me now, or I'm leaving for Arizona. Right now, his answer was *not* likely to be what she wanted to hear, but what could she do?

First, she needed to head over to the hospital, check on Bryan, and put that ordeal behind her. After yesterday, she wasn't ready to face him again, but Martha was counting on her.

Twenty minutes later, as she looked into his hospital room, she was overcome with a sense of despair. As Bryan slept there in the hospital bed, he struck her as a broken man. She decided not to wake him.

The nurse told her his vitals were better, and his condition was stable. They were still waiting for a bed for him at a rehab center.

Mind spinning, she left the hospital and headed toward the beach. She parked near the boardwalk and walked to the end of the pier, hoping that being out there would give her the perspective it usually did.

Across the bay, the southern pier was awash in large breakers, but she was able to make her way to the end of the leeward pier. As the jetty angled toward the lighthouse, large swells gushed along the concrete breakwater, licking over the side like an enormous serpent's tongue. She had less than two days to let HR know her decision. By next week she could be back in Tucson, far from the man she loved and the world she now considered home.

For an instant, the dark water held a strange appeal. She could almost comprehend what her father might have felt. In one crashing roar, all the raging feelings that shrieked through her would be silenced.

She shuddered. She would never give in to such feelings, even if things seemed hopeless. She loved life too much. She'd decided long ago to live out her life and to live it fully. She'd always found a way to tackle her problems head on, and she would now. Though she'd battled with grief and despair, she'd never suffered from the kind of all-encompassing chronic depression that had afflicted her father.

After his suicide, Meghan had been tormented by anger, guilt, and depression. She'd studied hard and earned straight A's while feeling more alone in the world than she'd ever thought possible. One day at school she'd looked in the mirror and seen dull eyes staring back at her, eyes much like her dad's had been in his last months.

Although there had been a blizzard going on outside, she'd felt compelled to get away from her cramped dorm room. Bundled up in a long wool coat, boots, a stocking cap, and scarf, she ventured out into the snowstorm. She walked through the campus for hours, under the tall, bare-armed trees and snow-covered pines, silent tears spilling down her cheeks.

"And miles to go before I sleep," she said to herself, quoting a line from one of her father's favorite poems, "Stopping by the Woods on a Snowy Evening," by Robert Frost.

At dusk, she trudged back to her dorm through the deep snow. She climbed the icy steps of the old dormitory, stomped snow off her boots, and stepped into the vestibule. Once inside the lobby, she felt a rush of warm air and was enveloped by the inviting aroma of dinner.

Her spirits lifted as she heard strains of *Claire de Lune* being played by a student on the piano in the lobby. She caught sight of herself in the mirror in her long navy coat. Her cheeks were rosy from the cold, and her hair was decorated with melting snowflakes. Two friends gestured for her to sit with them. She approached them, smiling.

That was the moment she'd decided to embrace life rather than withdraw in despair. After dinner, her grandparents had called, reminding her how much they loved her. She'd choked back tears. "I love you too." They were her family now, and she was theirs.

She went on to join the university choir and dated a boy in her history class who'd been trying to ask her out all semester. She went with him to concerts, football games, mixers, and movies, and enjoyed the fun and excitement of being with her first real boyfriend. She grew more determined each day to be strong enough to face life, no matter what it held.

Even today, she wasn't depressed as much as distraught that Will had turned his back on her, refusing to let her explain. She understood that he needed time, but she didn't have the luxury of time.

She returned to her car and headed to Will's cottage. Though his Jeep was gone, she knocked on the door. She considered leaving him a note, but she'd already left messages on his home phone. Too bad he hadn't let her replace his cell phone that was lost in Lake Michigan.

She headed north until she reached Leland. She thought of her sad trip there after their breakup and then of her delightful visit there with Will on their wonderful color tour. She headed out onto the docks of the marina, hoping the sights and sounds of moored boats would help lift her spirits, but most of the boats were gone for the season.

Something always drew her to sailboats. She thought of her disastrous attempt at sailing on Lake Michigan and how the storm had thrown her together with Will. They had both believed it was meant to be. Now she wasn't so sure.

Crimson rays of the setting sun splashed along the lower edges of the dark clouds. She pulled up the hood of her new fleece-lined parka against the chill. Just before nightfall, she turned back toward Frankfort, heading south to her cottage on the edge of the woods. She drove slowly, scanning the sides of the road for reflections of the bright eyes of deer. She'd been warned that they often jumped out in front of cars, causing accidents.

She was down to the wire on her decision, and needed to find a way to calm down and analyze what to do. She was being asked to leave both Will and Bryan and move back to Tucson for a new position as a school principal. It was clear to her that turning this offer down would end her chances for career advancement with the school district and could even get her terminated. She would probably have to bow to the district's pressure to report for work next week.

She hadn't been crazy about being assistant principal, with all the discipline, but had considered it a stepping-stone to becoming a principal, where she could set the tone and policy for a school. Here was her chance, but it felt all wrong. Her stomach was in knots.

She picked up a pizza and a bottle of Merlot. Back at the cottage, she piled several logs in the fireplace, and placed kindling wood and newspapers around them to get a fire going.

Seated before the crackling fire, she poured herself a glass of the wine, took out a pad of paper, and drew a line down the middle of the page. At the top she wrote, "Accept Job at Lincoln High and Leave Michigan." On the left side she wrote "Pros," and on the right side, "Cons."

She hoped this would help her make a rational decision, but she couldn't bring herself to write anything down. It was really very simple. If she refused the position, not only would she lose her opportunity for career advancement and the chance to make a real difference as a school principal, but she'd probably lose her job, her income, and her health care. She wanted to stay in Michigan because she loved Will. But she'd lost his love and trust, and it was too late.

Her eyes filled with tears. She'd already lost everything she cared about and had nothing to gain by staying here. Will was avoiding her, and who could blame him? Finding out that his father had been alive all along had to be mind-blowing, but the shock of learning that his father was his mother's murderer *and* the other man in Meghan's life would be too much for any man to cope with.

Martha also seemed to be turning a cold shoulder to her. Of course she was angry. She even noticed people whispering about her when she went into town. Once again, her world had been smashed.

Her decision was clear. She tore off another sheet of paper and began to scrawl off a letter.

> *Dear Will,*
>
> *Please call me. I need to talk with you right away.*
> *I never meant something so beautiful to bring such ugliness, and I didn't mean to deceive you. I had no idea who Bryan was to you or that he even had a son.*
>
> *Love, Meghan*

She set the letter aside, added a log to the fire, and began a second letter.

> *Dear Bryan,*
> *Rage was your love turned inside out. Reverse the fabric, and you'll find the good man that you are.*

She closed the curtains, pulled a thin blanket around her, and stared at the crackling fire. Then she dashed off a third letter.

> *Dear Daddy,*
> *I'm so sorry. I should have stayed home and found a way to help you. But why did you leave us, when we needed you so much?*

She wadded up all three letters and tossed them into the fireplace. The flaming words rose upward through the chimney and disappeared into the cold, damp air.

CHAPTER 40

Wind whined through the trees, and something was rapping against the roof. It was probably only a branch, but Meghan's entire being screamed of something wrong. She glanced at her alarm clock. It was 4:47 in the morning.

She pulled up the covers, only to be awakened two hours later by a nightmare. This was the most vivid it had ever been—her father underwater, gasping for air. She saw it with such a terrible clarity that she couldn't drive it from her mind.

She decided to check on Bryan again later this morning but first needed to have a solid breakfast. She'd had nothing but a slice of pizza and wine since yesterday morning, and her head was throbbing.

She stopped at a nearby restaurant and ordered scrambled eggs, cottage fries, and orange juice. When it arrived, she remembered the marvelous breakfast Will had prepared with such loving care on the morning he'd told her he loved her, just before she'd broken up with him. All she could get down was a slice of toast and coffee.

She took two Excedrins, paid for the uneaten breakfast, wrapped the rest of the toast in a napkin, and headed to the hospital. Blinding rain pounded the windshield, making it hard to focus. When she saw a man standing on the side of the road, she felt as if her father were watching her through the rain. She could almost hear him calling her name, warning her.

"What do you want? Tell me!" she cried. She had to get to the hospital. She stepped on the gas, squinting. Her vision was blurred by both tears and rain as she drove up the hill. She leapt from her car and rushed into the lobby and down the hallway, coming to an abrupt stop in front of the doorway to Bryan's private room.

His bed was empty. She hurried to the nurses' station.

"Mr. James has checked out," said the nurse. "He left against doctor's orders. He said his son was coming to pick him up."

"His *son?*" Meghan felt light-headed. She stopped by a restroom and doused her face in cold water.

Still swollen and bruised, with elevated blood pressure, Bryan was supposed to have gone straight into a rehab program. Meghan couldn't picture Will picking him up and bringing him home and could not imagine Bryan agreeing to stay with Will.

She tried to call Will again, then drove out to his cottage. Seeing that his Jeep was still gone, she headed back to Frankfort.

Though Martha's message had said she'd be gone until later today, Meghan jumped out of the car and rapped on her front door. Then she went around to the back and saw the note taped to the back door. What would she tell Martha when she returned? That she'd lost Bryan?

She raced home, screeched into the driveway, and hurried into the cottage, hoping for some message that would make sense of things, but there were no messages.

For a fleeting moment, she considered calling the sheriff but decided against it. She'd been told that Bryan was with Will, and it was possible. Either way, Bryan would be furious to have that kind of attention. Worse, she might get him in trouble with the law, if what he'd said about killing his wife and brother were true. His name might still be on a wanted list for cold cases. Hadn't she heard something about there being no statute of limitations on murder?

She fought to stay calm, despite rising panic. Where *was* everyone? Once she tracked down Bryan and made sure he was okay, she had to find Will. She needed his input about her career decision, even if it *was* a bad time. She had just one day left to decide what to do.

Bryan had held his jealous rage in check, and for that he was thankful. No one had been seriously hurt this time—at least not physically. That he could no longer hold back a lifetime of unshed tears was of little consequence to him now. Once again, he'd lost everything, including what he'd been most afraid of losing.

His ugly confrontation with the son he'd abandoned had further traumatized Will and hurt Meghan, the only woman he'd loved since Susan. He'd also distressed his aunt, the one person who'd loved and stood by him all these years, raising his precious son as if he were her own. He owed his aunt Martha everything, yet had brought her only worry and misery. At least if they ever found him, he'd be considered a victim of the storm. No one would have to blame themselves.

Bryan felt a strange sense of peace as he rowed out into Lake Michigan in a small rented fishing boat, watching the approaching storm with resignation. From the northern sky came the billowing darkness that announced the approaching squall line. Angry gray clouds were forced upward by the encroaching mass of cold air. Waves rocked the small boat, and he steeled himself to the chill wind's assault.

Will nailed down the last of the shutters on a summer mansion perched on the high, rolling hills between Lake Michigan and Big Crystal. Working outdoors as a handyman and having tangible results every day had been a nice change of pace. Soon he'd have his symphony completed and would be ready to take the next step in his musical career.

He pounded each nail with intense concentration. Even the smallest task seemed to require enormous effort these past two days. His rage toward his uncle—his *father*—had dissipated. Will was at last free from the unexplained torment he'd battled throughout his life. Yet instead of relief, he felt as if his heart and guts had been ripped from his body.

The concept of Bryan as his father was a bizarre abstraction, but Bryan's relationship with Meghan was painfully real. Neither his uncle nor the woman he loved had turned out to be who he thought they were. Anne, the woman he'd thought he loved, had been an illusion.

He had to talk with his mom. He needed her support now more than ever, but when he'd stopped by her house, he'd found a worrisome note taped to her door. She didn't have a cell phone and had left no explanation, phone number, or address.

He wanted to sit with her in the kitchen and talk while she prepared dinner. She'd always been able to get to the heart of things, even while following a complicated recipe. He'd never told her how he felt about Anne, but she must have guessed. He hoped that someday Martha could help him make some sense out of everything that had happened. He wanted to talk with her about how he felt trapped in a web of deception. Yet *she* was at the heart of the greatest lies of all: who his parents were, how they'd died, and who she was to him.

Bryan had told Will yesterday that his adoptive mother, Martha, was also his great aunt. She and Bryan had a close relationship, and Will had been kept in the dark about that too. He'd always believed his Uncle Bryan was his only living relative. Martha had kept his past from him, and because of that, he'd gone through needless struggles trying to understand what had been bothering him.

It was so unlike her to go off alone without telling anyone, particularly in the midst of a crisis, with her nephew in the hospital. She was such a caring and sensitive mother, yet she'd left him alone to face this nightmare. He'd been deceived by everyone, including Anne.

He considered returning her calls but couldn't bring himself to pick up the phone. What could he say? He was still too angry to muster up a civil response.

He heard a faint rumble of thunder in the distance and hammered faster to finish before the storm hit. He could see it coming across Lake Michigan. Then he saw lightning. In frustration, he packed up his tools and climbed down the ladder. Now he'd have to return another day and set everything up again.

He loaded up quickly, started the Jeep, and drove along the west shore of Crystal Lake to his turnoff. As he pulled onto his property, he noticed the sky had darkened into a sulfurous hue. He swore under his breath as he spotted a small fishing boat nearing the point. Of all the boundless stupidity. He was tired of seeing careless boaters floundering as they passed the point.

The beacon light of the Point Betsie Lighthouse was still an official Coast Guard navigation light, but Will wished the lighthouse were still

manned. Computerized back in 1983, the lighthouse was now a historical building overseen by the county. With his cottage so close to
the lighthouse, Will was in the unenviable position of spotting boats in
trouble as they rounded the windswept point.

The thunder was louder. He scanned the horizon again. The fishing
boat appeared to be heading west, right into the approaching storm.
Damn!

He knew the Coast Guard number by heart but was suddenly drawing
a blank on it. He dialed 911 and reported the boat that was in trouble.

Outside, the wind roared and waves pounded the shore. He hauled
in two big logs for a fire. Even if his boats hadn't already been in storage
for the season, Will knew they wouldn't have been of much use in getting
past the huge breakers.

He decided to play some Chopin and try to get his mind off things
for a while. From now on, these careless boaters were going to be the
Coast Guard's problem—not his.

❧

The low hanging blue-black clouds darkened the sky over the rented
fourteen-foot aluminum boat. It was two in the afternoon but seemed
much later. Bryan knew the sheets of rain rooting along the surface of
the water were the angry snout of the predicted cold front. A shiver ran
through him as the icy wind penetrated his very soul.

All those empty years alone, and then feeling alive and in love, only
to be betrayed once again. The vision of his brother in bed with Susan
forced itself into his mind. Suddenly he heard an echo of his brother's
voice. "Guess you've gone and married yourself a little tramp."

"You bastard!" Susan's words screamed through his mind.

Now that he was about to die, was he finally starting to remember?

The barrage of hail that followed was so violent that Bryan dropped
the oars and covered his face with his hands. Enormous waves bore down
in a booming roar.

His heart hammered in his chest, and he felt the storm's terrible force with every nerve in his body. It was almost time. Pain, unbearable pain, was all he was, and soon it would be over.

He thought of Kate and Erin. He felt grateful he'd been able to help save Erin's life and reunite her with Kate. He'd come to love them both. At least he'd done some good along the way and had loved someone. He loved his son, Will, who despised him, and felt closer to his aunt Martha than he ever had in his life. He knew he would always love Meghan and Susan. He even loved his twin brother. He'd tried to *become* him, for God's sake.

"*I'm not Bryan!*" he cried out. Yet he'd stopped being Stewart a long time ago.

A feeling of radiance and love flooded through him. With a gut-wrenching jolt of regret, he realized that at this moment, he was more alive and at peace than he'd been in a long, long time. In that brief instant, he accepted the pain that he'd felt he could no longer endure.

"God forgive me." He took the crucifix Martha had given him from his pocket and clasped it tightly. He heard a loud roaring sound overhead.

The tiny craft was thrust high into the air on the crest of an enormous wave and then flung end-over-end through the air. As angry walls of water crashed down on him, Bryan realized, too late, that he wanted to live.

Will peered through his binoculars from the deck of his cottage on the dune, recalling how his second encounter with Anne was in a storm such as this. How close they'd been to becoming victims of the lake—then later, how close to finding true happiness together. He'd never been so happy in his life as during these past few months with her. Yet her alter ego, Meghan, had never been his. Thinking back, she'd made it crystal clear from the beginning that she was involved with another man. He'd never really known her.

Then his father had appeared from nowhere and destroyed his life, once again. "Like father, like son," Bryan had said, in words that had struck Will like a physical blow. Unbridled rage had driven his father to murder. Will wondered if he was any different. He'd been afraid Bryan would injure Anne, yet he hated to think of what he might have done to Bryan if she hadn't shouted at him to stop. Had his fear that Bryan was a threat to her been realistic, or was it distorted by confused memories of what had taken place so long ago? Something about Bryan's angry features had triggered Will's rage and deepest fears.

There were so many questions he needed answered—questions only his father could address. He reached for the hand-carved wooden whistle he'd made as a boy for an imaginary father, after he had carved a small boat for Jake. He'd never dreamed that his distant uncle Bryan was his father.

He reached for the phone and dialed the nurse's station to see if they knew when Bryan was to be discharged.

"Can you please hold?"

Finally the nurse came back on the line. "Mr. James checked himself out against doctor's orders. He told the orderly who escorted him out in a wheelchair that his son was going to pick him up."

"That would be me," Will blurted out, surprised to hear the words coming from his own lips. "And I didn't pick him up."

"Do you have a brother?"

"No." Not that he knew of, anyway. "Thank you for your help."

Will hurried outside, jumped into the Jeep, and raced back to Martha's house. He checked both doors and peeked in the windows. The blinds were closed, and his mom's note was still taped to the back door.

Could Bryan be with his mother or with Meghan? Were they all together somewhere?

He drove up the driveway to Meghan's cottage and saw that her car was gone. On the way out, Joel told him she'd been gone for most of the day, though she'd dashed back to the cottage a couple of times and left again in a big rush.

Maybe Bryan was staying overnight at a local motel. Will let himself into his mother's house, dialed the Betsie Bay Inn, and was told that Bryan wasn't registered there. He called other motels. After several tries, he called the Harbor Resort.

"Sorry. Mr. James is out."

"Did he say when he'd return?"

"I don't believe so. Just a moment. The desk clerk from first shift is leaving, and I think he spoke with him."

Will waited, while a muffled conversation took place on the other end of the line.

"Thanks for waiting. It seems that Mr. James asked our night desk clerk where he might rent a fishing boat to take out on the lake. He seemed very anxious to go fishing. Of course, we advised him against it, with this weather."

"Mr. James asked about how to rent a fishing boat for today, on Lake Michigan?"

"That's what I was told. Hopefully, he's just out in the bay."

"Thanks." Will headed to the marina and looked out. The only boats he could make out were docked or moored.

Meghan headed north on M-22 in one last attempt to find Will at home. She still needed food but was gripped by panic and an inexplicable sense of dread.

She raced to Point Betsie Road and turned off on the unpaved road that led to Will's place. Large breakers pounded the beach, and dark clouds rolled in from the southwest. Still no Jeep. She spun around in the sand without coming to a stop, then sped back to town. As she passed the Congregational Summer Assembly on the west shore of Crystal Lake, driving rain pelted her windshield, as if it were pummeling her throbbing head.

Will raced toward the harbor overlook, driving through a blinding wall of rain. The electrical storm seemed to have passed through, but no one should be out there in a small fishing boat in this weather, let alone an injured, alcoholic, old man who'd just left the hospital against doctor's orders.

He turned up the entry road to the Coast Guard station and saw parked cars everywhere. There must be something going on. He sped on to the Benzie County Sheriff's Office in Beulah, where one of his old friends, Jerry Carr, was a deputy. He squealed to a stop and raced up the steps, two at a time.

"Will! Good to see you. What's up?" asked Jerry.

"Hi, Jerry. I'm sure glad to see you. Any chance I could get an update on that 911 call I made about the fishing boat in distress out by Point Betsie? Is the Coast Guard on its way?"

"Hold on. I'll check." Jerry picked up the phone and punched in a number.

"The man in the boat could be my . . . my father." Will nearly choked on the word.

Jerry's eyes widened in surprise. "I'll see if I can find out." He picked up the phone and spoke a few words, but he mainly listened and nodded.

Then he returned to Will. "How do you take your coffee?" asked Jerry.

"Black. What's going on?"

"The Coast Guard was going to send out a rescue boat from Frankfort, but the waves are over their limit now. It would take them too long to get out there, anyway."

"So now what?" asked Will. "Someone's got to do something!"

Jerry poured coffee that looked like old motor oil into a Styrofoam cup. "As I understand it, our Coast Guard distress calls get routed through District Command in Cleveland, go to Sector, then go back to a unit operations officer at the station where they're assigned. It's done as fast as possible, but they go through the chain of command. They cover an enormous area. Luckily, a Coast Guard Rescue Copter out of Traverse City is returning from a rescue just south of here."

"Can they get there in time?" Will caught his cup as it started to go over. He took a sip.

"I hope so. If the weather gets too bad, they might have to delay. They're not supposed to fly into electrical storms, but I think that's passed through. Maybe they can come in behind the storm."

"You seem to know a lot about the Coast Guard."

"We work closely together, and my brother's in the Coast Guard."

"Where do you think they'd bring him in?"

"Probably Munson Hospital in Traverse City. They've got a helipad, and patients often wind up getting transported over there by ambulance anyway. I'll let you know. Now we just sit tight and wait."

"Looks like we've got no choice."

"Your father will be in good hands." Jerry frowned. He thought Will's dad was an ore boat captain who'd died years ago. "These Coast Guard rescue crews do amazing work. But if you know how to pray, this would be the time."

"US Coast Guard Air Station Traverse City, this is Coast Guard Rescue Copter 6500," said the pilot. "Small fishing craft sighted. Stand by."

The crew, including Shriver, the Rescue Swimmer, had just done a tough rescue in high waves and wind. They'd been heading back to the Coast Guard Station in Traverse City when they got the call that there was an individual in trouble in a small fishing boat, northwest of Frankfort.

A small boat would be at high risk under these storm conditions, where seas were too high to even take the rescue boat out.

As they neared the survivor, waves were at seven feet, air temperature at fifty-two degrees, and water was sixty-eight degrees. A thirty-five-knot left quarter head wind had been reported.

Shriver spotted an individual in a small aluminum boat moments before the boat was upended by a large wave. "Person in the water!" he reported. They'd have only minutes to rescue someone in a wetsuit, and this guy didn't look like he was wearing one. Not many survived more than a few minutes in the cold October waters of the Great Lakes. There was truth to the old sailors' maxim: Life jackets are to help find the bodies.

"Put wind off nose, one o'clock, wind is sixty off the nose. Roger."

The Rescue Swimmer moved to the doorway of the open cockpit, tethered by a harness and wearing a wetsuit and neoprene hood. As a Rescue Swimmer, he was an EMT, while the pilot, copilot, and flight mechanic were qualified in CPR and first aid. He scanned the water for a bobbing head or a life jacket, maintaining communication with the pilot through headphones.

The pilot angled the craft into the wind with precision, hovering as close as feasible to the survivor in the water below. The Rescue Swimmer adjusted the harness before he was lowered into the angry, dark waves.

The spotlight from the helicopter shone on an object hurling through the foam toward him. Damn! The victim wasn't even in a life jacket! Shriver swam toward the spot where he estimated they could intersect. He braced himself, reached out, and with one powerful grasp, seized the human projectile. He locked his arm under the man's shoulder.

"Hold on!" he yelled against the roar of the wind.

Dan felt the man's hand grip his arm. He radioed for the double lift.

When it was lowered down, he carefully positioned the survivor into the rescue sling so he could be hoisted up in a seated position, head elevated and legs not too low, which was important in cases of hypothermia. The man was trembling violently.

The cable started to whine, and the survivor was reeled upward, by increments. "Survivor fifty feet from aircraft. Survivor ten feet from aircraft. Survivor at the door." Then he was pulled into the chopper.

They lowered the sling back down for the Rescue Swimmer. As he was raised into the cabin, he felt the blood race through his veins, but he was oblivious to the effects of the cold on his own body. It was a great feeling to snatch someone from certain death.

The doors closed, and the helicopter began to ascend. One of the crew placed the survivor on the stretcher, rubbed him down gently with a rough towel, and wrapped him in special air blankets designed for hypothermia. Shriver took his vitals.

"Probable hypothermia, possible shock. Blood pressure elevated. Breathing on his own. Facial lacerations from a prior injury."

Shriver placed his hand reassuringly on the man's arm. "You're going to be okay," he said with more confidence than he felt.

The man shivered and tried to speak. His fist was clenched, as if he held something.

"Save your talking for later," Shriver said. "Just rest, and we'll get you over to Munson Hospital in Traverse City, where they can get you all warmed up."

"We're less than two miles out of Frankfort, and we're low on gas," said the pilot. "We're landing in Frankfort." The ambulance can make the call whether to take him to Paul Oliver or transport him over to Traverse City."

"Funny thing," he added a moment later. "They just told me our survivor's already registered at Paul Oliver, and he's supposed to be there right now."

Meghan pulled to the side of the road near the Frankfort Gateway arch to allow the ambulance to pass. She heard a deafening roar overhead and looked up to see a Coast Guard helicopter heading toward the small Frankfort airport. Then she spotted Will's red Jeep making a high-speed turn onto Airport Road.

With numbing dread, she followed him toward the small terminal building. She leapt from her car as leaves and sticks were sucked upward in a violent whirlwind as the chopper landed.

She stood beside the car and watched a stretcher emerge. *It was Bryan!*

It couldn't be! Her worse fears had come true. Another man she loved had killed himself. This time she was the direct cause.

She ran toward him. When she was closer, she could see that his face was red and uncovered and that he was tightly clutching something. He was still alive!

Tears streamed down her face as she watched him being transported to the ambulance. She felt Will beside her and reached out to touch his arm. He moved away.

Overcome with gratitude for being spared the fate he'd chosen for himself hours earlier. Bryan felt an unfamiliar sense of calm moving through him. It was time to come forward and confess his crime. No more living a lie.

Over the roar of the propeller blades and shrieking wind, he heard the voice of his rescuer. "We're on the ground now. You're going to be okay. The ambulance is right here to get you over to the hospital and stabilized. You take care of yourself now."

Bryan managed a thank-you, which didn't begin to express his deep gratitude. He felt bad that he'd risked all their lives in an attempt to take his own.

Two men approached with a stretcher and more blankets; then he noticed a man and woman standing together. Meghan and Will, as it should be. He relaxed his hand, which was sore from holding the crucifix so tightly. He felt himself sinking . . .

CHAPTER 41

Will sat stiffly in Martha's living room, across from his mother and Bryan, who had just been discharged from the hospital. He'd been treated for hypothermia, along with his original injuries, and released to Martha after refusing treatment in an alcohol rehab center. He claimed he'd already dried out and never planned to take another drink.

Will pulled at a loose thread on the cushion.

"Please don't pick at that," said Martha. "My mother did that needlepoint."

He pushed the cushion aside. "Where were you for the last two days, Mom?"

"We can discuss that later."

"No time like the present." Will tried to control the anger in his voice.

He noticed that Bryan's eyes were fixed on the framed photographs on the opposite wall, showing Will at different stages of boyhood. Most were of Will with his stepfather: Will and Jake holding a big stringer of fish, hiking, playing in the waves, and sailing. Jake had been there for him, while his birth father had masqueraded as a distant, absentee uncle.

Martha's new painting hung over the couch. Will wished he were standing on the banks of that wooded stream right now, casting for trout, like the man in the painting.

"Going out on the lake like that in a tiny fishing boat on such a stormy day wasn't a very good idea," Martha said to Bryan, as if he were a small boy who'd played hooky. "You should have checked the weather first. You need to take better care of yourself."

"You're right," Bryan said, looking down at his hands.

"You too, Will," she said. "You've risked your life too often this summer to save other people from drowning. I'm proud of you—but I hope you'll be more careful."

Will stared at her in silence.

"Maybe you've been out West for so long, Bryan, that you've forgotten how dangerous Lake Michigan can be, especially this time of year." His mother rambled on, still glossing over the truth, as if Bryan had only been careless.

Will set his mug down hard, splashing coffee onto the end table. "I didn't get the impression it was an accident. Correct me if I'm wrong." He looked at Bryan.

Bryan turned beet red. "You're not wrong."

Martha cast Will a warning glance. "You'd never try something like that again, would you?" she asked Bryan, as Will daubed up the spill with a paper towel.

"No, I wouldn't. I can promise you that." Bryan tightened his grip on the arms of the overstuffed chair. "I'm very sorry for what I've put you all through."

"We're just thankful you were rescued. I hope you know that I love you very much. You're welcome to stay here until you're stronger and feel ready to face the world again," said Martha. "You can rest up and get better. Tonight I'm making you both hot chicken soup, and Dutch apple pie. That used to be your favorite, Bryan."

"It still is." Bryan's eyes misted over, as if it were the nicest thing anyone had ever offered him.

"My chicken soup is known for its restorative powers." Martha smiled. "I've put countless people on the road to recovery with it."

Bryan coughed, shifted in his seat, and straightened the lace doilies on the arms of the chair. "I need to stretch my legs." He pushed himself up with considerable effort.

"Since you're up and walking around, I hope you're well enough to make an important phone call," Martha said.

"Is there a problem at my office?"

Martha turned to Will, "I need to speak to your father privately."

Bile rose in his throat. "I was just leaving."

All the lies. He felt detached from his entire life, like a stranger in his mother's home. He'd grown up believing his only blood relative was an uncle he hadn't seen in years, when all along, he'd been raised by his own great aunt. The woman he loved was not Anne, but *Meghan.* In her real life in Arizona, she'd been his father's lover. He stormed outside to get some fresh air.

When Will returned from his long walk, his mom was standing in the hallway, wringing her hands. "I think you should go lie down."

"I'm fine."

She touched his forehead gently. "You don't seem to have a fever. Be sure to come back for dinner. I'm making your favorite johnnycake, and the soup will help you too. Oh, and Will?" She gave him a pleading look. "It would be nice if you could stay over for a day or two."

"Stay here?" asked Will, holding the front door open.

"I'd really appreciate it." She glanced in Bryan's direction. "I might need some help. Be back by dinnertime. And shut the door before you let all the heat out."

"We should take him back to the hospital, if you ask me," Will said in a low voice. "Better yet, to the rehab program."

"That's not an option anymore," Martha said. "I'm the only one he has at the moment."

Will headed for the door. "I'll be back around five. I wouldn't want to miss your johnnycake. I'll stop and pick up some fresh honey from the farm." He leaned down to embrace his mom.

"Fresh honey would be *wonderful.*" She smiled through tears. "Everything's going to be alright. You'll see."

Bryan paced back and forth. Martha had told him that Sergeant Haggerty would be waiting for a call from him on Saturday at noon. She'd made it clear that she hadn't given out any information to the retired officer about herself, or Bryan. The decision was all his.

He couldn't figure out how she and Haggerty had made contact with each other, and she wasn't saying. There was no way she could have known that Haggerty was the one person who knew the truth.

Forty years ago, in his role of old family friend, more than as a law enforcement officer, Haggerty had discouraged him from rushing to make his confession. Why was the deputy anxious to speak with him now? Did he have second thoughts?

Whatever the reason, Bryan was determined to make the phone call. It was time to accept responsibility for the terrible crime he'd committed decades before. He was tired of living a lifetime of lies.

He downed another swig of coffee. Hand trembling, he dialed the number.

"Sergeant Haggerty? This is Stewart Jameson."

"Stewart. You're still alive! It's good to hear your voice."

"I left the state and made a new life for myself in the West."

"I tried to locate you for several years, to no avail. Nobody knew where in the hell you'd gone, and I had only myself to thank. When I ran your Social Security number, there was no activity, so I figured you must have died. Years later I made a few more stabs at finding you by searching online."

"Don't worry. I've decided to turn myself in now, and believe me, I'll never let on that you knew." No need for Bryan to get into how he'd managed to get a new identity years ago, including a new Social Security number and dropping two letters off his last name, but there had been ways.

"The official records vanished when we updated our filing system. You couldn't get convicted on it if you tried. In fact that's what—"

"I won't bring you into this," Bryan reiterated.

"There was new evidence found when the old farmhouse was finally sold," Haggerty said.

"It won't matter once I confess."

"Tell me, Stewart, where did you hide the weapon?"

"I've often wondered about that. There's not much about that night that I've ever been able to remember."

"Why do you suppose that is?"

"I'd had a lot to drink, like I told you. Or maybe I was in shock. I don't know."

"As I recall, you were probably in an alcoholic blackout."

"Probably. It wouldn't have been the first, or the last. I never was able to remember what happened after I saw them there together."

"Then how can you confess?" asked Haggerty.

"It's pretty obvious, isn't it? I was at the scene; I had the motive. I was the last person to see them alive."

"Forty years ago, you tried to confess a double murder to me," said Haggerty. "The weapon wasn't found until the house was sold to new owners. Two shots had been fired."

"One for each," said Bryan.

"Allow me to finish. The fingerprints on the weapon weren't yours."

"What are you talking about?"

"Your wife's prints were all over the handle—and those of a very small child."

"Susan's . . . and my son's?"

Suddenly he recalled his brother's ugly words to Susan that had screamed through his mind out in the squall. "Guess you've gone and married yourself a little tramp."

"You bastard!" Susan had cried. Had she reached into the nightstand for the gun?

"The evidence showed that your wife shot your brother, or as it says in the record, her husband. Then she turned the gun on herself."

Bryan forgot how to breathe. He felt as if his heart had stopped beating too.

"With our baby son nearby? I can't believe she would do that."

"You believed you'd done that," said Haggerty.

"And it's tormented me all my life. What kind of man would murder his own wife with his little boy in the next room?" Bryan's voice broke. "I tried to visit my son twice, but couldn't face him anymore."

"The little guy must have dragged the weapon away from the scene," said Haggerty.

"He was too small to do that."

"Apparently not. He was almost twenty months old and walking. We'd somehow overlooked a small chest under the stairwell when we'd searched the house. When it was finally sold, the new owners found the gun and reported it to the sheriff. A toy gun lay beside it, along with a stuffed bear. The chest must have been used as a toy box. Maybe the poor tyke thought it was another toy."

"I remember that toy box." Bryan's voice broke.

Haggerty cleared his throat. "I was the one in charge of the investigation and the one responsible for missing it."

"Are you trying to tell me that I didn't do it?"

"That's right," said Haggerty. "The case was reclassified as a murder-suicide. I was tremendously relieved. I'd lost a lot of sleep over what I'd done. What if an innocent person were one day accused of the murders?"

"Exactly. That's always haunted me." Bryan had subscribed to the local paper for over three years after the tragedy but never saw that anyone had been charged with the crime. When the Internet later became available, he did an online search and still found nothing.

"If that had happened, I'd have stepped forward and admitted to the cover-up," said Haggerty. "It never did, of course. When we learned the truth, I tried to notify you. It haunted me to think that you'd be carrying that guilt with you as long as you lived."

"And I have, but that's not your fault. What you'd told me at the time made me think. My confession would have devastated the family and ruined Susan's memory. But I'm the one who made that choice."

"I had good intentions, but what I did was wrong," said Haggerty. "It was the biggest mistake of my life. If I hadn't been covering things up, I know we'd have done a more thorough search of the house, and you wouldn't have had to carry that guilt with you for all these years."

"I'm having a hard time taking all this in."

"It wasn't an unsolved murder—or cold case—like your aunt had thought."

"How did you find my aunt?"

"I should have found her sooner, but she'd left town without a forwarding address soon after the adoption and so had Susan's parents.

They'd sold their farm and headed south, but no one seemed to know where they'd gone. I'm sorry I took so long to find you. *Damn sorry.* I knew that you blamed yourself. Fortunately, your aunt called me this week. Someone at the county courthouse gave her my number."

"Are you sure she didn't somehow persuade you to come up with all this to change my mind about confessing?"

"No, she didn't. I think she just wanted to know the truth about what had happened. She was careful not to give me any information about you. That's why I asked her for *you* to contact *me*."

"Why would I do that?" asked Bryan.

"I wasn't sure that you would, but after she called me, I felt a ray of hope. Before I died, I wanted to make sure you knew you weren't a murderer."

"You're absolutely sure about this?" His twin brother had always taken everything that should have been his. When he'd seen him in bed with Susan, he'd been angry enough to kill him.

"I have proof," said Haggerty. "I'll send you a copy of the whole file. When they were computerizing our records and getting rid of old files, I grabbed it and slipped it into my briefcase. I've hung on to it, just in case I ever met up with you again. I never gave up hope that I'd reconnect with you some day. Thanks to your aunt, I have. Give me your address, and I'll mail you the records today."

"You're serious," Bryan clenched and unclenched his right hand. Then he gave Haggerty Martha's address.

"I'll send it Priority Mail, with signature confirmation. I want to make sure it's delivered directly into your hands. You should have it by Monday or Tuesday. Good-bye."

"I'll be waiting. Thank you." Bryan sat with the phone in his hand, expressionless and unmoving. All these years he'd thought of himself as a man who'd murdered his wife and his brother, with his son in the next room. All these years of agonizing guilt and self-hatred. He'd turned his back on his own dreams, and on love. He'd lived a lie.

"If you'd like to place a call, please hang up . . ."

Martha let herself into the room, took the receiver from him, placed it back on the hook, and rested her hands on his shoulders. "I listened in. I'm sorry." She wasn't proud of her eavesdropping on the phone call, but she'd had to know.

"How can this be?" Bryan asked, voice breaking.

His aunt kissed the top of his head. "I always knew that you were a good man."

"That's a tough concept for me." Bryan's face reddened, and he blinked back tears. "It's going to be hard to wrap my mind around this."

"But you will, with God's help."

"Thank you for what you did, Aunt Martha. That took a lot of courage—and love. But now I need to be alone for a while."

Saturday evening, Will sat in the window seat in the front room of his childhood home, watching the rain splatter against the window. So Bryan wasn't his demon after all. Neither his father nor his uncle had pulled the trigger. He couldn't believe his mother had done such a terrible thing. He'd idealized her all his life, along with the father he'd thought had died with her.

Maybe he hadn't witnessed it after all, though the newspaper had reported he'd been found with his parents. Maybe his uncle, pretending to be his father, had been Will's monster. As a toddler, he could have sensed something very wrong and been afraid. Then he'd found them dead.

He heard Bryan pacing above. He thought of climbing the stairs and knocking on the guest room door to see if he was all right. He wanted to tell his father that he was thankful he hadn't died out in the storm, but decided to leave him alone until he was ready to come out.

Will looked out at the rain. Good smells emanated from the kitchen, and he was reassured by the sight of Martha in her apron. She'd finally explained to him where she'd been when she left town, and how everything had changed with two phone calls. He couldn't help but admire her courage. She'd taken a huge risk to find out the truth.

The doorbell rang. Meghan stood there, red-faced and dripping wet.

She asked to speak to Will in private, her voice tense. Just then, Martha announced dinner from the kitchen.

"It's not a good time," Will heard himself say.

"I understand. But please be sure to call me after dinner. It's important. I really need to talk with you *tonight*."

He didn't call her back. He wasn't up to another major confrontation right now. He would talk with her when he was calmer and less apt to say something he'd regret.

The next morning, she knocked at the door again, her face somber and eyes red, as if she'd been crying. "I waited for your call. Finally, I was forced to make a big decision on my own. The school district told me I have to report for work next Monday if I want to keep my job. They need me immediately as an interim principal at their second largest high school."

"I thought you were on leave."

"They canceled my leave. I need to report for work. So I've come to say good-bye."

"Good-bye?"

"For now, anyway. I'm on my way to the airport. We can talk on the phone." She handed him her Tucson number, forgetting it was disconnected. "Please call me."

Will stuffed the note into his pocket. What perfect timing on her part to make an exit. She could slip off into the sunset, leaving all the emotional wreckage behind. He'd like to do the same.

"How's Bryan doing?" she asked.

"He's been keeping to himself." He didn't tell her the big news. It wasn't his to tell.

"Do you think he'll stay here with Martha for a while longer?"

"Maybe so." He wanted to take her in his arms and plead with her not to go. But how could he, with his father, who still loved her, in the same house? If she really loved him, how could she leave him right now?

Meghan said good-bye to Martha, then turned to Will. Frozen to his spot across the room, he managed a wooden good-bye. Devastated, he watched her hurry off to a waiting shuttle van.

Every time Martha opened the door to Bryan's room, she saw him sitting there, motionless, staring out the window. He didn't eat, sleep, or speak, and he hadn't come downstairs since the phone call.

The following afternoon, Martha called him down to sign for a package.

Later she heard his muffled sobs. She thought of going in to comfort him but decided to let him be.

The next morning, she found him shaved and dressed, making toast in the kitchen. "Is Will around?" Bryan asked.

"He's gone back home."

"Maybe I could stop by to see him before I leave town. We need to talk."

"I'm not sure he's ready." Martha brushed crumbs off her apron.

"Aunt Martha," began Bryan, "I know I'll never be able to make it up to him for all the misery I've caused."

"All I want is for you and Will to find happiness. Today, just try to make a start with your new life," she said. "It will take a while, but don't give up."

"I won't. And I'll never be able to repay you for all you've done. You're the one person who's always stood by me."

"You're leaving already?"

"There are some matters at work that I need to deal with. I can't expect my chief engineer and secretary to stave things off forever. There's a groundbreaking ceremony I need to attend, and it would be nice to get a glimpse of the sun again."

"There have been a lot of dark days this month, that's for sure." Martha felt he'd reverted to being Bryan James, yet he didn't really seem like either twin. He was more like a unique amalgam of the two.

"Not so dark as it was." Bryan turned to face her. "But you know something, Aunt Martha? I'd always pictured myself reaching for the gun . . . pulling the trigger."

Martha looked him in the eye. *"You're no murderer.* Now you're going to have to face up to that fact. You've spent so many years punishing yourself for something you didn't do, it's going to be hard to change. You'll have to let go of all that guilt and move on—and that's not going to be easy."

He reddened, continuing to spread strawberry jam over his toast. "That pretty well hits the nail on the head."

CHAPTER 42

"Welcome home!" Kate burst into Meghan's office bearing a pot of bright-yellow mums and set them on her desk. She wore a rust-colored skirt, a black shell top, and a knit shawl that flowed with a wavy, earth-toned design.

Meghan leapt up to embrace her, then poked her head out the door to tell the secretary to hold her calls. "Thank you for the flowers. And I love your shawl. When did *you* get back?"

"I flew in from Virginia a few days ago with Erin. And I'm glad you like the shawl." She handed Meghan a large plastic bag. "This is for you. It's handmade in Appalachia."

Meghan opened the bag and removed a similar shawl in a different pattern. "Thank you so much. It's beautiful. And how's my favorite god-daughter?"

"Great, considering all she's been through. She enjoyed the family and got to do a lot of painting there in the Blue Ridge Mountains."

Meghan beamed. "I'm so glad she's getting back into her art."

"She was also a big help to my aunt. She lives in a large, older home that needs endless attention. She loved having Erin's company."

"I'm not surprised. I can't wait to see her."

"As soon as we get settled, we'll have you over."

"Take your time." Meghan smiled to cover her disappointment. She couldn't wait to see Erin and had planned on heading straight over to Kate's after work.

"You've finally got your nice, big office. Businesslike, and a bit intimidating—as it should be, now that you're in charge."

Meghan shifted uneasily in her executive chair. There was an oversized desk and chairs for visitors along the opposite wall. "Everything is the way Mr. Bronson left it, except for my Petoskey stone."

"The mums will help brighten things up until you get a few more plants and a painting or two. A round table over in the corner and a few comfortable chairs would be nice."

"Why don't you help me decorate it?"

Kate laughed. "You might not like what I'd come up with. Too casual."

"I'm not trying to be formal." Meghan folded her arms in front of her. "They told me last week to show up for work here on Monday. It caught me at a really bad time."

"Sometimes you have to move fast and not look back."

"I had to drop everything to keep from losing my job."

"And every*body*."

Color crept into Meghan's cheeks "What are you getting at?" She'd been so anxious to see Kate, but something was wrong.

Kate picked at the yarn on her shawl. "I'm worried about Bryan."

"Suddenly you're his number-one fan. That's quite a switch."

"He helped save Erin's life. So yes, I guess you could say I am his 'number-one fan' now."

Meghan looked Kate directly in the eye. "Is there something I should know?"

Kate flushed. "Of course not. But would you care, even if there were?"

Meghan felt a tightening in her gut. She'd missed Kate and had been thrilled to see her this morning. Yet she sensed hostility, which wasn't like Kate. Things seemed to be turning ugly, like everything else in her life. Or was she imagining it?

"So what are Erin's plans?"

"She's eager to see her friends and to start school next semester."

Meghan lowered her voice, almost to a whisper. "Even though Devrek and Maldonado are still at large?"

Kate frowned. "It's a huge worry. But, like you, she can't put her life on hold forever. She's going to live at home with me for the time being. Those bastards must be hiding somewhere south of the border, or overseas. Otherwise, they'd probably have turned up by now."

"That's what I kept telling myself. But didn't Erin hear Devrek's voice behind that motel?"

"That was three months ago. And how can we be sure it was him?"

"I'm sure she'd know his voice," said Meghan. "Are they getting anywhere with the investigation of the vanished treatment center?"

"As far as I know, they haven't found any sign of it, or anyone associated with it, except that guy who drove her to the motel. He's still in jail. If he's talking, I'm not aware of it. I worry about all those poor girls being held somewhere against their will."

"Won't the local authorities in Nevada or the FBI get to the bottom of it?"

"I hope so. Bryan's been trying to put pressure on law enforcement to keep it a priority."

"Good. And you're right that we can't keep our lives on hold forever. This is a good career opportunity, and I want to give it my best."

"I had the impression you might not want to come back," Kate said. "I thought you were getting pretty serious about Will."

"He wants nothing to do with me now."

"But I thought things were going so well."

"I can't get into the whole miserable story right now, but Bryan barged in unannounced while Will and I were sitting together in my rented cottage. There was . . . a terrible scene. Everything since then has been a total disaster."

"I'm sorry to hear that." Kate took off the shawl and laid it across her lap. She ran her hands over the soft yarn, as if to smooth it. "I hope you and Will can work things out somehow."

"I don't think so. It turns out that Bryan . . . is Will's father."

"That sure complicates things." Kate didn't sound surprised.

"When I went to say good-bye to Martha, Will's adoptive mother, Will and Bryan were sitting there together. Will wouldn't even look at me. I can't say I blame him, under the circumstances. What could I say? Sorry about that little detail I forgot to mention, that *I used to sleep with your dad*. And then explain to Bryan why I dropped him for his son?"

"You had no idea they were father and son," said Kate. "And didn't you let Will know from the start that you were involved with someone?"

"I even overstated it. For some reason, I'd told Will I was expecting a call from my *fiancé*."

"Sounds like you had a gut feeling that it might turn into something more."

"I made it clear that we could only be platonic friends. And we kept it on that level for quite a while . . . until we fell in love."

"Will sounds like a terrific guy."

"He is. When he found out there was someone I was hiding from, he wanted to know what was going on, so he could help. I didn't tell him, and now it's too late."

"Why too late?"

"I went by the alias Bryan gave me, even with Will. I never even told him my real name, where I grew up, or where I lived. I was waiting until Devrek was captured to tell him everything so he wouldn't have to be part of the deception. I'd assumed that would be soon."

"You and me both."

"Now I've become almost paranoid. I still struggle with fear that I'm being followed."

"Maybe you are."

"There's been no indication of that since May, when I left Arizona. I'd finally met a man I could love and picture spending the rest of my life with, and I shut him out. Before I had a chance to tell Will the truth, Bryan burst into our lives, looking angry enough to kill someone."

"I feel so bad for all three of you," Kate said. "How's Bryan doing now?"

"He's still in Michigan." Meghan began to straighten a pile of papers on her desk.

Kate hesitated. "I heard he was injured in a boating accident."

Meghan placed the Petoskey stone in her palm, focusing on its cool, smooth mass. "He was out on the lake in a terrible storm and had to be rescued by the Coast Guard."

Kate looked her straight in the eye. "What *really* happened?"

"Maybe you should ask him for the details. He seems to be keeping you pretty well informed. And I'm afraid I'm going to have to cut this short. I need to get back to work."

"I just wish someone would tell me the truth."

"It sounds like someone already has."

"When I talked with Bryan, he changed the subject, same as you." Kate eyed Meghan carefully. "It wasn't an accident, was it? The boating mishap?"

"No, it wasn't. But I really do need to get to work now. I've got a big backlog of paperwork, along with everything else that hasn't been done."

"How did Bryan get injured out in the water?" demanded Kate.

"He was already hurt. Will is very strong, and protective," Meghan said quietly.

"Will and Bryan . . . *fought* over you?"

"Aren't I the lucky one?"

"Maybe you are, if Will is half the man his father is."

"I can hardly believe my ears."

"Bryan used to infuriate me, but he risked his life to help me find Erin. I hope you realize he did it all as a favor to you." Kate flushed. "I know that I've always rubbed him the wrong way, and vice versa, yet he kept his promise to you to find your goddaughter. If that's not dedication, Meghan, I don't know what is."

Meghan's eyes teared up. She recalled the night when he'd risked his life to check her car for a bomb. "You're right. Bryan can be very courageous, and I appreciate that. But there's a lot you don't know about him."

"Like what?" asked Kate.

"He told me he murdered his wife and brother," she said, almost in a whisper.

"That's not true!" blurted out Kate.

"It's a cruel world out there," said Meghan. "Maybe we're all capable of murder."

"What we're all capable of is love."

"I've always been an idealist too. But the dark side of human nature won't vanish simply because we refuse to acknowledge it. Our enemies, and even the ones we love, may be more evil than we ever imagined."

"My God, Meghan. You sound so bitter. It's not like you."

"Maybe I've finally faced up to reality."

"I don't think so." Kate placed her shawl back over her shoulders and drew it around her. "Listen to me. I know I'm not the one who should tell you this, and now is not the time—but I can't allow you to go on thinking that Bryan is a murderer."

Meghan reddened. "What do you mean?"

"For all these years, Bryan believed he killed his wife and twin brother. But this past weekend, he found out that wasn't true. When his wife and brother were killed, Bryan was in an alcoholic blackout. His aunt somehow tracked down the deputy who was in charge of the case at the time. They hadn't found the gun. When they finally did find it, Bryan's prints weren't on it. The fingerprints were those of his wife and little boy."

"Little boy?" cried Meghan. "That would be *Will*, who wasn't even two!"

"The murders had been quietly reclassified as a murder-suicide, by his wife."

"Who . . . who told you this? No, don't tell me. It could only have been one person."

CHAPTER 43

Meghan stood in the doorway of Kate's adobe home wearing a faded blue sweat suit. It was Saturday morning, and she hadn't been invited over yet to welcome Erin home. She and Kate hadn't spoken since their tense meeting at school.

"What's wrong?" Kate was still in her robe.

"Everything. Can I come in?" Meghan was breathing hard. "Sorry if I woke you."

"That's okay. I need to get up. Come in, and I'll brew you some jasmine tea. Erin should be up pretty soon. I was going to call you today."

Trembling, Meghan burst into the room and locked Kate's front door behind her. "I'm anxious to see her, but that's not why I'm here. Someone broke into my house during the night. The police just left."

"While you were home?"

"While I was sleeping."

"Oh no! Are you okay?" Kate led Meghan back to the kitchen.

"I'm not hurt." There was a tremor in her voice.

"What did they take?"

"Nothing, as far as I could tell. The problem is what was left behind." Meghan dug into her purse and pulled out a folded copy of a note. "This was lying on top of my coffee maker."

Kate scanned the note: *You're beautiful while you sleep.* "When did you find this?"

"A couple hours ago."

Kate saw the terror in Meghan's eyes. "Do you think it was Devrek?"

"He was my first thought—but who knows?"

"How did he get in? Did he break a window?"

"No broken windows, and the doors were still locked. That's what's so chilling. He has free access to my home and could have easily killed me . . . or done whatever he wanted."

"You can't stay there anymore." Kate's hand shook as she stuffed tea leaves into the strainer. "Move in with us."

"And draw him to you and Erin? I shouldn't even be here now, come to think of it." Meghan's gaze darted from window to window. "He could have followed me."

"Then stay in Bryan's townhouse, with its twenty-four-hour guard at the gate. It's sitting empty, at least for another day or two."

"I can't do that." She rubbed her temples. "When the renters' lease is up on my grandpa's townhouse next month, I can move in there. You and Erin are welcome to stay there too."

"You need to move out today!"

"If it's Devrek, so do you and Erin. But what's the point of my hiding out somewhere, only to show up five days a week as principal of Lincoln High School?"

"At least you could rest easier when you're home—maybe even get some sleep."

"I can't stand to live in hiding anymore." Meghan's voice shook with anger. "This bastard is ruining my life!"

"Ours too," said Kate. "We've got to *do* something."

"I know. Why do you suppose he didn't kill me while he had the chance?"

"He seems to delight in terrorizing you, and maybe killing a school principal would put on too much heat."

"And this note won't?"

Kate handed her a cup of tea and looked at the note again. "This could probably have been spewed out by any inkjet printer. It may not be much of a clue."

"Clue or not, it shows I'm still being threatened by someone and that I'm still not safe in my own home."

"This is such a nightmare," Kate said. "I just can't believe that after all this time, the *only* lead on Devrek was Erin's report of hearing his voice when she was hiding in a trash bin—at least what she *thought* was his voice."

"It *was* him!" Erin stood in the doorway, blood rising up her neck into her cheeks.

"I believe you," Kate said, "though I'd much rather think you were mistaken and that he was somewhere far away."

Meghan rushed to embrace Erin, with tears in her eyes. "Thank God he never found you and that you're back home now with your mom. It must have been terrifying."

"How long have you been listening?" asked Kate.

"I just woke up." Erin leaned over to kiss Kate on top of the head and opened the refrigerator. "Can you squeeze me some fresh orange juice, Mom?"

"Any chance you could make us all some juice, honey? Meghan and I are in the midst of a serious talk. The paring knife and juicer are right there on the counter."

"Oh Mom. You just don't want her to know how much you still spoil me."

"I'd have never guessed," Meghan chuckled. "It's so great to have you back."

Kate put her arm around Erin's shoulder. "There's something we need to tell you."

"Can't it wait, Mom? I want to kick back for a while this morning."

"I'm afraid this can't wait." Kate handed Erin the threatening note. "Someone broke into Meghan's house last night and left this. She's afraid it was Dr. Devrek."

As Erin read the note, the fine hairs on her arms stood on end.

Karl Devrek was growing tired of his little terrorist game. It was too easy. The schoolmarm had a key hidden under a rock near her front door, like the trusting, small-town hick she really was. On a hunch, he'd reached under a blatantly fake rock, and there it was. Unbelievable, considering she'd known for months she was being stalked. It had been easy getting a duplicate key made before returning the original to its place.

Watching her sleep in her bed was a real turn on. She was completely helpless, and he had all the power. He could have killed her in a dozen different ways but didn't want to put an end to his fun just yet. She and the girl could run and hide again, like the prey that they were, but he would always be right there, hunting them down.

He was still enraged that his plan to abduct Erin in Kingman had been aborted. The guy making the drop was supposed to step outside for a smoke and then drive off. For months, Devrek had anticipated the moment the girl would look up in shock and realize that the man walking through the door of the motel room was the one she'd sent to prison, and that she was powerless under his control. Her horrified expression would have been priceless.

Unfortunately, the imbecile had gotten drunk, botched the carefully laid plans, and let the bitch get away. To top it off, the jerk had returned to the crime scene and managed to get himself arrested. Now the incompetent psych tech was in custody, no doubt spewing out what little he knew to the FBI. It probably wasn't much. He couldn't have known the drop involved Devrek, or he never would have been so careless.

Devrek figured the girl couldn't have gotten far from the motel that night, but the element of surprise had been spoiled. He'd sensed she was hiding in the dumpster, which disgusted him. If he'd seen or smelled her like that, it would have ruined things, permanently. He had no tolerance for germs or filth. He just wished he hadn't blurted out her name. If she was within earshot, he'd placed himself back in Arizona for the benefit of law enforcement.

Devrek was sure he'd get another chance to surprise her, and when he did, it would be on his terms. She would have to cater to his every whim for as long as he kept her alive—and his whims were quite involved. He would take his time. He would never forget her damning testimony against him at the trial. Nothing he could dream up would be too terrible for her.

As for the schoolmarm, for now it was enough to keep her terror-ized and destroy her career, as thanks for her testimony against him. No sense killing a school principal, with the FBI breathing down his neck. She'd already been forced to take a leave of absence because of the fire he'd set in her office. He wanted her to live in fear, to even doubt her own sanity.

Then there was the engineer. If anyone was to blame for his planned reunion with Erin getting derailed, it was him—and getting the girl back apparently wasn't enough for the bastard. Several days after his failed attempt to abduct her, Devrek received an anonymous text warning him that Bryan James was doing a lot of snooping around. He relished the thought of strangling the engineer with his bare hands. He got visceral pleasure from violence that was up close and personal, but that was too risky.

Through years of professional training in psychiatry, it became obvious to him that he was a textbook example of an abused child who'd become a sadistic, sociopathic adult. With impressive self-control, he'd learned to channel his rage and violent impulses so he never left a trail. He'd made it a point to keep a spotless record as a professional psychiatrist, until the girl had turned him in and the schoolmarm had backed her up in court.

During the trial, he'd arranged for Maldonado to take photographs and notes for him. Eddie had been loyal, which Devrek couldn't say about many others. But he knew too much.

Back when Devrek had first started running halfway houses and treatment centers, he'd always made it a point to know about the personal lives, family connections, and weaknesses of his employees for future ref-erence. Today, when he'd done a search on Maldonado, he'd run across an announcement of the upcoming wedding of his sister.

He figured the odds were good that Eddie would show up at the wedding, despite the risk of capture. If the authorities arrested him, the FBI would have bigger fish to fry—like tracking down Devrek, escaped convict and child rapist. Maldonado would most likely give them what they wanted in exchange for a lighter sentence.

He couldn't afford to take that chance. He'd set up a meeting with Maldonado, alone in the desert, but Eddie had family members who were connected, and Devrek feared a double cross. He decided to move fast, do the unexpected, and slip off in the ensuing chaos.

In September, Devrek had moved back to Tucson and created a new life right under everyone's noses. He'd shaved off his dark beard and mustache, bleached his hair white, and became a snowbird from Illinois. As a kid, he'd often visited his grandparents in Chicago, so he knew how to fit right into potlucks and bingo nights as a retired Midwesterner. It was perfect. He'd recently made quite a few "friends" in Tucson. He had to remember not to use mental health jargon and to feign an interest in the Chicago Bears. He often wore a cap with their insignia that he'd picked up at a sports shop at the mall. Lately, Devrek was living more openly in Tucson than he'd lived anywhere in his life. He found it quite humorous.

Whenever he needed to disappear for a while, he'd mention he was going back East to see the grandkids; then he would head to his remote ranch near Weaver. With ghost towns as his closest neighbors, there was no one nearby to snoop around or ask questions, and the few people he encountered usually kept to themselves.

Eddie waited at the Nogales port of entry on his way back into the States. He hoped he wasn't so nervous that the dogs could smell it. He had paperwork to cross the border, as Edward Costino. As Eduardo Maldonado, he was wanted by the Feds for kidnapping.

What concerned him more was that the crazy shrink was after him. Devrek had already arranged for a private meeting, supposedly to pay Eddie what he owed him for transporting Erin to the bogus center.

Eddie knew Devrek had founded the notorious New Horizon, originally known as Hannah's, and later as Ocotillo Center for Girls. He knew about the psychiatrist's penchant for kiddy porn, because he'd supplied him with it, and he knew that the doctor had molested numerous underage patients at his halfway houses in Tucson and Las Vegas. Erin hadn't been the first, or the last, and Eddie could name names. He had enough on the shrink to get him locked back up for the rest of his life, which put Eddie in grave danger.

The meeting Devrek set up with him was scheduled for a week from

Tuesday in a remote area near Dragoon. He planned to show up, but with plenty of backup. How dumb did Devrek think he was?

He regretted ever getting involved with the psycho shrink, and he was sorry he'd followed Devrek's orders to deliver Erin to Vegas. Eddie had tried to contact the Las Vegas treatment center last week, but their phone was disconnected. He hoped Erin was okay. She was a nice girl who he could have brought home to meet his mother. He just hoped his mother didn't know what kind of bastard her own son was.

After six months of lying low with relatives in Mexico, Eddie was short on cash and wanted to come home. He was tired of hiding out, and it hadn't even worked to keep him hidden from Devrek. Most of all, he wasn't about to miss his sister's wedding. After the wedding, things were going to be different. He would get back into legitimate photography, under the name of Costino, and start a new life for himself in LA.

CHAPTER 44

Tucson looked good to Bryan from his window seat as the jet broke through the clouds over the pass between the Rincons and Catalina Mountains. On the way back to Tucson he'd stopped off in Albuquerque to check on an engineering job. He was anxious to get home.

It was a sunny November day, with a few clouds clinging to the mountains. It should be perfect for the groundbreaking ceremony. The small planned community his firm had designed was about to become a reality.

He enjoyed spotting familiar landmarks as they flew the length of the city. Row upon row of mothballed planes at the Air Force boneyard glinted in the sunlight. The big shopping malls and parks were easy to spot, along with the red-brick buildings and football stadium at the university. Swimming pools sparkled like aquamarines, and as they circled to land he saw A Mountain. It was good to be flying over the sprawling desert oasis known as the Old Pueblo.

He could start his life again, free from immobilizing guilt. *He was not a murderer.*

His eyes misted over as they touched down and taxied to the gate. He paused for a moment on the steps of the commuter jet, raising his hand to shield his eyes from the glare. He didn't mind that the Jetway was out of order. From where he stood, he could see three of the beautiful mountain ranges that surrounded the city. His back still ached and he was tired, but it was great to be home.

Once in the terminal, he made his way down to baggage claim. He glanced through the crowd and spotted a beautiful redhead smiling and waving. Kate looked happy to see him, but Meghan was nowhere to be seen. It had been foolish of him to hope she'd come along with Kate to meet his plane. He wouldn't have wanted her to risk it anyway, after Kate's latest update on the threatening note Meghan found in her home. After all that had been done to keep her safe, the bastard was back at it again.

But he'd spent enough of his life weighed down by jealousy, anger, and guilt. There was no time for that anymore. He was grateful that Kate had offered to come.

"It was nice of you to meet me. I appreciate it."

"It's no problem," smiled Kate. "Erin wanted to come, too, but I'm still trying to keep her from being seen in public, after Meghan's latest scare."

"Good idea. How was your trip?"

"We both fell in love with . . . the area. Erin wants to have you over to see the pictures we took." Kate hesitated, adding, "Meghan wants to see them too. No sense showing them twice."

"Looks like she has her hands full with her new position. And it's still best for her not to be at your house as long as your daughter is there."

"This has gone on for too long. We have to live our lives."

"That's just what I intend to do." Bryan smiled. "Are you sure you're up for the groundbreaking?"

"Sure, why not? You can get your bags while I bring the car around."

"Meet you out front."

As he watched the baggage carousel, he reminded himself that it was time to put Meghan behind him and move on. He couldn't wait to get back out on the tennis courts and devote more time to overseeing the construction of the planned community.

But they could never completely move on until Devrek and Maldonado were behind bars, along with the ringleaders of the vanished center. As far as he knew, the girls were still being held somewhere against their will. He'd seen Erin's crumpled sketch of her friend, done the day she'd died. He couldn't get her out of his mind.

The baggage carousel jerked into motion, spewing out his single bag. He grabbed it, donned his sunglasses, and stepped outside into the bright sunlight. After the ceremony, he hoped Kate would join him for a leisurely lunch. He had a taste for Mexican food.

They turned off Oracle onto the bumpy dirt road that led to the Mica Ranch, soon to become a planned community. Beyond the high, rolling foothills of mesquite and paloverde trees loomed the steep north face of the Catalina Mountains.

Dozens of people were already gathered for the ceremony by the time Bryan and Kate pulled up to the brightly colored flags. Rows of folding chairs were lined up under a canvas ramada, and a large purple ribbon was in place, ready to be cut. The mayor arrived, along with the project's key investors. They seemed pleased Bryan had made it.

He touched base with his chief engineer, Sam Friedman, who was ready to represent the engineering firm if Bryan's plane was late. His stomach growled, and he thought again about lunch. He'd missed Tucson's great Mexican food. He might have enchiladas or chiles rellenos.

He felt himself relax in the cool, fresh air, with the gentle warmth of the sun on his back, and nearly dozed off during one of the speeches. Kate poked him a few minutes before it was his turn to speak and handed him coffee in a Styrofoam cup.

Moments later he walked to the dais and thanked everyone for coming. He made his comments brief and to the point. The new planned community would be designed according to the highest standards and would aim to create a sense of community. It would include shops, as well as homes, a large pool and other recreational facilities, and common grounds to be left as natural desert. Then it was time for the biggest investor to cut the ribbon.

After the ceremony, guests drifted back to their cars and drove off in a trail of dust, bouncing along the bumpy lane toward Oracle Road. Bryan stayed behind to review the soil compaction with Friedman and to look around the site once more before the work began. Kate waited under a large mesquite tree.

By the time Bryan headed toward Kate's VW, the only other vehicle remaining was a sand-colored Jeep. His thoughts turned again to lunch. He'd love to have a margarita, but after everything that had happened, he'd be ordering iced tea from now on. Maybe he would try a chimichanga.

Suddenly he heard a loud pop. A sharp pain tore through his back, and he crumpled to the ground.

Kate raced toward him, screaming, as the Jeep streaked off into the desert. Blood pooled on the ground beneath him.

"Lie still," cried Kate. "I'm calling 911."

"Damn it, Kate!" he groaned, squeezing her hand. "This sure is rotten timing."

✢

Meghan collapsed into her chair, her head in her hands. "No!" she cried. She played the message again, hoping she hadn't heard right.

Bryan had been shot in the spine and might be paralyzed from the waist down. It had happened within hours of his arrival in Tucson, at some event on the northwest side of town. He'd been airlifted to the trauma center, where he was in the ICU.

It wasn't fair! Bryan had finally been freed from the guilt of being a murderer, and now this? She couldn't bear it.

She dialed Kate, who broke down sobbing as she tried to tell Meghan what had happened. Though Kate was inexperienced in first aid, she'd been the only one there to keep him alive. She told Meghan she'd felt like she was floating above herself, terrified, watching herself staunch his bleeding with her skirt. She gave Meghan his room number at the hospital.

But Meghan wasn't going there—at least not until Bryan had been stabilized. The last time she'd visited him in a hospital, he'd gone out the next day to take his own life. The best thing she could do was to stay away.

The next day, she sent him flowers. Two days later, when he was transferred out of the ICU to another unit, she sent him a Bose radio, along with several audio books.

The only positive was the renewed media attention on Devrek's prison escape and the missing treatment center. The shooting made national headlines. They were all questioned by the FBI, and the investigations were finally getting priority treatment.

Meghan couldn't figure out why Devrek would have drawn that kind of attention to himself, after his successful getaway. Had he assumed no one would suspect him, or was someone else behind the shooting?

She was relieved that Kate was looking in on Bryan at the hospital. Kate and Erin had even offered to go home with him for a while as he convalesced. It was obvious to Meghan that it was only a short-term plan. It wouldn't be long before Bryan and Kate got on each other's nerves.

After that, it would be Meghan's turn. Though they were no longer a couple, she felt a sense of obligation to care for him until he could make other plans. He'd been such a great support to her when her grandfather was ill and after his death. Until recently, she'd been the main person in Bryan's life and had assumed they might marry. It was up to her to step up to the plate and do what was needed. Still, she didn't feel ready to face him, and she wasn't about to hurt his recovery by showing up at the wrong time.

Bryan had found out about her relationship with his son the hard way, yet she'd never told him, face-to-face, how much she loved Will. She guessed there would never be a good time to bring it up. Now that he was partially paralyzed, it would only make matters worse. And what would be the point? What she'd had with Will was in the past.

Will had turned his back on her when she'd needed him most. She was devastated by his cold rejection when she'd stopped by Martha's to say good-bye. She'd still hoped to talk things over with him before she left, but it had obviously been too late.

Meghan looked out at the six-foot, slump-block wall, not far beyond the sliding glass door. She tried to focus on the small cactus garden, refusing to give in to a feeling of claustrophobia. She'd rented the townhome the same day she'd received the threatening note. It was in a gated community and had a working alarm system in place. The long, narrow, boxlike town-house only had windows at the front, which looked out at the carport, and a sliding glass door in the back. She missed her bright, cheerful home, with its mature orange trees, flowers, fountain, and view of the mountains beyond.

She flinched when the phone rang, fearful of more bad news about Bryan. But it was Will's number that came up on her caller ID.

Hand trembling, she reached for the phone in slow motion. "Hello?"

"Meghan? It's me, Will."

"Will! It's so good to hear from you!" She tried to control the quaver in her voice. She and Will would finally get the chance to talk.

"I heard the terrible news about Bryan. I can't believe it. He was due for a change of luck, for the better."

"That's for sure."

"My mom and I wanted to help in some way. Maybe we still can. But that's not why I'm calling. I heard about the note you found in your bedroom. What's going on down there in Tucson? Who's trying to kill all of you? I don't understand!"

"I'm still being stalked, probably by an escaped convict I helped send to prison for molesting my goddaughter. I'm so glad you called. I've wanted to talk with you about this for a long time."

"Is what happened to Bryan related to that, or what?"

"I'm not positive, but I'm afraid that it is. Bryan helped find Erin when she was kidnapped. Since then, he's done his best to pressure the authorities to track down the escaped convict as well to find out what happened to the so-called treatment center where she was held against her will."

"Why don't you come back to Michigan? I could come out and fly back with you."

Those were the words she'd been longing to hear, yet she heard herself explaining why it wasn't possible. "I really appreciate your offer, but I've accepted a position here as principal of a large high school. I had no choice, if I wanted to keep my job. I wanted to talk to you about it but never got the chance. They're depending on me now."

"I wish you could get away from there, job or no job. Your life just might depend on it."

"What are you saying, Will?" Was he saying that he still loved her and missed her, despite all that had happened? That what he wanted most was to be with her?

"I want you to go somewhere safe. If that's Michigan, fine. If it's somewhere else, then go somewhere else. I don't want to pressure you to come here. Change your name and disappear again, until it's really safe to return to Tucson. You're in too much danger now."

"You remind me of your father. I'm sorry, that's not what I . . ." she stammered, instantly regretting her words.

"You said what you meant. I remind you of *him*—and not in a good way, from your tone of voice. You know, Meghan, it took a lot for me to make this call. I stuck my neck out to call because I care about you and your welfare, and so does my father. But since you've got us lumped together in your mind, there's nothing more to be said."

"That's not really what I . . ." She grasped for words to undo the damage. Yet Will *was* acting like Bryan, pressing her to go into hiding and give up her life again without any assurance he'd be there for her. He didn't even seem to care if she wound up in Michigan or somewhere else.

"If you need my help to get to a safer place, let me know. Otherwise, be careful and find some way to protect yourself."

"I will."

"Good-bye, Meghan. Have a good life."

She heard the line go dead. She set the phone back into the cradle and sat staring at the gray block wall outside the sliding glass doors. Then she put her head in her hands and sobbed.

CHAPTER 45

Kate kept Meghan updated on Bryan's progress. He was transferred from the hospital to a rehab center, where he struggled to gain back some mobility and functioning. After six weeks, he was released to go home and continue therapy as an outpatient.

"Erin and I are staying with him," Kate reminded her, as if seeking her blessing. "She can help while I'm at work."

"It's very generous of you both. Just be sure that's what you want to do. I know how he can get on your nerves."

It was so typical of her best friend to jump into something with both feet without thinking of all the ramifications, but Meghan was relieved. She needed more time before she felt ready to even face Bryan again, much less take on his care.

"It would be nice if you could come by and see him, as well as spend some time with me and Erin," said Kate. "We'd like you to come to dinner Sunday night."

"I'll let you know. And don't forget, whenever you need a break, I can take over. It's not fair for the entire burden of responsibility to fall on you just because there were problems between the two of us."

"That's crazy," said Kate. "You haven't even gone to see him yet, and I'm fine helping out. It's the least I can do, after all his help in finding Erin."

"Remember that I'm here if you need backup."

Kate paused. "You know, you're the second one who's made that offer."

"Really? Has Lois offered to help?"

"Will called a few days ago to relay his mom's offer to have Bryan stay with her while he recuperated. He said he could arrange to be there most of the time to help out."

"You're kidding me."

"Not at all," said Kate. "I thought it was a pretty generous offer, under the circumstances."

"That's for sure. Martha's in her eighties and has trouble getting around. Will would have to do most of the care, and I can't imagine that."

"Don't worry about it. Bryan declined the offer. He's got too much going on at work, especially with the new planned community underway. He told him that his life is here in Tucson."

"Good. It couldn't have worked. Will was so angry at Bryan that I'd rather not even think about how badly it might have gone."

"He was probably trying to help out his mom," Kate said. "He sounds very kind."

"He is." Meghan said with a tremor in her voice. "Will called me, too, offering help. Here I finally get a chance to talk to him, and I blow it as soon as I open my mouth! Will was getting real protective, and I made a huge blunder. I blurted out that he reminded me of his dad."

"Uh-oh," said Kate. "What happened?"

"It was too late to take it back. He told me to have a nice life."

"Oh, Meghan."

"I don't blame him. I've caused everyone so much misery, especially Will and Bryan."

"It's not your fault Bryan tried to kill himself." Kate was never one to mince words.

"Because of me, he felt betrayed once again—this time, by his lover with his son."

"But you didn't betray him. You told him the truth. He had his own issues, which had nothing to do with you. It wasn't at all like before. He'd never made any commitment to you. And you had no way of knowing that Will was his son!"

"That's true, but I feel so rotten about the whole thing."

"I think the best thing for you and Bryan to do is to face each other and talk. The offer still stands for dinner Sunday night."

"Like I said, I'll get back to you."

The next day, Meghan picked up the phone, then set it down again. Finally she punched in Kate's number and was relieved to get the machine. "I can make it for dinner Sunday. I'll bring a key lime pie."

On Sunday at six o'clock, Erin greeted Meghan with a warm hug and showed her in. She took the pie and disappeared into the rear of Bryan's townhome.

"I'll be with you in a few minutes," Kate called out from the kitchen.

Meghan found herself face-to-face with Bryan. She'd known he would be in a wheelchair, yet the sight of him was jarring. More striking than ever, he now sported a full mustache that was darker than his steel-gray hair. He wasn't the broken man she'd last seen in Michigan.

For an instant, she thought she felt his eyes reach into her like a caress, but he glanced away, and the feeling was gone.

❧

Seeing Meghan nearly left Bryan at a loss for words, but he smiled and extended his hand to her. "Hello, Meghan."

"You look good, but . . . different," she mumbled. "I don't mean—"

"The wheelchair?" Pity, as palpable as the chair beneath him. His resolve hardened.

"How is the principal of the second largest high school in the state?"

"I'm just interim principal."

"Congratulations are still in order."

"Thank you." Meghan sat down in a chair beside him. "I'm sorry I didn't come by sooner. It's just that . . ."

"No need to apologize." *Pity, and guilt.* He wanted no part of it.

"There's been so much to catch up with on the new job," Meghan said. "I just want you to know that I'm so sorry about what happened, Bryan—can I still call you Bryan?"

"Aunt Martha is the only one who sometimes calls me by my given name. And you need to stop apologizing."

"Fine. How's your physical therapy going? You look good, after all you've been through."

"Thanks. The therapy's going well. I'm getting back some function in my legs—more every day. I can already move a few toes. My spinal cord wasn't severed, just damaged."

Meghan smiled for the first time. "That's great news."

"I'm working hard with the physical and occupational therapists. I can't let up, because I'm determined to walk again. But enough about me. How do you like being principal?"

"It's a real challenge, but I've been preparing for it for years."

"And how do you like it?"

"It keeps me busy. Never a dull moment."

"You know, I always thought you loved your job most when you were choir director. Your face used to glow when you talked about your choir students and the school musicals you were directing." He often surprised himself lately by saying exactly what he was thinking.

"Maybe so." She hesitated. "I do miss it, but I need to give this time."

Kate announced dinner was ready. It was another spicy, vegetarian dish. Bryan craved meat, potatoes, and fresh vegetables that weren't all doctored up with weird spices, but how could he complain when Kate was working so hard to help him? Without her, it was hard to imagine what he'd have done. She seemed to know him well, yet accepted him as he was.

The dinner wore on, with strained conversation and interminable awkwardness. Meghan was clearly ill at ease, which he'd never seen before. Even Kate seemed tongue-tied. Had it not been for Erin's nervous, animated chatter, it would have been unbearable.

After dinner, Kate wheeled him onto the patio. "We can have the pie later, while we watch the slide show." Then she asked Erin to help her in the kitchen, a transparent ploy to give Bryan and Meghan more privacy. Meghan looked tense as Kate and Erin headed inside.

Bryan turned his chair to face her. Seeing her bathed in the glow of moonlight flooded him with desire. For a moment, he felt himself weakening, but he steeled himself.

"There's something I need to tell you," he said, starting to lose his nerve.

"I'd like to say something first," she said.

"Shoot." He noticed her flinch.

"I want to tell you how very sorry I am."

"Is this another apology?"

"I want you to listen this time. I know you felt betrayed by me, like you were before." Her eyes glistened with tears. "I'm so very sorry." She hesitated, as if gathering the courage to go on. "I can't bear that I caused you to . . . to try to end your own life."

"No one has that kind of power."

"That's what they say. I want you to know that in a few weeks, the lease is up for my renter, and I could move back to the condo next door. You'd be welcome to stay with me. We might need to have someone come in to help, but I've got plenty of room. You could take the master suite."

"Thank you for your kind offer, but if I need anything more, I'll arrange for more help in my home. I've decided to get on with my life."

"I'm glad to hear that." She squinted, as if trying to comprehend how he could get on with his life in his present situation.

"You've always been honest with me," he said, "even when I didn't want to hear what you were saying. In your letter, you told me you'd found someone new. And I know you had no way of knowing who Will was to me."

"Let's not talk about Will," she snapped.

He longed to comfort her and fought the impulse to take her in his arms, stroke her hair, and make her smile. This was going to be even harder than he'd imagined.

"I've found someone new, myself," he said. "I want you to be the first to know."

Her eyes widened, registering shock.

"Someone very special," he continued.

She waited.

He was losing courage. "I think it's important we be open with each other."

"Who is it?"

"I thought you'd have guessed by now."

Confusion clouded her features. "Is it Lois?"

"I'm referring to Kate," he said gently, realizing that she was completely in the dark.

Blood rushed to her cheeks.

He felt like a heel, but he hadn't been able to think of another way to get her to let go. Otherwise, she'd always feel a sense of obligation toward him. And she did have a right to know about the powerful bond—the love—that was growing between him and her best friend, Kate. "I hope this doesn't interfere with your friendship with her."

"I'm happy for you—for *both* of you," she stammered.

Though he wanted to make everything all right, and protect her from being hurt again, he forced himself to remember the pity he'd seen in her eyes. Her feelings for him had turned to sympathy and some misguided sense of duty. It was his son she should be with, and he would no longer stand in the way of their happiness.

"Will still cares for you, but he's probably hurt."

"Aren't we all? But don't worry about your son. I'm sure he'll have no trouble meeting someone new. This has been a very long day, and I have to work tomorrow. You've taken me quite by surprise, Bryan, but I wish you both the best. Good night."

Meghan managed to thank Kate for dinner and say good night to Erin, while maintaining a modicum of composure.

"You didn't see the slide show yet," said Erin.

"Slide show?"

"The pictures of Virginia, on my laptop."

"I'm sorry, Erin, but I'm not feeling very well. I'd love to see them some other time."

Meghan sensed that Bryan meant to say something more, but he wheeled the chair around and faced the other way, looking out the window into the night.

"Thanks again," she mumbled, slipping out the front door.

She'd agonized for weeks about how to find it within herself to become a caregiver for Bryan, and it hadn't even been an option. She wondered if she could ever speak to Kate again after this. Why hadn't Kate told her what was going on? Her best friend had encouraged her to face her fears and confront Bryan. Kate should have asked her if she'd like to come over for dinner and get kicked in the gut.

As Meghan prepared for bed alone that night, she was torn between feelings of anger and relief. Night after night, she'd lain awake hurting for Bryan and worrying about the pain she'd caused him. She'd agonized about how to tell him how she really felt, unaware that he wanted to be rid of her. While she'd struggled with her sense of duty to take care of him, he'd been falling in love with her best friend!

Tonight he'd almost seemed condescending as he tried to let her down easily. How could she have been so naïve? All indications had pointed to Kate, yet she'd been incapable of seeing them as a couple.

Suddenly it began to fall into place. She hadn't been talking to *Bryan*, not the Bryan she'd known. This man was the other twin. The Bryan she'd loved would never have fallen for her free-spirited best friend, Kate. This other twin, though handicapped, seemed more at ease and centered than Bryan had ever been.

And hadn't it really been over between the two of them since that night she'd flown off to Michigan last May? She hadn't realized it at the time, but looking back, that was when he'd raised an impenetrable wall between them.

Because of Bryan, she'd lost the love of her life. Now she would lose her best friend, and probably lose contact with her goddaughter as well. Once again, Meghan was alone in the world—more alone now than ever.

She wept until she finally fell asleep.

Bryan saw Kate come down the stairs in her multicolored silk robe. She started to brew some tea. They enjoyed having a quiet time at the end of the day, when they would read.

He pretended to be absorbed in a book.

"Did you and Meghan have a good talk?" Kate's back was to him as she filled the teapot with water. Her voice was tense and carefully modulated. It wasn't like Kate to hold back.

"Yes, we did. It went fine." For one of the most difficult conversations of his life.

"She seemed pretty upset when she left."

He drew his breath in slowly. "It's over between Meghan and me. I told her there was someone else."

Kate stood very still. "Someone else?"

"I told her how important you've become to me. How much I care for you."

"*Me?* I mean, I know we've become good friends, but . . . me? Are you sure?"

"I'm sure."

Kate went to him, kneeling at his feet, her head in his lap and arms around his waist. "I'd been trying so hard to get you two to meet together and talk with each other again. But when it finally happened, I felt almost physically ill. I was afraid you might get back together."

"That's not going to happen."

"How did she take it?"

"She'll need some time," he said, "but she'll be fine."

He hoped Kate couldn't feel his tears dropping onto her hair. Lovely Kate, possibly the best friend he'd ever had in his life. She could both infuriate and delight him with her spontaneity. He could be himself with her; and the honesty between them was as refreshing as a dip in a cool stream. Her generosity and spontaneous joy in little things filled him with a spirit of adventure. Still, there were limits, even to honesty.

There was no reason that she, or anyone, would ever need to know how the thought or sight of Meghan still affected him.

CHAPTER 46

"Shoo!" cried Kate, waving a broom at a fat squirrel munching on the last of her pansies. "These rotten squirrels have taken over the yard."

"It's their salad bar," joked Meghan, as she sat on Kate's back patio, snacking on sliced apples and Gjeitost cheese. Hummingbirds whirred around their ruby-red feeders, and large, cottony clumps of seed from desert broom swirled through the air. Whimsical metal sculptures of jackrabbits and javelinas lurked amid prickly pear and barrel cacti.

It was the first time they'd met since the awkward dinner together at Bryan's. She'd missed her best friend's company and had feared their friendship was over.

Kate poured iced sun tea for Erin and herself, then brought out hot coffee for Meghan.

"Thanks!" Though the iced tea looked better, Meghan was touched. Kate was an avid tea drinker who never seemed to have coffee in the house, and Meghan had always had to bring her own. Kate had obviously gone all out to make her feel welcome today.

Things had been pretty tense between Meghan and her best friend since Bryan blindsided her at dinner with his declaration of his feelings for Kate. Yet Kate insisted she'd been even more surprised than Meghan had been.

"Heaven knows what's going on over at my place." said Meghan. "I hired a gardener to look after my yard and citrus trees." With Devrek still at large, she was afraid to go there alone.

Erin burst through the sliding glass door, laptop in hand.

"Close the door," said Kate. "I don't want any more lizards in the house."

"Listen to this." Erin set her laptop on the table and hurried back to pull the door shut. "Eddie could be in town next weekend."

Kate stopped chewing and set down her bran muffin. "What makes you say that?"

"I was doing a search of his last name in Tucson. There's an Estrella Maldonado getting married Saturday at the cathedral downtown. She could be related to Eddie."

"It's a common surname," said Kate. "Who are the parents of the bride?"

"Jaime and Maria, but I don't even know if Eddie has family here. He never introduced me to anyone." Erin shook her head, scowling. "I was such an *idiot*."

Kate put her arm reassuringly around Erin's shoulders. "Don't beat yourself up. We all live and learn. I know you won't make that kind of mistake again."

"That's for sure. Here's a birth announcement for an Eduardo Maldonado—but it's in the 1930s." Erin's long, slender fingers danced across the keyboard. "Here's another one dated twenty-six years ago. The parents are Jaime and Maria. It looks like this might be his family!"

"Even if it is, would he be reckless enough to make a public appearance here in Tucson, where he's a wanted man?" Meghan asked.

"Totally. He's an arrogant jerk, and if this is his sister, how could he *not* go?"

Kate frowned. "We should probably take this up with the police."

"I don't know about that." Meghan started to bite at her nails again and jammed her hands into her pockets, disgusted. She'd never been a nail-biter, but now her nails were bitten down to the quick. "Now that I think about it, what could the police do? ID every adult male at the wedding? Unless they've already got mug shots of him."

Kate shook her head. "I found out that he's never been arrested, so no mug shots. Don't you have pictures of him, Erin?"

"Believe it or not, I don't, though he must have hundreds of me." Her face reddened. "But I could spot him anywhere. I need to be at that wedding."

"No you don't!" cried Kate. "You need to be as far away from it as possible. And Bryan would never go for something like that either."

"Then don't tell him," said Erin.

"It doesn't seem fair to go behind his back on this, after all he's done to help rescue you."

"Maybe not, but if we want to do it, we can't tell him. He'd put a stop to it."

"And he'd be right," said Meghan. "It *is* dangerous."

"It wouldn't have to be," countered Erin. "I've got an idea. After church weddings, people usually head outside to congratulate the bride and groom and throw rice or something. I just show up outside, dressed for a wedding. I don't even have to go into the church. When the wedding lets out, I blend in with the crowd."

"What if he sees you?" asked Kate. "I can't stand to think of him hurting you again."

"I'd be in the background, in disguise; and he'd never expect to see me there. He might think that I'm still being held prisoner at the center."

"Surely, he's heard about your escape," said Meghan.

"You'd think so. On the other hand, I wouldn't be surprised if he totally forgot about me once he dumped me off."

"What a bastard," said Kate.

"Don't I know it!" Erin's eyes flashed with anger. "But I'm sick of hiding out and being a victim."

"I can relate to that." Meghan felt tension building between her shoulders.

Erin stood up. "I'm going to be outside the church when that wedding lets out. If he's there, I'll turn him in."

"Then I'll go with you," said Meghan.

"I can't believe you're saying that," said Kate. "You're always the levelheaded one."

"We've waited patiently on the sidelines for months, hiding out as if we were the criminals. Maybe it's time we take action."

"You've got a point," said Kate. "Deal me in."

"What about Bryan?" asked Erin.

"We can't tell him."

"Thanks, Mom," said Erin. "Meghan and I will mingle with the guests as they leave the church. If I see him, I'll signal you, then you can call 911."

"I'd need to be somewhere close enough to see you." Kate was damp with perspiration, though it was a cool, dry morning. "That might be easier said than done."

"You could be parked across the street," said Erin. "If I see him, I'll take out a Kleenex and wipe my eyes. Tears of joy, and all that."

"Once you give the signal, we'll just slip away," chimed in Meghan. "I'll give you a lace handkerchief to use."

"Old-school," said Erin.

"Weddings are old-school." Meghan took a swig of coffee, feeling better than she had in weeks. They were finally going to *do* something about their plight, instead of running and hiding. And they were doing it together.

Kate pushed her hair away from her neck. "I still think we should get police backup. They could give us a panic button to press while they waited nearby in unmarked cars. I've seen that done on TV."

Meghan shook her head. "I don't think so. I've worked with quite a few officers at school, and I'm pretty sure they wouldn't want to place civilians in that kind of danger. And if we ask for their support and they direct us *not* to do it, then we can't do it."

"So you think we should do this without help from the police?" asked Kate.

"I'd love to have police backup," said Meghan. "But like Bryan, they'd probably put a stop to our plan if they knew about it."

"So how do we actually go about this?" demanded Kate.

"Let's just put ourselves in the vicinity of the wedding, like Erin suggested. If she happens to spot Maldonado, we call 911 and report his whereabouts. If not, we go out to lunch and forget the whole thing."

"Something tells me it won't be as simple as that," said Kate.

"Nothing ever is, but we can improve our odds by doing reconnaissance ahead of time. We'll check out the area around the church, including parking, and make sure we know the time when the service should be letting out. We'll research everything."

"And get new dresses," said Erin.

"Not to mention wigs," added Meghan. "You two stand out in any crowd with your gorgeous red hair. Do you think you could loan me and Erin some wide-brimmed hats, Kate?"

"My hats aren't the look you're after. And this is already getting way too complicated."

Saturday was a cold, crystalline November day. The mountains were dusted with snow, down to the four-thousand-foot-elevation. Fifteen hundred feet lower, and Tucson would have enjoyed one of its rare snow-falls.

The first step of their plan was for Kate to leave early and get a good parking spot across from the cathedral. Then she would walk to a nearby restaurant and kill time having lunch, while trying to stay calm enough to actually eat. Ninety minutes later, she was to head back to the car and sit inside with its tinted windows cracked open, pretending to be on her cell phone.

Since Kate's lime-green VW could be easily recognized, and Meghan was a school principal, they'd rented two beige cars to blend in. Wearing a brunette wig, faded jeans, a gray sweatshirt and black parka, Kate left Meghan's rental townhouse first.

It was still cold and windy an hour later when Meghan and Erin made their exit. They were glad they'd stopped by Meghan's unoccupied house the day before to get coats, despite Meghan's uneasiness at being there. She wondered if she'd ever feel safe there again.

The face of the mission-style cathedral was stark white in the midday sun. As Meghan drove slowly past the front, she was relieved to spot Kate's rented Honda sitting across the street, as planned. She was glad to see several women wearing dressy hats and coats as they headed toward the church on one of Tucson's rare cold days. Hopefully, she and Erin wouldn't draw undue attention to themselves in a city where women rarely wore coats and hats.

Meghan's mind raced as they drove around, killing time. What if they passed by the church too often and aroused suspicion, or what if Kate spent too long at the restaurant? So many things could go wrong.

The massive wooden doors of the cathedral were still closed, but mariachis now lined the steps leading up to the entrance.

"Mom's in the car now," said Erin.

"It's time to make our move." Meghan maneuvered into a parking spot several blocks away. They donned their sunglasses, coats, and new hats and strolled toward the cathedral, hoping to pass for a mother and daughter who could blend with wedding guests. Meghan took care to project a calm, relaxed manner, though her entire body felt coiled and ready to react. She and Erin smiled as they spoke, lingering to admire a small garden.

Minutes later the large doors swung open. The organ was playing the recessional, Mendelssohn's "Wedding March." When the bride and groom appeared in the doorway, the mariachis raised their bows to their violins, placed trumpets to their lips, and burst into song.

The bride was petite, with beautiful brown eyes. She looked angelic in her white lace gown. Meghan pushed aside a pang of guilt about what she was about to do, reminding herself that she didn't want Eddie to be able to hurt other girls like he'd hurt Erin.

As the crowd spilled out onto the street, Meghan took a deep breath and led Erin forward. They fell in with the crowd and applauded the newlyweds. Smiling, she commented to Erin about the loveliness of the bride. For a brief instant, she thought the mothers of the bride and groom might have exchanged a questioning glance, but they quickly turned their attention back to the receiving line. Tears flowed, trumpets and violins soared, and the sky rained rice.

Meghan managed to stay on the fringe of the group, but Erin was swept into the receiving line. As her goddaughter hugged the bridesmaids and kissed the bride with a nervous smile, Meghan tried to catch her eye, to no avail.

As Erin turned away, a bearded man at the end of the receiving line grabbed her by the upper arm. His eyes locked into hers. Her smile disappeared. She removed her arm from his, opened her purse, pulled out a lace handkerchief, and dabbed at her eyes.

It must be Eddie, and he'd recognized Erin! Meghan had to act fast.

Smiling, she stepped forward and took Erin firmly by the arm, steering her away from the group toward their rental car. Erin managed a warm smile. She hoped that Eddie's role in the receiving line would keep him occupied long enough for them to get away.

On their way to the car, they hurried past a white Crown Victoria. Meghan wondered if it was an unmarked police car. As they approached it from behind, she took a closer look. No one was in the driver's seat, but there was a man in the passenger seat with the window down. There was a distinctive mole on the back of his neck.

She stifled a gasp. The man in the car had white hair and no beard, but after sitting behind him in court for two weeks, she had no doubt that the hideous mole on the back of his neck belonged to Karl Devrek. Then she spotted a rifle across his lap!

They were too close to turn back. They had to keep on walking right past him. She held her breath, praying that she wasn't visibly trembling, and that the sunglasses, wigs, hats, and coats would keep them from being recognized.

When they were almost a block away, Meghan took Erin by the arm. "Follow me," she said under her breath, guiding Erin into a side entrance of the walled courtyard of the cathedral.

Erin made the abrupt turn beside Meghan, keeping up the brisk pace.

"Devrek's here, with a rifle," whispered Meghan, once they were inside the courtyard.

Erin paled. "Where?"

"In that white Crown Vic. Keep your head down." Ducking their heads, they ran to the rear of the church.

"Mom was parked pretty close to that car."

"You gave her your signal. By now she should be a mile from here, calling 911."

"I sure hope he didn't see her," said Erin. "Or us."

"He has no reason to know her, and she's in disguise," reassured Meghan. She hoped it was true, but had the impression that Devrek was very methodical and thorough. She regretted going along with this plan. What had she been thinking?

Behind the cathedral, Meghan led Erin down concrete steps to a basement entrance. "Let's sit down here, on the bottom steps. We're below ground level and out of sight." And hopefully, out of the line of fire.

Sitting beside Erin, she called 911 to report seeing Devrek in front of the church, armed with a rifle. Almost as an afterthought, she reported that Maldonado was in the receiving line.

"Officers are already en route to that location," said the operator. "Get to a safe place and take cover."

"We're doing our best. Tell them to hurry."

"What did they say?" whispered Erin.

"The police are already on their way. Your mom must have gotten safely away and made the 911 call." Meghan put her arm around Erin. "She must be okay."

Erin's eyes brimmed with tears of relief.

Suddenly an image of Devrek pushing his way into the church and firing at random flashed through Meghan's mind. Not only was he an evil man, but she was starting to wonder about his sanity. Showing up with a rifle at such a public place didn't strike her as his style.

She jumped up. "I need to warn the wedding guests. Stay here. I'll be right back. I'm going to try to stop anybody else from going outside."

Meghan hurried up the steps, opened the door, and entered the church from the rear. She followed the sound of voices down the corridor until she saw a doorway leading into the front of the sanctuary. Guests lined the aisles, slowly moving toward the rear of the cathedral and outside to the receiving line.

She spotted the priest near the doorway, listening to a police officer. Suddenly the priest started directing wedding guests to get away from the doors and move into the hallway. Then he stepped outside.

The mariachis followed him back into the church, still playing, as if it were a normal progression of the celebration. Guests poured back into the cathedral, looking worried and confused, followed by the frightened-looking bride, groom, and wedding party, minus Eddie.

"What the hell's going on?" shouted an older man.

"Get down!" she heard a woman cry. Another woman herded her children into pews and told them to lie on the floor. A baby was crying, and a young girl screamed. The groom guided his trembling bride to a middle pew and shielded her with his body.

Once everyone was inside, another officer announced that the cathedral was being put in lockdown. Meghan had to move fast to get back outside to Erin.

She edged out the door of the sanctuary and hurried back down the corridor, her pulse racing. She hoped she wouldn't be stopped by an officer—or by Eddie. She managed to slip out the way she'd come in, seconds before she heard the door on the landing lock behind her.

An officer stepped outside the rear exit, just above them. He made eye contact with her and signaled for them to stay down.

Devrek's car was blocked by a squad car. He stepped on the accelerator, rammed the car in front of him, then backed into the one behind him. He pulled up onto the sidewalk and scraped along the wall of a flower shop, pulled back out and slammed into another car. He was trapped.

"Lay down your weapons! Get out of the car!" ordered an officer over a bullhorn.

Devrek leapt from the car, rifle in hand, and dashed into the walled courtyard.

"Drop your weapon!" shouted an officer, pulling out his own firearm.

Meghan pushed Erin flat against the concrete. They lay there, facedown.

"Drop the gun!"

"Hell no! Drop yours!" she heard Devrek shout.

Shots rang out.

After a brief silence, they heard voices in the courtyard and a siren getting louder and louder, until it stopped very close to them. They crouched lower against the steps.

A few minutes later, Meghan peeked out of the stairwell. Police cars and an ambulance were in the courtyard, lights flashing, as EMTs worked on a bleeding man on the ground. One of them checked his vitals, shook his head, and spoke in a low voice to the others.

Standing beside her, Erin clutched the railing, her knuckles white. "I think it's Devrek. They've stopped working on him."

Meghan put her arm around her goddaughter, who was trembling.

"Is he dead?" asked Erin.

"It looks like they're handling it as a crime scene now—not a rescue."

They watched as his face was covered.

"He can't hurt anyone else now," said Erin.

Instead of the bride and groom driving off with loud cans clanging behind the car, two guests raced off in the bridal limo with the best man. During the pandemonium, Eddie got away.

He switched cars and made it to Nogales, where he was detained at the border and transported to the Pima County jail.

Within a week, the FBI located Devrek's townhouse on the north side of Tucson. It was listed under the name of Don Holden. When they searched the place, they found a large collection of child pornography, including professional photographs of girls from halfway houses, but Devrek had been careful to have no child porn on his computer. They found several different Nevada phone numbers, all of which turned out to be disconnected.

It wasn't until weeks later that the sheriff in Lawrence County, South Dakota, got a call from the sheriff of Meade County that the case of the missing girls from the vanished treatment center finally broke open. A group of Hell's Angels shared detailed information with a clerk at a Harley Davidson tee shirt shop in Sturgis, and asked him to call the sheriff. They wanted to be of help, but not to slow their trip or get involved with the law.

They'd picked up a terrified, battered girl hitchhiking. The girl had told them she'd escaped from a remote camp near Deadwood. She'd given them the exact location and said other girls were still imprisoned there. When they'd stopped so she could call the sheriff, she'd slipped away. She'd probably hitched another ride. They weren't sure if she'd even reported it.

But the story she'd told them checked out. By the time the FBI heard about it, the Lawrence County Sheriff's Department had rescued fourteen girls and arrested five staff members, including Dr. Randolph.

In a search of Devrek's home, the authorities had found a newspaper clipping on his desk about a ribbon-cutting ceremony event that was scheduled to kick off a planned community on the northwest side of Tucson. The name of Bryan James was underlined. There was also a receipt from a bar in Ludington, Michigan, where Will had brought Meghan to see the car ferry.

Sunlight beamed through the kitchen blinds at Meghan's rented townhome. She rolled out the dough for the piecrust, exerting just the right amount of pressure. She rubbed her hands on her apron. "I love to make homemade pumpkin pie, and it's a lot more fun doing it together."

Kate lifted a baked pumpkin from the oven. "Now comes the hard part."

"Maybe not. I stopped by my place to pick up the food processor. It's so great to be getting ready for Thanksgiving without worrying about whether we're being watched or are in imminent danger."

"Such a huge weight off our shoulders," said Kate. "And I'm so thankful that those girls at the center were finally rescued."

"So am I." Meghan frowned as she lifted the flattened dough into the pie pan. Then she pinched off the extra dough and crimped the edges.

"So what's wrong?" asked Kate.

"I just keep thinking back to that night I was alone on the bluffs of Arcadia and how terrified I was that it might be Devrek coming down the steps after me. It turned out to be Will, but it could have been Devrek. He'd been in Michigan last summer only an hour or so from where I was. Maybe he'd even watched my cabin from the woods."

"We'll never know. He had contacts in Chicago. Maybe he took a drive north along the lakeshore, then took the car ferry across the lake from Wisconsin." Kate cut the pumpkin into smaller pieces and fed them into the food processor. "But it's over now. He can't come after you anymore."

"It gives me the chills to think of it. Why do you suppose he didn't lay a hand on me that night he was in my home?"

"I'd rather not try to analyze his twisted mind anymore, now that we don't have to. But he seemed to delight in the hunt and in terrifying his victims."

"I had no sign of trouble in Michigan, but I never lost a gnawing fear that I was still being followed. I figured I was getting paranoid, but once I got back to Tucson, Devrek obviously wanted me to know he was still stalking me. Maybe he didn't want me on his turf."

"You weren't paranoid. You've always been a very stable, rational person."

"I always thought so, until this. I'm so thankful it's all behind us now," said Meghan. "But I still feel bad that we had to spoil that beautiful couple's wedding."

"I'll tell you what would have *really* spoiled their wedding," said Kate. "If it weren't for you and Erin, the bride's brother would probably have been gunned down on the church steps. Your courage and fast reactions may have even saved the bride and groom and other guests. As it turned out, no one got hurt except for Devrek. Now he can't hurt anyone else, and Maldonado's behind bars. You and Erin were able to track down those predators and bring this all to a head when the authorities couldn't."

"It wouldn't have been possible without you, Kate. The three of us did this together."

"Yes, we did." Kate poured the fresh pumpkin filling into the piecrust and washed her hands. "No more guilt trips."

"No more guilt trips," agreed Meghan. "We've got enough left over to make empanadas. We can have them later with hot cider. Tomorrow, I'm moving back home."

CHAPTER 47

The sun was still high in the sky as Will turned off onto the wooded road that led to Interlochen, the fine arts school that had once been the center of his universe. He was glad it was finally May. Whether the winter had been more severe than usual, or had just seemed that way, he wasn't sure. The long, dark days reflected the darkness of his mood whenever he thought about Meghan and how it might have been.

At least he'd managed to work on the orchestration for his symphony throughout the cold, overcast days while wind shrieked across Lake Michigan and snowdrifts piled high against his cottage. During the three days he'd been snowbound, he'd accomplished more than ever.

Now that he was finished, he'd need to make a decision about the next step in his career. He wasn't going to spend the rest of his life alone here on the dunes, pining for a woman who didn't love him. He considered going back on the concert circuit, but after years of living in different hotels, he'd had enough. He wanted to be home, and to spend time with his mom.

As important as Interlochen had been to Will while he was growing up, he hadn't made the short trip there since he'd returned to Michigan. This morning, Martha had given him a gentle push. She'd claimed she didn't feel up to going to the concert and hoped he could put her ticket to good use. When he'd asked if he should pick up Sandra, who always went to the concerts with her, she had told him she'd planned to go alone.

Once on campus, he felt almost as excited as he'd been as a boy. Students in their traditional navy knickers and red sweaters lingered around the cabin porches and under large oak trees, just as they had in his youth. He remembered Jennifer, with her blonde ponytail. She'd tied her sweater over her back just so, with the sleeves draped with careless perfection over her breasts.

He thought of Mark, Akio, and Jacob, friends who'd shared his love for music, the outdoors, and girls. They'd rehearsed together by the hour, swam and canoed whenever they could, and pursued their first loves on warm summer nights.

One foggy evening they'd gone skinny-dipping at a nearby lake. He could still remember the feeling of the cold water against his skin and the pure sensuality of that night. As he looked out at the mist-enshrouded lake, he pictured himself swimming nude with Meghan. His fantasy was so vivid that he could feel her body, cool and wet, against his. He pushed the image from his mind.

Jacob was a cellist with the Boston Philharmonic, Mark was director of a university marching band, and Akio was a full professor at Julliard. His friends had thrown themselves into their musical careers and never looked back.

Will continued on a wooded path toward the Bowl, the outdoor amphitheater where important performances were often held. He remembered how proud he'd been to perform on stage there with Martha and Jake in the audience.

Though Bryan had paid for his tuition to Interlochen, he'd never heard Will perform there—or play the piano anywhere. Hopefully that would change when he visited next week. Will had called Bryan every few weeks since he'd been shot. One day, he'd noticed that his father had sounded pretty down, and had surprised himself by inviting him to visit for a week in Michigan to do some fishing. He'd been even more surprised when his dad had accepted.

As he passed the old wishing well, he took a shiny penny from his pocket. He imagined Meghan standing beside him. He tried not to think of her. She knew where to find him but had made no effort to reconnect, and his attempt to reach out to her had been a disaster.

He tossed the penny into the well and made his wish. *I want to find a way to share my love of music.* Sunlight bounced off the bright copper coin as it plunked into the water, then drifted downward to the bottom.

Through the trees, he could make out the Kresge Auditorium. Covered by an overhead roof, the rear and sides were open to the fresh breeze off the water and the sound of rustling trees. On occasion, it could also be open to sharply angled rain.

His seat was excellent, near the front. The lake was silvery-blue, with sunlight dancing across the water. Will felt a knot in his throat as the conductor walked on stage and the World Youth Symphony Orchestra arose in unison. He was struck by the radiance of their young faces. Once upon a time, his eyes must have shone as brightly.

As the orchestra played Brahms, he saw a passing fishing boat. His mind drifted back to his life as a graduate student, with its intense competition and long hours of practice. Somewhere along the way, the sense of camaraderie and joy had disappeared. After earning his master's degree, he'd become lost in a whirlwind of concerts abroad, moving from one city to the next. No doubt about it—his days at Interlochen had been the highlight of his youth.

For Will, the music, woods, and wind off the water were inextricably intertwined. Being close to nature helped him create. He'd considered returning to Interlochen many times since he'd come home, yet he hadn't felt ready until tonight.

He thought back to the night Meghan had shared her dreams with him. When she'd happily recalled the impassioned performances of her choir students performing *West Side Story*, he'd pictured Interlochen students. Yet he'd never brought her here, much as she would have loved it.

As the music soared, he lost himself in musical movements that were the stuff of his very soul. He had no sense of time passing. Then it was over. As he stood to applaud, tears came to his eyes. He'd come home, after all these years.

⁂

Meghan spotted Kate sitting at their favorite table in the patio of the Prickly Pear. The acacia trees were in bloom in the courtyard, and Kate wore a white gardenia in her hair.

She leaned over to give Kate a hug. "You look more gorgeous every time I see you." She admired Kate's ability to carry off such a bold look. On anyone else, it would have been outrageous, but on Kate it was pure enchantment. She could see how Bryan had been drawn to her, though they were such opposites.

"Thanks." Kate smiled warmly. "I can't wait to tell you the news."

"Don't keep me in suspense."

"Erin's been accepted at San Diego State for fine arts. She's transferring there this summer. I'm going to drive her there, and I'll stay a while. It'll be great to get back to the ocean."

"I know what you mean," said Meghan. "I always love being around the water. But I didn't realize she was trying to transfer to San Diego."

"She wants to make a fresh start. You can fly over weekends to visit," promised Kate. "We'll go to the Seaport Village, Sea World, and—"

"The zoo! Remember the fun we always have there?" Meghan hoped they'd have some time to see the sights without Bryan. She still couldn't imagine him and Kate as a couple.

She and Kate rarely spoke of Bryan, who'd gone back to work in a power chair, after a few modifications to his office building. He was still getting physical therapy and continued to gain more function in his toes, feet, and even in his legs.

"We'll have plenty of girl time," Kate said. "Bryan's not coming until later."

"It sounds like fun." Meghan had dreaded summer vacation this year and was relieved to have something to look forward to. During the school year, she'd been absorbed with her new job as principal, with little time to dwell on all that she'd lost. Last summer with Will, she'd been happier than she could ever remember.

This summer, she'd be preparing for the next school year, working to improve the curriculum, reorganizing class schedules, and making plans to set a more positive tone at school. It would be nice to start out the year as principal, rather than jumping aboard late in the first semester. Still, she missed the joy of leading her students in song as well as the friendships with other teachers she'd had as choir director. As principal, there was a certain distance between her and faculty members.

None of that mattered next to losing the only man she'd ever really loved. A trip to San Diego with Kate and Erin might be just what she needed to help her get out of the doldrums.

The waiter brought their lunches—the turkey-avocado-bacon sandwich for Meghan, and for Kate, the large topopo salad, with layers of cheese, tomatoes, olives, sliced avocados, and refried beans in lettuce, served in a large, bowl-shaped tortilla.

"There's something else I want to talk to you about," Kate said. "We've both been avoiding the subject pretty well."

Meghan put her sandwich down. "The elephant in the room."

Kate's smile faded. "Bryan. I need to know if it's really over between the two of you."

"Of course it's over. But isn't it a little late to be asking?"

"Maybe so. But are you absolutely sure?" Kate looked into Meghan's eyes, as if trying to read the truth.

"I'm sure." Irritation crept into Meghan's voice.

Kate grew quiet. Then she asked, "What if I were to marry him?"

"Marry Bryan? Are you serious?"

"Very serious. But if you have even the *slightest inkling* you'd ever want to get back together with him, I wouldn't dream of it. You have to be honest with me—and with yourself. Take your time. You don't need to answer right now."

"I am being honest. But stop and think, Kate. You two are such opposites, and you've always gotten on each other's nerves. And there's so much involved. Are you really up for being a caregiver, maybe for decades?"

"He'd never allow me to care for him. He has his own help."

"I never dreamed you'd make it permanent. You're young and healthy. What if one day you wanted to have another child?"

"I'm not *that* young. That's not going to happen."

"And can he still . . . ?"

"Make love?"

"Never mind. It's not my business." Meghan flushed. She well knew of his great tenderness and skill as a lover, but he still wasn't walking, despite all the therapy. Though she'd heard he was getting more movement in his feet and legs and could transfer from the power chair to different furniture, she hadn't had the nerve to inquire about the full extent of his injury.

Kate turned crimson. "I . . . I don't know."

"The subject hasn't come up?" Meghan couldn't believe what she was hearing.

"I'm fine with things the way they are," Kate said.

"The answer is obviously no."

"It doesn't matter, don't you see? That's what's always ruined things for me. Now that Bryan's more relaxed and open, we enjoy each other's company."

"You always used to set each other off. What about his compulsive neatness? He loves meat and hates Asian food. I could go on."

"He has his space, and I have mine. He doesn't ask any more of me than I want to give."

"But Kate, you could be giving up so much. And how would you have your own space if you were married?"

"I've had sensitive lovers, but all their efforts and years of therapy never helped me get over being uptight. Sooner or later, a man finds out I'm faking. I guess it was spoiled for me forever by a boyfriend of my mom's when I was thirteen."

"I'm so sorry." Meghan said. "I had no idea. You never told me about that."

"Guess I never felt like bringing it up."

"It's impossible for me to imagine life without—"

"Sex?"

"Well, yes."

"I thought you'd given up all earthly pleasures in pursuit of your career."

"For now, but I'm leaving that door open. You'd be closing it forever."

"I love him, and that's all that matters."

"I hope you're right. But sometimes I wonder if any relationship . . ."

"Go on."

"It's too dark a thought for today. I don't want to spoil . . . your good news."

"You'd better get it off your chest."

Meghan arranged and rearranged her napkin in her lap. "It's just that things that start out with all the promise of a newborn can take such a dark, twisted turn."

"It does seem that way at times."

"Sometimes I feel like happiness is kind of like the Trojan horse . . . a deception, hiding something dreadful inside. I'm not sure I could ever trust my own feelings again."

"Oh, Meghan." Kate took her hand and squeezed it. "I'm part of this pain, aren't I? Your best friend with your lover."

"Ex-lover. There's something you need to understand. As soon as I left Tucson, Bryan threw up some kind of emotional barrier between us, before I even met Will. I haven't felt close to him since last May. From the first time I spoke to him from Michigan, I sensed he was shutting me out. Two months later, I wrote to tell him I'd found someone new, and things have been officially over since then. If Bryan and Will hadn't turned out to be father and son, I'd probably be with Will right now." Her eyes flooded with tears. "So do what's best for you, and stop worrying about me. I have no intention of getting back with Bryan."

Kate speared a slice of avocado, savored it, then set her fork down and looked across the table at Meghan. "Do you still love Will?"

"I'm afraid so. But I don't even exist to him. After what happened last fall, he's written me out of his life."

"Why don't you fly out to see him?" asked Kate. "He sounds like a caring person."

Meghan frowned. "You've talked with Will again?"

"Will's been calling Bryan every few weeks or so. He's invited his dad to come for a visit next week. They're planning to do some fishing."

"I can't believe it."

"It's true. Will called me first to make sure I was okay with the plan, and then to see if he should make any modifications to his cottage. I told him I thought the trip would do Bryan good and suggested he put in a ramp."

"How's he going to handle the flight? I can't imagine him getting through O'Hare."

"It would be tough for him to fly commercial right now. He'll probably arrange a private flight with Greg Gillespie. The guy is terrific. He's the pilot who helped in Erin's rescue. Bryan seems to be looking forward to the trip."

"That just proves how right I was to take myself out of the picture," Meghan said. "I'm glad they're getting together. That never would have happened if I were still involved."

"Without you, they'd probably never have gotten to know each other at all."

"Their meeting was a nightmare because of me."

"Maybe so, but you still care for Will, and I'll bet he still cares for you. At least consider reaching out to him so you can find out."

"Let's drop it. I'm sure Will has someone else by now, and even if he hasn't, it's clear he's not interested in me anymore."

"I could feel things out the next time Will calls," offered Kate.

"Don't you dare!" Meghan snapped. "And please don't mention his name again!"

CHAPTER 48

Will wheeled Bryan up the ramp he'd built to his cottage entrance. Maybe now he could start to get to know his father, before it was too late.

As they entered the living room, the afternoon sun cast long patterns of light on the wall, illuminating the oil painting of the dunes.

"Where did you get this painting?" his father demanded.

"My mom—Martha gave it to me last summer, when I first moved out here on the dunes. She used to have it over her mantel. It was always my favorite. Do you like it?'

"I'd thought all my work was lost in a fire, years ago."

"*You* painted it?" Will was incredulous. A part of his father—a tangible, visible expression of his spirit, had been with him all this time.

"I was an art major, once upon a time. An oil painter."

"It's the focal point of my home. It might have been nice to know it was done by my father. I'm sorry your paintings were burned. Do you still paint?

"I set them on fire myself, and gave up painting . . . after what happened."

"You gave up your whole career?"

"And took up my brother's," he said. "Look—I know I haven't been fair with you."

"Neither has Martha." Will frowned. "She should have told me you painted it. When she gave it to me as a housewarming gift, I asked her for the name of the artist. Now that I think back on it, she changed the subject."

"She was trying to protect you."

"I understand, but it would have been nice to at least know she was my great aunt."

"Don't be too hard on her. All she ever did was love you and raise you as her own. I'm sure she wanted to spare you the painful truth about how your parents died—not that she really knew the truth."

"What *is* the truth about my mother? I don't know much about her, except that she cheated on you with your twin brother. She doesn't sound like . . . a very nice person."

"Your mother was a *wonderful* person. She just made a mistake."

"Tell me about her."

Bryan looked down at his hands and then back at Will. Finally he responded. "She was kind and beautiful, barely more than a girl . . ."

Will listened with rapt attention, hardly moving. At times, his father's voice broke, and he stopped to pull himself back together, but he kept on. He shared the kind of details Will longed to know: lullabies his mother had sung to him, books she'd read to him, and that she'd had a generous spirit and enthusiasm for life. Will's eyes brimmed with tears as Bryan told him how much his mother had loved him.

"I've always loved you, too," said Bryan. "Wrong or not, I believed that the best way I could show it was to provide financial support and stay out of your life."

"At least I didn't grow up feeling abandoned," said Will. "Though I was."

"I believed I was a murderer and that you deserved better. Martha was the best woman I knew to raise you, and Jake seemed to be a terrific dad. I knew they loved you. Once I saw the three of you together, I gave up any ideas that I'd had of taking you back. I felt the best thing I could do for you was to let them raise you without my interference."

The clock on the mantel chimed one, jolting Will back to reality. More than two hours had passed since Bryan had started to speak. "Thanks for sharing this. It means a lot, but we have to start getting ready. We're due in Onekama by two-thirty."

"Then let's get going." Bryan took Will's hand and gave it a squeeze. Will wished he could walk along the beach for a while, to allow his heart to regain its normal rhythm and his brain to take in all he'd learned about his mother. After all these years, he was finally starting to get a sense of the loving woman she'd been.

He put the folding wheelchair, gear, jackets, sandwiches, and drinks into the back of the Jeep; helped Bryan up into the seat; and headed out. He couldn't remember the drive to Portage Lake ever taking so long.

He turned to Bryan, who hadn't spoken since they'd left. "I want you to know how much I appreciate your talking with me like you did. It must have taken a lot of courage."

"It was long overdue."

"Martha's glad we're having this week together," said Will.

"So am I." After a long pause, Bryan cleared his throat and coughed. "Since . . . I lost your mother, I've lived alone. It's not what I'd call an ideal life."

"I'm sorry about that," said Will.

"What about you?" asked Bryan. "Have you ever been in love?"

Color crept up Will's neck into his face. "Only once."

Bryan came straight to the point. "Were you and Meghan serious about each other?"

"So now it's my turn for blood-letting! Is that it?"

"That's not my intent. I just wondered how things were between you and Meghan before I showed up and ruined everything."

"I never knew Meghan. I once thought I loved a woman named Anne, but she was just a figment of my imagination."

"She's no figment."

"*You should know.*" Will was furious that his father would have the insensitivity to bring up the topic of the woman they both loved. It was the one subject certain to destroy any delicate bonds that could ever develop between them.

"I'm the one to blame, not her," said Bryan. "I gave her the alias and told her to use it until they captured whoever was after her. I let her know how important it was not to use her real name so that bastard couldn't track her down."

"You even renamed her? My God."

It was my own version of witness protection. It seemed to work until she returned to Tucson."

"I knew she was afraid of something. She always acted like she was being stalked."

"She was, by an escaped convict, up until last November. Hasn't she ever told you about what happened to that psychopathic, child-molesting psychiatrist?"

"No. We haven't been in touch."

"The bastard had been waiting outside a church wedding with a loaded rifle, probably lying in wait to kill the best man and whoever else got in the way. Meghan saw him and called 911. He refused to surrender and shot at the police. They shot back, and he was killed."

Will shook his head in disbelief. "There's not much she did get around to telling me. But I have to admit that she did tell me right up front that she wasn't available because she had someone back home." Will glanced at Bryan. "She never confided what was bothering her, but she did let me know she was involved in a serious relationship."

Bryan's face reddened and he swallowed hard. "I'd warned her not to confide in anyone."

"I guess she did whatever you wanted her to do."

"*Hardly.*"

Will felt the chill of Bryan's glare, though he was watching the road. "Sorry. But you were the one who sent her here and never told us."

"She had to get away from Tucson—fast. This was the safest place I could think of on the spur of the moment. There wasn't time to analyze everything."

"But why didn't you at least share your plan with my mom? She could have helped."

"I didn't want to burden her with it, or put her at risk. For the plan to work, no one could know. I didn't even tell Meghan where she was headed."

"You're joking."

"Not at all. I got in touch with the Larsens, who used to help us open and close our cottages. Our families had known each other years ago, and

I knew they'd owned a farmhouse with a rental cabin. I hoped Meghan could stay there briefly, until they captured the bastard who was after her. I never dreamed it would take so long to track him down."

"You must have had to tell the Larsens something."

"Only that *Anne* needed to get away for a while. They were in the dark about her identity and about her relationship with me."

Will lowered his voice. "Did they know who I was to you?"

"There's no way they could have."

"Because, over the years, Joan has asked some pointed questions about my adoption. She seemed pretty curious at times."

"I don't know what to make of that." Bryan paused. "But it seems to me that you and Meghan have a lot to talk about."

Will wheeled the Jeep onto the shoulder and came to a screeching stop. "Knock it off, dammit! The subject of Meghan is off limits!"

He felt his father's steadying hand on his shoulder. "I just want you to have a good life . . . to not be alone in the world, like I used to be."

"Used to be?"

"I've found someone. That's what you need to understand. As far as Meghan is concerned, I'm out of the picture."

"So am I!" Will steered back onto the road and floored it. "But I've got to hand it to you. You never run out of fight."

"I came close a few times. Too close." Bryan's jaw tensed. "Only God could have pulled me from those raging waters."

"God, and the Coast Guard."

"And *you*. Thank you for calling the Coast Guard for me."

"No need. I didn't even know it was you at first. But I'm glad I did. It wasn't time for you to die out there. It sounds like you've made a new beginning for yourself, and I admire your courage."

If his handicapped father could get on with his love life, then so could he.

Will made a mental note to call Ginger, the attractive librarian who'd been openly flirting with him. He thought of her infectious laughter and her thinly disguised interest in him. Life was too short to waste on grieving for what might have been.

For a brief moment, he had an impulse to call Meghan but thought better of it. After her abrupt departure, her cutting remark when he'd called, and her failure to get back in touch with him, it was clear he meant nothing to her. Whatever happened in his dad's world, it was over between him and Meghan.

❧

The large fishing boat was moored to a dock in Onekama at the east end of Portage Lake. Bryan shook hands with Tom Lebowski, Will's friend, and captain of the fishing trawler. Tom and Will hoisted supplies and fishing gear into the boat; then Will wheeled Bryan up a makeshift ramp. They both helped him into the boat.

Bryan missed his power chair, which let him feel somewhat independent. But this was all temporary, he told himself. He was determined to continue in physical therapy and push himself hard until he could get around with a walker, then a cane. His goal was to walk on his own again.

Once they were aboard, Will cast off, and Tom shifted into reverse. He and Will worked together efficiently, with little need for talk as Tom steered the fishing trawler across Portage Lake and out into Lake Michigan. Once they reached the desired depth, Will set up the downriggers.

As a boy, Bryan had often trolled for perch and lake trout and had done some fly-fishing, but he'd never fished with downriggers. He watched the setup with interest.

Will hooked lead weights about the size of tennis balls to the lines. Once in the lake, the poles bent toward the water like Robert Frost's birches, bowed by ice. If a fish was on the line, the poles would pop up. Then he was to grab the pole, set the hook, and start reeling.

"You ready to start?" asked Will.

"I'd like to watch you bring one in before I give it a go," said Bryan.

"Good idea," said Tom. "Why don't you go ahead and take the first one, Will?" Tom seemed confident there would be fish for everyone.

The surface of the water was smooth, with gently rolling swells. Bryan looked back at the enormous dunes through the mist and remembered the fun of climbing the sand dunes as a boy, along with the thrill of running back down in bare feet.

He became engrossed in reading the depth-finder with its jagged, moving graph of the lake's bottom. It reminded him of watching the stock market.

When Will's pole popped up, he grabbed it, pressed it against his abdomen, and reeled fast. Then he let the fish run with the line, careful to keep it from getting slack. Suddenly, Bryan saw a silver shimmer of light as the fish broke the surface. The line whirred as the fish streaked off. It disappeared for several minutes, then leapt from the water near the boat.

"Get it right up to the side!" Bryan had seen too many fine catches lost at the end, with botched attempts to net the fish. You had to get close enough with the net. He wanted to leap up and net the fish himself, but that was one more thing he couldn't do right now.

Tom landed the beautiful steelhead, iridescent in the late-afternoon sun.

"You've got yourself a real fine fish there, son." For the first time in his life, Bryan was the proud father, admiring his son's catch. Tears came to his eyes at the enormity of lost time and for the unexpected gift of this moment.

Tom drew three beers from the ice chest. Bryan asked for a Coke. He drank silently as the powerful engine rumbled in the bowels of the twenty-three-foot trawler. An eerie whine sang through the lines of the downriggers. Wind was coming from the southwest, and the swells had grown to rolling mounds of water.

Bryan thought of the last time he'd been out on the lake, heading into the squall. He felt overwhelmed with gratitude at being allowed to live, and having this chance to go fishing with his son.

Will passed around sandwiches and chips, but Bryan never got a chance to take a bite. The second pole snapped erect off the transom.

"This one's yours, Dad!" Will sounded excited.

Bryan grabbed the pole and jammed it hard into his gut.

"Looks like a monster on the screen!" shouted Tom, watching the long, vertical line on the depth-finder. "Must have been right under the boat. Get the tip up! Now reel, but not too fast. Don't give it any slack."

Bryan held up the tip of the pole with difficulty and began reeling downward, as he'd seen Will do. The fish was surprisingly strong. He continued in the same rhythm, reeling in and waiting as the powerful fish made a wide swing outward. Then he started reeling it in again.

Beads of perspiration formed on his forehead and sweat trickled into his eyes. He still couldn't get the fish within twenty yards of the boat. His back and arms ached.

"Let me spell you awhile; then I'll hand it back over," said Will.

"No, thanks."

"He's pretty red in the face. Is he okay?" Tom commented to Will.

"I hope so."

Bryan's arm began to throb, and his abdomen was getting sore. The wind grew chilly and the swells larger, rocking the boat unpleasantly. Finally, the fog dispersed, and he could make out the shoreline, several miles away. He was glad he hadn't eaten that sandwich.

"I'm doing fine, but could you throw my jacket over my shoulders?"

Will draped the parka over his dad's shoulders. "You feel pretty tense."

"It's sure putting up one hell of a fight!" said Bryan.

"It's been almost an hour," Tom said. "Let us know if you'd like one of us to jump in there for a while."

Bryan didn't respond, reeling harder. His heart sank as he heard the line scream out again. Then he started to make headway. He didn't want to build up slack and let his fish snap the line. He didn't want Will or Tom to help land—or maybe lose—the fish. He wanted to catch it himself.

Finally, it was close enough to see. He knew it must be tiring for it lay on its side for an instant. He jerked up the pole and reeled faster. The fish took flight to the north, and then . . . nothing! He reeled harder. "Damn. It's gone."

"Keep reeling, don't stop!" shouted Tom, maneuvering the cabin cruiser to keep the fish behind the boat.

Exhausted, Bryan kept reeling. Why did he want this fish so much?

Then he felt the tug. It made one more brief pass by the boat and started to come in.

"Careful . . . real careful. The line is only twelve-pound test," cautioned Tom. "It's huge! I think I better use the gaff." Tom reached for the pole with a large metal hook jutting out from the end. For the bigger ones, the gaff was the surest way to bring them in.

"Let's use the net," Bryan said.

"It's your fish, but I'd hate to lose her. She could be a record-breaker!" With considerable finesse, Tom netted the fish and brought it onto the deck, where it flopped around fiercely. "It's an enormous Chinook—a king salmon."

Bryan grinned. The great salmon was strong and beautiful, still battling valiantly for her life. Bryan had developed a bond with this magnificent fish and had come to respect it. It was a worthy prize. He was swept with a sudden wave of sadness that this was to be her last struggle.

Tom rushed to the bow for his scale while Will steered the boat. "Fifty-three pounds is last year's record. I think you've got a good chance! We've got to get her into ice water right away so she won't dehydrate before the official weigh-in." Tom raised a club over the Chinook to put a quick end to her.

Bryan gestured him away. He leaned over, unhooked the fish, and with considerable effort, pushed her back into the net and scooped her up. Then he grabbed the railing, pulled himself up, and flipped the king salmon over the stern. He watched her flounder for a few seconds near the surface, then dive straight for the bottom. Then he collapsed back into his seat.

Silence reigned for a full minute until Tom said, as if stricken, "I just wish I could have weighed her."

"I was picturing her mounted over my mantel," Bryan said. "Then it hit me that I didn't want to see her that way."

Will placed his hands on his father's shoulders, overcome with tenderness for the man who had been his demon. "You stood up on your own."

Bryan beamed. "That's right! It's a start."

CHAPTER 49

The party spilled out into the courtyard. Mariachis with their festive trumpets and violins led the way, followed by Erin, radiant in the white lace gown she wore to celebrate her confirmation as a Roman Catholic. She breathed in the cool night air as she entered through an archway of red bougainvillea.

Margaritas flowed freely, as well as wine and citrus punch. The long banquet table was draped in a bright tablecloth and was arrayed with tea sandwiches, mini chimichangas, rolled tacos, and trays of veggies, crackers, and cheese. A second table offered watermelons filled with melon balls, grapes, and strawberries, and a large cake decorated in Erin's honor.

A year had passed since she'd been dumped off at that horrible place in Vegas and held against her will. Each day she gave thanks for her freedom. Tonight she felt blessed to be safely back home with her family and friends. The dancing was about to begin on what was turning out to be one of the best evenings of her life.

At breakfast this morning, Bryan had presented her with the delicate gold crucifix that she was wearing now. He'd offered to give her this party and had made no attempt to mask his pleasure about her confirmation.

Her godmother, Miss Walcott, still hadn't arrived, though she'd been at the ceremony at church. Erin hoped it wouldn't get awkward again between her mom, Miss Walcott, and Bryan. Tonight was a celebration, and she didn't want anything to cast a dark shadow over it.

Not only was she happy to be confirmed in the church, she had something else to celebrate. She'd thrown herself into her art classes this semester to make up for lost time and had earned straight As. With glowing reports from her professors and a letter from the dean, she'd been accepted at San Diego State.

Last weekend, Bryan had painted with her out on the patio. He seemed to enjoy her company and was very interested in her art.

"Did you get a chance to paint much in Virginia?" he'd asked.

"There were so many amazing scenes I wanted to paint, but I finally zeroed in on a beautiful old watermill. I painted it at different times of the day and at different times in the fall."

"A bit like Monet's series of the facade of the Rouen Cathedral."

"So you're into art history, too."

"It's kind of a long story. I was once an art major."

Erin had turned to him in surprise. "I thought you'd just taken up art a few months ago. I wondered how you got so good all of a sudden."

"It feels great to reclaim a bit of that guy I used to be."

"Lately, I've noticed a new luminosity in your paintings. They're very good."

"That means a lot to me, coming from such a talented artist."

"Do you really think so?"

"I know so."

"Two of my professors suggested that I major in commercial art to leave more career options open."

"Stick to your guns," said Bryan. "You've got real talent and a passion for what you're doing."

After talking with him, she'd decided to keep her major in fine arts.

Erin had gravitated toward Bryan long before her mother had. She'd always seen him as kind, generous, and caring. Most of all, she could tell that he believed in her as a person. He'd helped save her life, and he was the first man she'd ever been able to trust. She glanced over the patio to see him in his power chair, smiling like a proud father. He waved her over.

Erin beamed. She reached down and kissed him on the head. "This is one of the happiest nights of my life, and I have you to thank for it."

Bryan swallowed hard and smiled. "Same here."

A hush fell over the room as Meghan appeared in the doorway. She wore a turquoise gown and a dazzling aquamarine pendant with matching earrings. She glanced through the crowd for Kate and Erin, trying to ignore the stares and whispers. She wished she were home reading. Everyone knew that she and Bryan had been a couple, and that now he was with her best friend. She reminded herself that she was the principal of one of the largest high schools in the state. She could do this.

Her stomach knotted at the sight of Bryan in his wheelchair across the courtyard, but tonight was Erin's night. She was determined to be cheerful and relaxed. She spotted Kate near the fountain, in a hand-cro-cheted, floor-length Oaxacan dress embroidered with bright flowers.

Looking radiant, Kate greeted Meghan with a warm embrace. "I'm so glad you're here!"

"I wouldn't miss this for anything. Everyone seems to be having a great time."

"I hope so."

"You've done a wonderful job with her, Kate. She's turning out to be a terrific young woman."

"She is, isn't she?" smiled Kate. "You've helped her so much, too. I hope you really enjoy yourself tonight. "

"I'm sure I will. I think I'll get something to eat."

Meghan edged toward the food, making friendly conversation with the guests, many of whom were old friends from Central High School. She would make it clear to everyone that Kate and Bryan had her blessing, so that things could finally stop being uncomfortable. She made her way over to Erin. "I'm so happy for you." Meghan's eyes teared up. "I've always been honored to be your godmother."

"I'm the one who's honored." Erin took Meghan's hands and looked into her eyes. "I hope you have a good time at my party—and I hope you'll always be a big part of my life."

Meghan embraced her. "Of course I will." She couldn't miss the meaning. Both Kate and Erin seemed worried about how she'd react to Kate's impending marriage to Bryan.

She needed to have a normal conversation with Bryan and put an end to all the tension. She noticed him watching her from under a large orange tree in a secluded corner of the patio. She would make this work, for Erin's sake.

She sensed she was being watched by several guests. If they were hoping for an awkward encounter between her and Bryan, they were going to be disappointed. She would simply greet him, have a brief and friendly conversation, and return cheerfully to Kate and the others.

Bryan smiled up at her. "It's good to see you."

"Same here. What a lovely party. Erin's in her glory. She's the belle of the ball."

"I'd say you hold that honor."

She felt her cheeks getting warm.

Bryan gestured for her to sit down. "It can get tiresome looking up at people all evening,"

"It must give you a stiff neck." She wondered if her face was visibly red. Was he deliberately trying to throw her off?

"You look lovely this evening, as always." He smiled again, warmly.

"Thanks. You look well too. I really appreciate all you've done for Erin."

"My privilege. It's nice to be able to give something back, after all I've been given."

"Oh, Bryan." Meghan's voice fell as she looked at him there in the power chair. "How can you say that?"

"I've been given a new beginning."

"You're not bitter?"

"I don't have time for that."

"I don't suppose any of us do."

"That's right." Bryan turned to face her directly. "And no time for misplaced guilt."

"Don't lecture me."

"I know that you've blamed yourself for . . . for what I nearly succeeded in doing out in the lake that day. When you tried to apologize to me, I cut you off."

"Let's not spoil a wonderful evening."

"I don't intend to. I don't want to ever spoil anything in your life again. First of all, I want to make it clear I would never try anything like that again—in case you wondered."

Her stomach started to ache. "Of course I've wondered. Is Kate behind this little talk?"

"Not at all. I made a terrible mistake that day, but out there in the storm, I changed my mind. I wanted to live. Miraculously, God gave me another chance. But when a man decides to take his own life, that's between him and his maker. No one else has that kind of power over someone else."

"I should have sensed how you felt and tried to help."

"I didn't want help at the time. You're simply not to blame." He paused. "You're not responsible for what happened to your father, either."

Meghan turned crimson. "Let's not bring my father into this."

"Kate told me that the way I tried to kill myself was a cruel choice, considering what your father had done. She'd assumed that I knew."

Meghan looked down. "Suicide is always cruel to those left behind, whatever the method."

"I'm sorry for all that I put you through." He looked into her eyes. "If your father could speak to you now, I'm sure he'd tell you to stop blaming yourself."

"You have no right to speak for my father."

"Hear me out. I've spent most of my life blaming myself for something I didn't do, and it poisoned everything. When someone takes their own life, it's their own decision."

"Yet those who cared for them are always haunted to think of what they might have done to save them—especially those who loved them the most." Her voice broke. "Thank God you didn't die that day. I'm so grateful you were saved."

"Something happened out there." Bryan touched his crucifix. "I had this in my hand when I was rescued. It was a miracle."

"I remember." She paused. "But there was no miracle for my dad."

"Whether there was or not, it's not because of anything you did, or didn't do. I know I'm not the first to tell you this, but you have to find a way to accept that, and let it go. And even though it wasn't your fault, maybe you have to learn to forgive yourself."

"I know that you're right, but it's not that easy."

He looked intently into her eyes. "Stop blaming yourself, and that's an order."

"Domineering as ever." A smile broke across her features. "As if you could order someone to change how they feel."

"I just did." Bryan took her hand in his, and squeezed it, his eyes moist.

She laughed through her tears. "You *are* still the same old Bryan, aren't you?"

"Yes, and no—but enough of that. This is an evening for celebration, so go back and join the party. Have a wonderful time."

"Another order?"

"Call it a directive. Enjoy yourself."

"Alright then, I will. And, Bryan, what you've said to me . . . means a lot. I know this comes from a deep place . . . and that you really care. I promise to take it to heart."

Feeling shaky and almost weightless, Meghan drifted back across the courtyard, surprised at the powerful impact of his words. She'd been told many times that she wasn't responsible for her father's death, yet somehow Bryan's words had penetrated her very soul. He knew what he was talking about. It was almost as if he *had* been speaking for her dad.

She was suddenly overcome with a sense of boundless goodwill toward Bryan, and toward Kate, Erin, and all the guests, including those who'd been staring at them, whispering.

Kate reentered the courtyard carrying a tray of veggies. Meghan hoped she hadn't seen the tender gesture that Bryan had shown when he'd squeezed her hand.

The band played *Mambo No. 5*, and Meghan got out on the dance floor with an old friend from Central High and started to cut loose and enjoy herself. She loved to dance. But when they played "*When I Fall in*

Love," she was once again floating across the ballroom at the Grand Hotel in Will's arms. She had to fight back tears. Unlike the lyrics of the song, it had not been forever.

✍

Erin was helping out a friend at a local art gallery. Kate and Bryan had the house to themselves. Kate had started to enjoy teasing Bryan, sometimes spending the better part of an afternoon driving him ever closer to the edge of helpless ecstasy. At first she hadn't expected him to respond. He'd allowed her to explore his body at her leisure, never commenting when she showed no interest in being pleased in return.

Tonight Bryan suggested they try something different. "Come and lie beside me," he said tenderly. "Just let me be close to you."

Kate had never confided to Bryan about her problem. He'd seemed satisfied with being pleasured himself. This afternoon she felt playful and relaxed, and allowed him to gently caress her. She held her breath and remained still.

Suddenly she grew tense. "Let's not do this anymore."

"Whatever you like." He moved away. Bryan had come to suspect that something had happened to Kate to make it bad for her.

She began to cry, great silent tears. "No. Don't stop."

A shudder of excitement ran through him. Yes, he had grown to love her, his lovely Bird of Paradise. Not in the same way he'd loved Meghan, but every bit as much. With her, he'd found an honesty and openness he'd never known before. Now he would give something back.

Time slipped by unnoticed as the sun sank behind the mountains and they made love. After a time she held him closer and cried out.

Holding her tenderly in his arms, he saw tears in her eyes.

"Are you alright?" he said, gently brushing away a tear.

"Never better," she whispered.

CHAPTER 50

Every time Meghan heard *Pomp and Circumstance*, she got goose bumps. Tonight, as the graduating seniors filed out onto the field, she was nearly overcome with emotion. She couldn't remember a better rendition of the graduation march. She marveled at the band director, who'd worked miracles with the undisciplined, discordant group of high school students. Many had come to him unable to read music, and few could afford private lessons.

Helping the seniors get to this point had been an enormous challenge after such a year of turmoil, but with a concerted effort by teachers and counselors, most had managed to meet their requirements to graduate.

These beautiful young people were about to go out into the world to make their marks. Their lives were filled with promise, as every sentimental commencement address maintained. As their principal, she felt a sense of closure and celebration—something she'd missed when she stopped directing concerts. Ceremonies like this were not only a rite of passage for the graduates, but also a tangible reward for parents and faculty who'd struggled for so long to show them the way.

She thought back to the night when she and Will had enjoyed the Northern Lights together. She'd put her dreams for an ideal school into words, and Will had taken her seriously. He hadn't chided her for being a hopeless idealist.

Her own high school graduation had been darkened by the death of her mother. By the time she'd graduated from college, she'd lost both her parents; but her grandparents had come all the way from Tucson to Maine to see her graduate, which had meant the world to her.

To the southwest, the sky was getting darker. She thought she might have heard a faint rumble of thunder but didn't hear it again. Though they'd predicted a 20 percent chance of rain, she'd never heard of graduation being rained out in Tucson. The monsoons normally didn't start until early July, and even if it did rain somewhere in the city, most places probably wouldn't get wet.

She'd opted not to go to the contingency plan to move graduation to the auditorium. That would have upset a large number of students and their relatives, as the auditorium could only seat a fraction of the crowd that was already in the stadium. She'd been introduced to family members who'd come from as far away as Vermont and Guadalajara, Mexico. Now she wondered if she'd made a mistake. If there was lightning nearby, she'd have to call off the whole event.

Last year she'd missed graduation while she was in hiding. Thank God that was all behind her. Now she could stop living on the defensive and start working to shape the future of the school. She hadn't grown to love her new job yet as much as she'd loved being choir director, but being a high school principal had its rewards.

In addition to serving as principal, she'd volunteered for several district committees and had still been able to continue singing in her church choir. She had little time to herself, but that was just as well. She couldn't afford to waste energy agonizing over all she'd lost. Some things weren't meant to be. Still, she missed seeing Kate every day and missed the camaraderie she'd once had at Central High. Most of all, she missed Will.

Her first semester and a half at Lincoln High had been a long haul. She'd had to intervene in conflicts among different gangs and student cliques. She'd met with representatives from each group, and together, they'd come up with a plan to work out differences. Once a month, there were cultural events during lunch hours in the courtyard. One month it would be Western music, the next month mariachis, and after that a Chinese lion dancer, always with a focus on sharing and mutual respect. Each class had adopted a nursing home. The residents loved the attention and treated the students as grandchildren. Tonight, she felt her persistence was starting to pay off.

Then she smelled the pungent scent of greasewood that often preceded rain in the Sonoran Desert. She looked off to the west and saw the sky was getting ominously dark.

After the presentation of awards, there was an unexpected pause. The senior class president stepped forward and invited Meghan to come to the podium. He read from a plaque, "Our senior class wishes to express our appreciation for all you've done to help us believe in ourselves, learn to work together, and prepare for the future." He handed her the plaque and shook her hand. "Thank you, Miss Walcott."

She thanked everyone, then addressed the parents and seniors, emphasizing her pride in their accomplishments and their spirit of cooperation. She blinked away tears. She wished her parents or grandparents could see her now. No one who cared for her was here to share this moment with her. Even Kate was miles away at Central's graduation.

She imagined Will in the stands, applauding enthusiastically. She had a bad habit of picturing him everywhere. If only he could have been here to share this special moment with her—but she wasn't about to let herself dwell on sad thoughts right now.

The name of the first graduate was announced. The graduates filed to the front, one by one, as their names were called out in alphabetical order. Meghan shook their hands and congratulated each student by name while nervously watching the sky.

She felt the first drop of rain when they got to the *R*'s. She was thankful they were near the end of the alphabet, but she knew there were still over forty to go. By the time they got to Paul Wyden, the final graduate, fat raindrops splattered off students' caps and gowns. Paul took his diploma in his hand, turned to the crowd, threw his cap into the air, and let out a loud whoop to the cheers of fellow graduates. Family members roared with applause, then surged onto the field to find their children. They'd made it just in time. As Meghan moved off the stage, cameras flashed, and lightning danced across the sky west of the Tucson Mountains.

She recalled her father walking toward her on her own graduation night. She'd felt that his tears had not been tears of joy, as her mother hadn't lived to see her graduate.

There was a dash to get the electronic equipment under cover as the downpour began, and the crowd quickly dispersed. The sound of car engines and honking horns outside the stadium was muffled by sheets of rain drumming against the metal bleachers.

Finally she was the only one left in the stadium, except for a man still sitting under an umbrella in the stands across the field. He wore a dark windbreaker, and it was hard to see him through the driving rain.

He began to make his way down the bleachers and headed across the field toward her. Her heart raced. He'd been here after all, waiting until the very last moment to show himself and surprise her!

She walked toward him, trying to catch her breath.

"Will?" she called out.

"Tim. Tim Stanley from the *Arizona Daily Star*. I'll be glad to share my umbrella, Miss Walcott, though from the looks of it, I'm too late. You're drenched."

Not Will. Disappointment struck her with sudden ferocity—a physical pain that nearly doubled her over.

"I've heard that several top universities have been recruiting your seniors this year," said Tim. "I've done stories in the past on drugs and gang activity at Lincoln High. I'd like to write something positive."

Meghan pushed her wet hair off her face, struggling to comprehend the reporter's words. She was glad it was raining hard. Hopefully the reporter couldn't see her tears of disappointment.

She accepted his invitation to coffee and dessert. Though she was sopping wet, she couldn't turn down a request for such an upbeat interview about the school. Any other time it would have delighted her. As they headed toward the exit, the lights of the stadium went out.

Over decaf coffee and a bagel, she provided the reporter with the information he needed. She had to dig deep within herself to give him a friendly, upbeat interview. Afterward, she stood by her car, letting the cool rain wash over her. This night was a highlight in her career. She'd never forget it. But now she was face-to-face with the gaping hole in her life.

※

Once home, Meghan took a long, hot shower, then put a frozen pizza in the oven and poured herself a glass of wine. As the pizza baked, she spread out the summer school schedules and began to go over them.

She read the first page three times before she realized she hadn't comprehended a word of it. She imagined Will beside her, sharing her joy in the graduation ceremony. He would have understood all that it meant to her and reminded her that the year was over and it was time to relax. She swept her hand across the table, flinging the schedules to the floor.

After her fantasy that Will was waiting for her after graduation and the devastating disappointment to find out that he was *not* Will, she could no longer deny that all the accomplishments in the world meant nothing without him.

She grabbed the phone and keyed in his number. As always, she hung up before it started to ring. It would be 1:23 a.m. in Michigan, and he would be sound asleep—possibly with another woman.

It was too late to fix things over the phone, especially after their disastrous long-distance conversation last fall. Communicating by phone hadn't worked with Bryan, and she couldn't risk it again with Will.

She went online and booked a flight out at 12:15 p.m. the next day. Plenty of time to get a decent night's sleep, throw a few things into a suitcase, and get to the airport.

Meghan hurried through the corridor at O'Hare. When she'd passed through it a year ago, she'd had no idea what to expect at the other end. She still didn't.

Suddenly it dawned on her that she was about to do what Bryan had done. She was going to show up unannounced. And she would probably find exactly what Bryan had found—the one she loved in someone else's arms.

She tried to picture Will opening his door to see her standing there. Would he be shocked, angry, cold, and rejecting— or would he be happy to see her? At least she'd ring the doorbell. She wouldn't barge in, like Bryan had done. If Will chose not to answer or cracked the door open to tell her that this wasn't a good time, she'd be discreet and make a polite exit. Or *would* she?

She still had a few minutes before boarding, and she owed him a heads-up. What had possessed her to fly to Traverse City without letting him know? If he didn't want to see her, she still might be able to catch a flight back to Tucson this evening.

She punched his number into her cell phone, steadying her shaking hand.

"Hello?" Will's deep voice resonated through the line.

"Hi. It's Meghan." Her voice faltered.

"Meghan?"

"You've forgotten so soon?" Her heart pounded wildly.

"Lord knows I've tried." His voice was strained. Was someone with him?

"So how have you been?" she asked, fumbling for words.

"Very well, thank you," he said coldly.

"I'm glad to hear that."

"So you care how I'm doing?"

"Of course I care," she said.

"You've a strange way of showing it."

"What could I do? You made it clear you wanted nothing more to do with me." Meghan saw the flight attendant open the door to her boarding gate. Passengers from the arriving flight began to filter out.

"Is that what you think?"

"You told me to 'have a good life,' and I can't blame you," she said. "I shouldn't even be calling you now."

"Then why *are* you?"

"Just a crazy impulse. Hold on. I need to hear if they're calling—"

"Flight 4047 is now boarding for those requiring special assistance."

"What's all that noise in the background?" asked Will.

"They're calling my flight. I'm at O'Hare, in Chicago."

"I know that O'Hare's in Chicago."

This conversation was worse than she could have ever imagined. It was time to board the flight, and she had nothing more to lose. She had to get to the point before he hung up on her.

"Are you alone right now?" she asked.

"Are you?"

"Yes, I am. But I thought you might be seeing someone."

"I have been," he said.

Meghan steadied herself against the pillar. She'd wanted to know. *Now what?*

"Her name is Linda. She's a lovely person—a librarian."

Another kick in the gut, but what did she expect? She tried to think of how to end the call.

"I broke up with her after a few dates," he continued. "I had no choice."

"Why is that?"

"I was in love with someone else."

"I see." This miserable conversation was getting worse by the minute, and she had to find a way to end it fast. He'd had more than one serious relationship since they'd parted. This was a terrible mistake.

"*Do* you see?" asked Will. "I doubt it. I broke up with her because I'm still in love with this woman from Tucson, the one who left me suddenly without a real good-bye and who never once called or even wrote."

"Are you saying what I think you're saying, Will? Hold on. I've got to board now, or I'll miss the flight."

"Why did you call me, after all this time, knowing full well that you wouldn't have time to talk? What do you take me for?"

She didn't have time to elaborate. "I take you for ... the man I love."

There was silence at the other end of the line. She heard him exhale. "Don't say that unless you mean it, Annie."

"Of course I mean it. I've never stopped loving you, not for one moment. I don't blame you for being angry, and I know I had no right to call you like this while I'm en route. But this is the last call for my flight, and I have to get on the plane—*or not*. Tell me whether to get on. Just say the word, and I'll catch a flight back to Tucson."

"Which flight?" he demanded. "You never said where you're headed."

"Flight 4047 to Traverse City. I decided to come see you. I know it's crazy, but—"

"Get on the plane, Annie! I'll be there to pick you up."

"You *do* want me to come?"

"You have no idea how much." His voice broke. "I've missed you, Meghan Anne. God, how I've missed you. Now get going, or you'll miss your flight!"

In Traverse City, Will was waiting, his deep-blue eyes burning into her, his hair tousled by the wind. It all came back, like surf breaking around her—what it was like to laugh, to make love, to share the joy of being alive with the man she loved.

NORTHERN MICHIGAN,

SIX YEARS LATER

Will and Meghan sat on the long porch of the old Victorian inn, looking out at the glistening water. White pillars framed the poplars and cedar trees along the shoreline of the small lake. The clink of horseshoes being thrown and voices of children at play dispersed into the wind.

The moon's halo the night before had foretold the gentle rain early this morning, and the chill in the August air had been replaced by a warm breeze from the south. The day emerged a hazy blue, as if time had been gently rolled back to the beginning of summer.

Only low dunes separated them from Lake Michigan, but it was another world in time and place. Far-removed were the dark times when her life had been derailed by an escaped convict, and when she'd nearly lost the man she loved. She reached for his hand and they strolled together to the water's edge.

They stopped to admire a miniature lake and village created by two small girls. Its tiny houses were made of sand and colored pebbles, and its trees from sprigs of cedar. She'd always loved helping their twins build similar towns in the sand.

"I miss the boys," she said. "I hope they're doing okay."

"We just talked to them last night. They're fine." Will's blue eyes sparkled in the sunlight. She'd never known any man so vital or thoroughly alive.

Meghan hoped their five-year-old twins would enjoy Disneyland and their weeklong visit in the West with Kate and Bryan. Todd would be the first to hop on the new rides, but Devin would describe all they'd seen and done. Todd might come home singing a Disney tune, and Devin would make them drawings of his favorite characters. Each of their sons was unique, and Meghan and Will took care to encourage them both. Meghan loved being with them and watching them grow, but she'd been looking forward to this time alone with her husband.

Bryan, Kate, and Erin would arrive with the boys in a few days and stay for a short visit. Meghan couldn't wait to see Kate and Erin, and had learned to set aside her discomfort with Bryan, for the most part. After all, he was grandfather to her sons. After two surgeries, intensive physical therapy, and much determination and hard work, Bryan had not only regained his ability to walk, but had hired a trainer to help him try to get back into tennis. Erin was teaching art and preparing for her own show at a gallery in Tubac.

Meghan had moved to Michigan when she'd married Will, and had been fortunate to find a position doing what she most loved—teaching high school choir. At first she'd had to commute over an hour each way, but last year she'd landed a position at the local high school. She felt blessed with her students and many new friends who'd welcomed her into their world.

Will was an instructor of piano at Interlochen, while still composing. His first symphony had been played there by the World Youth Symphony Orchestra. Last fall he'd performed it with the Boston Symphony Orchestra, with Meghan sitting up front, next to his proud mom. Martha was delighted that he'd found his musical place there at home, and even was organist at her church, with Meghan as choir director. Most of all, she was happy that Will, Meghan, and the twins were part of her daily life.

The late-afternoon sun cast diamonds across the waves, as three children played catch in the shallow water with a large multicolored beach ball. Suddenly the ball was scooped up by a gust of wind and skipped across the waves, just out of reach. A man dragged his boat into the water, climbed in, pulled the tiny engine's starter cord, and began a slow-motion pursuit of the ball, like a man chasing a dream.

The breeze caressed her skin, moving gently through her hair. As they stood hand in hand watching the slow-motion chase, their heartbeats were indistinguishable from the soft lapping of the waves. There was no sense of urgency. It was as if they were suspended in time on an endless summer afternoon.

ACKNOWLEDGEMENTS

I am blessed with a wonderful family, and would like to thank my terrific husband, exceptional parents, and entire family for their encouragement, support, and helpful input.

I have benefited from Tucson's rich creative environment that supports authors, including the Tucson Festival of Books, Pima Writers' Workshops, Arizona Mystery Writers, and the Society of Southwestern Authors. I want to thank my writing groups, Sunset Writers, with special thanks to Nancy Andres; and a writing group in Frankfort, Michigan. I appreciate Elizabeth Day for her ongoing help and support for my novel, and my book club and other friends for their encouragement.

Countless knowledgeable and generous people have helped me with their expertise in areas where I lacked experience. U.S. Coast Guard Air Station Traverse City pilots and public affairs officers, U.S. Coast Guard LTJG Chris Breur, and LT Dan Schrader, were very informative and helpful regarding Coast Guard rescues; as well as US Coast Guard Station Frankfort. I'd like to thank Josh Cheek of Cops 'n' Writers, and Mac McClung, for help on police matters; and Ellie Gaudino for her informative input. I also appreciate the many others who have helped provide encouragement and needed information along the way.

Thanks go to artist, Katie Iverson, who encouraged me to do the cover painting; and artists, Elaine Pekarske, Bonnie Brennan, and others for their helpful input. I want to thank Guillermo Escudero, photographer of the author photo and cover painting.

Finally, I would like to thank my wonderful editor, Nancy Buchanan;

author, Ethyl Lee-Miller, for encouraging me to make contact with the publisher, Wheatmark; Grael Norton, Wheatmark acquisitions manager; and Lori Conser, Wheatmark senior project manager, for her excellent work in helping bring the novel to fruition.

ABOUT THE AUTHOR

Mary Anne Civiok is an artist, writer, and retired school social worker. She holds an MSW from Arizona State University and a BA in Spanish from Michigan State University. A native of Michigan, she lives with her husband in Tucson, Arizona, and enjoys water sports, dancing, and long walks. Her belief in the potential of people to overcome enormous obstacles with courage and compassion has been a driving force in her work with students and their families, as well as in her writing.

Made in the USA
Middletown, DE
05 November 2017